FINDING DAISY

January 1936. Sarah, a young executive at a Yorkshire mill, returns home to attend her grandfather's funeral, blissfully unaware of the shock that awaits her when his will is read. The twists and turns in the next few weeks see her meeting an old flame and find her striving to unravel the mystery of a long-hidden family secret. But what of Daisy, the terrified child she meets on the train?

FINDING DAISY

FINDING DAISY

by

Val Margerison

Magna Large Print Books
Long Preston, North Yorkshire,
BD23 4ND, England.

British Library Cataloguing in Publication Data.

A catalogue record of this book is
available from the British Library

ISBN 978-0-7505-4434-4

First published in Great Britain 2015 by Amazon Paperback

Published in Large Print 2017 by arrangement with
Val Margerison

Magna Large Print is an imprint of Library Magna Books Ltd.

Printed and bound in Great Britain by
T.J. (International) Ltd., Cornwall, PL28 8RW

This is a work of fiction. All characters, organisations, and events portrayed in this novel are either products of the author's imagination or are used fictitiously.

To my friends at the Baildon Scribblers,
Shirley, June M and June S for their
valuable help and support.

Chapter 1

1936

The tension began to ebb as she relaxed into the plush of the Pullman car, welcoming its warmth and comfort on such a night as this. She pulled down the blinds, shutting out the rain-spattered blackness, and gave herself up to the pure enjoyment of travelling, cocooned and protected from the winter just abandoned at Kings Cross Station, well aware that a far different winter awaited her in the north. The past couple of days had seen Sarah in a flurry of hasty plans, of telephone calls, of meetings cancelled, of emotions in a whirl. The regular tattoo of the train as it flew over the track soothed her spirit and made her drowsy. She was roused briefly as the train slowed and drew into a station. She lifted the blind a little. A glance outside revealed passengers huddled into their collars, gratefully hurrying to board the train, escaping the flurries of sleet which swept the platform. 'Retford', announced the white lettering. With crossed fingers Sarah hoped that her compartment would remain empty as she heard the banging of doors. The guard's whistle was answered by a hoot from the driver, signalling the 'off', and the great engine huffed its way out of the station. Good, she still had the compartment all to herself and Sarah snuggled up into her corner. Just over half way home, she thought, as the regular clickety-clack lulled her into restfulness and sleep.

The door to the corridor slid back slowly, opening just enough to reveal that Sarah was the only occupant. A pair of inquisitive eyes surveyed the scene rapidly, the door opened a little further and, in a flash, closed again just as silently with a small person on the inside. Moving furtively the child first made sure that the blind covering the window onto the corridor was fully down and tried peeping under and round the edges to find out whether or not she could be seen from the outside. If anyone had been watching it would have seemed a strange manoeuvre for a child of her age. With great care she climbed onto the corner seat diagonally opposite to Sarah and curled into as small a ball as possible, tucking her dark, curly head under one arm and arranging her coat about her small frame. To the casual observer she could pass for someone's jacket thrown onto the seat. Two wary eyes kept a steady watch on the quiet figure asleep in the other corner, eyes that were very far from sleep, eyes that held fear in their depths, eyes that darted towards the door at the slightest sound from the corridor. She could not have been more than six or seven years old.

The train battled on through the snow and sleet. A sudden rattling over points caused Sarah to stir and she opened her eyes. Blearily looking round she fumbled behind the fur cuff of her coat to find and consult her watch. Almost half an hour had passed since the short stop at Retford and Sarah raised the blind a little to peer out of the train. The weather had worsened considerably. Between heavy clouds there was occasional sight of a full moon which allowed glimpses of a countryside dusted with white and she could see snowflakes hurtling horizontally past as the train flew through the night. Sarah stretched her legs and sat up to straighten her shoulders. The bundle of clothes in the other corner stirred almost imperceptibly, catching her attention. Sarah looked up to the luggage rack, vaguely wondering if her raincoat had fallen down while she had been asleep. It was then, her gaze falling once more onto the bundle, that she noticed those bright, blue eyes watching her every move.

'What?...Who?...' She stopped as a slight commotion in the corridor and raised voices, muffled at first, soon carried clearly into her compartment as the door slid open. A man's voice, trying to sound cultured and polite, but failing to convince, said, 'Excuse me, so very sorry to trouble you, madam. We are looking for our daughter.' At this point a woman appeared at his side, dyed blond hair with a red pill-box hat, her face half covered by black open netting which wound its way back to the top of the hat to a gathering held down with a red flower. Sarah took in all of this in a matter of seconds as the man raised his trilby and spoke. She was also aware that the bundle in the corner had shrunk very slightly and, as she gave it a cursory glance, she saw those eyes again. They were wide, brilliant, and flashed across to Sarah such terror in them that she could almost feel the fear in herself. She stood up, steadying herself against the swaying of the train and walked the few steps towards the door. As she took hold of the door frame she had placed herself and the loose raglan coat she was wearing between the anxious couple and the bundle on the seat. The man was speaking again.

'It's our little girl, you see. Playing games with us, she is, the naughty child. One minute she was right beside us and the next, nowhere to be seen. You can see how upset my wife is.' He turned to the woman who was peering round his shoulder and trying to see into the carriage. Was that a nudge he gave her? The woman's face crumpled into a grimace as she fished out a handkerchief, dabbed at her eyes and began to wail, 'Oh! Oh, where's my baby? How could she run off like this? Leading us such a dance, she is.' The man patted her hand and turned to Sarah.

'You haven't seen a small girl, have you, miss? About this high?' The image of those terror-stricken eyes came so vividly into Sarah's head that it took her a fraction of a second to make up her mind. Sweeping an arm around to indicate its emptiness she said, 'As you can see, I am the sole occupant of this compartment and have been so since I left Kings Cross. I'm afraid I cannot help you. I would suggest you go and report your problem to the guard. And now, if you will excuse me...' So saying, Sarah slid the door closed and locked it.

There was no movement from the curled-up child as Sarah checked carefully both the blinds on the corridor side and drew down the cover on the door. To give the impression that she might be sleeping she turned off most of the lights, leaving only the one over the figure still cowering in the corner to illuminate the scene. Afraid of alarming the child still further Sarah quietly sat down beside her and waited a full minute before speaking. When she did so it was in a soft tone and slowly, 'Well, now, what's all this? I wake up to find that someone has decided to share my compartment, someone who came in as quietly as the thistledown fairy! I wonder who she can be?' Sarah kept her voice gentle and made no move to touch the child. She could not even see those bright eyes now and all she could hear was muffled sobbing which gradually became softer as she remained still and waited. Sarah tried again.

'Please try not to cry. You'll be quite safe with me. I'll do nothing to hurt you or frighten you. The door is locked, so those people can't bother us again just now.' At the mention of 'those people' the small bundle began to tremble, heart-rending gasps and sobs shook the child, making Sarah dare to ask the direct question in the hope of eliciting some reaction other than this distressed weeping.

'Those people, are they really your mummy and daddy? If so, I shall have to tell them you're here after all.' The little girl shuddered, her tear-stained face, very white, appeared from somewhere inside the heap of clothing and she made a valiant attempt to pull herself together.

'No, no, no mummy and daddy.' The words were almost whispered and came amongst little sobs which the child was trying to control. Sarah was not sure whether this meant that the couple were not her parents, (which Sarah had suspected), or whether the child was saying that she had no parents. It was enough, for the moment, Sarah thought. It was enough to let her decide to offer the child her protection until the end of the journey when she would be able to hand her over to ... whom? Probably the police would be best. Let them make the necessary enquiries, return the child to her rightful place. Whatever was going on with the trilby-hatted fellow and his scarlet-clad lady she could not stand by and see a child so obviously distressed and terrified, so utterly petrified of those people who claimed her as their own, that she had escaped their clutches on a moving train. While Sarah sat and thought, deciding what she must do, the child's sobbing began to subside.

'No-one can see us in here, you know. Maybe you'd like to sit up so that I can see you properly. You do believe that I'm your friend, don't you? We can just have a little talk and you can tell me all about yourself and why you were crying so much and, perhaps, you could manage to help me to eat my bar of chocolate.' Sarah's time spent as a nanny in Switzerland had made her feel at ease with children and she knew from experience that a bit of chocolate was usually guaranteed to inspire confidence.

'My name is Sarah,' she said as she found the chocolate bar and busied herself with its wrappings. 'I hope this hasn't melted. No, it's alright. So, a piece for you and one for me.' Sarah tried to sound normal, as if it was the most ordinary thing in the world to be sharing chocolate on a train with a runaway child. Suddenly, 'I'm Daisy,' announced the little girl but said no more as she filled her mouth with the proffered confection and dispatched it in a flash, her eyes fixed upon the remainder of the bar held on Sarah's lap.

'Another piece, Daisy?' The only reply was eager nodding of the dark curls as Daisy abandoned her foetal position within her oversized coat and sat up close to Sarah, her tears forgotten, for the moment at least. It occurred to Sarah, as the chocolate disappeared at speed, that this child was hungry ... very hungry. The days were long gone when Sarah carried sandwiches. Nowadays she always used the restaurant car. Travelling for the business meant she could claim such expenses, but she usually popped a packet of biscuits into her bag in case she was peckish but not in need of a proper meal. Two bright, blue eyes followed her every move as she reached for her smaller travel-bag and began fishing about inside it.

'Aha! Even better than chocolate when you're really hungry,' cried Sarah, whisking forth a small, oblong tin filled with Scottish shortbread. Daisy now shrugged off the rest of her coat, her eyes growing big in their sockets as she shuffled to the edge of the seat, letting her legs dangle down, reaching only half way to the floor. Sarah offered the biscuits and Daisy ate ... and ate. The poor mite, thought Sarah, I wonder when was her last meal. She asked the question.

'Don't know, lady,' came the reply. The shortbread, however, worked wonders and, coupled with the drink of water that Sarah never travelled without, Daisy was transformed from fear and trembling to giving Sarah a trusting but shy smile and a, 'Thank you, lady,' in a small voice.

'You're welcome.' Sarah smiled in return and patted the seat beside her so that Daisy moved to sit close to her.

'You must call me Sarah,' she said, 'not "lady".'

'Why?'

'Because that's my name, Sarah Grange. Have you another name besides Daisy?'

As if a button had been pressed a flow of words was suddenly released.

'My name is Daisy Elizabeth Francis. I am six and three quarters. I live with a lot of other children in the Children's Home because I haven't got a mummy and daddy. Mrs. Johnson looks after us and she's nice but I don't like Samuel and Kevin 'cos they're too bossy and sometimes I play with Jennifer and my bestest friend's called Anna and we sleep in the same dorm'try and we go to school and sometimes she cries ... not at school, she cries in the dorm'try and Mrs. Johnson says that's silly 'cos there's nothing to cry for, and, one day, my mummy and daddy might come to find me ... and Anna can come as well.' Daisy's speech came to an abrupt stop as she saw another biscuit on offer. It took Sarah a moment or two to take in this stream of information. She smiled and Daisy smiled back, her elfin face lighting up as she responded to this grown up person who seemed so interested in what she had to say.

'Tell me some more,' said Sarah. 'What do you like at school?' This, she thought, was safer ground than talking about anything else.

'I like sums and Anna does, and I'm good at reading and a bit good at writing,' this last said with a slight screwing up of the button nose and a rueful grin. She knew her shortcomings, did Daisy.

'When I was at school,' Sarah said, 'I didn't like sums at all. I wasn't very good at arithmetic, but I loved to write stories and, do you know, my favourite thing of all was music.' She would have said more, but Daisy suddenly jumped off the seat, her diffidence forgotten, and began to dance, providing her own music with the song, 'The Grand Old Duke of York', as Sarah clapped the beat and joined in with the song too. As the performance came to an end Daisy clapped and jumped back onto the seat next to Sarah. She found herself quite captivated by the child who, while she danced, seemed to be transported into a world of her own. The narrow space between the long seats provided her with all the stage she needed as she balanced and twirled, twisted and stepped in perfect time to the song she sang. Sarah marvelled at the grace and spontaneity that Daisy possessed and also at the speed at which a child, any child, could recover from tears. Daisy's plain, serviceable, grey skirt and white blouse, topped by a green school jumper were all somewhat too large for her slight frame, but, in her heart, she was Isadora Duncan. As her confidence in Sarah's friendship grew, Daisy told her a little about the two people who had caused her fright.

'This lady came to the home and talked to Mrs. Johnson. Then she came again with that man. They were ever so nice and brought me a new doll and I got very excited 'cos they said they know where my mummy and daddy live. They told Mrs. Johnson they would take me to see them and they might let me stay for ever.' As she spoke her face lost the glow it had had when she had danced. The deep anxiety returned; she sat closer to Sarah.

'They came for me yesterday.' The child's voice had dropped to almost a whisper and her head was bowed. Sarah gently put an arm round her small shoulders.

'Something happened? They didn't take you to your mummy and daddy?' Daisy's tears threatened to start all over again and Sarah drew her into the crook of her arm, her heart saddened by the child's distress. She was unable, because of her age, to put into words what had actually happened, so Sarah said, 'Never mind, Daisy. It doesn't matter now. You're quite safe here with me. I'll look after you till we can get you back to where you belong. There, that's better...' Daisy lifted her face to Sarah and managed a weak smile.

'Let's talk about something else, shall we? Listen to the noises that the train makes. It says, "We're nearly there, we're nearly there ... it won't be long, it won't be long..." Sarah and Daisy made up jingles to match the rhythm of the train.

'My teacher told us a poem about a train,' said Daisy, 'I liked it. There were fairies and witches and flying along and seeing things from out the windows.' Daisy danced over to the offside of the train, almost overbalancing as the carriage leaned, caught by a particularly strong gust of wind as it rounded a bend, and peeped under the blind.

'We can't see anything, 'cos its dark,' she said.

Sarah smiled and drew from her memory, repeating the lines that she, herself, had loved as a child.

'Faster than fairies, faster than witches,
Bridges and houses, hedges and ditches,
And charging along like troops in a battle,
All through the meadows the horses and cattle.
All of the sights of the hill and the plain
Fly as thick as driving rain,
And ever again, in the wink of an eye,
Painted stations whistle by.'

'That's it!' laughed Daisy, coming alive again and clapping her hands. 'Do some more, please.' Her blue eyes sparkling, she snuggled up to Sarah and waited for her to go on.

'Here is a child who clambers and scrambles All by hims... My God! What's happening?'... Sarah was stopped in her tracks by the sudden, violent and explosive crash. Her mind was slow to register events, for what followed seemed to happen in slow motion. A shrill scream from Daisy, her arms wrapped tightly round Sarah's waist, the shattering of glass, the popping of light bulbs and the carriage rolling and pitching, throwing them to the floor as it reared and catapulted luggage across the compartment. Sarah's arms were round the child, at the same time trying to protect herself from flying glass as the lamps were torn from their sockets. The blinds were ripped and hanging loose. She could see sparks flying, hear screams, smell the searing screech of metal on metal. Another and another massive eruption of the train until Sarah wondered would it never stop. The terrifying noises as the train came to grief seemed endless as she and the child clung together on the floor. It was as if a separate part of her mind, detached from her body, was trying to analyse the sounds and make sense of the chaos. Then, just as suddenly as it began, everything stopped. Total blackness enveloped them and an utter, palpable silence fell, save for the continuous wail of the great engine's steam whistle.

Chapter 2

In the hallway of their Victorian house on the outskirts of the city John and Alice were preparing to leave.

'Are you sure you wouldn't like me to go to the station?' came a voice from the sitting room. 'The road might be quite treacherous later on.'

'Thanks, James, but, if we are to slide into a wall, I feel it might be better if I, and not a twenty-year-old, were at the wheel,' laughed John. 'Besides your mother and I are not too decrepit, yet, to get out and walk if we have to and there's plenty of time before Sarah's train's due.' John's attempt at jocularity, James knew, was a cover for his deep seated sadness at the death of his father. The arrangements for grandfather's funeral had kept him and mother very much occupied during the past few days. It would be a big family-gathering.

'Oh, well, alright, if you insist, but take care, the pair of you,' James said as he came out into the hall to see them off. Secretly he was disappointed. For one thing he would have liked to meet his sister from the train. He hadn't seen her since October because she had left for London before his return from Birmingham last week. For another he would have really enjoyed the chance to drive father's new Rover. Perhaps, he thought, the old man didn't care to risk his gleaming new motor in the hands of his smart-Alec son. James sat down again on the settee and mused on the experiences of his first two years spent learning to be a doctor. That first term his daily task, along with other students, had been to dissect, disembowel and dismember a grey slab of what once had been a human being. And then working amongst all manner of the living variety, learning, so fast that it was almost impossible to believe, about the human condition both sick and well ... and then playing hard in order to redress the balance of his sanity. This, thought James, is what father is not aware of, at least, not as yet. Perhaps he'll notice in a little while that I've grown up! He moved over to the cocktail cabinet, dismissed its contents, and went off to the kitchen in search of a beer.

'Can I get you something, Mr. James?' Jennie Parker was sitting toasting her toes beside the kitchen fire. She was cook, housekeeper, maid and friend to Alice Grange. Few people kept servants these days, and certainly not in the numbers that had been common thirty years ago. Jennie had worked for Mrs. Grange's mother-in-law and now, at seventy, she was glad to have a home here and to serve out her days with the family of which she had become a part. There was great affection on both sides.

'Just fancied a beer,' said James, 'don't trouble yourself, Jennie. I can find it myself.' And he did just that with a swift descent to the cellar.

'And a good deal faster than I would have done it,' chuckled Jennie.

'I'm not used to being waited on nowadays,' said James, 'and, besides, it's time you took a rest occasionally.'

Jennie watched him making for the sitting room and thought how well he had turned out. Well, not only James. There was Sarah making her way as a designer in textiles, earning herself a place in her father's business, Penny away at teacher-training college, and David, fifteen already, and doing well at school by all accounts. Eeh, dear, how fast they do grow up! Jennie relaxed again in her rocking chair and dozed off.

In the sitting room James flicked through the evening newspaper. They were still rejoicing that England had, for the first time ever, beaten New Zealand at Rugby last weekend. The Royal family continued their Christmas holiday at Sandringham. The King had been seen riding his white pony but had been unable to join in his favourite sport, shooting, because of inclement weather. The number of unemployed continued to rise. The weather forecasters warned of imminent gales about to hit the south-west and move northwards. James put down the paper and leaned over to reach the wireless, which stood on a small table near the end of the sofa. He switched it on and tuned in to the sounds of a dance band and sat back to enjoy its energetic and tuneful music. He was not sure how long he had been sitting there when the music was suddenly faded out.

'We interrupt this programme from Broadcasting House to give a Police Message,' said the cultured tones of the announcer. James gave scant attention. 'There has been a serious accident involving the L.N.E.R. express from London at a point just north of Bawtry. Those with relatives or friends known to be travelling on the 2.50 from Kings Cross are advised to telephone the police for further information.' James felt an icy coldness run through his veins and, for a second or two he froze like a statue. His sister's train ... his sister was on that train. He leaped to his feet, strode three paces across the room and back again to stare at the wireless in disbelief and growing fear as the words of the announcer seemed to echo in his head, 'serious accident', 'express from London'. Suddenly his legs were, somehow, unable to hold him and he sank down onto the sofa, his elbows on his knees and his head between his hands. He closed his eyes tightly, as if to try to concentrate his thoughts that were dashing wildly about in his mind. A deep breath and he composed himself, knowing that he must be calm, now, and decide what should be done. No use panicking when the most important move at present was to get hold of his parents, be with them for support and, between them, discover the details of the accident and find out where Sarah was and whether or not she was hurt. He decided to try to get to the station. His parents would be there by now and may well have been informed about the accident. They would be frantic, he thought. Why is it that troubles never come singly? Putting on his overcoat James went towards the kitchen in search of his Wellington boots. He wondered what he should tell Jennie, not wanting to alarm her before he had some more definite information. The shrilling of the telephone in the hall startled him and he almost ran to pick it up.

'Hello,' his voice was strained, 'this is...' He heard the coins drop and the line cleared. 'James, is that you?' His father's voice was anxious. 'We're here at the station. I've had to wait ages to find a free telephone. Sarah's train has been delayed, they've told us. We don't know, yet, what the problem is, but ... what? Just a minute, James, your mother is trying to tell me something....' James sensed that his father was holding open the kiosk door. He heard enough down the phone line to know that his parents were now hearing the news that he already knew and he, too, listened with growing anxiety.

'It is with regret that we must inform those meeting passengers on the 2.50 train from King's Cross that this locomotive has met with an accident a few miles south of Doncaster.' A silence fell on the station concourse as the announcer continued: 'We believe there have been some minor injuries to passengers and we are doing all we can to provide information as quickly and accurately as possible. Would relatives and friends please go to the Station Master's office.'

'James, are you still there? Did you hear that?'

'Yes, father. Please try not to worry. Stay there. Take care of mum and I'll be there with you as soon as I can. You...' The pips cut off his words.

What was there to say, anyhow? James's heart was heavy. Not knowing the full truth of what had happened just made things worse. The railway people were being very cautious in what they said, naturally. But they do not broadcast Police Messages, thought James, unless there's serious cause for concern. He hurried back to find his boots. What should he tell Jennie?

'I have to go out, Jennie. I shouldn't be too long, but don't wait up.'

'Tell her nothing,' muttered James to himself as he let himself out of the front door. 'Tell her nothing, until there's something to tell.'

The lofty, Victorian splendour of the Exchange Station in the centre of Bradford was the source of great civic pride. It was designed with soaring arches of decorative ironwork, elegant pillars supporting its roof which was furnished with glass to allow in as much daylight as possible. Comfortable waiting rooms with cheery fires in their grates and warm rest rooms offered refreshments to travel-weary passengers. The maroon and cream livery of the London and North Eastern Railway was echoed everywhere in the paintwork, while smartly clad porters hurried about their business. On any normal day there could be felt a buzz of excitement as people crowded on and off the trains. Even though it might be a little quieter during the evening, especially during the dark, winter months, nothing could have prepared James for the silence which greeted him when he, at last, arrived there to find his parents. There were still noises from the locomotives going about normal duties, still the hisses of steam, still the rattle of carts as the post-van was loaded and doors closed. But there was an uncanny quietness pervading the scene as James saw the group of anxious faces gathered together beside the Station Master's office. He hurried towards it as he saw his mother running to meet him, his father just behind her.

'Thank you for coming, James,' said Alice. 'We're so worried. They don't seem to be able to tell us anything further at the moment apart from the fact that the train has been de-railed and they think that there are some casualties. No-one has any details yet because the weather is so bad that even some of the telephone lines are down. We have been asked to be patient and wait a little longer. They are trying to reroute the 'phone calls but you can imagine how busy the lines are.' James was thankful that his mother was not the sort of woman to go to pieces in a crisis. Alice was eminently sensible and level-headed. An optimist, too, she would, even now, refuse to entertain thoughts of the worst scenario. She would be patient, she would jolly along her husband who had, for goodness sake, had enough to cope with over the past week since the sudden passing of his beloved father.

'Come on,' she said now, 'let's go and warm ourselves up with a cup of tea. You must be frozen, James.' They went into the restaurant. It was full of others, all awaiting news of the accident. They all spoke in low voices, trying to keep each other's spirits up while hiding their own fears. John ordered tea for three and they managed to find somewhere to sit down. The man on the next table nodded to them and said, 'They should hear something soon. I'm here to meet my uncle and aunt. I guess you must be expecting someone, too?' It seemed a superfluous question, James thought with a spurt of irritation, but, he had to agree, it helped to talk to someone else who was going through the same experience.

'We came to meet our daughter. Let's just hope that no-one is badly hurt.' Alice smiled at the man encouragingly.

James remembered that he hadn't told them about the message on the wireless. He opened his mouth and shut it again. No use causing further alarm. Telling them would not help. This waiting was getting him down. He finished his tea, looked at his watch, got up and walked onto the platform. Several others who had found it impossible to sit any longer were pacing up and down.

'May I have your attention, ladies and gentlemen.' This was no longer the loudspeaker system, but the Station Master in person who had come down from his office carrying a paper in his hand. James hurried to join his parents as everyone immediately re-grouped in the restaurant eager for news, yet fearing what he might have to say.

'I can now give some further information about the accident, although, at this point, I cannot give out the names of passengers who might be injured. I cannot stress too strongly to you all the deep regret of the Company at this distressing event. Be assured that everything that can be done will be done to assist you and those who are involved in the accident. We now know that the engine and seven of the ten carriages have left the rails. Darkness and wintry weather have caused major problems in communications and we apologise for your having to wait so long for information.' The man cleared his throat. He was finding it difficult to speak. He went on, 'The police and ambulance services, aided by local people and the St John's Ambulance are working at the site of the accident and are, gradually, moving all passengers away from the track. Those who are injured are being taken to Doncaster hospital by ambulance or by coach and, in some cases by private motor cars whose owners have offered to help.' The man paused again and James felt the tension in the room increase as people realised that he was not, at present, in a position to tell them the whereabouts and condition of their own friends and relatives. He placed an arm around his mother's shoulder as the man continued.

'There were two hundred and fifty four passengers on board all of whom will be taken to Doncaster for care and attention. I understand that local church or school halls have been opened close to the hospital for those who do not require hospital care. We are providing a special train to transfer those relatives who wish to travel to Doncaster this evening. It will leave from platform six. As soon as I receive any further news of its time of departure you will be informed. Meanwhile, please will those who wish to travel on the special train register their names and addresses, plus the names of the people they wish to locate, at the main ticket office. Thank you.'

It remained very quiet as he made his way through the crush and back to the office, followed by eyes resentful, anxious, tearful and angry. A flurry of conversations began all over the room, many voices raised in concern at the very lack of information that had taken him so long to impart.

'I can't go to Doncaster,' wailed one young woman, 'I've left my baby with a neighbour just for an hour or two.' She was close to tears. 'How shall I find out about my husband?' Another station official appeared looking harassed and tired and said that news of relatives would be relayed by telephone to anyone who could leave a contact number. Those who preferred this service were urged to go home now and wait to be called. By no means had everyone a telephone in their homes but kindly friends, neighbours and even local public houses could be relied upon to relay messages in an emergency. Almost half of the anxious, waiting faces melted away to find their way home. Of the rest, which included John, Alice and James, most went to find a 'phone, inform their households that they would not be back tonight, and made their way to the ticket office to organise their journey to Doncaster.

'Keep your pecker up, love,' John gave his wife a gentle squeeze and she smiled wanly into his face. 'We must be positive and strong for Sarah, however she is when we find her. Come on, James, take your mother's arm and let us get on with it. It looks like being a long night.'

It was almost four hours later when their train drew into Doncaster station. It had taken at least two hours to organise a special train, to man it and to alter the schedules of other services so that the 'special' would have a clear line on which to run through to Doncaster. By now there was some semblance or order about the whole event. People were detailed to take their names, ask whom they sought and to direct them towards taxis which would take them, hopefully, to their loved ones. Alice's face was white as the three of them were approached by a girl in a St. John's Ambulance uniform. The girl smiled kindly.

'Would you give me your name, please,' she addressed John.

'Mr. and Mrs. John Grange,' he answered, forgetting entirely that James was there. The girl consulted her list.

'You will be looking for a Miss Sarah Grange?' All three of them nodded, unable to speak. 'Then I must direct you to the hospital.' Alice's hands flew to her face, her eyes wide and fearful as she stared at the girl.

'What has happened to her? Is she badly injured?'

'I'm very sorry, I don't have any other details,' said the girl, gently, 'but if you would go with this gentleman he will show you the way to a car that will take you there. The staff will fill you in on your arrival.' She gave Alice an encouraging smile. 'Try not to worry, they're all in good hands now.'

The journey to the hospital took less than ten minutes. It seemed like an age. No-one talked as their own thoughts dwelt anxiously on what they would find at the end of it.

Chapter 3

They had been thrown together on the floor of the railway compartment which was lying at a crazy angle in the pitch darkness. All Sarah could hear was the high wind and the wail of the steam whistle growing fainter and fainter until it finally faded and died away.

The sound of a small whimper brought Sarah back to reality and she wondered for a second how long she had been here on the floor. Had she been unconscious? Why was she so cold? Her befuddled brain gradually began to focus, to realise where she was, what had happened. A sudden thrill of terror swept through her as she remembered the child, her frightened companion whom she had promised to protect until the end of the journey. Daisy! Where was she?

Sarah's whole attention was now focussed upon Daisy, her own predicament disregarded. 'Daisy, I'm here my poppet. Where are you? Are you alright? Are you hurt?' With relief she welcomed the reply, 'I'm cold ... can't see anything. I can feel you, Sarah. I'm glad you've woken up at last to talk to me.' It was only then that Sarah realised that she had her arms around Daisy's slight body and that it was shaking violently. She must have kept tight hold of her as they were thrown around by the crashing train. From the child's last remark Sarah deduced that she had, indeed, been unconscious for a time. As her mind became clearer she recognised the need to re-assure and comfort the terrified child who had waited, Lord knows how long, in the pitch darkness, for signs of life to return to her new friend. Again she asked, 'Are you hurt, Daisy? Have you bumped your head?'

'No. I don't think so.'

'Can you move your arms and legs?'

'Yes.' And Daisy gently unwound herself from Sarah's arms. 'We're under the seat. I can't sit up. Why is it so cold, Sarah?'

'The windows of the train are broken, the wind is blowing through. Do be careful, there will be broken glass everywhere.' Daisy crawled slowly out from the confined space below the seat, never letting go her hold of some part of Sarah's clothing, until she could sit up. Sarah prepared to follow, only then realising that she herself could not move more than a little and that, when she tried to withdraw her legs, she experienced such a stab of pain that she was obliged to return to her original position without delay. She ran her hand down her leg and found, to her horror, that both her ankles were pinned to the floor by the pipe that served the compartment with its heating. Any attempt to move her lower body was swiftly curtailed by the agonising pain from her trapped legs. She remained quite still as she spoke again to Daisy.

'We must try to keep ourselves as warm as we can until someone comes to help us,' she said, trying to sound normal. 'Someone will come, Daisy. They will come and get us out and then you'll be alright.' Sarah tried to pull herself together and to keep as still as she could. If she lay still it wasn't too bad, she could bear it. Try to think of a way to keep warm, she thought. Where was that jacket that Daisy had on? Was it safe for Daisy to try to find it?

'Daisy, hold my hand and try to reach up to the seat. If you feel your jacket, pull it down.' Daisy took hold of Sarah's right hand and stretched her arm upwards. It was there. As she pulled it a shower of broken glass and wood-splinters fell on them, but they had the most important item ... a means of staving off a little of the bitter cold which swept through the carriage.

'Come and cuddle up by me, now,' she said to Daisy. 'Listen. We must listen for people coming and we must stay here on the floor because my foot is trapped.'

Daisy did as she was bidden, creeping as close to Sarah as she could, pulling the woollen jacket over their shoulders. Daisy sounded tearful as she whispered, 'Oh, dear, poor Sarah. I hope the people will come very soon.' Daisy put her arms round Sarah's neck and held her tight, trying not to cry as the wind rattled the torn blinds and brought flurries of sleet across the blackness.

Sarah's attempts at normal conversation, to allay the child's fears, were becoming increasingly difficult. At times she almost cried out but she must not ... for Daisy's sake. The two of them, strangers until a very short time ago, huddled close together under the jacket. She drew deep breaths of the icy air and was thankful, for once during this nightmare, that she was lying down. Daisy's voice came to her, as if from a long distance.

'Mrs. Johnson says it's good to sing if you're scared. Shall I sing for you, Sarah?'

'That would be lovely.' Sarah's voice was weak.

'Twinkle, twinkle, little star, how I wonder what you are...' sang Daisy's small voice and Sarah closed her eyes and prayed that help would come soon.

Distant at first but definitely coming closer the welcome sounds of the rescue parties approached.

'They're coming, someone's coming,' whispered Daisy into Sarah's ear. 'Will they get us out? You won't leave me, Sarah, will you?'

'No, I won't leave you. I promised to look after you, didn't I?' Sarah was surprised at the strength of feeling she had for the child, even through the haze of her weariness. 'They'll soon have us out, sweetheart, and take us somewhere safe and warm.' Vaguely she began to wonder what she would do about her young companion after they were rescued. I'll think about that later, she decided. Later, when we're out of this hell-hole.

Lights appeared. Men with powerful torches were approaching along the track. Voices called to each other, matter-of-fact, purposeful and businesslike. Sarah listened closely, trying to assess from their comments what they were seeing of the crash. As the lights came closer she knew that their wait must be nearly over. The corridor side of the train, where she was trapped, was lying on the embankment. There was no chance of getting them out that way. Quite suddenly a ladder was thrown against the opposite side and a torch-light beam flashed around, picking out the figures lying under the seat.

'We're here,' Sarah called, weakly.

'Someone in here, Jim,' shouted a voice. In a gentler tone he called across the compartment, 'Are you hurt in there? Don't worry, we'll have you safe and sound as soon as we can.' The man leaned into the wrecked car as Daisy managed to scramble out from under the seat, calling to him, 'Come and help her, she can't get out by herself.' The little girl slipped and fell as she tried to cover the sloping floor to the door.

'Let's get this door open if we can, Arthur,' called another voice. The ladder was removed, as was the torch, leaving them once more in darkness. Daisy slid back, crying softly now, to stay by Sarah.

'It's all right now, Daisy, we'll soon be safe.' Sarah was by now very frightened indeed because her legs had stopped hurting, she could not feel them at all. She wondered how long it would be before they would be able to release her. There was much more noise outside now. It seemed as if scores of people had descended suddenly upon the wreck, all intent on rescuing those unfortunate enough to be caught up in this tragedy on this bitterly cold night. It was true. Fire engines, police vans and ambulances were converging on the area and the rescue operation was, by now, in full swing, hindered as it was by a howling gale and driving snow.

'That's done it!' Sarah heard another voice as the door of the compartment was suddenly flung back. A rush of freezing air hit Sarah's face, forcing her back to consciousness when she had been on the verge of passing out.

'Come on, love, let's have you out. Give me your hands,' said the officer to Daisy as the torch-light shone in.

'But, what about...?' Daisy looked back at Sarah.

'We'll come for your mum in a minute, sweet-heart. Just try to reach my hands. What's your name, love?' Gently he dragged Daisy from the teetering carriage and handed her to someone who wrapped her in a blanket. 'Her name's Daisy,' he said as with comforting words and gentle hands she was taken across a snowy field to the roadside where the ambulances and vans waited.

Daisy looked back. She saw an expanse of darkness with pinpoints of moving lights as the rescuers continued their work. It was still oddly quiet when they reached the vehicles on the road, and, after checking for obvious injuries, Daisy was bundled into one of the ambulances, another blanket wrapped round her. Someone brought a mug of hot chocolate, placed an arm round her, and sat down beside her.

'My name is Dr. Pearce,' said the young man. 'I thought you'd like a warm drink while you wait for them to get your mummy out. It won't take them long, Daisy, then you'll be off to hospital together, just for a check-up.' Daisy sipped the cocoa thank-fully as Dr. Pearce told her that he worked at the hospital and that he would be there to help to look after all the people from the train-crash and would see her later. Daisy liked Dr. Pearce. He was nice, she thought, but a few minutes later he was called to see to someone whose head was bleeding. She did not see him again that night. Daisy waited and watched as a procession of people was brought across from the train. With each new arrival her dark eyes searched for Sarah. Most people who could walk were led to a motor coach which ferried to and from the hospital. Daisy was put into the ambulance to wait for the woman whom everyone had assumed was her mother and, until now, there had been no opportunity to explain that she was not. Suddenly Daisy was aware of a commotion outside the ambulance, raised voices, people running, the doors being thrown open and several of the rescue party hastily pushing a stretcher onto the bench opposite her.

'Where's the driver? Get this thing on the move, pronto, lad,' called one of them as the ambulance driver appeared from the gloom. 'This case can't wait. You'll have to step on it, Pete, this chap's in a bad way, but he's young, thank God. You'll need to use the siren and ... well, just do your best. Good luck!' The doors were slammed, the vehicle screamed off into the night, the young man on the stretcher moaned as the ambulance crew attended to him. Daisy clutched the blankets about her, watching everything with dark, apprehensive eyes. After about ten minutes they seemed satisfied that their patient would survive the journey.

'I think he'll do, now, Charlie. Just tighten that strap a bit, will you. There may be some sharp bends. Not much fun in these conditions.' The nurse turned and suddenly noticed Daisy sitting in her corner, holding on grimly as the vehicle threatened to jolt her from her seat. 'Hello! Who have we here?'

'I'm Daisy,' she said.

'Well, Daisy, what a surprise. We were so busy

that we didn't see you. I expect you've been waiting for someone who's still in the train. Poor little thing! You must have been horrified when we rushed you away. Never mind, we'll make sure there's someone to take care of you at the hospital until somebody claims you.'

They arrived, a short time later, at Doncaster hospital. Daisy was taken into a large reception area, full of light and warmth and nurses bustling to and fro. One of these, a kindly girl who told Daisy that her name was Nurse Taylor, checked her over for injury, found she had only a few scratches and said, 'You just sit here, Daisy, until they bring your mummy. You were with your mummy, weren't you?' And after a slight hesitation, Daisy answered, 'She couldn't get out 'cos her legs are trapped.' Then the tears began again as she wondered where Sarah was and if they had got her out safely. The nurse could see how utterly exhausted was this little girl and how worried about her mother. She gave Daisy a hug and said, 'Look, Daisy, I'll find you a place where you can see the door easily so you'll be able to run to mummy the minute she comes.' The nurse hurried away to the next job. It was going to be a long night. Better get on.

It took them over an hour to cut her free. By some miracle only one of Sarah's ankles had been broken though this was bad enough. They had given her a temporary support for the leg and some pain relief for the journey to Doncaster Hospital. It was after two-thirty in the morning when Sarah was carried through the hospital doors into its bright lights, warmth and safety.

The scene that greeted this latest evacuee from the doomed night train was one that she would always remember. The entrance hall and corridors were full of people, most of them in shock and many suffering dreadful injuries. The latter were being attended to as quickly as possible while those, like Sarah, whose injury was not life-threatening, were patiently waiting to be seen. Strangely there was little to be heard apart from the murmuring voices of the staff as they went about their duties. Sarah now had time to take stock of her situation, to wonder how she would contact those at home who were expecting her arrival. She decided that she would telephone as soon as she could, but, meantime, she scanned the faces around her for sight of Daisy.

But of Daisy there was no sign. Sarah, as soon as she had been allocated a place to sit and wait her turn to attend for X-ray, stopped several nurses as they passed and enquired after a little girl. None had seen her. Sarah began to panic. Again she asked anxiously,

'Excuse me, nurse. Do you happen to have seen a little girl called Daisy? She has dark, curly hair and...'

'Oh, yes.' Nurse Taylor stopped on her way past and smiled. 'She's waiting for her mum, just over there.' She pointed to a chair close to the door. It was empty.

Chapter 4

By four a.m. Sarah was quite frantic. Nothing, it appeared, had been seen of Daisy since the young nurse had left her, still wrapped in a blanket, on a chair near to the hospital entrance. Sarah's mind was full of unanswered questions, at the same time her brain refused to operate with any degree of clarity. She knew that the events of the past eight hours or so had been traumatic in the extreme and no wonder she felt so confused and exhausted. Trying hard to stay awake she recalled the telephone call from her mother shortly before she embarked upon this journey.

'We're suddenly in the grip of ice and snow, dear,' she had fussed. 'Make sure to wear sensible shoes, Sarah. Even the short walk to the car could be hazardous in your elegant high heels. And, apart from the problems of getting about, Lord knows how they'll manage to prepare the ground for the old man's resting place. Typical, isn't it? Just like him to choose the worst frost in years to shake off the mortal coil. And your grandma's insisting that they bring him back from Morecambe to lay him in the family grave over at Shipton.' Sarah allowed herself a smile. Her mother had prattled on in this vein for some time and Sarah knew that it was bluster to cover her real sadness at the death of her father-in-law. For, in spite of his stiff, Victorian attitude, he had been a real family man at heart. Alice had become extremely fond of him, although it had taken a few years for her to learn about his kind heart and generous nature.

The hospital staff had been wonderful, coping with this major emergency, treating the injured with dedicated care whatever their state. Sarah knew, too, that she had been one of the lucky ones. From snippets of conversation overheard she learned that there had been fatalities and, when she allowed her thoughts to dwell upon those sudden, terrifying moments a few hours ago, she was not surprised. They had put her leg in plaster up to the knee, given her something more to help with the pain and provided welcome tea and biscuits and as much sympathy as they had time to offer. More serious patients needed them and so Sarah found herself, for the moment, back again in the waiting room. Others were there who, like Sarah, were sitting waiting, stunned and shocked, but glad to be alive, waiting for friends or relatives to come to take them home, or waiting for some kind of transport to enable them to complete their journey. Sarah had telephoned her home a few minutes ago. After what seemed like an age she had heard Jennie's anxious voice down the line, 'Hello. This is Mr. John Grange's residence.' Jennie was not at all at ease with telephones.

'Jennie, this is Sarah speaking. I need to talk to mother or father.'

'Oh, Miss Sarah, I was so worried about you all. There's no-one here but me. Where are you? Are you alright? Your parents went to meet your train and then Mr. James left, too. They telephoned to tell me that your train was delayed and not to expect them back for some time. They were all going to Doncaster by special train.' At this Sarah felt relief, just as if a warm infusion had been injected into a vein. It travelled through her body swiftly and she breathed a deep sigh. Soon, she thought, they'll be here. She felt as vulnerable as a child at this moment.

'Now Jennie, you mustn't worry any more. I'm not badly hurt, just a broken ankle and that's in plaster now. You go to bed and we'll see you tomorrow. O.K?'

'Thank you, Miss Sarah, I'll not go to bed, though. I'll not be able to sleep. I think I'll bank up the fire and bake a cake or two to welcome you home.'

Sarah smiled. 'Goodbye, Jennie. See you tomorrow.'

Sarah rang off and hobbled awkwardly on her crutches towards the waiting room. The place was less crowded now. Many patients had been admitted to the wards, some had been taken home and those who could continue their journey on other trains had gone back to the station. Weary nurses and doctors still moved about, their work not finished yet. As Sarah struggled to walk back to her seat she caught sight of a figure coming towards her. He wore the white coat and stethoscope that singled him out as one of the doctors. He stopped in his tracks when he saw her and Sarah gripped hard on the crutches, her face suddenly drained.

'Sarah?' he exclaimed, his face wreathed in smiles of recognition. 'Sarah!' He came briskly to her, took her gently by the shoulders and looked into her face. There was no answering smile from Sarah. Her face grew even whiter and her legs gave way altogether as she lost consciousness. She would have fallen heavily had the doctor not gently lowered her to the floor. The young nurse came to assist and they laid her on her side.

'Sister Jones was right, we should have admitted her, but we had no beds left,' said the nurse, loosening the clothing at Sarah's neck.

'Can you find a trolley?' The doctor's quiet voice carried authority but also revealed his concern. His eyes never left Sarah's face while the nurse fetched the trolley. Sister Jones hurried over. Between them they lifted her limp body onto the trolley.

'I was afraid that this might happen, doctor. Miss Grange said she thought she might have been knocked out for a time. She must be admitted for observation; a bed must be found for her. Nurse, go and see what you can do.' As Nurse Taylor sped off towards the wards a group of people entered the main door, just in time to see Sarah being wheeled into a side-room.

'There she is!' James and his parents rushed past the reception desk to follow Sarah's inert form, their faces anxious. Sister looked up in annoyance at this intrusion.

'Would you be kind enough to wait outside,' she almost snapped, glancing over her shoulder briefly. She was one of the old school who considered that relatives were nothing but a nuisance, that the patient was best served by qualified staff in the absence of any distractions.

‘These people are her parents; I am her brother. Surely we...’ James’s words were interrupted by the young nurse bursting into the room, breathless.

‘Sister, they’ve found a bed in ward four and...’

‘Nurse!’ Sister’s voice was icy-sharp. ‘I trust you did not deem it necessary to run?’

‘Sorry, Sister,’ she panted, ‘but they sent me to fetch Doctor Pearce. There’s an emergency on ward eight. Please, doctor...’ With a last glance at Sarah, the young doctor left the room. The Sister’s attention was focussed entirely on her patient, those who watched quite unaware that her unconscious state was a recent occurrence. As the nurse checked Sarah’s pulse and stroked her forehead, finding it cool and smooth, Sarah stirred and opened her eyes. The family, who had stood by in silence, refusing to be banished from the room, came closer now.

‘Welcome back, Sarah,’ said Sister Jones, her tone gentle and kind, ‘your mother and father are here to see you.’ And she made way for them as they each took one of her hands.

‘Oh, I’m so glad to see you,’ Sarah whispered. There were tears in Alice’s eyes, tears of utter relief that Sarah could speak to them. ‘I’m afraid I have a broken ankle, but that’s all.’ That’s all, thought John, that’s all? The girl had been unconscious for hours and had not even been allocated a bed in this God forsaken hospital!

‘You stay here, I’m going to find out what’s been happening,’ said John and marched off, ignoring entirely the bewildered nurses who stood watching Sarah.

'How are you feeling, darling?' Alice's voice was full of concern.

'Tired, so very tired,' came the reply and Sarah's eyes closed again.

'Sister!' cried Alice, 'She's gone again.'

'No, Mrs. Grange, she is just exhausted. She's sleeping now and that's the best thing for her. We'll take her to the ward, make her comfortable and leave her to rest. Then you and your husband can come with me and we'll have a cup of tea and a chat.'

John returned looking aggrieved since he had not found anyone in authority to speak to. Alice took his arm and they saw their daughter settled onto the busy ward.

'Come with me, now,' said Sister Jones, 'let her sleep. It's the best medicine.'

The winter dawn was breaking as they sipped tea in the Sister's office and learned that Sarah's sudden fainting spell was probably due to delayed shock, that she had seemed alright after her ankle had been set and that, most likely, they would be able to take her home after they had run a few more tests. Last night had been the busiest that Sister Jones could remember. At times the place had seemed like a battlefield. Details of the train crash had filtered through gradually. Of the two hundred and fifty-four passengers, two hundred and fifty-two had been accounted for. Sadly, sixteen had lost their lives and, of the rest, twenty-one had serious injury. Most had survived with nothing more than shock and cold. By now the hospital was beginning to return to normal. It had been a frantic few hours.

There was a knock on Sister's door.

'Come in!' Sister Jones apologised to Sarah's parents as the door opened and Nurse Taylor entered.

'Excuse me, Sister. Is it alright if I go off now?'

'Of course, nurse. I thought you finished your shift at seven.' It was now after nine.

'Yes, well, we were all so busy, Sister...' she looked embarrassed.

'Thank you, dear. It was good of you to stay. Off you go, now.'

'Er ... did they find that little girl, the one Sarah Grange was asking about?' ventured the nurse. Sister looked blankly at her, evidently ignorant of any child. Nurse Taylor went on, 'A little girl told me that she was waiting for Sarah. I told her to sit near the door so that she would see her mother the minute she arrived. Later, when Sarah came back from the plaster room, the child was not there. But Sarah did ask me if I'd seen her.'

'There must be some mistake,' interrupted Alice, looking puzzled. 'Sarah is not this child's mother. She has no children, she is not married and she was travelling alone from London.'

'My dear, you must have made a mistake. You know how many people we had through here last night. It was pandemonium at times. And, if the child had gone, she had, obviously, been claimed by someone else, her mother I expect.' The young nurse made as if to speak again, but changed her mind. Sister was probably right. It had all been a misunderstanding in the confusion of a chaotic night's work. She would go home and get some sleep. It had all been quite overwhelming and she knew she would have to be alert to work again on the night shift at eight o'clock.

'Yes, I must have been mistaken. It was a very busy night. Goodbye, Sister.' Nurse Taylor left, still looking puzzled.

'You must both be very tired, too, since you've obviously not slept last night,' said Sister Jones. 'Might I suggest that you take rooms at the George, stay tonight and give Sarah another twenty-four hours to recover. They will want to carry out some tests with Sarah when she wakes and another night here will do no harm, especially when she knows that you're near at hand. The George is just around the corner; I can recommend it. I am going off duty myself now, but, perhaps we'll meet again tonight.' She shook their hands and told them not to worry, Sarah would be fine.

They had not long to wait for James who came for them in a shiny new Morris, hired from the local garage and drove them to the George. The worry and tension of last night had taken its toll on all of them. Alice thought she had never been so glad to see an hotel room in her life. The pale pink satin eiderdown was all she noticed about the room as it beckoned her to lie down and rest. John ordered lunch and dinner, explained their visit and made sure there was a telephone in their room.

'Will it be just the one night, sir?' asked the receptionist.

'I certainly hope so,' said John. James took himself off for a walk. He needed some cigarettes, anyway, and a brisk walk would do more to revive his spirits than lying in a hotel bedroom. He found the park nearby. How beautiful the trees looked with their black tracery picked out in sparkling white. The sun was bright and the snow crunched under his feet. It was good to be alive on a day like this and thank goodness his sister was alive, too. He refused to contemplate what might have been, what he had feared so dreadfully when he had heard the wireless message and rushed to the station. James drew on his cigarette and blew smoke into the frosty air, his step light with relief that his sister was coming home. Reaching the railings at the edge of the park he had to walk up a short slope to gain the gate. At the top of the rise the trees petered out and he could see across to the valley below. There seemed to be a great deal of human activity going on down there. He screwed up his eyes against the sun and saw the great black scar cutting through the snow, the massive steam engine lying across the track, derailed at both ends. He saw the carriages, piled up like toys thrown about by an angry child, only the last three remaining, by some miracle, on the line and looking, at this distance, perfectly normal. Men were to be seen with crowbars wrenching off doors, climbing inside to retrieve luggage and personal belongings and others, loading them onto tractors with trailers since no other vehicle could cross the field. A crane was being towed by the same means. At both sides of the track he could see what appeared to be an unusually large number of police, working as teams, combing the area around the train. Using their truncheons they poked under the bushes close to the track while others, in a line, climbed the embankment on the other side, their heads lowered, examining the ground. James watched for a while as the enormity of the accident and its consequences slowly filled his mind. Sarah was, indeed lucky to have been so slightly injured. He shuddered as he turned away. With his back to the sun he made his way down, his step no longer springy, his face thoughtful. In a few years' time, he thought, I may find myself patching up the poor souls after accidents such as this. It was a sobering thought.

James regained the George Hotel and was thankful that it was opening time at the bar.

'I'll have a pint of best bitter, barman, please.' He found the beer refreshing. It helped to relax his tired bones.

'Been for a walk, sir?' said the barman, glancing at James's wet shoes and the bottoms of his trousers which were dripping water onto the floor. 'Lovely morning, sir. Pity about them poor folk on that train last night. We 'ad quite a few of 'em in 'ere. Them that wasn't 'urt, o' course.'

'Yes,' said James, 'a great pity.' And, feeling that the jolly barman intended to regale him with stories of the crash and its aftermath, James drained his beer and made for the door, but the barman was not prepared to let him escape so easily.

'You'll 'ave 'eard about the police 'unt, will you, sir?'

'Er ... no,' answered James, edging towards the door.

'Seems there's a couple o' folk missin'. They called in the constabulary to 'elp look for 'em.'

'I'm very sorry to hear that,' said James, politely,

finally making his exit and climbing the wide staircase to his room on the first floor. There he lay on the bed, staring at the ceiling until he heard his father knocking to tell him that it was lunch time. They went down together, the three of them, all rather lost in their own thoughts.

'A penny for them,' Alice said, taking John's hand across the table. John looked at his wife and his son.

'If you must know, I was thinking how unevenly life throws its arrows at us. You go jogging gently along, sometimes for years, and then, "Pow!" two or three hefty jolts hit you all at once. Why can't Fate space these things out at more regular intervals?' He grinned ruefully. 'It's dad's funeral on Monday.' James recalled the scene from beyond the park and thanked God that it would not be Sarah's during the same week.

'Visiting time!' said Alice, always to be relied upon to raise the mood. 'Come along, let's go and see Sarah.' It was not far to the hospital, so they walked. Alice kept their spirits up with cheerful chatter, seeming entirely unworried about her daughter. Deep down, however, she knew that nothing was ever certain in this life and she was old enough to know that there is almost always another hurdle to contend with sooner or later. And they all knew that Sarah would need to draw strength from all of her family to make a full and complete recovery.

Sarah was sitting up in her white bed with a welcoming smile for them.

'Hello, darling, you look wonderful,' said Alice, kissing her daughter.

'Oh, yes, sure I do in this chic hospital gown,' she laughed.

'Looks just great on you, sis. Watch out, you'll start a new trend,' James joined in the banter, grinning at his sister.

'Can you come home with us tomorrow?' John, as usual, got straight down to the important question.

'They think so. All the tests have been fine so far, but they want me to stay until the last test is through, just to be sure. I should be ready by lunch time at the latest, they said. Anyway, how come you're all still here? You must be tired out.'

They told her about the decision to book into the hotel, about the hired car, even about the improvement in the weather. Pleasant things they talked about. No-one mentioned the accident.

'Good! Now sit down, all of you. James, pull up that chair if no-one else needs it, and listen while I tell you about what happened to me on the train ... no ... before the crash. It's quite a weird tale and a bit of a mystery as well.'

And she began at the beginning and told them about Daisy.

Chapter 5

After her very welcome visitors had left Sarah spent some time resting her leg and talking to other casualties from the train. There was an elderly lady in the next bed who had been badly cut and bruised. Her husband, she told Sarah, had a head injury and was in a poor way. It was such a worry, not knowing how long they would have to stay here. Sarah sympathised and encouraged her to tell about what had happened last night. It seemed to help their recovery to talk over their frightening experience. The two of them, one very young, one at the opposite end of life's journey, seemed to be a source of strength to each other, lightening the load until they found themselves laughing about some aspects of the event.

'You certainly need to have a broad mind when you find yourself in hospital,' said Sarah's new friend. And, in a whisper, she went on, 'I could have died when that young doctor insisted that I take off my corset so that he could examine me.' With hindsight it was something to giggle about. Before long a little group had formed round Sarah's bed, attracted by the hilarity, all agreeing that it was good to speak to others who had been through the same ordeal.

'At one time last night, I thought I might not live to see the morning,' said one, 'but look at us now, all patched up and mended.' Sarah smiled at the woman as they made to move back to their own beds.

'Before you go, let me tell you about something very odd that happened last night,' said Sarah, suddenly seeing an opportunity to quiz these women about Daisy. 'Most of you will have been in the waiting room at some time when we were all brought from the train. There was a little girl. She had come to sit with me for part of the journey and was with me when we crashed. She was brought out first and, well, I had hoped to see her again. Did any of you see a child on her own?'

'What was she like?' asked a tall woman who had her arm in a sling.

'Dark, curly hair, a pretty face with blue eyes. Quite small, though she told me she was six and three quarters. She had on a grey school uniform.' There was some thoughtful shaking of heads until one said, 'I saw a small child, probably a girl, wrapped in blankets, sitting near the door, when they brought me in. She seemed to be asleep.' Sarah's face lit up. This agreed with Nurse Taylor's account.

'What time was that, do you think?' The girl considered.

'It's hard to say,' she said, 'I sort of lost track of time. But, I guess it must have been somewhere between twelve thirty and two in the morning. I can't be sure.'

'Well, thanks for that, anyway,' said Sarah, thoughtfully. But, where had she gone after that ... and with whom? Sarah felt sure that Daisy would not have gone willingly away without seeing her again. She made up her mind to ask questions of the night staff, if she could, before she left the hospital and, for once, she was thankful that she would be staying another night.

The group of women moved away, leaving Sarah alone with her thoughts. She fell into a light doze and memories of her grandparents filled her mind.

Grandpa Grange was gone. It had been so sudden. Until now there had not been a moment to muse over his loss. When had she seen him last? It must have been almost two years ago when she had returned from Switzerland. Yes, she had made a special visit to see the pair of them during the summer of '34 because she had not seen them since before she went abroad. During her four-year absence they had decided that the fresh sea air of Morecambe would be just the thing for grandma's health, so retirement to Morecambe it had been. She had learned that they had bought a bungalow quite close to the sea front.

Sarah snuggled down into her hospital bed enjoying the memories of that visit. She had imagined something small and pretty but, to her surprise the taxi had drawn up outside a pair of wrought iron gates through which she had glimpsed sloping lawns and a white-walled ... well, yes, it was a bungalow, it was pretty, but it was certainly not small. They had greeted her warmly, her grandma and grandpa, but with that certain reserve that was always theirs.

'We've missed you, my dear. Welcome back! It's good to see you looking so well. The tea's in the pot. What do you think of our new abode?' Sarah recalled how she had tried to answer that question with care. She could hardly say 'What do you want with a huge place like this?' could she? But before she had had time to reply grandma had been laughing and saying, 'It's your grandpa's fault! You're right to wonder, you are wondering aren't you, at the size of the place, but, you see, we both want to feel that we have room here to have John and Alice, David, James and Penny and yourself to stay; your friends, too, if they'd like to come. We've not regretted it. Hardly a month goes by without one or other of them here to keep us company.' Mrs Grange's face was wreathed in smiles. 'And now you're home you must come as often as you want.' The pleasant recollections faded as Sarah fell asleep.

The puzzle of Daisy's disappearance was never far from Sarah's mind. An argument was raging in her head. Was it or was it not up to her to instigate enquiries into the whereabouts of a child who had merely chosen to share her part of the train? And what of the two people from whom Daisy was running? Of all the women encountered on the ward and those whom Sarah had seen about the hospital since her arrival, none had resembled the woman in the red hat. Where was she? Where was her companion? Perhaps they were among the dead. Where, if that were the case, would that leave Daisy?

Sarah had been gazing through the window behind her bed. She was surprised how quickly the bright, sparkling, winter afternoon turned into the darkness of evening although it was barely five o'clock. She began to look forward to visiting time. Alice had promised that they would be back about seven after an early dinner at the George. She closed her eyes and thought over the period between Daisy's rescue and the time when she came to, lying on a trolley, with her mother and father holding her hands. For all she struggled to remember, she could not recall why she had fainted. She remembered coming back from the plaster room, searching all the time for Daisy. She could remember the telephone call to Jennie and that she had scanned the faces of the crowded room for sight of the couple who seemed to be the cause of Daisy's terror. But in vain. All three had vanished. Sarah, her eyes still closed, the better to concentrate, had to admit that she was not prone to fainting fits. She was level-headed and immensely practical. So what had induced so dramatic a reaction in her? And then she remembered. Sam. For some weird reason she had imagined she had seen Sam, coming towards her, his expression one of delight and surprise. It wasn't Sam, of course, how could it have been? But, yes, it was the shock that had made her pass out. The impact of suddenly seeing him again after all the trauma of the evening had been too much. Now she remembered the dizziness that had spread from the top of her head and taken away her senses. After that, she thought, they wheeled me in here and left me. All I wanted was to sleep. I must have been half asleep already to think I saw Sam Pearce after all these years! What tricks one's brain can play sometimes. Sarah opened her eyes, still thinking about Sam. He had been her first real boyfriend. He was everything a girl could wish for; tall, handsome, with dark wavy hair, kind, considerate and full of fun. Sarah took a drink of water, plumped her pillows, moved the heavily-plastered leg to a more comfortable position and lay back, giving herself up to memories of seven years ago. Her eyes closed again and she was back at school.

She and Madeleine attended the Girls' Grammar school just outside the city. Sam was at the same school but the boys' and girls' departments were kept strictly apart, even though they were housed in adjoining buildings. As they grew older, however, the young people inevitably found ways around the rules, such is human nature. Maddie and Sarah had been friends since they started at kindergarten when they were four years old and throughout the roller-coaster ride of childhood and adolescence they were inseparable. Sarah was the sensible one, quiet, sensitive, hard-working, with a mischievous sense of humour to balance her serious side. In contrast Madeleine was head-strong, clever and high-spirited. They were popular with their schoolmates and a perfect foil for each other, the one with her long, blond hair, fair complexion and fine features, the other, tall, dark and athletic with elegant good looks. Mad the Bad they called her, since she was for-ever disregarding the rules. Sarah smiled as she recalled her friend, flying in late to an English lesson or daring to walk out without her hat ... a heinous crime according to the headmistress. Sarah sighed. She did miss her. During the years since they left school, Maddie would turn up, out of the blue, from time to time, full of apologies for not having written. She would hug Sarah, and they would go off, arm in arm, chattering, catching up on the latest gossip. True to form, Madeleine had shunned the idea of college or university. The stage was her magnet and nothing was to stand in the way of her determination to 'tread the boards'. So, Sarah had not seen very much of her dearest friend during the past few years as Maddie pursued relentlessly her ambition to be an actress and Sarah, herself, had spent some time in Switzerland. That last year in the confines of the 'nunnery' as they jokingly called their school, was one crammed full of memories, happy and otherwise. Sarah almost giggled aloud as she recalled how excited they had both been when their parents had, at last, agreed to allow them to go to the cinema with two boys. (Maddie had, of course, been to the pictures with David once or twice already, but no-one was supposed to know). David had brought Sam who had been asking for weeks to be introduced to Maddie's beautiful, blond friend. They had sat in the darkened cinema, in the double seats thoughtfully provided by the management for those of an amorous disposition, and shyly held hands. Sarah and Sam had eyes for no-one but each other from that day onwards. The next time they went out together, they went alone, enjoying a long, summer walk and a picnic on the moors. It marked the beginning of many such excursions. They had enjoyed playing tennis together, swimming at the municipal pool or in the park where there was a beautiful outdoor Lido, marvellous when the weather was hot. They had walked, talked and listened to the dance bands, learning, hilariously, the latest dance steps. Whilst Maddie had a new boy every other week Sam and Sarah needed nobody else. It had been an idyllic summer, a time for growing up, for embracing the future with enthusiasm and hope.

Sarah breathed a deep sigh. Wonderful, magical days were those. She kept them locked deep in her heart where they were safe from the trauma and desolation of subsequent years.

She had been day-dreaming. It must be nearly time for Sister to graciously allow the visitors into the ward. It was then she saw him again. He was coming towards her bed, his dark hair and tall figure unmistakable, though more mature. And he was grinning broadly. Sarah's heart leaped as she pulled herself up against the pillows and drew up the sheet to hide that awful hospital gown. Steady, girl, she told herself, get a grip on your feelings and, especially, your tongue. He was not a figment of the imagination after all.

'Sarah, thank goodness they haven't sent you home, yet.' He took both of her hands in his. 'I wanted to come and find you last night but we worked until after five a.m. I was utterly exhausted and I knew you'd be asleep. I got home to the digs and slept the sleep of the dead. Woke up just in time to get back on duty! This is my first port of call.' Sarah found herself unable to speak, merely gazing at him as she listened to his words which almost fell over each other as they tumbled from his mouth.

'I saw you last night, just for a minute or two. You fainted. I guess the dreadful time you had in the crash had just caught up with you. Anyway, you were just coming round when I had to rush away. It must have been awful. Poor Sarah! I could hardly believe it was you. How do you feel now?' He stopped for breath, his eyes searching her face for a clue to her reaction at his appearance. Sam's torrent of words had given Sarah a few moments to compose her thoughts and to arrange her face into an expression of welcome. Her heart was pounding. She felt he was certain to notice. Self-possession came to her aid and she smiled brightly.

'Oh, Sam, it's lovely to see you. Come and sit down. You must tell me how you come to be working here. I was amazed when I saw you coming down the ward. How long have you been in Doncaster?'

'This is my first year out of Medical School. I'm doing my Junior Housemanship here. This was the nearest place to home and, when they agreed to have me I jumped at the chance. Only been here since last September. I'd had enough of London so decided to apply to hospitals in Yorkshire so that I can see the old man a bit more often. Besides, I missed the moors and dales more than I ever thought I would.'

'So did I. Miss the Yorkshire countryside I mean, when I was away in Switzerland,' said Sarah. 'Switzerland has its own brand of beauty which I loved, but the colours of home, with everything so fresh and green, were a welcome sight when I came back.'

'When was that? How long have you been home? Where are you living?'

'Hey, slow down, one question at a time,' Sarah laughed. He hadn't changed! Still as charming as ever. But, thrilled as she was to see Sam again, she must be guarded and careful in her conversation with him, at the same time seeming to be the carefree girl he used to know. She, like him, was more mature, had grown into a woman in the intervening years since their adolescent romance.

'I returned to England two years ago and now I'm living back at home with mother and father, not to mention James, Penny and David. James and Penny are away most of the time, so there's just David and me.'

'What are they doing with themselves, the older two?' Sam enquired.

'Penny decided to train as a teacher. She's ideally suited to it, so she's away at college. James is following your example ... he's a medical student.'

'Poor chap! I wonder if he knows what he's let himself in for,' laughed Sam.

'And you,' he looked earnestly into her face, 'what about you?' There was no opportunity for her to answer for, simultaneously, the bell sounded for the visitors to enter and a nurse, looking anxious, hurried over to Sarah's bed.

'Oh, there you are, Dr. Pearce. Dr. Andrews sent me to find you. He's been waiting for the notes you took from Mr. Jackson this afternoon. He doesn't look very happy.' Sam pulled a face for Sarah's benefit which made her smile.

'That's the Registrar after my blood!' said Sam. 'I'll have to scoot. No doubt he'll have a few cutting remarks about my idleness, but I'll eat humble pie for the boss. I'll come back and see you later when I can escape from his clutches. Here come your visitors I think. Toodle-oo!' Sam hurried away, passing Alice, John and James as he went, but they were too intent on seeing Sarah to pay him any attention.

'Darling! You look so well tonight. How's that leg?' said Alice, kissing Sarah.

'Was that your doctor we saw as we came in, dear? He looks very young.' John laughed. 'It's a sign of ageing when the doctors and policemen start looking like boys,' he commented, twinkling at his wife. How to handle this one, wondered Sarah, quickly marshalling her thoughts.

'Oh! That was Sam Pearce. He doesn't work on this ward. I knew him at school, years ago. He remembered me and came to say "hello". He was, er, a friend of a friend of Madeleine's.' This was very true!

'Nice for you to see a friendly face here,' said John. Sarah guided the conversation to other matters.

Assuming that she would be discharged tomorrow she wanted to know about the plans for Grandpa's funeral. With all that had happened since Thursday lunch-time, when she had set off on her journey northwards, the purpose of it had been almost eclipsed. John and Alice explained the arrangements for Monday. There would be a service at the Anglican Church where the family had worshipped for three generations, followed by interment at the nearby cemetery.

'It will be just the family and close friends at the cemetery,' said John. 'I expect there will be quite a number at church to say goodbye to him.'

'And Jennie's preparing a light lunch for everyone who comes back to the house afterwards,' added Alice. 'There'll be all the family and a few close friends.'

'How's grandma coping with all this?' asked Sarah. 'It must have been a double shock when she heard about the train crash. I haven't even asked where she is at the moment.'

'Mother's coping very well. His death was not entirely unexpected but it was very sudden even so. She was badly shaken and really needed the family round her. She's at Annie and Jim's now. I expect she'll stay for a while after the funeral but she'll go back to Morecambe when she's ready. Remember, your Grandma is thirteen years younger than father and she has plenty of life to live yet, God willing.' They talked until the visitors' bell rang. They would telephone in the morning and come to pick her up as soon as they were allowed.

'Sleep well, see you tomorrow,' they bid each other goodnight.

The ward became quiet again, the lights were lowered; patients were expected to retire early and to rise early in the mornings. The ward was run on regimented lines and woe betide anyone who broke the rule. Sarah was not a rule-breaker herself, but she chuckled as she thought how Madeleine would fare in a place like this. She was wondering if Sam would turn up again at her bedside. She hoped he would. It had occurred to her that he might know something about Daisy. He might have seen her, talked to her, treated her, even. He might know where she had gone ... and with whom. Do come, Sam!

Dr. Pearce was delighted at the warmth with which he was received at her bedside at twelve-thirty a.m. He had been a trifle doubtful about disturbing her at this hour. Sarah had had her eyes closed, but she was not asleep and she sat up as soon as she heard footsteps approaching.

'Sam! You're still here! I thought you might have gone home.'

'No, I'm covering nights all this week. Sorry I had to rush off this afternoon, but all in the line of duty, as they say.' They were both whispering, the ward was dark and most of its inmates asleep. There was a movement from the desk at the end of the room where Sister sat, bending over some paper-work, under the light from a reading lamp. The crackle and rustle of her crisply starched apron heralded her approach, though her rubber-shod feet made no sound on the floor. Junior doctors, in her opinion, had a very great deal to learn and she would endeavour to ensure, at every opportunity, that lessons were learned. What did that young pup think he was doing, disturbing one of her patients at this time of night? And Sister Jones bustled across, determined to put a stop to this nonsense.

'Doctor Pearce!' Her stage-whisper would have woken all but the deepest of sleepers. 'Would you mind telling me what you are doing at the bed-side of one of my patients, on my ward, at this hour of the night.' Sister Jones could be formid-able when she chose. Sam was slow to respond. He was not good with formidable women, especially Ward Sisters. Sarah came to his rescue. She must not have him sent away now, not now, when she needed to ask him about Daisy.

'Dr. Pearce,' she said, 'is a very old friend of mine. We were at school together but we haven't met for years. He was called away when he visited me this afternoon after only five minutes. I would like to talk to him, please, Sister. I promise we'll be very quiet.'

'That's right,' said Sam, 'we'd like a chance to catch up. I won't stay long.' Sister Jones con-ceded defeat, her expression one of doubtful disapproval, clasped her hands under her ample bosom and rustled back to her post. There might, indeed, have been the vestige of a twinkle in her eye as she returned to her work at the desk.

They talked in low voices, fearful of disturbing other patients and so induce the wrath of Sister Jones. Sam began, taking her hand, 'You know, Sarah, it seems as if the last seven years have melted away. I feel as if it were only yesterday that we were together, walking over the moors.'

'I know what you mean, Sam,' she replied. It was the same with Madeleine. Whenever they met after a long period of time they always picked up their relationship as if no time had elapsed. Sarah felt this was the sign of true friendship. She felt no awkwardness in Sam's presence even though she knew that it might not be so very easy to take up where they had left off. She had changed ... everything had changed, and yet nothing had changed.

'Tell me, first, how you came to be travelling on that train,' said Sam.

'I was on my way back home. I'd been in London presenting some of our latest fabrics to the Guild of Master Tailors, along with several other companies, of course. The conference runs until Saturday, but I was returning early because Grandpa Grange has died. It's the funeral on Monday.' Her face clouded. With the dramatic events of last night, the sudden re-appearance of Sam, the mystery about the child, she had almost lost sight of the reason for her journey north.

'I'm sorry,' said Sam. 'As I recall he's the one who retired to Morecambe, yes?'

'You've a good memory, Sam! Yes, they moved for the sake of grandma's health, to get away from the mill chimneys, really. They love it there.' Before Sam could launch once again into his questioning, Sarah cut in with one of her own.

'Listen, Sam, there's something I've got to find out before I leave tomorrow, something that's been on my mind all day. To cut a long story short I want to find out the whereabouts of a little girl who came to sit with me on the train. No-one seems to know where she went after she was brought in here. Did you see her? She's small and dark. I was really worried about her ... she was so scared, running away from something ... I promised to help her ... we got separated ... I don't know what happened to her and...'

'Hey, wait a jolly minute. Not so fast, Sarah! Why don't you start at the beginning and tell me everything.' Their voices had become slightly raised. They were aware of indignant rustlings from the direction of Sister's desk.

'Why don't you put on a robe and we'll go and talk in the day-room,' whispered Sam.

'I only have my coat, that'll have to do. Hand me that crutch, Sam and I'll hang on to your arm.' Sarah was eager to leave the quiet ward. She hated the thought of disturbing others who wanted to sleep. They indicated to Sister Jones that they would soon return as Sarah hobbled along, finding Sam's company strangely comforting. They passed several other rooms, down a short corridor and gained the darkened dayroom where Sam found them both a chair and switched on a lamp.

'Now,' he said, 'start at the beginning.' When

she finally stopped for breath Sarah searched his face for a reaction. She found she had the folds of her coat tightly wound around her hands and there were tears in her eyes as she told him how the little girl, who had trusted her, had simply disappeared.

'As far as I know there was only one child, around that sort of age, aboard the train,' Sam said. 'I saw her while we were with the mobile units on the roadside. It was only a brief meeting. There were so many people! My job was to assess each casualty as they were brought out and direct them towards the appropriate vehicle ... you know, ambulance to hospital, bus to the church hall, that sort of thing. It was during a lull between patients that I had a minute to see to the child. Now that I really think about it, I'm sure it was Daisy. Yes, I remember, Arthur carried her over the field. He told me her name was Daisy. They were trying to get her mother out but the child had hardly a scratch. I think she came over here in one of the buses.' Now Sarah was hanging on every word, anxious but hopeful.

'One thing I missed when I told you Daisy's story,' she put in. 'They all assumed that I was her mother. I was in too much trouble myself, with my legs pinned under the seat, to have a sensible conversation with anyone about the mistake. I don't know what Daisy made of it all ... what she was able to tell anyone. Perhaps she was too scared to speak, or, maybe she thought that I would sort out the muddle when I got to the hospital. I suppose it was natural for people to think I was Daisy's mother since there was no-one else in our compartment.'

'So,' said Sam, 'where do we go from here?' The implication that they would be looking into the mystery together was not lost on Sarah. Sam was thoughtful. 'I could ask around the staff tonight and see some of the day staff before I go off duty tomorrow morning. What worries me most is what happened to that couple? Surely they, too, would have come over here after the crash. Let me have a word with the chaps who ferried the people into town on Thursday night. Someone's got to know something. I can ask Gerry, too. He's a police sergeant, he might have some news of them.'

'There isn't a lot of time,' Sarah said, 'I think I'll be going home tomorrow afternoon.'

'But I'm not going anywhere! I spend most of my waking hours in this place!' Sam sounded cheerful about the fact. 'I'm just your man to keep my ear to the ground. I'll let you know by telephone if I find anything. And don't worry. After all, this little girl isn't really your responsibility, you know.'

'Oh, but I'll always wonder if I don't get to the bottom of this, Sam, and I'm so glad you're here and willing to help.' She squeezed his arm, a simple action of gratitude, and suddenly there appeared a slight tension between them. It was as if this natural action had re-awakened a familiarity long forgotten and it surprised them both. Sam cleared his throat.

'You know,' he said, 'we've been so busy discussing your waif and stray that we've had no time to catch up on the last few years. It seems that fate meant us to meet up again, Sarah. I don't want to lose touch with you again. It's still there, isn't it, that special something between us?' He went on quickly, before she could reply, 'I'll need your 'phone number to let you know anything I learn about Daisy. It will be alright, won't it, for me to ring ... to ... well...' The words trailed off into silence as he looked into her face. What was she thinking? Her expression was distant and strange. Lord! Was there somebody else? How stupid of him to believe that a girl as lovely as Sarah would be unattached. Fool! No wonder she had withdrawn her hand and was sitting slightly further away.

'Sarah, I'm sorry. I should not have barged in like that. It's just that I hoped you might feel the same. I had no business to assume you are just as pleased to see me again. And it's really too bad of me to put you on the spot like that. I hope you can forgive me. Come, I'll walk you back to the ward. Sister'll think we've absconded.' He tried to sound jocular, to make light of his clumsiness. Sarah remained strangely quiet, smiled at him and took his arm. She felt it would serve her purpose at the moment to keep him in the dark as to affairs of her heart, but she was quick to put him at ease as they made their way along the passage again.

'That's alright, Sam. I am pleased to see you again. You must know that, but just now I've only three things on my mind, Daisy, the funeral and getting my foot healed. That's quite enough for anyone, don't you think?' She smiled up at him. 'Come on, let's leave the rest till morning.'

'Don't forget to collect any luggage you had with you on the train, will you?' said Sam. 'All the stuff was cleared from the train by the police. Yours should have been put in here.' He pushed open a door. The empty side-ward had been used to store cases and bags and assorted personal items. 'Shall we just check that yours is here? Save you time tomorrow?' Sarah leaned against the wall as he switched on the light. The luggage was piled up neatly, the empty bed held smaller things, umbrellas, briefcases, hats and coats.

'Here's your case, I think. Your initials? Sarah?' But Sarah was not listening. She was staring at the things on the bed. Sam's eyes followed her gaze which was fixed, mesmerised for a moment, on a woman's hat. Bright red, with a scarlet flower on the crown and netting that had seen better days.

'What is it?' asked Sam. 'You've gone quite pale.'

'That's her hat, the woman seeking Daisy on the train.' Sarah made a lightning decision then, dismissing any consequences in favour of taking a risk.

'Quick, Sam, pull out my case, yes, that's the one. Put the red hat in it.' Sam hesitated, perhaps not realising the significance of the hat at first.

'Don't you see, it could give us a clue to who she is.' Sarah's impatience at his slowness had her hopping on one foot towards the middle of the room, anxious to execute the theft herself.

'Hey, steady on! That's the way to get more broken bones!' He steadied her and helped her to the foot of the bed. 'Don't move.' He swiftly opened her case and popped the red hat inside. 'This your briefcase, too?' She nodded. 'I'll put them together here, then you can collect them when you leave. Come on, now, back to bed and

I'd better make tracks to get some work done.'

In the early hours Sarah lay awake. There would be no time until after the funeral to follow up her lucky find amongst the luggage, but at least she had something to go on. Meantime Sam's enquiries may turn up something. She prayed that, wherever Daisy was, she would be safe from harm. She was glad that time had not allowed too many of Sam's questions about the past. Perhaps some day she would tell him. She had not even told him about Andrew, quiet, faithful Andrew who was always there, had always been there, and who had promised to wait for her until she felt ready to make a full commitment to him. This was the first time for days that she had given him a thought. Poor Andrew, he would be wondering why she was not home yet. Perhaps he had 'phoned the house and Jennie would have told him about the accident. She knew he would be there, at the funeral, on Monday, ready to be by her side whatever the day might bring. Gradually her rambling thoughts settled and Sarah slept.

Chapter 6

Another X ray showed that her ankle was set correctly for a full recovery and Sarah was relieved that she could go home with her parents and brother straight after lunch. The four of them were welcomed by Jennie who insisted on plying them with tea and cake in front of a roaring fire that she had made in the sitting room. Sarah sat with her foot on a stool simply enjoying being at home. Alice needed to make several telephone calls, the first to her parents to tell them they were all safely home and to assure them that their grand-daughter was recovering from her ordeal. They were very close, Alice and her mother. Sarah watched through the door into the hallway as Alice talked to Granny Ambler. What a handsome woman Alice was with her delicate features, so like her own, but with dark brown hair worn longer these days, caught into a soft ribbon at the nape of the neck. She was forty-two, her graceful figure, slim and elegant, looking perfect in the flowing lines of current fashion. She sat erect, her posture modelled on that of the Queen whom Alice admired affectionately, from afar. Like many she was a dedicated follower of the doings of the Royal family. She was answering her mother's anxious enquiry.

'Yes, mother, she's just fine, already quite nippy on the crutches. She has to keep the plaster on for six weeks, but she insists on going back to work well before that ... yes, I hope she will take a couple of weeks off first. It must be very tiring at first, learning to move around with the crutches. John says all she needs now is a parrot on her shoulder... Yes, I'll tell her, and we'll see you at church tomorrow... That's right, we'll be there.' Alice returned to the fireside. 'Granny sends her love, and Poppa says you've to take it easy and do as you're told with that foot. They're both so relieved that you're safely home.'

James, having delayed his return to Edinburgh in order to attend his grandfather's funeral, had been to take the hire car to the local depot and was just coming through the front door, dashing the slush from his shoes.

'There's been a fast thaw today,' he commented. 'But there's not much sign of the wind dropping. The main roads are almost clear but our drive's a sorry mess. Before I come in to get warm I think I'll shovel a clean path to the front door, shall I, mother? Be safer for all the visitors.'

'Thank you, James,' called Alice, as the telephone rang in the hall, 'and see who that is, would you, before you go out.'

'Hello, this is 7249, James Grange speaking... Yes... Yes, she is. You'll have to give her a minute to get to the 'phone. Hold on!... It's for you, Sarah,' he called. Sarah struggled to her feet and into the hallway. It was Madeleine.

'Oh, how lovely to hear from you,' said Sarah, her smile lighting up her face. 'Where are you?'

'I'm here, at home. I came round, hoping to see you on Friday and Jennie told me what's been happening. You poor old thing. How's the leg, and how are you?'

'Learning to hop!' laughed Sarah. 'Did they tell you about Grandpa Grange?'

'Yes, and I'm very sorry. You must all be very upset. He was a lovely chap and so kind and generous. You know I stayed with them for the whole summer season a couple of years ago when I was playing in Concert Party in Morecambe. I'll be at the funeral, of course.'

'Listen, Maddie, why don't you come over this

evening? We'll be finished dinner by eight, then we can do a bit of catching up. I assume you're not working at the moment?'

'It's called "resting" in the business,' retorted Madeleine, laughing. 'If the family won't mind I'll pop over later, as you say. Gosh! It must be almost two years since I saw you.'

'Well, that's settled, then. See you round about eight fifteen.'

Sarah knew that no-one would mind a visit from Madeleine. There was such a lot to tell her and so much to hear about her friend who seemed to lead a far more exciting and glamorous life than she did. And, despite being very tired after these few, stressful days, Sarah did not intend to go to bed early tonight. There was just a chance that Sam might call her.

A few minutes later Sarah had to struggle once more from her chair to the 'phone. This time it was Andrew.

'At last!' he said, 'your 'phone's been red hot for the past two hours. I've been so worried, sweetheart. Such a dreadful thing to happen to you, and on top of Mr. Grange's death, too. How are you feeling?'

'Yes, it has been a busy line. I'm alright, thank you, just a bit shaken up and sore. But I'll soon mend.'

'I want to hear all about it, but more than that, I want to see you. I could call this evening, bring flowers and comfort?' Andrew sounded hopeful. Sarah's own reaction to his obvious concern surprised her.

'That's really kind, Andrew, and I do appreciate

it. But could we make it another time? Tomorrow afternoon, perhaps? I'm so tired, my ankle aches and I've just said that Maddie can come this evening. Girl-talk, you know. And then I must get an early night. Sorry!' She hoped she did not sound rude, offhand. Nevertheless she was heartily relieved to have Maddie's visit as her excuse.

'That's O. K., I understand. You're bound to be tired. I'll see you tomorrow, then. Sleep well!'

Whatever is the matter with me? Sarah thought. Normally I'd be only too pleased to see Andrew, anxious, even. The sudden reappearance of Sam, she knew, had ruffled her composure and disturbed the equilibrium of her present, well ordered life. Was she going to be able to deal with his renewed friendship? One thing she was sure of, now that they had met up again, her feelings for Sam were very different from those she had for Andrew.

Penny had been to visit Grandma Grange during the afternoon and David had been playing football with the school team but by six-thirty they were back and Jennie was in her element, preparing dinner for all the family. It was not often, these days, that they all sat down together. Sarah was obliged to describe the events of Thursday evening to them all. They were intrigued by her tale about Daisy and full of sympathy for her injury and the frightening experience. James, with a twinkle in his eye, interrupted with, 'Funny how you forgot to mention a certain young doctor we saw hurrying from your bedside. I suspected him of being responsible for the colour in your cheeks.'

'James! Don't tease,' said his mother. Sarah was

thankful for the sound of the telephone that brought this altercation to an end. James ran to pick up the receiver, returning in a moment doubled up with mirth.

'Dr. Pearce ... for you,' he announced with a flourish. And, sotto voce, 'What did I tell you?' Sarah almost hit him with her crutch as she hobbled out of the room. She closed the door behind her.

'Hello, Sam.'

'Sarah! Glad you're safely home again. I'm really pushed for time. It looks like a busy night on the wards so this will have to be quick. I thought you'd like to know that I spoke to Gerry, you know, that policeman friend of mine, just before I came on duty. He was interested to hear of your encounter with that couple on the train. It seems that the number of people taken off the train didn't tally with the check that was made after the train left Grantham. There were two short.'

'Ye-s,' Sarah was beginning to grasp the implications of this report. Sam went on.

'They were searching for anyone thrown from the train, perhaps lying injured, when James watched them from the park on Friday morning. They didn't find anything.'

'Did you tell Gerry about Daisy?'

'Yes, I did. He was very concerned and promised to make some detailed enquiries. This was the first time a missing child had been mentioned. She would have been included in the count that was made as the passengers came off the train. Anyway, Gerry said he'd talked this over with his sergeant. They're still a bit worried in case these two missing people are still out there, somewhere, needing help. Otherwise, why should they not have turned up at one of the refuge centres on Thursday night? The only other likely explanation is that they didn't want to be found. That, says Gerry, raises suspicion that they were up to no good.'

'That was my impression, too,' said Sarah, 'they were certainly very oddly behaved. But I only saw them briefly. I could have been mistaken.'

'Gerry says that it would help if you could give a description of the pair. Their real concern is to find the child, of course. They really need to talk to you about Daisy. So far, all they have is my account of seeing her by the road. They are questioning the nursing staff now. Someone must have cared for her that night.'

'Look, Sam, tell Gerry I'll be pleased to help if I can. I could talk to the police over the 'phone tomorrow.'

'Good. Now I have to get back to work. I'll be in touch again very soon.'

Sarah stood by the telephone, her thoughts miles away, for several moments. She jumped violently when the doorbell rang right beside her. Through the stained glass panel she could make out a tall figure, still unmistakable as her childhood friend. Throwing the door open wide she greeted her with delight.

'Maddie! Right on cue! Come in, do. I've so much to tell you.'

Chapter 7

Joe and Doris Smithson watched the stricken railway carriages as rescue workers lit the scene with their torches. The bitter cold quickly seeped into their bones, the sleet driving through their thin clothing as they knelt hidden in the bushes beside the track. Joe was furious at the turn of events, his wife simply terrified and shaking with cold. He had called her a 'stupid woman' when he dragged her away, protesting, from the wreck. He had forced her into this death-trap of a hiding place, threatening further violence if she attempted to move or reveal their presence.

'Shut up,' he hissed now as she tried again to reason with him, her teeth chattering, her breath rasping with strangled sobbing. 'Just bloody well shut it, or you'll have 'em over here with those torches. Get behind that bush and keep your 'ead down.' And to reinforce his orders he propelled her forcibly backwards, catching her off-balance. There was a dull thud as her head hit the ground. Joe continued to watch the passengers as they left the train. He was pleased with himself for silencing his wife so totally. She knows who's the boss around here, he thought, grinning. There was a deal of hammering on one of the carriage doors, followed by the door's opening. Joe watched, unseen, as the men lifted Daisy out and someone began to take her across the field.

'Come on, now,' he whispered, 'we'll find out where they go with her.' There was no response from his wife. 'Doris! Come on, move, can't you? Stupid bitch,' he added under his breath. He turned to see if she was following, went back and saw her lying, motionless on the ground.

'Get up!' He took her by the shoulders and shook her roughly. Doris opened her eyes. They were glazed, unfocussed, empty. 'Oh, my God!' With one eye on the retreating figure carrying Daisy he made a snap decision. 'Stay here, don't move. I'll come back for you later. I have to see where they take the girl.'

Joe kept to the shadows at the edge of the field, skirting the open area where the snow lay. He might be noticed, even though it was dark, if he crossed the open ground and footprints, he knew, were less noticeable close to the hedge-bottom. He could see the lights of the vehicles waiting for the passengers as he gained the road some way further up. From here he reckoned it would be a simple matter to walk down to the group as if he were some local farm worker on his way home after a late night out. He stuffed his trilby inside his coat, undid the buttons and belt of his trench-coat and tied the belt untidily round his waist. Sauntering slowly past, his unsteady gait belied the fact that his wits were far from dulled by drink. It took him only a few seconds to see where Daisy was placed in the ambulance and to hear where she would be taken. As soon as he had cleared the arc of lights he retraced his steps to the track-side bushes. With Daisy's whereabouts certain for the moment he had to get his wife out of this field and into somewhere warm and dry. He regretted being so harsh with her, now. It was often like this, he reflected as he negotiated his careful route around the edge of the field, he the one to charge ahead, she the one to think things through, plan, prepare, take time. Sometimes it made him so impatient he just flew into a temper and hit out at her. But this whole affair wouldn't even be under way, for God's sake, if it hadn't been for Doris's idea and her careful scheming. His remorse grew and his steps quickened as he approached her hiding place. What had he done?

She was lying where he had left her. She had curled her feet up to her body and wrapped herself as best she could in her coat.

'Doris! Doris! Wake up, oh, God, please wake up,' he whispered, lifting her off the cold earth and putting his own coat round her shoulders. She stirred, opened her eyes.

'You're back. Don't tell me ... you're sorry you lost your temper, you're sorry you left me here to freeze, you don't know what came over you, you're sorry! Well just get me out of here first and then we'll talk about how sorry you are. You're lucky I'm not another of those dead bodies they've been carrying out of that train. Come on, get me somewhere where I can dry out and get warm. My head's splitting and there's no chance I'll be able to think straight till we find a roof over our heads.' It was a tirade he felt he deserved and Joe was all solicitude as they made their way to the road, struggling against the strength of the wind.

It was about two hundred yards downhill to a crossroads where four country lanes met. It must have been a staging post in the days of horse travel because there were not one but two hostelries on opposite corners. Both shone welcoming light from the windows in spite of the late hour, after midnight in fact. Joe was almost carrying Doris as they came to the Dog and Gun, pushed open the door and were met by an astonished landlord.

'Tha's a mite late in't' day, lad! Niver mind, bring thi missis ower t't fire an' a'll get it blazin' fo' ye. Whativer's 'appened t't' pair o' ye?'

'Thanks, landlord,' said Joe, producing the tale that Doris and he had invented as they battled through the sleet. 'Our car broke down. We left it a good mile up the road, pushed it into a gateway and walked. That fire's the best thing I've seen all day. I don't suppose you have a room for the night, have you?'

'I daresay mi wife'll fit you up with summat. We don't 'ave much call for rooms in't' wintertime, but give us 'alf an hour and we'll see you all right. Can a get ya summat t' eat? Or a sup?'

'I just want to be dry and warm,' said Doris. 'Maybe a sandwich, though, would make us feel better.' The fire was huge, filling the inglenook with its comforting warmth and it was not long before Doris was feeling half human again and ready to tackle the next item on the agenda of this eventful night.

They must have Daisy back. It was a delicate problem. But, here goes, thought Doris. She asked the landlord did he have a car. No, he said, but the man next door ran a taxi and did Doris want to fetch something from her car?

'Well, no. It's more serious than that. You see we

had our little girl with us when we broke down. We spoke to some ambulance men on the roadside, asked them for help. They told us they were far too pressed to help, but, if we wanted to walk to the nearest pub, they would take our daughter over to the hospital with their patient and we could collect her when we had found accommodation. She would be saved the long, cold walk through this awful weather. We have to pick her up as soon as we can ... from the hospital ... in Doncaster.' Doris rattled through this fabrication as fast as she could, hoping that it did not sound too far-fetched a story. Luckily the landlord, though good-natured to a fault, was not too bright. He accepted the scenario as painted by Doris without analysing it for flaws. Why should he, indeed? He suggested that Joe should go and rouse the taxi-driver and drive to the hospital without delay. The Smithsons could not believe their luck. Within the hour Joe was being driven into the nearby town.

It was just after one o'clock, the taxi waiting outside, when Joe appeared in the crowded lobby of Doncaster Hospital. No-one paid him any attention as he found Daisy, sleeping, on a chair near the door. In a second he gathered up the blankets and the child and hurried out into the night. Daisy woke briefly as the cold night air touched her face. The blankets were warm and cosy, she was sleeping the deep sleep that only childhood offers and she was carried quickly to the taxi. She slept until Joe laid her down on the bed next to his wife in the small bedroom in the pub.

'Well done, Joe. You've been quicker than I expected,' whispered Doris.

'She was easy to find, just inside the door.'

'Did anyone stop you?' she asked anxiously.

'No, they were all too busy. The place was full. I don't think I was even noticed but I didn't hang around to find out.' Daisy stirred and sat up regarding the two of them with eyes suddenly wide with apprehension. She looked round at the room and back at Doris and Joe, drawing up her knees and hugging them to her chest.

'Are you hungry, Daisy?'

'No.'

'I got a nice glass of milk for you. I know it's very late and we should all be asleep, but a little drink might help you to sleep again,' said Doris, her voice gentle and kind. 'We've all had a fright on the train and we were so worried when we couldn't find you. We looked everywhere, Daisy. Where were you?'

Joe joined in. 'Please have some milk, Daisy. We're sorry you were so scared on the train. Where did you go?' Silently the little girl accepted the milk and drank most of it without uttering a word, still taking in her new surroundings and watching these two strange adults warily. They were being kind to her now. They seemed like different people.

'Never mind, Daisy, we needn't talk any more now. We're all so tired. Look, there's a small bed just for you. We can talk in the morning,' said Doris. And she laid the child on the bed, covered her and wished her goodnight. As they made themselves comfortable for what was left of the night, Doris whispered, 'Remember, Joe, this will only work if the child is not afraid of us. We can't have her running off like that again, so keep a check on that temper of yours and watch your tongue tomorrow. O.K?'

Mine host and his wife provided a hearty breakfast for their unexpected travellers and made a great fuss of Daisy. They showed her pictures of their grandchildren and produced a box of toys to amuse her while she waited for Joe to pay the bill and order the same taxi as they had used last night. The weather had eased somewhat and the prospect of a thaw was confirmed when the morning sun rose like a huge yellow balloon, bathing the snow-covered land in pink and silver. As they drove through the Christmas card scene Daisy was captivated by it, her face pressed to the taxi window, her fears of the previous night obliterated by the excitement of the moment. Her stomach was full, her clothes dry and Doris said they were going to Leeds. This was better than school, anyway, she thought, and these people were not so bad, after all.

At the railway station Joe found, not surprisingly, that trains to Leeds were cancelled until the track was cleared later in the day, they hoped. They could go via York, but that could take most of the day.

'We'll try the bus-station,' decided Doris. It would be less expensive, anyway, she thought. They had spent almost all the money that they had saved for this weekend with Daisy on their room, breakfast and taxi fares and Doris was worried. Joe was not good with money. If it were in his pocket he would spend it, so Doris held the purse-strings. There was a bus leaving for Leeds at ten o'clock. Joe bought tickets and they found a cosy corner in the station cafeteria. A copy of the *'Rainbow'* lay on a table, abandoned by its first reader and eagerly seized upon by Daisy. As she immersed herself in the antics of Tiger Tim and the Bruin Boys, Doris and Joe talked in undertones over the cup of coffee they were sharing.

'When are we going to tell the child?' asked Joe.

'Later rather than sooner is my preference,' answered his wife. 'My mind's in a complete whirl at the moment since all that stuff last night and the lies we had to tell to get her back. I'm having trouble getting my thoughts back on track. Oh, dear, a pretty bad phrase to use, under the circumstances,' she smiled ruefully at Joe. 'What say we stick with what we said at the Home, for the time being. Give me time to iron out any wrinkles, you know, in case she knows more than we think she does. No use rushing and digging a hole to fall into. I thought I had it all worked out, but now I'm not so sure. It occurred to me that we never asked that Mrs. Johnson how much she's been told about her past, if anything. Let's leave it as it is.'

'Right,' said Joe. He had every confidence in Doris, of course, but this was by far the most ambitious escapade they had tackled yet and he could not help but feel a bit nervous. Think about something else, he said to himself, and aloud he remarked, 'It's a pity you lost that hat. I liked it. What happened to it?'

'I'm not sure. It must have fallen off somewhere in the field. I didn't realise, till we got to the pub, that it was missing. There'll be another where that one came from, more than likely, but, yes, I liked it too. Rather a classy little titfer. It came from one of the best milliners in Leeds.'

'You just wait, sugar, before long you'll be able to buy all your clothes from the best shops in town and I'll have a Crombie overcoat and some real alligator shoes. We'll show 'em right enough. We'll be proper swanky folk when our daughter comes home.' Doris lowered her voice and signalled to Joe to do the same. The pair of them had become quite animated during the last exchange.

'You did check on the house again, didn't you, on Thursday ... before we left?' she murmured.

'Yeah ... it's right enough. Called away unexpected like till the end of the month. All tickety-boo there,' grinned Joe.

Daisy said little during the journey on the bus. She felt glad they had not asked again where she went when she had found Sarah on the train. Her young mind was keen enough to realise that she did not want to share this encounter with these two, even though, at present, they were being nice to her. She remembered, with a slight shudder, how the man had shouted at the woman, how he had taken her aside, pushed her against the wall at the railway station. He had put his face close to hers and said awful things to her and shaken her by the shoulders as they waited for the train to take them to Leeds, that dreadful train that had crashed off the rails and hurt Sarah. She knew they were arguing violently and that it was something to do with her. She thought she had done something wrong, but she did not know what it could be. In the end he had marched over to Daisy, grabbed her roughly by the arm and had almost thrown her into the train. She remembered falling and grazing her knee, then turning to see the man going back for the woman and pushing her rudely as he followed her onto the train.

Daisy looked steadily out of the window of the bus. In one way she wished they would talk to her, tell her more about where they were going ... and why. In another she was relieved that they let her alone. At least they seemed calm and friendly just now. Better not risk making the man angry again. Still she felt uneasy. The prospect of this outing, when it had been put to her at the Home, had thrilled and excited her. Now she was not so sure about it. She thought about Sarah and wondered where she was now. When I grow up, she thought, I'll go and find Sarah and say thank you for looking after me on the train. Daisy thought that anything would be possible when she grew up.

The scene through the window had changed. There were now more houses and large buildings. The bus went under bridges where Daisy could see the railway running overhead. They stopped now and again for passengers to get on or leave the bus and each time Daisy wondered if it would be their turn to get off. She ventured to ask, 'Are we nearly there, yet, at Leeds?'

'Not quite, dear, another half an hour or so I should say. Then we have to take the tram. You'll like that. Have you ever ridden on a tram, Daisy?'

'I don't think so,' said Daisy, doubtfully. 'I might have seen a picture of one.'

The tram was the best part of the journey for Daisy. Doris took her hand as they came out of the station and Daisy gazed around at the centre of the big city. There was a large, open space surrounded by tall buildings, a garden at its hub with a huge statue of a man riding a horse. The front legs of the horse were raised, as if it was about to jump into the air. Daisy could not take her eyes off it. She had never seen anything like it and her feet began to drag behind Doris as she tried to keep this amazing sight in view. On the far side of the square a large hoarding carrying advertisements leaned at a crazy angle, blown over by the gale and now being attended to by a gang of workmen. This, too, caught Daisy's attention and Doris began to lose patience with the child.

'Come along, Daisy, or we'll miss our tram,' she cried, pulling the child's arm as Daisy twisted and turned, trying to take in the unfamiliar scene of City Square.

There were rails set into the ground, just like the ones Daisy had seen on the train track, but she could not see any trains here.

'This is our stop,' Joe told her, as, suddenly they came to a halt and joined a small row of people waiting beside a signpost. They, too, were watching the attempts of the workmen to sort out the mess of the fallen hoarding. One of them said that the wind had blown the structure onto a passing tramcar and that five people had been injured. No-one could remember a worse storm.

Daisy had time to look around the square now. She saw several vehicles that she took to be the trams, circling the square, stopping and starting with a great amount of clattering and squealing. She could not make out which end was the front of these huge, strange things which hissed and clanked their way along the rails. One of them came towards her and she took several steps backwards, only to be grabbed by Joe.

'Here we are. Up you go, Daisy!' They seemed to be getting on at the wrong end. There was a wheel to steer it with and lots of brass levers and a man in uniform who looked like the driver. Daisy was very confused.

'Let's go on top,' said Joe and Daisy was helped to climb some very steep, iron stairs. It was a bit like a bus when you got inside, except that the seats were made of wood and had very straight backs. They were followed up the stairs by the man in uniform, who shouted, 'Tickets, please!' and made Daisy jump. She watched, fascinated, as he produced three tickets from a small clip-board strapped to his chest and put the money for them into a leather bag held by another strap. Once they had found a place to sit Daisy could not remain silent any longer. She bombarded Doris and Joe with questions. They could not tell her who was the man on the horse, but they knew all about the trams and how they had a space at each end for a driver so that they could go up and down the line without having to turn round. Joe showed her how the wooden seats could be moved to face in either direction, and he pointed out to her, as another tram passed them, the long pole that carried electricity to drive the vehicle. Daisy ran to the front. You could see everything from the top of a tram, she thought.

She was really beginning to enjoy herself. The tram bowled along, swaying from side to side as it left behind the elegant buildings of the city. Daisy saw row upon row of red brick houses, close together and seeming rather dark and forbidding. There was very little snow here. The tram jerked to a stop several times and she turned round to see if Doris and Joe were ready to get off, but they still sat there and waved to her, smiling, as she stayed, glued to the view from the front of the tram. Gradually there were fewer of the tightly packed streets. Now she could see trees, a park where children were playing on swings and men were enjoying a game of football. Here the houses stood in gardens where lawns still had a covering of snow and the occasional snowman could be seen, gently melting in the sunshine.

'Come along, Daisy. Ours is the next stop,' she heard Doris calling. 'Hold tight as we go down.' Daisy scrambled off, still clutching the comic she had found at the bus station. She stood on the pavement, wondering which of these lovely houses belonged to them.

'Just a little way to walk, now. Then we'll be home to have a nice cup of tea,' said Joe.

But Daisy's legs were tired and her smile had faded by the time they reached the dingy, basement flat which was home to the Smithsons.

Chapter 8

Daisy regarded the houses they passed as Joe's 'little way to walk' extended to twenty minutes steady trudging along the Leeds pavement. They were all large, imposing homes with gardens shielding them from the road. Trees lined the pavement and, had she been older, Daisy would have recognised this as a wealthy residential area that had passed its best more than a decade ago. An adult passer-by would, perhaps, have noticed weeds growing in the driveways. Porches displaying half a dozen bell-pushes revealing multiple occupancy hinted that the street had seen better days. Peeling paint-work, grubby curtains and a general air of decay would have been evident to the average observer, but Daisy thought it was all wonderful ... until her legs began to ache and she found it hard to keep up with Doris and Joe.

Quite suddenly they turned in through a gateway whose double gates stood back at odd angles and Daisy followed as their feet crunched on a gravelled drive. The handsome front door was ignored as Doris led the way round the side of the house. Another entrance here had a flight of stone steps leading downwards to a door that Daisy could barely see at first.

'Here we are, home at last.' Joe found the key to the basement door. Daisy was relieved when he struck a match and a gas jet hissed and burst into life, bathing the doorway in its warm, yellow light.

'They've got the electric upstairs,' said Doris, 'but they never bothered with down here. I don't mind, really.' Daisy wondered whether Doris was speaking to her and, if so, what she should say in reply. She did not know what to say so she held her tongue and, as usual, used her eyes and ears to full advantage. This was not at all what she had expected but, as she no longer felt so afraid of these people, she was eager to take in her new surroundings and to make the best of it. All the same she did wonder when they were going to mention the main reason for this visit to Leeds. She thought they had told Mrs. Johnson that they knew where her real parents lived. They had talked together for a long time, Mrs. Johnson, Doris and Joe, while she had sat waiting outside the room. Daisy was used to this sort of thing. Children were never told anything. It was as if nothing mattered except that they were fed, kept clean and clothed and sent to school or to church on Sundays. Sometimes Daisy felt like shouting at the top of her voice, 'I'm here! I'm a big girl. I can understand.' But, of course, she never spoke these thoughts. She had learned at a very early age that life progressed much more smoothly if you held your peace, did as you were told and tried not to annoy the people who were looking after you. Indeed Daisy was ahead of her peers in maturity of this kind and often found herself looked to for support and counsel by them. Already there was an old head on those slight, young shoulders. She was not surprised that the people who might be her parents did not come to the Home themselves. She was not really excited about seeing them. After all, it was not the first time that someone had claimed to be her father and mother. Twice before couples had been to see Mrs. Johnson, talked a lot, looked at her and gone away. Other children at the Home told her that the same thing had happened to them. So Daisy was not filled with hopeful anticipation She had learned to take each day as it came, to accept what fate sent her way and not to waste time in fruitless dreaming. Secretly she kept one small dream locked away in the deepest corner of her heart. It was that, one day, perhaps there would be someone special who would stand by her bedside, stroke her forehead and kiss her good-night. She hardly ever took this dream out to examine it because she always found that it made her want to cry. It would never do to let the dream out now. No, she thought, not now.

Joe had lit three more gas mantles, and what was left of the afternoon sun managed to filter through the grey net curtains at the window which was half above and half below ground level. Daisy looked around. It was a large room. It was dominated by a huge, black iron cooking range with a fire-grate in the centre and an oven at each side. It occupied the whole of the chimney-breast and was topped by an elaborate mantel shelf supporting a number of pots and pans. Joe was even now rolling up newspaper as kindling, adding a few sticks of wood and pieces of coal and trying to coax a fire into life.

'It'll all look a deal more cheerful when the fire's lit,' said Doris, looking at Daisy's solemn little face as she watched Joe. 'We'll have the kettle boiling in no time, you'll see.' Doris had hung up her coat on the back of the door. 'Do you like tea, Daisy? Or will you have milk? I hope the milk will be still fresh. It should be, it's been so very cold these last two days.' She busied herself getting out cups and saucers from a very tall cupboard that filled the recess to the left of the range as Joe's fire made steady progress and he swung the kettle round on its hook to hang over the flames.

'I like tea, thank you,' said Daisy. There was a deep window sill below the sash with a couple of cushions forming a makeshift window seat and Daisy could see the rest of the room as she perched on the edge, her legs dangling. At each side of the fireplace sat a shabby armchair. A bare wooden table with four plain chairs around it occupied the centre of the room and was now adorned with a surprisingly pristine cloth, cups and saucers, three plates and knives and forks. At the back of the room an old Chesterfield took up most of the wall space and on the other wall a dresser with a mirrored back reflected Daisy's face. To its left there was a closed door.

'There, now,' said Joe, sitting back on his heels, 'the kettle will soon be boiling.' He got up and went to the other large cupboard to the right of the fireplace and opened both its doors. Daisy was surprised to see a sink with two taps and a draining board concealed inside here and she watched as Joe washed his hands clean of the coal dust.

'Come and wash your hands, Daisy. And, by the way, if you want the toilet, tell me and I'll show you the way. It's at the back.' Daisy dutifully washed and they sat down to cold ham and tomatoes and bread and butter, followed by tea and some sweet biscuits. As they ate Doris encouraged Daisy to talk about her life at Mrs. Johnson's.

'Are you happy there?' she asked.

'It's alright. Mrs. Johnson's kind to us. Mr. Johnson tells us stories about the railway. He works in the signal box sometimes and sometimes he helps to look after us.'

'Have you always lived with Mrs. Johnson, Daisy?'

'Ever since I can remember,' said the child, thoughtfully. 'I did live somewhere else when I was very small but I don't remember, don't know where it was. I think I didn't like it there.' Doris and Joe exchanged a glance. 'But I know I had a mummy and a daddy of my own when I was a baby.' This was stated as a matter of fact and with a brief nod of her head. There were no wistful longings attached to it.

'Well, now,' began Doris, seizing this fortunate opportunity, 'tell me what you know about your real mummy and daddy.'

'I don't know anything,' said Daisy, simply. 'But I think they are dead.'

'But hasn't Mrs. Johnson told you how you came to be living with her?'

'No, they don't talk about things like that at the Home.'

Doris had cleared away the remnants of the meal, there was a cheery fire, and with darkness outside, the room had taken on a cosy, even comfortable aspect. Joe had gone to sit in one of the armchairs and Doris found a pouffe for Daisy to sit on as she took the other armchair, saying, 'Well, now, Daisy I think it's time to have a little talk. Come and sit where the fire can warm you.' Daisy had begun to look a trifle uncomfortable and was reluctant to settle down.

'Excuse me, er...' She did not know how to address these people. If their name had been told to her, she had forgotten it since Thursday afternoon when Mrs. Johnson had told her she was to be allowed to spend the weekend with them. She was suddenly acutely embarrassed and she looked at the floor.

'Oh!' exclaimed Doris, 'you poor child! I expect you need to go to the toilet. Is that right?'

'Yes ... I don't know what you're called.'

'Of course you don't. Silly of me! But, come along, we'll see to urgent matters first.' Daisy held Doris's hand and followed her to the W.C. at the back of the house. They were soon back by the fire and Doris, nodding to Joe, began again.

'We have to tell you quite a lot, Daisy. So much has happened to us since we picked you up on Thursday, what with the train crash and everything, that there hasn't been time to sit down with you and talk. But, first things first. You must call me Auntie Doris and that is Uncle Joe.'

'That's right,' said Joe who was sitting forward in his chair listening closely to what his wife was saying. 'We hope we are going to be good friends, Daisy.' The child looked from one to the other expectantly. Somehow, in the firelight, they seemed so close and affectionate. Daisy's earlier fears were quite forgotten.

'Auntie Doris,' began Daisy, shy at using this

new form of address, 'do you really know where my real mummy and daddy are?' Her sudden directness seemed to startle Doris.

'Well, love, we're not quite sure, yet. Let me start at the beginning and tell you how we came to be knocking at Mrs. Johnson's door and asking if Daisy lived there. You see, Uncle Joe and I have some friends, a couple who live just a short way from here. The lady has been quite poorly for a long time but she is better now. They had a little girl, almost seven years ago, but when she was only about a year old the mother became ill ... too ill to look after a baby. The father had to go to work and look after his sick wife as well. It was too much for him to care for a baby as well. Sadly, they had to leave their baby in an orphanage to be looked after by some other kind people.' Daisy's eyes never left Doris' face as the story unfolded. She had reacted slightly at the word orphanage, but said nothing. Now she spoke softly.

'I think that's what they called the place where I lived before I came to Mrs. Johnson's.'

'An orphanage?' Daisy nodded

'Think very hard, Daisy,' Joe cut in. 'Can you remember anything at all about that place? You said you thought you weren't happy there.' Daisy wanted to hear more of Doris' story. She did not want to think about the past. But Joe asked again, though Doris gave him a warning look.

'You were very small, but you might remember if you try.' Daisy looked at Joe.

'Well,' she said, slowly, 'I remember the fire.' Joe sat forward in his chair.

'What fire, Daisy?' He took her small hands in

his and he could feel them trembling. 'Where was there a fire?'

'At the ... um ... at that place,' said Daisy and she was trying not to cry. Doris came to her rescue.

'Never mind, we won't talk about that, Daisy,' she said, a slight shake of her head directed towards Joe. 'Let me tell you a bit more about these friends of ours. After a very long time the lady got better and remembered that she had a little girl who she had not seen for all those years. She told her husband that now it was time to have their little girl back. She felt quite well enough but when they tried to find her it was no easy matter. Some people told them that their little girl had been adopted and gone away. We promised to help them to search for her. We've been to lots of children's homes. When we talked to your Mrs. Johnson we thought it was just possible that you could be the right little girl. That's when she agreed to let us take you away, just for the weekend, so that our friends could see you. We can go there tomorrow before we take you back. Would you like that, Daisy?'

'Yes, Auntie Doris. Yes, please.' Daisy was not sure if she had understood everything that Doris had said, but there was a feeling of excitement growing inside her that was competing with the overwhelming tiredness that had crept upon her as she sat by the cosy fire.

'Then we'll go in the morning. You're almost falling asleep sitting up, Daisy. You must be exhausted. Come with me and I'll show you your bed.' She followed Doris through a door that she had not noticed before. It led into a large bedroom where there was a double bed and a single. Doris lit a paraffin lamp and carried it with them as she showed Daisy round the gloomy room. She gave Daisy the night clothes that Mrs. Johnson had packed for her and, when she was ready, tucked her up in bed.

'Sleep well, Daisy. Goodnight.'

'Good night,' Daisy answered with a yawn and was asleep almost instantly. Doris returned to the living room.

'Well, I think that all went to plan after that terrible to-do last night. I think we deserve to congratulate ourselves. How about a tot of whisky, Joe?' The bottle looked suspiciously low when she took it from the cupboard. 'Have you been helping yourself?'

'You don't miss a trick, do you? Who bought the bloody stuff anyhow?' growled Joe.

'Never mind. All set for tomorrow? Got the house keys, have you? Right! Now, go to the telephone box and check on trains back to Grantham. We've got to be sure they're running again on that line. No! Leave the whisky alone till you come back.' Doris poured herself a generous measure and held the bottle until Joe had put on his coat and left to do her bidding. She sat down in front of the fire. He could be such a fool, that Joe. Better not let him drink much tonight, she thought, or he'd be likely to put his foot in something tomorrow. She smiled to herself. If all went well they would be in clover before the summer ... big house ... motor car ... who knows what. And Joe could have his crocodile shoes. She savoured the strong spirit as she waited for him to return.

Chapter 9

Sarah was glad of a quiet day on Sunday. She and Maddie had sat up late on the previous night catching up on each other's doings since they had last met. Sarah was delighted to hear how her friend's stage career had looked up since her lucky break three years ago when she had landed a key role with the Concert Party in Morecambe.

'I was just so lucky,' she had told Sarah. 'The leading lady had fallen sick and they needed someone who could sing and dance and look a little like her. I knew all the numbers, was able to learn the dance routines fast and I found I fitted in with the company just like that.' She had snapped her fingers and laughed. 'Like most things in life, I happened to be in the right place at the right time ... with the right face on! That's when I fell lucky again. Well, no, it was my barefaced cheek really, arriving on the doorstep of your grandparents' house and begging for digs.They were so kind to me and offered to have Josie as well. She's a girl I've known since rep. days. She was in the show, too. We stayed with the Granges for the whole season and couldn't have been better looked after. I haven't seen Mr. Grange since then. I was so very sad to hear that he'd died. I wrote a note to your grandma and sent her some roses. I never met such a kindly man ... once you got to know him properly, if you see what I mean.' Madeleine had grinned apologetically but Sarah had understood. Grandpa Grange looked like one of those gentlemen seen posing in Victorian photographs, very stern and stiff.

'Yes, you did need to know him. I think he hid a real shyness behind those whiskers,' Sarah had answered, her eyes misting over. 'He was a darling at heart. I shall miss him dreadfully.' Sarah had gone on to tell Maddie the strange story of the child on the train who had disappeared after the crash. Maddie had been anxious to help in any way she could and the two girls had agreed to try to find Daisy, once the funeral was over. Maddie's best piece of news was that she was to appear in the Pantomime at the Alhambra Theatre, taking over from another dancer at the end of next week.

'It's *Cinderella* with Reg Bolton as Peter the Page. I'm so excited to be joining the Tiller Girls, even as a stand-in. It's a great opportunity and, who knows, could lead to a permanent position. Bradford Panto's always a good one, a nice long run until the end of February and chance to really get to know the Company. I'll be able to stay at home with Mum and see you almost every day.' Sarah had laughed at her friend's bubbling enthusiasm.

'And will there be the famous line-up of Sunbeams again this year?' she asked, remembering how some of her friends at Primary school would have given anything to have been chosen to appear in this unique troupe of child dancers.

'Yes, of course there will. And I've heard they're planning to put some of the adult dancers on wires and fly them around the auditorium. That'll be a major attraction, don't you think?' They had parted about midnight, full of plans for the following week. Sarah had sat a while longer beside the dying fire after Madeleine had left, wondering why, after sharing so much with her friend, she had not mentioned her meeting up with Sam again. Ah, well, that was something that would wait until next time, she decided.

So, Sunday passed fairly uneventfully, giving Sarah time to collect her scattered wits. The others had gone to church in the morning leaving Sarah, with her leg up on the sofa, listening to the wireless. Jennie was busily preparing ham for the funeral tea tomorrow and was in her element. She, too, enjoyed the music and encouraged Sarah to turn up the volume so that she could hear it in the kitchen. Sarah smiled to herself as she heard Jennie's voice warbling away as she joined in with the music. It was a miracle that either of them heard the telephone ring at about eleven o'clock.

'Telephone for you, Miss Sarah,' Jennie called, coming through, wiping her hands on her apron. And Sarah hauled herself onto her one good leg and hopped into the hall. It was Sam.

'Hello, Sarah. How are you today?'

'Oh, jogging along quite well, thank you. It's good to hear you. Everyone's gone to church except me. Are you working today?'

'No, it's my day off. I'm ringing from the Police Station. Gerry says they are pretty certain, now, that two people left the scene of the train crash without coming for help. I've been asking the hospital staff if anyone saw Daisy. Nurse Taylor saw her, as I did on Thursday, but nobody remembers seeing her after midnight or thereabouts. Nurse Taylor remembers putting her near the door to watch for you. After that ... nothing. Would you be willing to have a word with Gerry? Tell him about the couple you met on the train?'

Gerry took the receiver and Sarah gave a description of the man and woman who had come into her compartment looking for a child, saying she was their daughter. It was not a very detailed description Sarah apologised because they were only with her for a matter of a minute or so.

'The woman had on a suit, I think, under a navy coat, quite neat and smart. She had high-heeled black shoes and a red hat with veiling and a flower. The man was not very tall, dark with a trilby hat and a fawn raincoat with a belt. I don't recall much more than that. Oh, and the woman's hair was bleached-blond.' Sarah waited for some response from the other end. 'Gerry...?'

'Sorry, I was getting it all down in writing,' answered Sam's friend. 'This is excellent! There's plenty for us to go on here. Sam's already given us a good description of the little girl, Daisy, isn't it? Thank you very much, Miss Grange. You've been most helpful. I'll hand you back to Sam now.'

Sam added his thanks. 'And I'll be thinking about you tomorrow. I hope everything goes well ... if you can say that about a funeral, that is. I'll call you again tomorrow evening. Oh, and by the way,' he suddenly dropped his voice, 'that certain item in your suitcase remains strictly "*entre nous*". Cheerio!'

Sarah went to the kitchen to share a cup of coffee and a chat with Jennie who had finished all but the last minute jobs and was ready for a chance to sit down.

'I do enjoy a houseful but all this takes more out of me than it used to do,' she puffed as she carried the last tray into the cool-larder off the back kitchen.

'What are your plans tomorrow, Jennie? I expect you'll want to go to the church with us.'

'Aye, I'll attend the service but I can't say I'd relish standing around the grave-side. I shall say my goodbyes to Mr. Grange and then come back here to make sure that everything's ready for later on. He were a grand chap. I were very fond of him, you know. He were kindness itself when we lost our Frank over in that awful war in France ... and when my Jack were taken in '22 your grandfather made sure I'd not suffer poverty. You won't have had the chance to go see him, then, at the Chapel of Rest, Miss Sarah?'

'No, Jennie. But I wouldn't want to, anyhow. I'd much rather remember him as he was. I wouldn't want to spoil those memories by seeing him lying in a coffin, cold and stiff.' Sarah shuddered.

'Me neither,' said Jennie and the subject was closed.

When the family returned from church Andrew Marsden was with them. Almost a head taller than any of the Grange men he was easy to pick out in a crowd and with hair that had retained the fairness of babyhood he was unmistakable as he walked with them down the drive. Sarah had never seen a man with hair as blond as his and she did not fail to notice him when she had started working at her father's offices at the mill. John Grange had taken him on three years ago to deal with the sales side of the business and found him to be an excellent ambassador for Grange Mill and a real asset to the firm as he found markets for the fine worsted cloth. When Sarah had joined her father's company a year or so after Andrew, she had soon become aware of Andrew's importance to the firm and, more to the point, his striking looks and friendly, easy-going nature. He, on the other hand, had fallen for Sarah as soon as they met. He made frequent opportunity to visit the design office to discuss with her the latest patterns, yarns and dyes. They became firm friends. Alice and John watched their relationship develop with evident pleasure. What could be better than an alliance between their daughter and this young man who, John confided to his wife, was destined to join the Board of Directors in the fullness of time. But Sarah was not ready or willing to enter into a romantic liaison. Now, as she waited for the family to return she smiled as she recalled the last time she had seen Andrew. He had called in to her office to wish her good luck with the London trip and, once again she was aware that his efforts to beguile her were not very far from the surface.

'I hope you have a successful meeting. Bring us back bags of orders won't you? But, of course, who could resist your charms? I'm sure I don't know how I'll survive without you.' And his arm slid around her waist.

'Get away with you, Andrew!'

'But you do know I'm serious, don't you. Let's have dinner together when you get back?'

'Oh, Andrew, you must know that I value and cherish your friendship, but, please, don't ask me for more than that. I can't ... well, I just can't. I'm sorry!'

'Well, I guess I shall have to accept that ... for now. But I'll not give up altogether. I'll keep trying until I see you walking down the aisle with somebody else!' Sarah knew that, in the meantime he would be content to be in her company and she would be glad of his. She was also sure that his patience would not last for ever.

Alice came in first and went straight through to the kitchen. Sarah heard her asking Jennie to lay another place for lunch. On the way to the hall to take off her coat she popped her head round the sitting room door.

'Sarah! I've invited Andrew to lunch. I felt sure you would like to see him and it's not often he can spend time with all of us at home.'

'Good idea,' replied Sarah, 'of course I'm delighted he can stay.'

'Am I glad to hear you say that,' said Andrew as he came into the room. 'Yesterday I wasn't sure whether you cared, since you preferred Maddie's company!' The twinkle in his eye told her that he was only teasing her. He came over to the couch and gave her a kiss. 'How's the wounded soldier, then?'

'I'm being pampered like a lady of leisure. Come and sit down here and talk to me until lunch is ready.'

'Help yourself to a drink, Andrew, and get one for Sarah, would you,' called John from the hall. 'I'll be with you shortly.'

'G and T?' said Andrew, opening the cocktail cabinet. He was more like one of the family these days.

'Mm ... lovely, just what the doctor ordered,' answered Sarah. 'I've had a lazy, quiet morning to myself and now I'm ready for a bit of good company.' James, Penny and David were followed into the room by Alice and John. John carried fresh supplies of coal for the fire.

'Now that we're all together,' said John, leaning on the edge of the mantelpiece, savouring his dry sherry, 'there is something I need to tell you. It concerns only the family so I hope you don't mind, Andrew. No, no, there's no need for you to go,' he said, as Andrew made to leave the room and take his drink into the dining room. 'It's not a private matter.' They all sat down and gave him their undivided attention. 'I had a message from Tom, the solicitor at Uttley, Uttley and Ross. He has asked me whether we will agree to his dealing with father's Will after the funeral, tomorrow. He would usually invite us all to the office, perhaps a couple of days after the funeral, but he has to attend Court every day next week and possibly longer. He sends his apologies and hopes that we will not find it an intrusion if he comes, say, about four o'clock. I have said that, unless he hears to the contrary, he may do so.'

'Better get it out of the way, don't you think?' Sarah addressed her sister and brothers in general. There was a murmur of assent around the room and Alice smiled.

'Well, that's settled, then. Sarah's right, better get it over and done with.' There was a tap on the door and Jennie announced that lunch was ready. They moved into the dining room somewhat subdued, but the mood soon changed as lighter matters entered the conversation and Penny entertained them with stories of her first attempts to control a class of six-year-olds during her recent teaching practice.

During the afternoon Andrew took Sarah out for a run in his car. Normally they would have walked. Both of them were fond of the open air, tramping over the moorland or scrambling along the limestone screes that outcropped among the rolling, green valleys of the dales. Many a mile they had covered together enjoying the peace and freedom of the countryside, both of them aware that the trade that employed them both owed its success to these hills which supported sheep and these streams whose soft water washed the wool in earlier days. While they drove today Sarah told him about the horror of Thursday night. It helped to talk about it, helped her to put the experience behind her. She told him about Daisy and how she had disappeared, about Sam's turning up at the hospital, about her fainting fit, even about her injury and its treatment and how scared she had been. Andrew was a good listener and encouraged her to bring her fears into the open. For the first time the gravity of what could have happened to her and to Daisy too, overcame Sarah and she found herself crying. Was she crying about the railway accident? Was she crying over the loss of her grandfather? Was she crying because she had lost Daisy? Was she crying because meeting Sam again had entirely disturbed her equilibrium and threatened to send her thoughts spinning out of control? A vast sea of emotion, an amalgam of all that the last three days had thrown at her, suddenly needed escape and her natural self-control broke down. Andrew stopped the car, put his arm round her, and let her sob her heart out on his shoulder. He stroked her long, fair hair, and held her close to comfort her until the sobbing subsided and she mopped her eyes with his handkerchief.

'Oh! Andrew, I am so sorry. I don't know what came over me. What must you think of me?'

'No need to be sorry, darling. You just needed to let it all out. You've been through a lot these past few days and I think you've been very brave. Shall we make for home now? There's not much daylight left. Come on, old girl. Pecker up!'

Later, as he drove home Andrew could not help wondering if Sarah's distress had anything at all to do with this fellow Sam. He was astute enough to realise that something or someone had managed to raise an emotional storm in Sarah. And who better than an old boyfriend, especially one she had never mentioned before? He was determined not to allow anything to come between him and Sarah but he knew that he must tread carefully as he fostered the relationship. Pressing her too hard to make a commitment to him would certainly send her off in the opposite direction as would any attempt on his part to elicit information about this former boyfriend, if that's what he was. Nevertheless he wished heartily that this person did not exist at all. He found himself unnerved and anxious by Sam's evident part in Sarah's life, however far in the past it was. But he knew also that it would never do to reveal these feelings to Sarah. He would have to remain patient, support and love her from a distance and continue to hope that she would return his devotion some day. A deep sigh escaped him as he let himself into his bachelor flat which overlooked the municipal park.

Chapter 10

The leaden, melancholy skies reflected the feelings of the Grange family as they gathered on that January morning to lay to rest their oldest member. George Albert Grange had been born as the British Empire, which seemed to have spread all over the globe, grew larger by the day. Victoria reigned over a land that held influence from Canada in the west to the farthest east in New Zealand and where life for George was safe, secure and comfortable. Unusually, for that time, George was an only child. His mother, having barely survived his birth, was unable to bear any more children and he grew up as a member of a privileged society, the Victorian middle-class family. His father, a successful architect, had been closely involved with the building of both Leeds and Bradford as these two places grew from small settlements into grand and elegant cities as the revenue from world trade flowed in.

George could have been forgiven for becoming

just another wealthy man's son who accepted the good life as his birthright but, as he grew older, he began to notice the poverty that existed alongside the easy-living that was his lot. Not only did he notice the difference between his class and that of the workers, but he also determined to try to do something about it if he could. It worried him that whole families lived, often in one room, all but the smallest working at the mill, taking home hardly enough to feed themselves. George, at seventeen, could see that there was money to be made from weaving sheds and discussed with his father the prospect of going into this trade himself.

'But,' he had said, 'I want my mill to be different. I want to build a large enough mill to employ several hundred people. It's my belief,' he had continued, trying to enthuse his father to back his idea with practical help, 'that people will work better if they have somewhere decent to live, so I want to build proper houses for them at low rents. I want them to have running water in those homes and freedom from damp and rats. What do you say, father? Will you help me to design and build such a place?'

George Grange's father had taken little persuading and with his financial backing and professional help, Grange's Mill had risen from a field site by the river. By the time he was twenty two years old George had seen his ideas come to fruition and he was the director of his own mill. He had a lot to learn and a great deal of debt to pay back but he felt so proud when he heard it said that a chap would give his eyeteeth for a job at Grange's. He considered it ample repayment for the years in which he had spent every waking moment learning about the manufacture of woollen cloth from the fleece to the loom and putting his knowledge into practice to the advantage of himself and the many men and women he employed.

George had continued to run his mill from the office on the first floor where he had a view over the river until he was sixty-seven years old. The years between had seen him repay his early debts and become one of the most successful and wealthy men in the county. Throughout his life, however, he never lost sight of his aims to see that his success was shared by those who worked with and for him and his death touched countless hearts.

He had trained John in the business from a very early age. Even before he had left school, John would spend time, when he could, with his father or elsewhere in the massive building learning all there was to know about producing fine cloth and selling the finished product. George's other two sons, Arthur and Frederick, had both chosen different careers and so there was no conflict of interest when George retired and left the mill in John's capable hands.

Retirement from his beloved mill had not been easy for the old man. It had been his life's work but he knew he must now take a back seat and let John do things his own way, though he was glad when John asked him to retain his seat in the boardroom. His decision to move to Morecambe was partly to do with his wife's need to live where the air was fresh and clean but, more importantly, it was to remove himself physically from the temptation to visit the mill too often and, heaven forbid, to be thought to be interfering there. Nine years had passed, happy ones for the most part, for George and Edith. There was a good railway service to carry them to visit their four children and to see the seven grandchildren and the family remained close-knit and always interested in each other's activities.

Edith Grange was thirteen years younger than her husband and since moving to Morecambe her health had returned. At sixty-five she was active and full of life, playing bridge and enjoying a game of golf as well as being an accomplished needlewoman and a keen gardener. Today, however, her thoughts were on none of these things as she prepared herself for the ordeal that she had to bear, the final goodbye to her dear George. The arrival of the hearse threatened to start her tears again but Edith was made of stronger stuff than that, she told herself, accepting the support of her daughter and son-in-law and walking bravely to the car, her head held high.

The sad procession of cars was watched by many silent faces as it made its way to the church. The hearse was followed by five black limousines carrying the family groups. Sarah, like the rest, was dressed in formal black. She sat beside David and held his hand for a few moments during the journey. At fifteen her brother was struggling with his emotions at the best of times but today, she knew, he was trying desperately hard to be grown up and sensible. There was a strong bond between the oldest and youngest of Alice's children and they walked together behind their parents and grandmother into the church.

It was a large and imposing building with seating for three hundred and fifty or more. Apart from the places reserved for the family there was not an empty seat to be seen. It was a mark of George Grange's standing in the community that so many people had come to say goodbye. The service was one of celebration for a life that had been lived with honesty and care for others. His sons, Arthur, Fred and John all said a few words of thanks for their father's life and the choir led in the singing of his favourite hymns. Sarah simply stood with the tears falling silently down her face. She could not sing, she could only feel. She was relieved when this part of the proceedings was at an end. She turned to follow her mother down the aisle and, for the first time, saw Andrew. He smiled across at her but she could not find a response to him, merely nodding formally. It was not over yet.

It was many years since the graveyard around the church had become full. These days people were buried in the huge municipal cemetery and thence was the final procession of the cortege. Apart from Andrew and a few close friends, only the family attended the graveside. Andrew came to stand beside Sarah and she found herself glad of his support. Afterwards she admitted that this was the worst part of the day. She turned away as they lowered the coffin into the ground, walked quietly from the group and stood looking up at the grey sky. She took a deep breath and whispered, 'Goodbye, Grandpa Grange.' She found Andrew beside her again and took his arm as everyone drifted slowly back to the cars, shaking hands, talking and comforting each other as they went. Sarah was glad. Now she could try to forget all this and remember him as he was, full of life and energy and love for her.

'Come on,' said Andrew, 'let's go and help Jennie open the sherry bottles! Why don't you come home in my car?' So she did, casting off the black hat the minute she reached the car and shaking out the blond hair that had been tucked up inside it.

'I hope I'll not need that again in a hurry,' Sarah said as she tossed the hat into the back seat.

As everyone gathered at the home of John and Alice the mood changed. For one thing they were able to get warm after the chill of the cemetery. Cheerful fires burned in each room and the sherry warmed them as they stood about waiting for the last arrivals. James found a radio station playing a programme of his favourite Big Band music and, with his mother's permission and that of his grandma, he allowed its swinging melodies to provide a subtle background which did much to help them all to relax. Before long everyone had arrived. Edith Grange sat in the big chair by the bay window and received the affectionate words of her family as they came, in small groups, to share her grief and offer comfort. Sarah sat with her for a while.

'How long will you stay with Aunt Annie?' Sarah asked her.

'Oh, just a few more days I think my dear,' she said. 'There are a couple of things I must do, things your Grandpa wanted me to see to, and then I shall be back to the sea air. I have to learn to live on my own now, but there are many good friends over there. I shall not be so very lonely. And, Sarah, I shall expect you to spend a day or two with me before you return to work. You seem to be coping terribly well with that cumbersome limb! Perhaps a spell at Morecambe would help to pass the time. What do you say?'

'Yes, I'd enjoy that, thank you, grandma. But we'll talk about it later. Here's Uncle Arthur to see you. Have you seen that moustache he's sporting?' Sarah tried to muffle her giggles but not before Arthur had spotted her and guessed the reason for them.

By mid-afternoon, the gloom of the morning behind them, the assembled Granges were sitting about the house in groups, largely determined by age. The six cousins present had repaired to the kitchen whence hoots of laughter came from time to time as they shared jokes that may not be suitable for the older generation. Even Celia joined in. At twenty-five and studying music she was the oldest of them, the only child of Annie and Jim Barker. Grandma Grange had been staying with them since the death of her husband and Celia had tried hard to comfort her by playing the piano for her. Celia inherited her musical talent from her father. He was an amateur musician. Music was his release from the boredom of a mundane job working at the Council offices in the city. Sarah enjoyed the company of her cousins. They were all so different and yet they shared the same blood and heritage. Andrew was now an accepted member of this younger set, never very far from Sarah, and now doubled up with mirth at some story that James was telling about a student who had drunk so much beer that he turned up for a ward round the next day unable to stand straight. The consultant had not been pleased when he had crumpled into a heap on the floor and quietly fallen asleep.

'No! It wasn't me!' James hooted with laughter as they all pretended to disbelieve him.

'They seem to be enjoying themselves,' said Edith as she sat with her children in the other room. 'I'm glad. They should have something to laugh about at their age. By the way, John, what time are we to expect Tom Ross?'

'He should be here within the next half hour, mother,' said John. Alice stirred herself and began to clear away some of the remains of their lunch. Jennie came in to help and soon there was space for everyone to gather in the same room to hear the last Will and Testament of George Grange. Edith knew that her husband had gone to great trouble over his will to make sure that no-one would feel aggrieved or neglected. He had commented that there was nothing like a will to set the cat among the pigeons. He did not want his family falling out, he had said, but it is not easy to suit everybody. He had spent hours with his solicitor, making sure that his wife would be adequately provided for. Indeed, she could live in luxury for the rest of her life, should she wish to do so, but George had known that Edith would never dream of squandering his wealth. He could but hope that his other bequests would be used as carefully. And then, he had confided to Edith, when he had revised his will for the last time, there was the knotty problem of what to do about Sarah. There had been more discussion about this than about all the rest of his will. There were only three people alive now who knew what George Grange had agonised over and what he had finally decided to do. Today there would be four.

Mr. Thomas Ross arrived at the door promptly at four o'clock. He was known to them all in some degree and was on first name terms with John and Alice. Andrew came over to Grandma Grange to wish her goodbye and Sarah went with him to the front door.

'Don't look so worried,' he said, squeezing her hand. 'It'll be all over soon and I'll see you later.'

Tom had already paid his respects to Edith Grange and now he waited for them all to settle down to hear her husband's Will. She could not help wondering what was passing through the minds of the people in this room. There might be a few surprises, but none as great as awaited Sarah. Edith felt a surge of apprehension as she waited for Tom to begin. 'Good afternoon to you all,' said Tom Ross, arranging his papers into a neat pile on the table. 'May I add my own sincere condolences to the many that I know you have received. George will be sorely missed and I am proud to have been counted among his friends.'

It was a straightforward and fairly uncomplicated document that Tom had to read to them. The widow was, of course, the main beneficiary receiving the house in Morecambe and all its contents and a substantial sum of money plus the value of certain stocks and shares. Ownership of the mill having already passed to John as his legacy, the balance of George's considerable wealth was to be divided between his other three children equally after certain other bequests were settled. To Jennie Parker came a sum of five hundred pounds in recognition of her years of service and friendship to him, his wife and family so that, when she needed to retire or had to have hospital care she would want for nothing. Several of George's colleagues, now elderly themselves, were remembered for their loyalty during the early days at the mill. There was a murmur of approval from the family, especially when Jennie's legacy was read out and again when they heard that the hospital and two local Children's Homes would benefit. Finally Tom announced that the last section of Mr. Grange's will was rather unusual but, none the less, perfectly legal. It concerned his seven grandchildren. Tom Ross cleared his throat and read from the document.

'At the time of writing my will I have seven grandchildren living.' Here Tom Ross read out a list of their names and ages. He continued, 'It is to these young people that I address my remarks. I have watched with pride your coming into the world and I hope that each of you knows my deep affection for you. It is for this reason that I have taken the unusual step of speaking to you through the medium of my Will to explain my actions at this time.' Tom Ross paused and noticed the puzzled looks that were passing between Sarah and her cousins. He resumed his reading.

'It is my firm belief that each man and woman must work hard for a position in life. Receiving too much, (financially), too soon is a sure deterrent to putting in serious effort to make one's own way. It is for this reason that I have decided against providing my grandchildren with a ready-made income. It is because I love each one of you that I am anxious for you to make a success of your lives and this can only come about through hard work and dedication to your chosen career. My legacy to you, therefore, is as follows:

For each of my grandchildren whose names are set out above I bequeath the sum of one hundred pounds and a personal letter.' Tom Ross was obliged to pause as a ripple of whispered comments passed round the room and glances exchanged between the cousins. Edith watched all this with interest. Tom cleared his throat politely, like a butler about to announce dinner, and silence fell once more. He continued. 'Of the two it is the letter which carries the more importance. I have watched you all grow from babyhood with great pride and affection and I think I know your hopes and aspirations. I have tried, in my letters to each of you, to give you some wise advice as you begin the journey into adult life. Each letter is as different from the others as you are yourselves. Your letters, I stress, are in my own hand, sealed and placed in the hands of my solicitors, Uttley, Uttley and Ross, until after my death.

'Finally, it is my specific wish that you read your letters in the privacy of your own rooms and take to heart the advice they contain. Thereafter you will be at liberty either to share the contents with whomsoever you wish or retain their confidence as you might if we had had a private conversation. This last is up to you as it is also up to each of you to make the best use you can of the small bequest I have made you. Make it grow by your own efforts and by your own undoubted talents and may God bless you all throughout your lives.'

Edith scanned the faces of her children's children. There was silence as Tom concluded his reading. She wondered how each of them would take George's words. She had been privy to the general idea that he wanted them all to start on equal ground and, after all, she thought, a hundred pounds was not to be sniffed at. It had been a fortune when she was a girl. But Tom was speaking again.

'I can hand you all your envelopes today, apart from your son's, Fred. Bertie will have to collect his from the office, since I am honour bound to deliver them personally. I think, ladies and gentlemen, that our business for today is completed. May I thank you all for your kind attention.'

'Let me offer you a drink, Tom,' said Alice. As Tom accepted a cup of tea the company prepared to go their separate ways. Sarah took her letter and put it away to read later when the guests had all gone. It was a very strange thing for the old man to do, she thought, but then he must have had good reason. One thing with which her grandfather would never have been labelled was eccentricity.

It had been a trying day for everyone. Alice felt utterly exhausted by the time the last folk had left so she was grateful when Sarah and Penny told her to go and sit down while they helped Jennie to finish off in the kitchen. The sisters had cajoled James and David into returning all the furniture to its normal place. The four of them were anxious to read their letters from grandfather and Jennie was walking about the house in a daze of disbelief at her good fortune.

'Bless 'im,' she said to Sarah, ''e were a gentleman to the end.'

It was early evening before Sarah had a chance to be alone with her own special envelope. Looking at her grandfather's strong, copperplate handwriting she slowly broke the seal. Gradually the colour drained from her face and she sank down onto the window seat. Taking a deep breath she began again to read her grandfather's words.

Chapter 11

'My dear Sarah,

I know you will be obeying my instructions and reading this alone in your room. I hope you will forgive an old man for his elaborate and unorthodox approach to the making of his will and will understand that these special arrangements are all for your protection. Let me explain my dear.

It has come to my knowledge, quite by accident, that I have a great-grandson. You will know, far better than I, the circumstances of his birth. It is a secret that you have had to carry close to your heart for six years and now I know of it too, as does Grandma. We have spoken of it to no-one but each other and, of necessity, Tom Ross.

Knowing you as I do, Sarah, I have imagined the

courage with which you must have faced the difficulties that beset you, the despair you must have felt, the disgrace you must have, at all costs, hidden from the family. You are a good girl, Sarah. I know that, too. Grandma and I feel that you must have loved someone very deeply and that you sacrificed everything to protect this family from dishonour.

I cannot leave this world knowing that, somewhere, there is a child of my blood who may need my help. The wealth that became mine in life will be of no use to me when I go to meet my Maker. I could not, without making public the existence of your son, leave money openly in my will. I have, nevertheless, found a way which, with your help, the boy may receive a sum to provide him with a good education at least.

There is another envelope lodged with Tom Ross that you must collect when you are ready. He is unaware of the contents but knows he must hand it to you when you ask for it. From that point on I place my trust in you to trace the child, discover in what circumstances he lives and decide upon the best way to use the money that is at your disposal for his welfare. It will not be an easy task for you to undertake. It will disturb the past and may cause you heartache on the way, but it will be worthwhile in the end, Sarah.

You may wonder why I have not acted upon the knowledge of your child during my lifetime. There are many reasons for leaving it until after my death, most of which need not concern you. Suffice it to say that I did not want to risk bringing the subject out into the open for fear of its reaching the wrong ears. The last thing I wanted to do was to hurt, alarm or embarrass you. You are older now and better placed to deal with a situation which may cause some sadness. I know no details of the birth of this child, only that he was offered for adoption. You must find a way to ensure that his adoptive parents receive the money and that they use it only for his benefit until he reaches maturity. One thing more, Sarah; if you should find the child in difficult or unhappy circumstances – for who knows what may happen to him – you will be at liberty to use his money, held in trust by you, to relieve any suffering and give the child a good start in life. I leave the ways and means of this undertaking to you, my dear with complete trust and confidence. May God be with your endeavour.

Your loving grandfather,
George William Grange
Witness, Thomas Ross LLB
Dated this twelfth day of December, one thousand, nine hundred and thirty-three.

Sarah placed the letter carefully on the small table and stared out of the window at the remnants of snow that lay about the garden, illuminated by the lights from the downstairs rooms. She was cold but otherwise unaware of any feeling whatsoever. She sat perfectly still. In the light from the sitting room windows she could see a cat creeping softly along beside the hedge, stalking some unknown prey. Sarah watched it, her brain refusing to focus on any other subject, as it wound its way out of sight towards the kitchen garden. She was in a daze, she knew. The silence in her room was palpable and the deep sigh that escaped her lips broke it for a second. Sarah reached for her crutches and hauled herself onto her feet, thinking that physical movement might jolt her brain into action, and drew the curtains against the darkness outside. The lamp on her side-table shone a pool of light onto the paper she had been reading. Sarah walked to the door, then changed her mind, came back, picked up the letter and sat down on the bed to read it again.

Her natural level-headedness and practical turn of mind were gradually taking over and when she had read her grandfather's words a third time she felt the mental haze begin to lift, allowing her to marshal her thoughts. How kind he was, to go to all this trouble to leave money for the child and to protect her from exposure. Sarah wondered how he had found out about the baby, but quickly put those thoughts to one side. If he had wanted her to know, he would have told her in the letter, surely.

All sorts of emotions crowded her mind now, as she pondered over his words and the whole event of six years ago came flooding back; memories that she had put away for ever, or so she thought. Yes, grandpa, I did love someone very much. The memory of how she had said goodbye to that love, with a smile to cover her broken heart, and of the following few tragic months up to her sixteenth birthday when she had lost a part of her very soul brought such a surge of renewed grief that Sarah felt she would die of it. Lying prone on her bed she buried her head under the eiderdown to stifle her sobs and gave herself up to wave after wave of anguish. She felt again, as if it were yesterday, the pain of saying goodbye to Sam and the true bereavement of losing her child to strangers. How had she borne it? How had she managed to go on living, to do all the things she had done during the past six years? No sooner had the clarity returned to her mind than she was once more engulfed in a morass of disordered and confused emotions, blinding her to coherent thought and banishing all self-control. She was unaware of anything apart from the pain of heartbreak and misery so suddenly resurrected from the past. She felt her sobs would tear her apart yet, even as she lay there, a small voice somewhere in her head told her that she must pull herself together. This was old grief, very real and extremely painful just now but this was something she had once learned to cope with. This was just the shadow, the returning spectre of her earlier trouble. She had faced it then. She must face it now. Not only must she face it, but she must also take action to follow her grandfather's instructions and she must do it gladly for his sake and the sake of her lost child. She sat up, listened. She heard music playing downstairs and after splashing her face with cold water and putting on a trace of make-up Sarah folded her letter, placed it in her pocket and went out onto the landing. She squared her shoulders and made for the stairs.

Alice had one foot on the bottom step and looked up to see Sarah coming down.

'Hello, darling. Let me give you a hand. Are you alright? You've been up there so long we wondered whether you'd decided to turn in.' Alice smiled up at her daughter. 'Come and sit by the fire with me and your father. The others have all gone to bed to read. Daddy fancied a bit of Elgar to calm us before we go up, not to mention another cup of tea.'

'I'd love a cup, too. And if you're not too tired, I'd like to talk to you both. About my letter from grandpa, you know.'

It was quite obvious to her parents that Sarah had been crying, even if Alice had not heard her sobbing through the bedroom door. Her eyes were red-rimmed and her whole aspect dejected and weary. In contrast her voice was light and calm as she offered to pour the tea.

'Thank you, dear,' said Alice. 'You know you need not discuss it with anyone unless you really want to.'

'I know, Mummy. But this is something I need to share with you both. I need your help. I need your love and support. I can't face this alone.' As the words came tumbling out Sarah's composure faltered for a moment, though she fought back the tears, which threatened to overwhelm her again. 'It would be easier if you were to read the letter for yourselves ... if you wouldn't mind. You're sure that everyone has gone up? We won't be interrupted?'

'They all said goodnight,' said John. 'I assume that Grandpa's letter has disturbed you in some way. Of course we'll help if we can. I'm certain it cannot be as bad as you think.' He joined her on the couch and placed his arm around her shoulder as Sarah drew from her pocket the letter.

'Don't read it aloud,' she whispered, getting up and walking a few paces away. 'Just read it together.' Alice came to sit beside her husband and Sarah watched their faces as they read. The moments of silence seemed endless to Sarah as she tried to predict their reaction from their faces. They had known all about the baby, of course, and like Sarah, they had put the whole episode behind them. Sarah remembered the love and understanding she had received from these two at a time when she had not expected any and, indeed, believed that she deserved none. Alice spoke first, very softly, voicing her initial response, 'How could he have learned about the baby? Come here, darling, and sit down. You must be in a state of total shock.'

'I wasn't able to believe it at first. It has taken me quite an hour to calm myself enough to come down. My mind's still in a whirl, but I don't think I shall cry any more. It doesn't matter how he found out, does it? Now I have to work out how to go about following grandpa's instructions.'

'That's right, my ever practical daughter,' said John as Sarah joined them gladly on the settee. She was not sure how much longer her legs would hold her up. John was smiling at her. 'Just like the old man to provide us with a challenge, even from the other side of the grave. And just like him to want to help, too. Perhaps your broken ankle's a blessing in disguise, darling. At least you'll have time to think out a plan of action without having to fit things round your usual work routine. But you won't have to do it entirely alone. We'll do whatever we can to help, you know that, don't you?'

Sarah sat there with her parents' arms round her shoulders and felt very humble. The idea of resurrecting the past and contacting her child's family was one that Sarah could hardly contemplate.

'I really can't start making any plans just now,' Sarah said. 'So much has happened over the past few days, I feel I need some time to absorb it all, think carefully and plan accordingly. Once I have made a start it should not take long to trace these people. In a strange way I seem detached – as if this child has nothing to do with me – as if the task I have to do is simply for someone else – as if ... oh, I don't know how to say it...'

'I think that's quite understandable. After all, you had no contact with either the baby or those who adopted it. Being detached seems to me the best way to approach it, the only way, really to protect yourself from further heartache. It would be folly to become involved with the child after all these years. Father's letter seems to imply that you should carry out his wishes from a distance,' John said, trying to sound encouraging. 'Whatever your course of action is to be over the next few days or weeks, it's surely time for us all to go to bed now. We've all had a trying time. What say we sleep on it? Poor Sarah! You've had one darn thing after another piled upon you since last Thursday.' John stood and took Sarah's hands, helping her to rise from the sofa. 'Come on! There's nothing that won't wait until morning.'

'You promise you won't breathe a word of this to anyone?' whispered Sarah.

'Darling! Need you even ask it?' said her mother. 'Just go up and I'll bring you a cup of hot chocolate to help you sleep.' Sarah gave them each a grateful hug, put the letter carefully in her pocket and swung her heavily plastered leg quite expertly as she went into the hall.

'I'm getting good at this!' she exclaimed and John laughed.

'That's my girl,' he said, 'bouncing back already. No need to worry, everything will soon be sorted out. Just try to look on the bright side, my love. Think of the good that will come of this task that Grandpa set you and don't dwell on difficulties before they arrive. Never cross bridges before you come to them, Mother always says. It's good advice, mark my words. Come on!'

They were halfway up the stairs when the telephone rang and Sarah suddenly recalled Sam's words, 'I'll ring you again tomorrow evening.'

'That's probably for me,' she said, and went to answer it.

'Hello, Sarah Grange speaking.' Why did she feel so breathless?

'Sarah, it's Sam. I've been thinking about you all day. How was it? Did you have decent weather? I expect everyone's gone home by now. I'm sorry to ring so late. Hope you hadn't gone to bed.'

'We were just going up. It's been a tiring day, but it all went off alright. Grandma was pleased to see all the family together and there was a huge crowd in church.'

'I'm not surprised at that. I remember him, you know ... met him just the once at your home. But, how are you?'

'I'm fine; becoming quite agile on these crutches in fact. Have you any news of Daisy or the two missing persons?'

'The police have assumed that the other two passengers have continued their journey under their own steam. No law against that, of course.

The little girl probably went with them. That, again, is O.K. if they had the right to be in charge of her. One thing is sure, no-one has been found around here and Gerry's Inspector has decided that no further action needs to be taken. Gerry's not too happy about it, though, and means to continue discreet enquiries a bit longer. He was off duty today and intended to ask a few more questions locally. I haven't seen him today.'

'Well, it remains a mystery. I'm beginning to think I must have dreamed up Daisy. If it wasn't for the fact that you and that nurse had seen her too, I'd truly doubt she really existed,' said Sarah. 'You will let me know if Gerry does unearth any new information?'

'Of course I will.' There was an awkward pause. Sarah found herself too tired to concentrate on polite conversation, yet she did not want the call to end. She was glad when he spoke again.

'Gerry's been working it out, you know, what might have happened on Thursday night after the nurse left Daisy. It's his guess that the couple came to collect her late that night. They may have caught another train or, perhaps, spent the night somewhere around here. Today he said he would ask about the hotels and guest-houses in case someone gave them a night's lodging. It's a long-shot, but Gerry's a very determined little ferret.' Another pause, then, 'Sarah?'

'Yes, I'm still here, Sam.'

'This isn't easy over the telephone, but I must tell you that I've thought of little else but you since we met up last week. I wonder, may I see you again – soon, I mean? I have some days off due to me and I wondered if I might come and visit you.' Sarah's heart leaped into her throat, or so it felt. He sounded so young, so eager, so much like the Sam of the summer of '29. 'Sarah? If you would rather I didn't, please say so ... if it's inconvenient?' Still she did not reply. What is the matter with me? screamed the voice in her head. Pull yourself together, girl.

'Sorry. I'm so sorry, Sam. Yes, of course, do come to see me. It will be lovely to be able to talk without the confines of the hospital.' Sarah found herself warming to this idea at a rapid pace. 'Come, yes, come as soon as you can. When are your days off?'

'Wednesday to Saturday. Four blissful days without the fear of being called to the wards any moment of the day or night. I shall call father straight away and tell him to expect me. He still lives in that rambling old house in Wellington Road. Rattles about in it all by himself. He'll be tickled pink to hear from me! I'll pick up all the latest from Gerry and I'll be with you on Wednesday afternoon. Oh, Sarah! I can hardly wait. Have to go now, darling. Goodnight, sleep well.'

'Goodnight, Sam,' she answered softly.

Sarah sat down at the foot of the stairs. Her mind was once more a jumble of thoughts and emotions and she put her head in her hands and closed her eyes for a few moments. Such a lot to think about. So many plans, so many decisions to be made. Life had, in one fell swoop, become complicated, difficult, exciting and demanding. She was tired.

'I'll think about it tomorrow,' she said quietly.

But already, in her heart she knew she was going to tell Sam about the baby ... his child. Sam would help her to find him. Sam would help her to carry out Grandfather's dying wish. She climbed the stairs, went to the bathroom to brush her teeth and prepared herself for bed automatically, her mind busily engaged with a million thoughts.

Alice came in with the promised cup of hot chocolate.

'There, I didn't forget. I always think that hot chocolate calms the soul when you feel life's in a turmoil,' she said.

'Oh, Mummy, what would I do without you? Sit down, please ... stay for a moment.' Sarah patted the bed and her mother sat beside her as she accepted the warm drink gratefully. 'That describes it exactly, Mummy ... a turmoil. All of a sudden I feel my whole world has been turned upside-down. The train crash, the little girl who asked for my help and then disappeared, the injury, the hospital, the funeral, even ... all these I could cope with. But Grandpa's letter has really shaken me. The more I think about it, the more distressed I get. I can't think straight. It's all come flooding back as if it were yesterday.' She dissolved into tears again. Alice took her hands in hers.

'We never really talked about it, did we, darling? It was all too painful at the time. Would it help to talk about it now? Lay a few ghosts to rest, perhaps? I don't want to pry into your private thoughts, but you know I'm ready to stand by you, to listen if sharing things will help.' Sarah dabbed her eyes and managed a watery smile.

'But it's so late, you must be tired out.'

'Never mind that, Sarah. We're not too tired to just sit here and talk for a while; try to put things into perspective, are we, love?'

'My mind keeps going back to the day when you and Daddy took me over to Scarborough. Remember? I watched the crowds of summer visitors enjoying the sunshine as we drove through the town and wished we were only there for a holiday. I was very scared that day. I remember thinking that everyone believed I'd gone to Lausanne. Only Madeleine knew the truth. The thought that I may not contact anyone for weeks and weeks, until I really got to Switzerland frightened me more than having the baby that day. The Convent gardens were full of roses, heavily scented, and I can't smell roses now without recalling the fear that gripped me that afternoon.

'The nuns were kind to me after you'd gone, well, most of them were. I never told you much about my stay there, did I?'

'No, darling. You wanted to put the whole episode behind you. It was perfectly understandable,' said Alice.

'During the day I worked with the nuns in the kitchen and helped the housekeeper with her jobs. I had plenty of studying to do in the evenings but I never went out of the grounds. It felt a bit like being in prison ... like a punishment. The only person I wrote to was Maddie. I looked forward to her letters and, of course, to your weekly telephone calls. Somehow the weeks passed, the baby grew inside me and I spent what little spare time there was learning French with Sister

Marie-Paul. If it hadn't been for the expanding girth I'd hardly have known I was expecting; I had no health problems, luckily.'

'You were very young, sweetheart. You told me at the time how frightened you were as the time came nearer for the baby to be born. Were you able to talk to any of the Sisters about your fears?'

'Oh, yes. The convent had been a women's sanctuary for about fifty years and some of the older nuns had lived normal family lives before deciding to join the convent community. It was a very worldly Order. I guess it had to be to do the work it did so well. Sister Ruth was wonderful. She even told us about how a baby was born ... she had had a child of her own when she was younger, you see.'

'Darling, you said "us". I thought you were the only girl staying at the convent just then.'

'Oh, no. There were two others besides me. One was about my age and the other was in her thirties. She had been badly beaten by her husband and had lost her baby. She had been very ill and needed rest and protection. The other girl was seventeen. Her baby was born the same week as mine. I think she came from York. Her parents had turned her out. Of the three of us I was the luckiest. At least my parents hadn't done that. Poor girl! She had no idea where she would go after she'd had her baby.'

Alice was listening intently as Sarah warmed to the telling of her story, a story never before broached by either of them. She realised now what a mistake it had been to suggest that it should never be mentioned though Sarah herself had felt that it would be for the best at the time. A case of 'see it through and forget it'. Having a child is a life-changing experience. Giving birth, parting with the child and then pretending that it never happened was a tremendous burden for a young girl to carry. Alice saw it all with new understanding merely by hearing Sarah speak of it.

'We should have talked of this long ago, Sarah. It was wrong of me to suggest otherwise and I feel very guilty. In a way Sister Ruth was doing what I should have done. Oh, darling I am so sorry.'

'Mummy, we all did what we believed was right for us at the time. There was no other way. And I could have chosen to tell you all this before, couldn't I? I just thought it was best left in the past. Don't be sorry. Anyone can know better with hindsight.'

'Your Grandpa doesn't what a storm he's raised, does he?' said Alice.

'He has made it possible for me to tell you these things and, now that I've begun I'd like to share it all with you. You've no idea how much better I'm feeling already.'

'Then, go on, Sarah. Tell me the rest.'

'The nuns had been approached by a local lady doctor who knew that sometimes they needed adoptive parents for babies born at the convent. She had a couple, her patients, who could not have their own child and were desperate to adopt. Sister Ruth told me about them, though girls were not always informed about such things. They sounded so nice I was sure my baby would be well looked after by them. I told the nuns that I didn't want to see the baby, that they must take it away the minute it was born and they agreed. I knew that, if I held it I wouldn't be able to let it go. It was born on my sixteenth birthday, well, you know that bit, don't you. I never knew that it was a boy.'

'And a week later you were on your way to Switzerland,' said Alice quietly, the tears falling onto the counterpane unheeded.

'To be transformed into a "Young Lady",' added Sarah, smiling now. 'Please don't cry, Mummy. It was all a long time ago, you know.'

'I just wish we had done things differently, that's all. You had too much to bear all by yourself. You were very brave, very brave.'

'No, Mummy. I just did what had to be done. Thank you so much for listening. I think we'll both sleep well now.' She gave Alice a hug and kissed her 'goodnight'. 'Daddy will wonder where you've got to.'

Alice thought that John was asleep when she crept in beside him.

'That was a long cup of cocoa,' he whispered. 'What kept you?'

'Heart to heart,' Alice said, yawning, 'long overdue.'

In the silence of her room, after her mother had left, Sarah continued to re-live the time, six years before, when she gave birth. Sister Ruth was there to hold her hand, to encourage and advise through the hours of struggle and pain which led up to the moment when this new life was pushed, with all the force that Sarah could muster, into the world. Sister Ruth said it had been an easy birth. Sarah wondered how anyone could survive a difficult one. This had felt as if her body would split into two and she was utterly spent and exhausted. She had closed her eyes and lain back on the pillows as they lifted the child from her. She heard the baby make its first squawking cry as it was carried away into another room by Sister Josephine, the young nun who was helping Sister Ruth that day.

'Well done, Sarah! All's well with the child; healthy and strong with a good pair of lungs,' said Sister Ruth. 'Just a bit of tidying up to do now and then we'll leave you to sleep.' And she had slept, she did not know for how long. She had woken later when it was dark, feeling very strange. The emptiness inside was not due only to the physical absence of the baby's body in her belly. It was a dark and endless emptiness, filling her whole being like a huge, black cloud, and yet she had felt a sort of freedom from the thing that had taken over her life so completely. It was not a happy freedom, but it was, she knew, inevitable. The milk flowed into her breasts that night and the nuns gave her something to drink which, they told her, would help to dry it up. The pain that was hers to bear for the next few days was sharp, burning and never to be forgotten, though the pain of the birth faded very quickly.

Sarah remembered making a speedy recovery, physically at least. She was moved from the hospital block back to her old room where she was soon well enough to pack her bags and leave the convent. The nuns who had been so kind to her waved goodbye as she set off for the school in Lausanne where she was to complete her education. This was yet another adventure into the unknown and one that needed Sarah's undivided attention. From the day she boarded the ferry to France she did not see her native land for more than four years.

Sarah finally fell into a peaceful sleep. Now, at last, she felt calm and able to face the challenge that lay ahead without the gnawing fear that had gripped her only a few hours ago. She had laid the ghosts to rest.

Chapter 12

Doris Smithson finished her whisky and went to the window to look for Joe. The telephone box was less than half a mile away and he had been gone for well over an hour and a half. She was angry. She had thought that her promise of a drink would have brought him back smartish, but she guessed the lure of the public house on the corner was too much for him. She considered going out to look for him but felt she should not leave Daisy alone in the flat, even if she was asleep. Pacing up and down did not help but she did it all the same. Another hour passed before she heard his feet on the gravel and watched from the window his staggering gait as he tried to find the door to his home. She flung wide the door and ran outside. She was far from sober herself as she grabbed his arm and dragged him into the flat.

'Where the hell have you been all this time? I

really don't need to ask, do I? You stupid fool. How the blazes are we to make a good impression tomorrow with you half cut and bleary-eyed.' She ranted and raved at him, at the same time conscious that they must not wake the child in the next room.

'Hel-lo, shweetheart. Am I late? Shorry. Just had a pint on the way. Everything hunkydory is it? Go-od. Think I'll 'ave that whisky now. Little nightcap. What d'ya say?' No amount of admonishment had any effect on Joe. He just flopped down on the Chesterfield and held his arms out to Doris. 'Come 'ere, ya gorgeous creachure. Let's 'ave a bit o' slap an' tickle!' Doris went in the opposite direction and opened the doors to the concealed sink, filled a small saucepan with cold water and proceeded to pour it over Joe's head.

'Let that be a lesson to you,' she hissed as the shock hit him and he lost the power of speech. 'I'm off to bed. You can stay there. I'll see you in the morning.' Doris stormed through the connecting door and turned the key in the lock. She was seething with fury but she made not a sound as she prepared for sleep and got into the big bed alone. She lay there for a while, her eyes open and tried to calm down. She knew that she would have to have her wits about her with a vengeance in the morning. I should never have let him out of my sight, she thought as she finally dropped off to sleep.

Children have a way of waking with the dawn and Daisy was no exception.

'Come on, Auntie Doris, it's morning, wake up.' Doris sat bolt upright in alarm. It took several seconds for her to focus conscious thought.

'Oh, yes, so it is. Good morning, Daisy, did you sleep well, my dear?

'Yes thank you. Where's Uncle Joe?'

'Let's go and find him, shall we?' said Doris, climbing out of her warm place to brave the chilly bedroom. Funny how children never seem to feel the cold very much, she thought as she pulled on a robe. 'Are you ready for some breakfast, Daisy? Shall we have some toast?' By this time they had moved into the living room and Doris was unsure of what she might find – or what sort of state her husband would be in. To her surprise the curtains were drawn back, the sun was streaming into the room and a fire crackled in the grate. Joe was washed and dressed and was busy setting the breakfast table. Doris was stunned. What had got into him?

'Good morning, ladies! May I offer you a cup of tea? The toast will not be long.' Doris could only stand and stare at him, open mouthed.

'What's the matter? Isn't anybody hungry?' If Doris watched him very closely she could discern an occasional wince as he turned his head and a definite avoidance of the light from the window. Otherwise no hint of the hangover he must surely be suffering. She was amazed but also extremely relieved. Today might not be so bad after all. Joe came over and whispered in her ear, 'I'm trying to make up for last night. Really sorry I am, should never have called at the pub. I've been up since six drinking coffee and trying to pull myself together.'

'I couldn't be more relieved,' said Doris, drily. 'See that you keep it up.' Her heavy sarcasm was not lost on him. 'I expect you thought of the consequences of spending today in a heap on the couch. You could probably see your Crombie overcoat disappearing in a puff of blue smoke. For goodness sake, Joe, keep a clear head and don't give me any more frights like that.' She turned her attention to Daisy and soon they had all eaten a good breakfast, washed, dressed and were ready to go out by ten o'clock. Doris had told Daisy that they would be going to visit the people who had lost touch with their little girl.

'They haven't seen their child since she was quite a baby, so they might not be able to decide straight away whether you are the one. Today we're just going to have a chat with them ... get to know each other a bit. Do you know whether you have any photographs of yourself when you were a baby?' Daisy thought for a minute.

'There is a little book of photos in my box at Mrs. Johnson's.'

'Are they photographs of you, Daisy?'

'I don't know. Some's babies, some's grown ups. I don't know their names. I might ask Mrs. Johnson if you like.'

'That's a good idea.' They walked along one tree-lined road after another in bright sunshine, Daisy in between them, holding a hand of each. The houses here were smarter, slightly newer, slightly smaller perhaps than those where Joe and Doris lived. Each had its own garden and a few had motor cars parked at the gates.

They came to a house painted green and built of red brick. Daisy liked the wooden gate and ran her fingers along the centre where struts of wood splayed out like the rays of the sun. The same motif was echoed in the coloured leaded lights in all the windows of the house. Joe rang the doorbell and they all stood on the path expectantly. There was no response from indoors, nobody seemed to be at home. Doris walked round the side of the house and came back looking puzzled.

'They don't seem to be here,' she called to Joe.

'Well, then, we'll go inside shall we? They gave me the key in case they weren't back. They must have been delayed.' Joe produced the key to the front door and opened it. It did not occur to a six-year-old that this was rather a strange situation as she followed the two adults into the hallway.

'I do love this house,' Doris was saying to Daisy as she led her by the hand into a room to the right of the hall. 'This is the lounge.' The room was quite large with a semi-circular bay window giving a view of the garden at the front. There was a thick Chinese carpet covering nearly all of the floor and coloured in gentle hues of grey and blue and pale pink. The velvet curtains were a deeper blue and fell down to the floor. There was a long settee and two matching chairs and little oak side tables here and there. In one corner stood a standard lamp with a huge pink shade. Daisy watched as Doris wandered round the room stroking the soft furnishings and looking at some fragile ornaments that stood on shelves in a glass cabinet. The fireplace was made of pale blue tiles and was quite the latest fashion with a matching hearth on which stood, at one side a brass 'companion set' and at the other a group of small green and blue rabbits of different sizes. Daisy's eyes grew wide.

'It's very posh,' was her only comment as she stood quite still by the door, as if in fear of being told off if she stood on that pretty carpet. Daisy had never seen anything quite like it in her life.

'Come and see the dining room,' said Doris, taking hold of the child's hand and leading her across to the other side of the hallway to another front room. 'Isn't it just lovely?' Doris seemed to be speaking more to herself than to Daisy. 'It's just what I've always dreamed of.' She walked round the elegant, modern dining table, straightening some of the chairs which were place around it. 'Come on, Daisy, let's go and have a look at the back room and the kitchen.' All this time Joe had been sitting at the foot of the stairs. He just seemed to be waiting for them. 'This is my favourite room. Don't you think it's wonderful with the glass doors leading out to the garden? They call them French doors, but I'm not sure why.' Doris sat in one of the armchairs. Daisy had never seen chairs like these. They were, she thought, like a lot of boxes, fastened together to make a place to sit. They were covered in smart velvet material in shades of black, grey and orange and patterned all over with what she thought looked like triangle shapes, all muddled up. There were orange triangles fixed to the walls and she saw that these were lights when Doris told her to watch as she switched them on. 'Topping, aren't they? Better turn them off!' Doris was clearly enjoying herself hugely. 'Come on Daisy, look at this wonderful kitchen.'

She swept the child along in her enthusiasm, showing her the ultra-modern kitchen with painted cupboards set against two walls, a deep sink with wooden boards at each side to drain the pots, a big gas cooker that sparkled in the sun from the window and a door which led to the back garden. Hardly had Daisy had time to see all this than Doris was off again, this time back into the hallway and up the staircase. Soft carpeting covered the stairs and passage leading to the bedrooms. Reaching the landing Doris stopped, took hold of Daisy's shoulders, and turned her around.

'And, what do you think of that?' she exclaimed, breathlessly. Daisy found herself facing the biggest doll's house she had ever seen. It was as tall as she was.

'It's alright, you can take a peep inside, if you like,' said Doris.

'Oh, but it's not mine,' said Daisy, her small hands firmly stuffed into her coat pockets. 'I mustn't touch.'

'Please yourself!' answered Doris, gaily. 'Now, where...?'

'Time to go,' came a sharp call from Joe who had remained at the foot of the staircase.

'Oh, but we haven't seen everything yet.'

'Doris! I said, "Time to go". Now!' Doris' feet hardly touched the stairs as she flew down, dragging Daisy behind her like a rag doll. They were outside on the pavement again before the child could catch her breath. When she did so, she asked, 'Where were the people? We didn't see the people. You said I might be their little girl. Auntie Doris!' But they were marching along quickly now and Daisy could hardly keep up, her feet running along between them. Before too long they slowed to a more sedate pace and turned their steps into a leafy park where Daisy could see children playing and babies being pushed out in their prams. Daisy had no eyes for these, however, as she turned first to one and then to the other, trying to gain an answer to her questions. It had not been like they had said. There was nobody there. She was on the verge of tears when, at last, they noticed her again.

'Now, Daisy, there's nothing to cry about. Look, we're almost at the café. How about an ice-cream?' Doris stopped and knelt down beside her. 'Come on, dear, let's have no tears. We hope you'll have a smile instead of a sad face when we've shared another little secret with you. Come along, they have lovely strawberry ices here.'

It was a pretty café with wicker-work chairs and tables both inside and along a verandah at the front. It faced towards the bandstand which stood a short distance away.

They stepped up onto the veranda and paused as Daisy asked, 'What's that, Auntie Doris?'

'It's a bandstand. On summer Sundays there's a band playing. Elegant ladies and gentlemen will come and sit at these tables to listen to the music and drink tea,' Doris told Daisy. 'Ordinary people, like us, will sit on the grass or on the deck chairs provided by the park-keepers. Everyone enjoys the band.'

Daisy looked with interest at the hexagonal wrought iron structure with its platform in the centre and its bright blue paint. 'Will the band be here today?'

'No, not in January, love. Much too cold. Let's go inside and get warm.' The aroma of toasted teacakes and coffee drifted past their noses. Joe looked at his watch. 'It smells good doesn't it Daisy?' Daisy managed a nod and a half smile.

'It's long past lunch time and I for one could do with a sandwich. What about you, Daisy. Are you ready for a bite to eat?' Daisy's disappointment back at the house was tempered by the idea of cakes and ices. She could see the cakes set out prettily on the counter and her mouth watered. 'Mmm...' she said.

A waitress dressed in black with a spotless white apron asked them what they would like and waited, notebook in hand, for them to decide. Doris ordered ham sandwiches, an ice-cream for Daisy and tea for her and Joe.

'You can choose a cake as well, when you've finished your ice-cream,' promised Doris. The tears were long forgotten as the dainty sandwiches appeared and Daisy discovered that she was hungry.

There were only three other people in the café. Two sat in the far corner with eyes for no-one but each other and one elderly gentleman, smoking a pipe and reading a newspaper sat warming himself beside a radiator next to the counter. 'I guess we'll be quite safe here from being overheard, Doris, don't you agree?' whispered Joe. As Daisy was nearing the end of her ice-cream, the waitress came to their table carrying a three tiered cake-stand, the like of which Daisy had never encountered before. Daisy was fascinated as the waitress turned it round and round and asked her to choose one of the many confections it held. She shyly pointed to a chocolate éclair, whereupon the waitress whisked the cake onto her plate with a pair of silver tongs.

'Thank you,' said Doris to the girl, 'that will be all for now. Would you bring the bill in about ten minutes, please?'

'Yes, madam.' As Daisy wondered how to tackle the eating of this extravagant cake Joe and Doris drew their chairs closer to hers.

'Try cutting it with this,' said Joe, handing her a piece of cutlery that looked like a cross between a fork and a knife. Daisy was nonplussed.

'Let me do it for you, dear,' said Doris. 'Now, Daisy, there's something we have to tell you, but it's going to be our secret for a little while, just the three of us. Do you understand?'

'Yes,' said Daisy, her mouth full of cream and pastry and her bright blue eyes full of surprise.

'Well, you see, dear, when we came to Mrs. Johnson's to take a little girl called Daisy out for the weekend, we had to tell a little white lie.' Daisy's surprised expression turned to one of doubt.

'What's that?' she asked. Doris' carefully planned speech came to an abrupt halt at this unexpected interruption.

'It's ... er ... well, it's when somebody doesn't tell the truth, but for a very good reason.'

'People should always tell the truth, Mrs. Johnson says. It's bad to tell lies.'

'Yes, well, it usually is, Daisy, but sometimes grown ups do it ... well ... because...'

'Because keeping a secret is more important?'

offered Joe, helpfully.

'Yes, I suppose so.' Doris' voice was uncertain. This was not going to be easy. She made a fresh start.

'We told Mrs. Johnson that some friends of ours are looking for their little girl, so she let us take you with us. Yes?'

'Yes,' said Daisy, 'we went to their house and nobody was there.'

'That's because they don't exist Daisy.' Another blank stare from the child who frequently did not understand what these people were talking about.

'We made them up, Daisy. There were no friends at that house. Nobody lives there at the moment. That house is going to be ours. And, Daisy, this is the big secret ... we think that we are your real parents. We can't be sure, yet. That's why we played a pretend game to start with. But, now that we've got to know each other, wouldn't it be lovely if we are your real mummy and daddy?'

'I don't know.' Doris and Joe looked at each other and back at Daisy and nobody knew what to say for a moment. A wrong word at this point could scuttle their plans altogether. It was imperative to keep the child on their side, to retain the level of trust that, she hoped, they had built up so far.

'When are we going back to Mrs. Johnson's?' Daisy looked utterly confused and lost. Those blue eyes held a haunted look and the cream cake was pushed aside unwanted. Joe was sure he had been right when he had suggested keeping quiet for the time being. Doris had insisted that they had set up enough of a rapport with the child to have earned her trust. In fact it seemed as if the whole idea had backfired on them. The purpose of this time with Daisy was to get to know her, find out as much as they could about her background and what she could remember about her early life, glean as much information, in fact, as they could to back up their story. It was stupid to confuse the child today, just when he felt they were getting somewhere.

Daisy's young mind was very muddled. After a bad start she had begun to like these two people. Now they were talking about telling lies to Mrs. Johnson, saying they might be her parents, asking her lots of questions, telling her that they made it up about the people in the lovely house. In spite of the ice-cream and cake she suddenly wanted to go home. She could not understand it and she wanted to go home ... to Mrs. Johnson ... right now.

This was not at all the reaction that Doris had expected. It had all gone wrong and it was up to her to try to put the plan back onto the rails. The waitress brought the bill, they paid for their lunch and left the café with Daisy trailing disconsolately behind these unpredictable adults and swiftly retreating into her shell. This was the child's main line of defence when she was unhappy, worried or confused. No amount of cajoling would persuade her to talk to them again. She was polite and distant in a way that would not have been surprising in an adult. It was alarming to encounter it in a child of not quite seven.

'Would you like to go to the pictures, Daisy? I think *Robin Hood* is on at the Odeon.' This was too much for Daisy. She did not know what the 'pictures' were, nor what an Odeon was. She was frightened and tired. She began to cry.

'No, thank you. I want to go home.' It was all they could get out of her. Joe looked at his watch. If they could catch a train they could have her back by seven or eight at the latest. He had asked about the line-clearance and knew that the trains were running to schedule again.

'If we hurry, we should be able to do it, Doris. Shall we abandon the rest of the weekend and take her back home now?' Doris, looking dejected, was also angry at the turn of events.

'I'm beyond making any more decisions. Yes, alright, let's do that. Let's try to salvage what we can ... do things her way ... keep her happy. We can drop the key off at the estate agent's on our way to the station.' They called at their flat to collect Daisy's things and took the tram into town. Three hours later they were on the doorstep of Mrs. Johnson's house.

'Goodness! I wasn't expecting you till tomorrow,' said the round, smiling face of Daisy's foster mother. 'Is everything alright? Come in, come in out of the cold.'

Daisy ran straight to Elsie Johnson and buried her face in her flowered apron. Elsie looked askance at the Smithsons and Doris wondered frantically how they might explain their early appearance and, more importantly, the child's behaviour.

'Oh, Mrs. Johnson, we had to bring her back

today. She began to feel unwell – about lunch time wasn't it Joe? – and she kept asking for you. I don't think it's anything serious, but we thought it best to bring her home. I couldn't do with the poor child fretting you know.'

Daisy turned her face towards Doris and Joe. In her eyes there seemed to be the wisdom of centuries as she looked at them with a mixture of anger, disdain, defiance and fear. She knew they were telling lies again. She knew also that her own version of what had happened would not be sought. Doris was moving towards her and she backed away slightly.

'Now, Daisy, dear, you'll be fine, just tickety-boo in no time, won't she, Mrs. Johnson? We'll come and take you out again another day.' Doris was at pains to calm the troubled waters that threatened to wreck their boat.

'Run along now, Daisy. Say "goodbye" and thank these kind people for taking you out. I'm sure they've been to a lot of trouble to give you such a special outing. You can tell me all about it later, dear.' And to Doris and Joe she said, 'Perhaps you would be kind enough to step into my sitting room where I can offer you some refreshment and we can talk.' Daisy mumbled her thanks as her best friend, Anna, ran down the stairs to greet her. As Elsie Johnson ushered her guests into the room that doubled as office and sitting room she heard the children chattering as they climbed the stairs to the day-room. Anna had missed her friend and wanted to know all about the weekend.

'And we went on a train and I tried to run away and the train had a crash and I went to the hospital and ... I got lost ... and they found me again ... and...' Daisy's disjointed sentence staggered on as her voice became high-pitched and anxious. '...And it was snowing. And ... oh, Anna, I wanted to stay with Sarah! I did, I did, but I lost her.' Mrs. Johnson was on the point of closing the door when Daisy's words floated down to her and she stopped, her eyebrows raised in surprise. She could hear no more of what Daisy was saying as she closed the door and prepared for the interview with Doris and Joe. Late it may be, but she was determined to get to the bottom of this. Something did not feel right. Elsie was a shrewd woman and she had hesitated a little when the Smithsons had first approached her. Now she was uneasy but it was hard to say why. They had seated themselves on her couch and she came to sit opposite them.

'I'm so sorry you had to alter your plans,' she said. 'A pot of tea will be here directly; I'm sure you'll be ready for a cup. Perhaps it would help if you tell me how you got on with Daisy. Have you had a pleasant weekend?'

'Very nice, thank you,' answered Doris. 'I hope Daisy has enjoyed herself. I think she just got a bit homesick, if you see what I mean, so we brought her back early.'

'That was good of you. Ah! Here comes our tea.'

'Thank you. You are most kind.' Doris was being excessively polite. At all costs this woman should not think badly of them. All the same her carefully staged composure was severely shaken when she found herself entirely stumped by Mrs. Johnson's next remark.

'Tell me,' she asked, 'who is Sarah?' Blank expressions passed between Joe and Doris and back to their questioner.

'Sarah who?' said Doris foolishly, looking in vain at her husband for help.

'I really don't know. I just overheard Daisy speaking about someone of that name. I also heard her telling Anna that she had run away.' Elsie poured the tea and handed each a cup. Her expression gave away nothing of her concern over what might have transpired between Daisy and these two people during the past three days. She had overcome her initial misgivings about their motives. After all, she thought, it was not her place to put obstacles in the way if there was any chance of finding a genuine family for one of her charges. And they did seem to know things about Daisy's history, however vague and unproven, that she did not. Nevertheless, she was glad that Daisy was safe home again. She would talk to the child later.

'Run away?' Doris was saying. 'No, it was hardly that. But we were accidentally separated when we joined the London to Leeds train. It was so crowded, you see, and for a few minutes we didn't know where Daisy had got to. You know what children are like – they move so quickly. And then, of course, there was the railway accident.'

'Whatever do you mean?' It appeared that Elsie had heard nothing of this event. Joe spoke for the first time.

'Oh, it was nothing for us to worry about; it didn't affect our section of the train. A couple of carriages, far up the line, had come off the rails. Everyone had to leave. I think a few people might have been hurt, and, of course, we could not continue our journey. That was when we found Daisy. She was in the corridor looking for us and quite frightened. We were so relieved to find her, I can tell you. We had to spend the night in a local hotel and went on to Leeds the next day.' He hoped, fervently, that Mrs. Johnson had not read anything about the crash in the papers. If she had, she gave no hint of it.

'And, when you finally reached your destination, did you have a pleasant weekend? Did you manage to introduce Daisy to your friends?' Doris, now at pains to stop Joe's elaborations, hurried to reply.

'Yes to the first and, sadly, no to the second question. We took Daisy to their home this morning but, unfortunately, we found our friends had been called away, quite unexpectedly – a family matter, we assume. Such a shame. I hope we may take her there on another occasion.' Doris glanced at the clock on the mantel-shelf. 'If you will excuse us, Mrs. Johnson, we must be on our way. Thank you so much for that welcome cup of tea.' They stood to leave.

'I hope we may come back quite soon and take Daisy out again?' suggested Doris. Mrs. Johnson hesitated for a moment.

'Why don't you leave it until the better weather?' She needed time to make her own enquiries about these people. 'I could suggest an outing for her birthday would be lovely. She would have something to look forward to.'

'Her birthday?' Once again Doris was unsure of her ground.

'Yes, towards the end of March – the 26th it is,

as far as I remember. One moment and I'll check for you.' She consulted some papers held in a small filing cabinet in the corner of the room. 'Yes, March 26th, 1929. Daisy will be seven.'

They were walking down the driveway, well out of earshot of Elsie Johnson who stood by the door, waving them off, when Doris spoke again to Joe.

'Is it possible? After all the careful work I've done, I just can't believe it. Joe, do you realise, this cannot be George Grange's great-grandchild?' Joe stopped in his tracks just beyond the gate and stared at his wife.

'What do you mean? Doris! What is it? You look quite pale.'

'The child was born in January, 1930. Daisy's birthday is in March! Don't you understand? We've traced the wrong child!' Joe continued to gaze at Doris in stunned silence for several seconds as he slowly took in this information. Doris took his arm and propelled him gently along the pavement.

'Come on, Joe! Mrs. Johnson maybe watching from the window for all we know. Act normally, for goodness sake.' After a few moments thought, Joe said, 'So ... it could have been a boy, after all.'

Chapter 13

The day after Grandpa Grange's funeral dawned bright and sunny. Sarah woke refreshed. She had slept soundly after the long talk with her mother and would have leaped out of bed on a morning like this and run down the stairs had she not been hampered by the plaster on her leg. As it was her mind was alert, ready to start the day and put into action at once her plans to trace her son. The leg was nothing but a nuisance, slowing her down, perhaps, but certainly not to be allowed to prevent her from going anywhere or doing anything she wanted. In fact, its worst aspect was, she decided, that she may not immerse herself into her usual luxurious bath full of lavender-scented bubbles. She hopped along the landing to the bathroom and conducted her ablutions the best way possible. Each day since the accident she had discovered new ways of coping with her disability, so by now, she was able to move about with comparative ease. In the dining room Alice, John and Penny were already enjoying the first cup of tea of the day. John would be away to the mill before long and he would drop Penny at the station on his way there. She had to go back to college and it would take most of the day to got to Bournemouth.

'Morning all,' said Sarah, helping herself to toast and marmalade. 'What time is your train, Penny?'

'Nine forty-two. It shouldn't be a bad journey. The weather's brightened up almost all over the country according to the wireless. Have you read your letter from Grandpa, Sarah? Mine was really nice. He said he was proud of me for going in for teaching. He said there was nothing more worthwhile than guiding the minds of our young people and told me I had his permission to ask Grandma for any of his books that might help me in my studies.'

Sarah smiled. 'That was good of him,' she said. 'Grandpa had collected quite a library over the years. There's bound to be plenty that'll be of use to you. He loved Shakespeare and had lovely, leather-bound copies of all his works. It will please grandma to see them being used again.'

'What did he have to say to you, then?' Penny asked.

'Mine was a lovely letter, too,' said Sarah. 'Wasn't it an unusual idea of his to leave us all something so personal and special?'

'Typical of the old man,' said John. 'He could be relied upon to surprise folk with his novel ideas. Good Lord! Look at the time. Come along, young Penny. I can't do with being late at the office and I have my taxi duties to accomplish first. Let's get your luggage into the car. We must be off by eight-thirty at the latest.' Alice glanced at Sarah. They must have known that father had purposely distracted his younger daughter from further conversation about the letters. Penny went upstairs to say goodbye to her brothers and collect her bags. Both James and David would sleep until eleven if left undisturbed. She rattled their doors.

'Come on you lazy good-for-nothings! I hope you'll both be up by the time I come back for the Easter holidays.' Then she and John climbed into the Rover and disappeared down the drive. Penny was leaning out of the window of the car, waving and calling to her sister to look after herself and have that leg ready for a game of tennis by the end of term.

'She's really enjoying College life, isn't she?' said Sarah as she and Alice returned to finish their breakfast together. 'I can't imagine her as a respectable schoolteacher, though. She's still such a tomboy and so young.'

'Listen to the staid old-timer!' laughed Alice. 'I expect she is quite different when she's away from home and family. Now, dear, what plans have you for today?'

'I should like to go into town to Tom Ross's office,' answered Sarah. Her mother smiled.

'Can't wait to find out what surprises there are in Grandpa's other envelope?'

'Well, I can only assume it contains money. That was the implication in the first letter. As soon as the solicitor's office opens I shall telephone and make an appointment to see Tom,' said Sarah. 'And I've decided that the first thing I must do after that is to arrange to visit St. Faith's.' Alice nodded. Quietly she said, 'Going there again will not be easy for you, will it, dear? Are you sure you can cope? Would you like me to go with you?'

'Perhaps. It's very kind of you to offer, but my plans are not very clear at the moment. Give me a couple of days to work things out, mummy, and then we'll see. I need to take it one step at a time and the first step is to see Tom Ross.'

Sarah desperately needed plenty to occupy her mind today. Tomorrow she would see Sam again and waiting another twenty-four hours seemed endless. She would tell him all about the baby – how he was born at St. Faith's long after their relationship had ended – how she had refused to name the father – how she had fled the country. As well as wanting to protect herself and the family from the disgrace of an illegitimate birth, Sarah had been determined not to ruin Sam's chances of a University place and his dream of becoming a doctor. She had blamed herself entirely for her pregnancy and she knew that, if she had told him, Sam would have insisted on marrying her, getting a job, any job, and would have given up all thought of Medical School. She could not do that to him. She loved him too much. She would see it through alone. She did not consciously think of it as her punishment, exactly, but she did know that she had been at peace with herself after coming to her decision. She could honestly say that she had never had a moment's regret about the way she had handled the situation. All these years later Sarah looked back at these events with a certain amount of pride and also some surprise that she should have managed so well when, after all, she had been little more than a child at the time.

'Your father left in such a flurry that he forgot his newspaper,' said Alice, picking up the *Times* from the table. 'He usually spends breakfast time half hidden behind it.' She opened the paper, passing quickly through the pages of advertisements for motor cars, the January Sales, the situations vacant, until she reached the headlines and news articles. There were several photographs of the havoc caused by the storms of the past few days.

'Just look at this, Sarah. Flooding at Ullswater caused the Lake to join up with Brotherswater and the gale blew the roof completely off a cottage at Patterdale. Trees are down all over the country and there's been some loss of life. It's my guess that a tree-fall or landslip was the cause of your train crash. It says that the storms have been the worst in living memory.'

'I suppose that's possible. I'm quite sure that the dreadful weather was in some way to blame for the accident. Is it reported in that paper?'

'Not that I can see,' said Alice. 'It may have been in Friday or Saturday's paper. We were all too busy then to even open a paper. Here's a photo of a hoarding blown across the road and into a tramcar in Leeds. Five people injured. On the whole, though, we've been luckier here. We do get some degree of shelter from the Pennines when the North Westerlies do their worst. Ah, well, this won't buy the bairn a new bonnet, as they say. Time to get on with the daily round. Are you happy going to see Tom by yourself, dear?'

'Yes, thank you, mummy. It's better that way. I'll be fine.'

Sarah had finished dressing and had on a smart business suit and a neat little hat. She had arranged to see Tom Ross at ten forty-five. The taxi was waiting at the door at ten fifteen and Sarah called to her mother, 'I'm off now, mummy. See you at lunch. Toodle-pip!'

'Goodbye, dear, and take good care of yourself,' said Alice, coming to the door to see her off.

Arriving at Uttley, Uttley and Ross Sarah was shown into the waiting room whose décor reflected the serious purpose of this establishment. The floor was covered with expensive Turkey carpet, predominantly deep red with strong blues and greens, lightened in places with areas of cream. Comfortable leather chairs and sofas and a small table with a pile of magazines were provided for waiting clients. The walls were half-panelled with dark, shiny mahogany. It all looked impressive and prosperous and Sarah felt small and insignificant, a bit like Alice in Wonderland, she thought to herself, when she had become tiny after eating the toadstool – or was it the bottle labelled 'Drink Me'? She was still pondering over this question when a voice politely enquired, 'Miss Grange. Would you come this way, please?' She was led by a young woman along a corridor to the door of Tom Ross's office.

'Miss Grange to see you, sir.' The young woman melted away as Sarah's feet sank into the deep velvet blue carpet and Tom ushered her to a chair.

'Forgive the formality, Sarah. It's just the way we are here. Please, sit down and make yourself comfortable. No need to ask why you are here, eh?' He chuckled and Sarah began to relax.

'Grandpa told me in his letter that you have another envelope for me,' said Sarah, coming directly to the point.

'Yes, indeed, that is so. It will take a few moments to complete our business. While you wait for me to get the papers would you take a cup of coffee?'

'No, thank you, Mr. Ross. It's not long since breakfast,' she said while her eyes took in the massive mahogany desk and elegant wooden filing cabinets which stood along the sides of the room.

'One moment, then, my dear,' said the solicitor. He took from one of the cabinets a large brown envelope and handed it to Sarah. It was a larger package than she had expected, and quite thick. Tom was speaking.

'If you will excuse me for a moment, I must ask one of the partners to join us. Please leave the envelope unopened until the handing over is witnessed.' He pressed a buzzer on the desk and a secretary appeared from the adjoining room.

'Would you ask Mr. Uttley to come in, please, Jane?' Edward Uttley was introduced to Sarah. He read aloud a short statement confirming that George Grange's wish that this package should be handed to his grand-daughter, Sarah, in the event of his death and that this transaction was duly carried out in the presence of... Sarah's attention wavered as Mr. Uttley's voice droned on with legal jargon until she was asked to add her signature to theirs on the document.

'I would suggest opening it when you get home, my dear. Would you like us to call a taxi for you?'

'Thank you, Mr. Ross. You're very kind.' Sarah left the severe formality of the solicitor's offices with relief and with the precious envelope safely stuffed into her handbag. At home she went straight to her room, sat down on her bed and opened it.

It contained a letter, little more than a note, from

her grandfather and a smaller, sealed envelope. When she opened the latter she was amazed to find it crammed with five pound notes. The note accompanying it said,

'My dear Sarah,
I have decided to leave the money for your child in cash. No doubt it is an unusual method, but it was the only way to do it to avoid its being traced. I could not have left a cheque because it would have to be recorded through my bank and, subsequently, through yours. Take great care of it until you find your son. There is five thousand pounds. Good luck, my dear.
Your loving grandfather,
George Grange

Sarah pulled the banknotes from their envelope carefully and laid them on her bed, fanned them out and gazed at them in utter amazement. They were mostly new, crisp and white, fresh from the mint, and took up less room than old notes would. She could hardly believe that they amounted to five thousand pounds. Such a vast amount of money was hard to comprehend and she touched the notes, felt their texture between her fingers, tidied them into a neat pile and carefully returned them to their packet. What should she do with such a fortune to keep it safe until it was needed?

She placed grandpa's second letter inside again, took down a hat-box from the wardrobe shelf and put the whole thing under the box's lining paper, replacing the hat on top. With the money hidden, for the moment, in her wardrobe Sarah went slowly down the stairs to find her mother.

Alice was in the kitchen with Jennie. They were about to sit down to a snack lunch together, a bowl of Jennie's home-made vegetable soup and a slice or two from a crusty loaf.

'We set a place for you, Sarah. I expected you back in time to join us. Come and warm yourself by the fire.' Alice drew up a chair for Sarah.

'Lovely,' she said. 'Nothing could be better after being out in the cold.' They sat, companionably, enjoying Jennie's nourishing broth and talking, mostly about the weather and about yesterday's funeral.

'Grandma Grange asked me if I'd like to spend a day or two in Morecambe with her,' said Sarah. 'What do you think?'

'An excellent idea, that's what I think. In fact, you could go back with her, perhaps? She may be glad of the company when she faces the house without Grandpa. It won't be easy for her. Why don't you give her a ring?'

Edith Grange would have admitted to no-one her apprehension at facing her home without her husband at her side as he had been for most of the past forty-odd years. She was a spirited woman, not given to over dependence on her husband as were many of her contemporaries, but she knew that going home would be hard. She greeted the idea that Sarah should accompany her to Morecambe with pleasure and relief.

'You see, some good has resulted from your broken ankle after all, Sarah. You couldn't have come with me if you'd been at work, could you?'

'When are you thinking of travelling?' asked Sarah.

'Saturday afternoon or Sunday morning. Which would suit you best, my dear?' Sarah thought about this for a moment or two, then decided to suggest Sunday. That would give her plenty of time to spend with Sam.

'Well, that's settled then,' said her grandmother, 'I shall collect you on the way to the station. I'll telephone to tell you what time to be ready. Goodbye for now, my dear, and thank you. I shall really enjoy the company.' Edith would also have time alone with Sarah, she reflected, in which to talk over George's legacy to the child, to clear the air over the secret that she had known and kept for the past three years. It would be a joy to be able to speak about her great-grandchild at last. Edith began her packing for her homeward journey with a far lighter heart than she had ever hoped for.

Later, when they were alone, Sarah confided in her mother the events of the morning visit to Tom Ross. Alice's reaction at the idea of such a vast sum of money lying at the bottom of a hat box on the top shelf of a wardrobe was nothing short of comical. Speechless amazement, her mouth opening and closing in soundless wonder, was followed by a torrent of words, spoken in breathless whispers as she took to pacing up and down the room.

'How much did you say? But it's a small fortune! In your hat-box? Good Lord, Sarah, you'll have to find somewhere safer than that to keep it.' Alice stopped her pacing suddenly, her worried expression clearing. 'Of course! I'd almost forgotten. Your father had a small safe installed. It was about the time that he took over from Grandpa at the mill. He felt he needed a secure place for private papers that he brought home to work on occasionally. Since they got the big, fireproof safes at the office, he's never used it. I think there's the jewellery that came to me from great-aunt Jessie still in there. It's terribly valuable; a necklace and earrings of rubies and pearls and black amethyst as I remember ... but far too heavy for me, not my style at all.' Alice was given to loquaciousness when excited and Sarah smiled and gave her mother a quick hug.

'Well then, that's the answer to the problem. I'll ask daddy as soon as he comes home to put it in the safe. Where is it, by the way?'

'In his study, built into the desk behind a dummy drawer. You'd never know it was there.'

'That's very true,' laughed Sarah. She was mightily relieved when, later that day, John showed her the safe and the cash was secured until she should need it. Since only a few hours ago when she had learned of grandfather's bequest Sarah had been so busy that there had not been any time to ponder over how she was to proceed from here.

The more she thought about it, the more confused she became and the task ahead of her seemed daunting. What if she failed to find the child? It was well known that adopted children were usually well protected and that discovery of their origins could be made particularly difficult. It was thought best that the new life with adoptive parents should be just that ... a new life, a fresh beginning. The reason for the adoption, whatever it may have been, was left securely locked in the past and contact between the child's two families actively discouraged. In most cases, thought Sarah, these arrangements were undoubtedly for the best, a clean and permanent break.

For the first time since the birth of her baby Sarah began to wonder about how, and by whom, his adoption had been arranged. At the time she had been grateful that all had been taken care of, that she was free to continue her life more or less as planned, that the baby had gone to people who would love him and that was that. Sarah's mind was running along lines it had never done before. She began to realise that her mind had blocked out of conscious thought everything that had to do with her child from the moment he was born and taken away from her. It was, she now knew, her way, the only way, to protect herself from the trauma of the whole episode and she had done it with a thoroughness that, until now, had been entirely successful.

Sarah was sitting, as she often did, on the window seat in her room, the book she had tried to read lying on her lap as she stared through the window at the wintry garden, her mind wandering about in a maze of thoughts and considerations. Her grandfather's words were only now beginning to take on real meaning ... she had to find the child that she had abandoned ... she had to discover his home and family ... she had to ensure that the legacy was duly and legally delivered for the child's benefit. Only now did the enormity of the task ahead of her truly begin to take shape and she suddenly felt overwhelmed by a surge of emotions that threatened to shake to its foundation her level headed, practical outlook. The finding of the child may or may not be easy, she thought, but in itself it is a task requiring common sense, factual enquiry, perhaps even a little detective work. This she could handle. The stirring up of feelings she had once refused to face was another matter entirely and Sarah knew, beyond doubt, that she was fearful of the task that faced her now. Alarm, anxiety, apprehension mixed with a long suppressed sorrow all combined to give her a heavy heart. This was going to be the hardest undertaking of her young life and she would have to square her shoulders and summon up all her courage to carry it out.

She sighed and took out Grandfather's letter to read it for the umpteenth time. His affection for her shone through the writing, comforting her as she read. Placing the letter carefully away again she looked at her watch. Almost time to go and help Jennie prepare the supper. Another thought came to her then. By this time tomorrow she would have talked to Sam. She would have Sam to help her to shoulder the burden, to see this thing through. With a lighter heart she went downstairs.

Chapter 14

Sam drove up to the house in his father's old Austin Seven soon after lunchtime and Sarah was ready to greet him at the door. At dinner the previous evening she had reminded her parents about the young doctor from the hospital in

Doncaster whom Alice, at least, had thought she had recognised. Since their return home there had been so much to do that somehow the old school-friend who had suddenly materialised at the hospital had not gained a mention. During the period of their friendship Sam had visited the house on only a few occasions, usually quite late in the evening to bring Sarah home. Alice and John were used to frequent invasions from their children's friends and were apt to pay scant attention after their first introduction. Sarah and Maddie were always out and about with a crowd of young people and were known for invading Jennie's kitchen where they could always rely on a welcome. Sam had been just one of the crowd as far as John and Alice were concerned and they had never been aware that this young man was so particularly attached to their daughter. Sarah, at the time, had been content to allow them to believe that her jaunts into the countryside and visits to the cinema were in the company of a group of friends, Maddie included. In her heart of hearts she had known that, at fifteen, her parents thought her too young for a steady boyfriend. It was a deception of sorts, she admitted to herself, that she had not asked permission to go out alone with Sam for fear of being denied that privilege. It was Maddie's belief that what they did not know they would not worry about and Sarah was too besotted with Sam to argue with her.

There was, therefore, nothing to point John and Alice towards suspecting Sam of involvement with Sarah's pregnancy; indeed, by the June of that year when Sarah had revealed her condition to her parents, Sam had already left for London. His degree course began earlier than most and he needed to settle in and find his way around, he said, get to know people. Sarah had told him that she would write but that it was too soon for either of them to feel tied to the other with so much studying for him to do and finishing school for her the following term. It broke her heart to cut the ties with him, to appear so carefree and happy while she knew that his child grew inside her. They had written, a time or two, but Sam was soon to find his new life so utterly absorbing, his time so full of the work and play of a medical student, that the letters stopped coming. Sarah was glad. She had to leave soon herself. Everyone except her parents (and Maddie) believed her to have gone to Europe to enjoy a short holiday before starting at the school in Lausanne in the autumn. The fiery intensity of their relationship during the early months of 1929 was a treasured memory. Life had to take a new direction ... for them both.

Hearing the approach of his car, Sarah hurried to greet him. She was nervous. She hoped it did not show. How ridiculous, she thought, what is the matter with me? I didn't feel like this in Doncaster. But now it was different, welcoming him over her own threshold, the place where they had kissed goodnight, the place where they had said goodbye so long ago.

'Hello, Sam! Do come in. It's good to see you. Let me take your coat. Did you have a good journey from Doncaster?' I'm talking too much, she thought. Gabbling! Calm down, for goodness' sake.

'Thank you, Sarah, it's lovely to be here. How's that leg of yours?'

'Oh, it's alright. I try to forget about it as much as I can. Come through and say hello to mother.' Alice was in the hall and greeted Sam warmly.

'How are you?' she said, smiling. 'It has been a long time, but I do remember your being among the school crowd who used to fill the house from time to time.' Alice was too polite to add that she thought he had matured into a handsome young man with his dark, wavy hair, clean-shaven face and some of the most sparkling blue eyes that she had ever noted in a man.

'Mrs. Grange, it's lovely to meet you again,' he said, his open, friendly grin crinkling the corners of those eyes and making them twinkle. 'I was amazed when Sarah turned up in our casualty department, I can tell you.' He turned to Sarah, a more serious expression on his face. 'I'm just so relieved that she was not more seriously injured. Such a worry for you all.' Sam took hold of Sarah's hand for a moment and looked into her eyes. She felt her heart turn over. 'Mrs. Grange, may I offer my condolences on the death of your father-in-law?'

'Thank you,' replied Alice, and turning to her daughter, added, 'Why don't you take Sam into the sitting room, dear, while I put the kettle on?' Returning shortly with a tray of tea Alice saw the two of them deep in conversation.

'You two seem to have plenty to talk about so I'll go and do some shopping if no-one minds. Jennie's taking a nap for an hour or two. Her legs are aching badly after all the work she did before and after the funeral. Enjoy your tea! I'll be back in about an hour.' She departed, a basket on her arm. They were alone.

'Gerry must have spent a good deal of his own time, then, making enquiries?' Sarah was saying.

'He felt sure that the people missing from the passenger list wouldn't have gone far that night and it was too cold for anyone to have spent the night in the open. Anyway, he asked at all the hotels in the town and drew a blank there. Then he began looking at the pubs that had accommodation and thinks he has tracked the couple to a pub called the Dog and Gun, just half a mile from the railway track. A man and a woman checked in there very late, very wet and muddy, very anxious!'

'But did they have a child with them?' interrupted Sarah.

'They told the landlord that their daughter was being cared for at the hospital. Then they took a taxi and went to collect her. Gerry says she looked about seven with dark, curly hair. He spoke to the taxi driver who lives by the pub.'

'It must be Daisy!' Sarah was excited. 'What else did Gerry find out?'

'The taxi took them all into Doncaster the next day and dropped them at the railway station. The ticket officer had a vague idea that a couple with a child enquired after trains to Leeds but they went off when they were told that no trains were running on that line until the clearance was completed.'

'Leeds? At least that tells us where they were heading,' said Sarah, leaning forward, forgetting entirely to pour out the tea. 'Anything else?'

'Gerry's in the right job! He's like a ferret when he's on to something. Doesn't give up! He traced them onto the bus to Leeds. The conductor clearly recalled the three of them from your description. They went to the terminus in Leeds. I'm afraid that's where we lose your little girl, though. Where they went after that, who knows? Shall we have some of that tea before it's quite cold? Here, let me do it.' Sam poured and Sarah sat deep in thought, accepting the cup absent-mindedly as she tried to work out how best to look for Daisy, for she was now more determined than ever to find her.

'It seems pretty certain that these two people must live in Leeds. I wonder what they're up to.' For the moment Sarah's attention was entirely focussed on Daisy. After a few minutes she said,

'I think this needs to be approached from a different angle. I wonder if we could find Mrs. Johnson's? Find the orphanage where she lives? What do you think, Sam?' Sam did not answer immediately. He was gazing, entranced, at her face. 'Sam?'

'What do I think? I think that you are the most beautiful girl I ever met. I think I must have been crazy to have agreed to part with you all those years ago. I think that I am still in love with you, Sarah.' He was leaning forward, gently taking her hands in his as he looked into her face. 'I think I never stopped loving you. Fate has brought us together again, Sarah. No other girl has ever made me feel like this. Yes, I'll do anything to help you to find Daisy, I'll do anything you want, only say you feel the same. Please, Sarah.' His words tumbled over each other as Sarah's mind swerved away from Daisy's story and centred on Sam who was now kneeling beside her chair, his head on a level with hers. Sudden though it was, and in the middle of a different conversation, Sarah found herself utterly defenceless and her arms went round his neck as naturally as night follows day. She buried her face in his collar and breathed in the so familiar scent of him. It was like coming home after a long journey.

'Oh, Sam, dear Sam,' she said, 'of course I feel the same.' Their kiss was gentle and tender. Sarah felt the years since their parting melt away like mist in the sunrise. She drew back and saw that the tears in her own eyes were mirrored in his. A piece of coal tumbled from the fire onto the hearth, breaking the spell, bringing them both back to reality with a start. Sam jumped up to retrieve it and to smother a few sparks that had fallen onto the carpet. Sarah joined him by the fire, suggesting a seat on the sofa...

'So that we can keep an eye on the fire, you understand,' she said with a twinkle.

They returned, when at last they began to talk again, to the subject of finding Daisy, discussing the possibility of tracing her through the orphanages.

'My uncle might be able to help, as long as we can invent a credible reason for our enquiry,' said Sarah. 'He works at the council offices and has something to do with the Social Services. I'll ask him when I get back from Morecambe.'

'Morecambe?' said Sam.

'Yes, I'm to travel back there with Grandma Grange. I shall stay only a couple of days, just to see her settled in. We're going on Sunday. I've always been very fond of them and since Grandpa's enormous generosity ... well ... it's the least I can do.'

'What do you mean?' Of course, Sam knew nothing of the Will, did he?

'Are you ready for a long story?' said Sarah, suddenly full of doubt and fear at the thought of telling Sam that she had been a mother, not to mention that he had been a father. Could she do it? Now that the moment had come, could she say the words, could she, should she, confide this long held secret to Sam? When she had sat in her room planning this moment it had seemed so simple, so easy. Yet now grey mountains of misgiving loomed on the horizon and a million qualms and fears had her faltering, indecisive, suddenly tongue-tied.

'Is something the matter?' asked Sam.

'No, er, no. It's just that something of the gravity of what I have to tell you has only just hit me. To explain what I mean about grandpa's Will I need to tell you something that I've known and come to terms with years ago.' She paused and took a long breath, looking at his face. 'I have only just realised how much of a shock it may be to someone hearing it for the first time.' Her gaze fell to her hands, twisting nervously in her lap. 'I ... I'm really not sure how to start. In fact I'm scared ... oh, not of you, Sam.' She smiled at his horrified expression. 'It's just that meeting up again has been fantastic and I'm so afraid that what I have to tell you might ruin everything. Oh, what a mess I'm making of it all.' Sam took her hands and found they were trembling.

'Darling, what on earth could spoil what we have? Look at me. Never mind the long story, just give me the potted edition and we can fill in the details later, if need be.'

'You're probably right,' she said, 'but before I tell you, you must understand that you will be one of a handful people to know my secret and I need you to promise that, whatever your reaction, whatever you may think of me, you will respect this confidence at all costs.'

'Lord! How serious you look!' He was on the point of laughing at her solemn expression when she put a hand on his arm and looked down at her feet as if to say, 'if you make fun of me I shall go no further'. He was chastened.

'I am serious, Sam.'

'Then you have my promise.'

Sarah spoke very quietly now. 'Just over six years ago I had a baby. It was on my sixteenth birthday.' She waited a moment, trying to judge his reaction. He did not move or speak, just continued to look at her and hold her hands tightly. She went on quickly and in a stronger voice, 'Grandfather Grange found out. I don't know how. He has left a great deal of money for the benefit of the child. I am to administer this part of his Will personally.' A pause. 'The baby was adopted, of course.'

The silence in the room was palpable. Sam, after what seemed like several minutes, measured by the loud ticking of the clock on the mantelshelf, got up and walked to the window. He stood there for the longest time before turning to face Sarah. There was a strange stillness about him, an indefinable expression on his face. When he spoke it was very softly, almost as if to himself.

'Sixteen? You were sixteen? Then the child was mine?' It was more a statement than a question and Sarah was shocked and alarmed at the tone of his voice. Her reply was almost a whisper as he came to sit heavily in the chair opposite.

'Yes, Sam. The baby was yours, of course.'

Sam bent his head into his hands, covering his ears and closing his eyes. In spite of the roaring fire a chill had fallen on the room. Sarah was bewildered. This was not how it was supposed to be. She was not sure how she had imagined he would take the news of his fatherhood, but this was certainly not it. His reaction, in its very silence, was frightening her. She had no idea what was going through his mind. His face had lost its colour and, although he had not moved, he seemed to be a million miles away from her. His gaze was fixed on the carpet as he struggled to find words that would express his feelings. Finally he stood up, walked away from her. She could see his knuckles were white. He spun round to face her.

'Why, Sarah? In God's name why did you never tell me?'

'I ... er...' He did not wait for her answer but spoke as he paced the room.

'How could you have kept this from me? Did it never occur to you that I had a right to know? Whatever possessed you to keep a thing like this to yourself?' Sarah could hear the rising anger in his voice though he still spoke quietly. 'All these years and I had no idea. You were fifteen then. I had made you pregnant and you had so little faith in me that you couldn't tell me? Didn't hold me in that much esteem?' He snapped his fingers towards her. Returning to the opposite chair he sat down and saw her stricken face. All the anger and hurt fled from his own as he took her hands again, suddenly contrite. She could not speak as she fought back tears, managing only to shake her head desolately.

'Oh, Sarah, what on earth am I saying? I'm sorry, so very sorry. It must have been awful for you. A child! My child! And you felt that you had to cope without my help and support. Why? I can't take this in! My head's full of questions. Why didn't you tell me? Why cut me out like that?'

'I told no-one except my parents of my pregnancy. No-one knew, Sam. I had to protect the family from such a disgrace. To this day I've told no-one the name of the baby's father. Maddie knows but only because she guessed. It was obvious to her. Involving you at the time was just not an option. You were about to go away to train as a doctor. It would have made things far too complicated. And what could you have done, anyway?'

'I, well, I certainly wouldn't have left you to face it all alone. I don't know ... I guess I'd have got a job, married you, stood by you ... tried to support you and the baby.'

'And you would never have become a doctor.' Sam had no answer. He could not refute this. 'I knew that would have been your reaction. That's why I didn't tell you. What a waste it would have been. No, Sam, neither of us was ready for marriage. Adoption was the only solution.'

'Perhaps it was, but you were wrong to go

ahead and make that decision alone. The child was as much mine as yours.'

'I know. I know, but at the time I saw it as solely my problem, my body, my fault, even. I felt entirely responsible and I was deeply ashamed, Sam. I was desperate to keep it secret. I thought how many lives would be affected if this disgrace became known. Believe me, I had many weeks to ponder and make my decision. I still think it was the right one.'

'To deny me the knowledge of my own...' he stopped short. 'What, Sarah, a son or a daughter?' That edge of anger showed again in his voice.

'I can't tell you that. I never knew ... I ... wouldn't let them tell me.' She covered her face, whispering, 'I made them take it away, I never saw our baby.' As she spoke these words aloud for the first time she broke down and sobbed.

'Oh, Sarah! I just can't imagine what you must have gone through. I need to ask so many questions but I know I'm not ready to deal with the answers.' Once again he left his chair and paced the room. 'All I can feel is stunned disbelief, but I know you would never lie to me about a thing like this.' Thank you for that much, at least, thought Sarah, wondering what he would say next. She was watching the scene through a vague haze of disbelief as if observing actors in a play, detached from reality. He had turned away from her but now he came and stood before her. He spoke, this time stiffly, formally, rather as he would to a complete stranger.

'You will have to excuse me, Sarah. I need to be on my own for a while. I'm in great danger of saying things I'll regret. I need time to think, time to come to terms with what you've told me and time to sort out all the questions I need to ask. No, don't get up; I'll see myself out. I'm sorry, Sarah, but I can't help the way I feel. I'll telephone. Just give me a couple of days.' She looked at him, saying nothing. She knew that she had taken a huge risk in telling him. She realised that this could make or break their relationship. Right at this moment it looked as if it might be 'break'. But she … she knew, also, that she could not carry on seeing Sam and not tell him. She heard the front door close behind him with the dropping of the latch and silence descended on the house.

Alice was puzzled when she returned from the grocer's to find the house empty of all but Jennie who was just coming down, refreshed after her rest. There was no sign of the car that Sam had arrived in either.

'Hello, Jennie. Where is everyone?' Jennie had no idea, she said. Alice went into the kitchen to put away her purchases and was surprised to find a note, in Sarah's hand, lying on the table. She read, *'Sam had to go. I fancied a bit of fresh air, so I have gone round to see Maddie. I'll be back in time for dinner. Love, Sarah.'*

'Well! What will that girl think of next? Imagine, walking out on a pair of crutches! Mind you, she said, only yesterday, that her potted leg wasn't going to stop her doing things if she could help it. Thank heaven the weather's fine at the moment.' Alice busied herself with putting away the groceries while Jennie began preparing the meal for the family. But Alice could not help wondering at this sudden change of plan. Something about it struck her as odd.

It had taken Sarah only a matter of seconds to realise that she must get out of the house before her mother returned. Alice would be sure to see straight through any story she might invent to account for Sam's sudden departure since she could hardly trust herself to speak, never mind appear calm and collected. Her emotions were in a tangle, her mind in a whirl when she picked up the telephone and dialled Maddie's number. Please don't be out, Maddie, she prayed. She was not sure what time her friend had to leave for the theatre each evening. The ringing tone stopped and she heard Maddie's voice at the other end with utter relief.

'Maddie! It's Sarah. I need to talk to you. May I come round?'

'Of course! Whatever's the matter? You sound dreadful.'

'Not over the 'phone. I'll be with you in ten minutes. And, thanks, Maddie!' She slammed down the receiver and grabbed her coat from the hall-stand. Putting it on was a struggle with nobody to help, but Sarah hardly noticed in her haste to get out. Swinging expertly between her crutches she was soon well on the way to her friend's house, the disaster of the afternoon running through her brain like a repeating horror film. It was not that she felt that Maddie would know what to do, but she knew she would listen sympathetically. What was there to do anyway, she thought as she covered the ground with long strides. With Maddie she could be completely frank and honest, since her friend was the only person who knew the truth, the full story, of what had happened six years ago. Sarah felt acutely aware that the brief conversation with Sam had ruined what had promised to be the happiest day of her life, the sweet reunion with Sam. She would give anything for a chance to live the last hour again, to have the chance to speak different words to him, words that would have kept him at her side, not driven him away. But it was done. It was too late. She was desolate.

Maddie had been watching for her and the door opened as she approached the house. In spite of the exertion of walking with such difficulty Sarah's face was pale, her eyes like dark pools. Maddie did not try to hide her alarm when she ushered her inside.

'Good grief, girl, look at you! Come and sit down. I'll get us a drink. You look as if you need a strong one!' Maddie closed the door to the small study where they sat and Sarah sipped the brandy, feeling it burn like fire as it went down. Its warmth spread comfortingly around her body, forcing the tightly held muscles to relax. A little spot of colour returned to each cheek and Maddie waited, a look of concern for her friend on her face.

'A trouble shared is a trouble halved, they say. Whatever it is, you're not on your own, Sarah,' she said. There were tears as she poured out the events of the afternoon and Maddie listened without saying a word until Sarah had finished.

'Oh, Maddie, I'm sorry to land on you like this,

but I had to have time to calm down a bit before seeing Mummy. I really think she'd guessed that there might be something special between us. What am I going to say to her, Maddie?' In spite of the seriousness of Sarah's anxious face Maddie could not resist a wry smile.

'I thought your mother was fixed on your marrying Andrew! What is she doing encouraging other men into your life?' Sarah could not answer this, especially just now, when her head was so full of other considerations. So she ignored it, repeating her first question.

'What shall I tell her?'

'Look,' said Maddie, 'he said to give him a couple of days, yes? And he is a doctor, isn't he? Couldn't you say he'd had a call back to the hospital for some emergency or other. That'll do, surely, to allow the dust to settle. Then, if he turns up again, or even if he doesn't, nobody will be any the wiser. Sounds to me as if the whole thing has hit him like a thunderbolt, knocking him completely off balance and he has simply turned tail and run. I reckon he'll do one of two things after what you told him has really sunk in.'

'Go on,' said Sarah, gloomily.

'He'll come back in a few days, ask you to forgive him for running out on you and give you all the support he can, or...' Maddie hesitated, wondering how jocular she dare to be at a time like this in a brave effort to lift her friend's mood. Sarah's gaze remained firmly on the carpet as she said, 'Or...?'

'He'll emigrate.' Sarah's head shot up and she glared, horrified, at Maddie until she saw the tongue-in-cheek expression on her face and the twinkle in her eyes.

'Oh, you ... you beast!' In spite of herself she felt the clouds lift a little and her tears gave way to a rueful, watery grin. 'Trust you to put things into perspective, Maddie! Whatever Sam does now, comes back or avoids me like the plague, I'm no more on my own with the problem than I was before, am I?'

'Quite right. And, by the time you've spent a day or two in Morecambe you'll have had time to think things over quietly and decide what you want to do next. No use worrying over Sam. Leave him to sort himself out. Look, Sarah, why don't you give yourself a break from all this serious stuff? Come to the theatre with me this evening! I can easily get you a seat. *Cinderella* is great escapism. Just what you need at present. Go on, give your mother a ring; tell her I'll drop you off after the show. What do you say? Come and have a laugh and forget your troubles for a couple of hours.'

'Thanks, Maddie. I don't know what I'd do without you, really I don't. I can't say I'm wild about Pantomime, but it certainly beats putting my head in the gas oven!'

'That's more like it! Come along, 'phone your mother and we'll have a bite to eat before we go.'

Alice was relieved to hear Sarah sounding relaxed and unconcerned about Sam's curtailed visit and delighted that she was planning an evening out.

'It'll do you good, dear. I hope you enjoy the show. Andrew rang, by the way. He said he would try to catch up with you before the end of the week. Goodbye; give my love to Maddie and tell her to break a leg!'

Maddie had a little Morris, a car which really belonged to an elderly aunt who no longer felt able to drive it. She had told Maddie that modern day traffic was too fast and dangerous for her but if Maddie thought she could cope with it she could use it with pleasure.

'Try to stop me!' Maddie had said. A dancer, a member of the chorus-line driving herself to the theatre, well, it was unheard of. Maddie was immensely proud of the little motor and kept it in tip-top condition. Sarah had to fold herself up carefully to accommodate the potted leg in the front seat as the shiny, maroon and black saloon chugged off cheerfully with the two girls who had been friends all their lives.

'If you like I could drive you over to Scarborough one day next week,' said Maddie. 'Might be easier than train and taxi, getting to St. Faith's. Have you decided when you want to go? It is the first call, isn't it, I think you said, on the search for the child?'

'Maddie, you're a diamond! Mummy offered to come with me. It was sweet of her, but I would feel easier with you.'

'That's settled then,' said Maddie.

Afterwards Sarah wondered how she had managed to laugh so much and so heartily the very evening of the debacle with Sam Pearce. The show had been excellent with a cast who enjoyed themselves as much as the audience, all the usual slapstick humour and outrageous characters of traditional Pantomime and brilliant dance routines and music. There was no doubt about it, thought Sarah, laughter is the best medicine. Who was Sam Pearce, anyway? Just someone from her youthful past whom she had learned to forget. What right had he to blunder back into her life, upsetting her ordered existence, playing havoc with her feelings and then dropping her like a hot brick when things turned difficult. Sam Pearce could fizz up and burst, she said to herself. She could manage very well without him, thank you very much, just as she had for the last six years and more. She was made of sterner stuff.

When Grandma Grange telephoned the following day Sarah had no reason to object to going back to Morecambe with her three days earlier than planned. Heavy snowfalls were forecast, she told her, and, if it were all the same to Sarah, she would like to get home before the weekend.

'Of course, Gran. We can be off as early as you like on Friday morning.' Sarah packed a bag, glad of something positive to do. Glad, too, that she would not be at home if Sam Pearce came knocking at the door before he went back to Doncaster Hospital.

Chapter 15

1933

The early months of 1933 were tough for Doris and Joe Smithson. When they had married nine years earlier Joe had a good job in a busy blacksmith's shop in Dewsbury, the small Yorkshire town where they lived. He had served his apprenticeship from the age of fourteen and was now able to turn out ornamental ironwork with skill and speed. Joe most enjoyed shoeing the horses and he was good at it, boasting that he could have an old shoe off and a new one on in eight minutes flat when the forge was running well and hot. The firm had won the contract to keep all the Council's horses shod so Joe was never idle. The coal merchant, the milkman, the grocer, the Royal Mail, all needed to be kept on the move and Joe's firm saw to them all and thrived. Hard, physical work over the anvil provided an outlet for Joe's naturally hot temper and contact with the gentle animals he cared for taught him patience. He was proud to take home enough pay to keep himself and his young wife in simple comfort and they were happy. Children would come along when they were ready, they had told each other in the early days, but they had waited in vain and the optimism with which they had started out together began to fade along with fears over Joe's employment prospects.

The repercussions from the sudden failure of the American Stock Market, four years earlier, were still being felt by the rest of the western world. Although such places as Wall Street meant little to Doris and less to Joe, they were all too well aware that the economy of their own country was struggling to provide employment for all. The war that had coloured their young lives as they had grown up and which was to be the final settlement of quarrels between nations, seemed to have settled nothing. As Doris, being the one who took time to do it, read the papers she discovered uncertainty, anxiety and fear over what was now happening in Hitler's Germany.

'Have you read this, Joe?' Doris turned the newspaper so that he could see the headline, 'Tremendous Fire Destroys Reichstag – Communist Youth to blame says Herr Hitler'.

'Can't say I'm particularly bothered,' answered Joe. 'It's all a long way from Yorkshire and what can I do about it anyway?'

'Oh, but if you can believe what the papers are telling us this chap Hitler is out to take over Europe. He's behaving like a dictator if you ask me. He's outlawed all political parties apart from his own Nazi's and, it says here, he's arrested all one hundred members of the government who were Communists. None of them can stand for re-election.'

'Let's hope it's all a storm in a teacup, Doris. Nothing for us to worry our heads over.' Joe seemed less than interested and Doris felt like shaking him.

'Nothing to worry about? You should have a look at the paper yourself sometimes, Joe. This article says the he's deporting all people who are not of pure German blood. I'm not quite sure what that means but I am sure it doesn't seem right or fair. And something else – where was it?' She shook out the paper and turned to the bottom of the page. 'Yes, here it is. It's reported that Germany's re-arming, mustering troops and preparing for a war. If that's not worrying I'd like to know what is! We're only just recovering from the last lot ... remember? All those boys who marched off, never to return?' Doris shuddered. She did not pretend to understand politics properly but she valued her right to vote and believed fervently in democratic government which she understood as fair and just. She tried to talk of these matters with Joe but he was really not concerned. His chief worry was over his own livelihood and paying the rent. Reluctantly he took the paper.

'Let's have a look, then. What else is there about Germany?'

Joe turned the page. 'Here's another picture of that Hitler chap. And look who he's shaking hands with!' Doris looked. It was the Prince of Wales. In common with half the women in England Doris admired Prince Edward, the playboy prince. She thought he was the most handsome and charming man in the world as he graced the photographs of the upper classes at the races and society weddings. Yet here he was paying a visit to the German capital, being greeted warmly by the Chancellor. Surely, thought Doris, he wouldn't be there if there was any doubt about the intentions of this man Adolf Hitler.

'Oh, well,' said Doris with a sigh, 'I guess you might be right, Joe. Maybe I am worrying over nothing. I suppose politics, kings and governments are big enough to look after themselves. My first priority at the moment is to make a good home for us and the family we hope for.' She gave Joe a hug and went off to make a pot of tea.

To their dismay, however, the swift arrival of motorised transport quickly decimated the number of horses working on the streets and before very long Joe's employer, with great regret, told him he would have to let him go. Joe came home that night to tell Doris he had lost his job.

'You'll soon find something else, love,' Doris had said, but, try as he would, Joe could find no other work. Gradually he came to feel useless, depressed, unwanted and angry. Until now, Doris had been blissfully unaware of her husband's tendency to the short temper and black moods that now became a part of his life and she was at a loss to know how to deal with him. To add to their troubles they found they could no longer afford to rent the little house of which they had both been so proud. Gradually Joe lost interest in looking for work, took to spending long hours in the public house wasting what little money they had on alcohol to dull his disappointments. Doris began to despair. It was then that she realised that, if she did not take charge of the situation they might both end up begging on the streets like so many others she had seen. Joe tottered home from the pub one night to find her waiting up for him. Grimly determined she sat him down, sobered him up and made him listen to her plan.

'There's nothing for us here in Dewsbury, Joe, you must see that. We're behind with the rent, there's no work for you, so the only thing to do is go where there is some work to be had. And it is probably going to be me that finds it! I know you've tried but now you're making things worse with all this drinking. I'm not going to put up with it any longer, Joe. Something has to be done, so I've decided!'

'Oh? You've decided, have you? And what'll you do if it doesn't suit me, whatever it is that you've decided?' There was a sneer in his voice, a defiance in his tone.

'If it doesn't suit you, my lad, I shall go ahead without you, leave you to stew and...'

'You'll what? Now, look here,' he shouted, 'You're my wife and you'll do as I say, do you hear?' Joe got up from his chair, rather unsteadily, took a step towards Doris where she sat, quite calmly, looking up at his red face, lost his balance and sprawled onto the floor at her feet. Doris stood up, seeming to tower over him. Her voice was steady and carried a note of finality. She spoke quietly.

'A husband in a state like this I can do without, Joe. I married you because I loved you ... and in spite of everything, I still do. But I can't follow you down into the gutter.' She stepped over him, walking over to the mirror that hung over the fireplace and looking at her reflection said, 'I am going to move to Leeds. It's a big city. There's work there, I know there is, and work for women, too. I might learn to be a secretary, I might find a job in one of the large stores or be an usherette in a cinema. Don't you see, Joe, I want to help us to drag ourselves out of this mess. You seem to have given up altogether. You can come with me or you can stay here, it's your choice.' She came back to kneel beside his inert figure. 'I wish you'd decide to come, but if not, I'm going anyway. Oh, and by the way, I've already given notice on this place. We have to be out by the end of next week.'

And so it was that their roles in the partnership were reversed. Doris took charge from that moment and Joe reckoned he would probably be better off staying with this woman who seemed to have such faith in the future just when he had lost all of his. He may live to regret it, but going with her to Leeds seemed the better option just now. Two weeks later they moved into a damp and dirty basement. Doris insisted on controlling what was left of their meagre funds, allowing Joe pocket money and, when he went out for a drink, she went with him. No better way of getting to know people, hearing about the area they lived in and keeping an eye on Joe, she thought.

It was not easy to make a home out of a hovel, but Doris did her best, even chivvying Joe into giving the range a coat of blacking. With little else to do Joe knuckled under and helped with the improvements to their gloomy rooms. Bit by bit they made acquaintances here and there, mostly at the local pub, the Bell and Bottle.

It was through one of these, a woman called Trudi, that Doris heard about the vacancy at the firm of Uttley, Uttley and Ross.

'Mae's bin there for years,' Trudi told Doris as

they sipped port and lemon, both of them keeping a weather eye on their husbands' consumption of ale. 'She goes in early in t' mornin', does t' steps and front door, polishes that theer brass plate that 'as all t' names on, like, and then she does the 'all and stairs so's it's spick an' span when t' lawyers comes in ta work. After, about haf past five, like, she comes back an' cleans an' dusts t' offices. Well, they weren't arf upset when Mae got sick. They were used to 'er, see, an' Mr. Uttley said as 'ow it weren't easy ta find a person they could trust, like Mae. Ee, poor Mae! I'm reight sorry for 'er.' Trudi's voice dropped to a whisper and she leaned closer to Doris. 'It's women's trouble, yer know. Poor lass 'as to 'ave everything tekken away. She'll not be back at work fo' months if I know owt abaht it.' Doris wondered whether someone like herself might be acceptable as a replacement for poor Mae? Until Mae was well enough to return to work, you understand.

'I can't see why not,' answered Trudi. 'It'd tide the pair o' ye over till Joe finds summat else. Why don't ya call an' ask?'

To Doris' amazement the following day she was told by Miss Cheadle, the receptionist at Uttley, Uttley and Ross, that she may present herself for interview on Wednesday afternoon at three p.m prompt and that Miss Cheadle would meet her in the front lobby. She would, said Miss Cheadle, be advised to appear smartly dressed, neat and clean, for old Mr. Uttley required nothing short of the best from his staff.

'Ee, by 'eck,' said Trudi, when she heard, 'all that, just for a cleaning job! Fancy!'

Doris was thoughtful as she sipped her drink, making it last, for their refreshment during their visits to the pub were strictly rationed by her own determined efforts to make ends meet. She looked at her new friend, noticing the fashionable cut of the suit she wore which married awkwardly with her demeanour and the way she spoke. She assumed that it had been given to her, perhaps by her employer, for Trudi worked as a maid in one of the wealthy Jewish households in Alwoodley.

'To be clean and neat costs nothing,' said Doris. 'Getting something smart to wear on Wednesday is quite another matter.'

''Ave yer never bin to a Jumble Sale? Great place ta lay yer 'ands on summat good if yer can put up wi' second-'and finery.' Trudi laughed at Doris' expression, stood up for a moment and turned round to show Doris the full effect of her undoubtedly expensive suit and blouse. 'Yes, this came from one o' them,' she winked mischievously, 'like nearly all my clothes. Yer'll never guess what I paid for this lot.' Doris was impressed. 'They 'ave one first Tuesday in t' month. Come with me, if yer like. Yer don't allus get stuff as good as this, but it's worth a look.'

From then on Doris and Joe's wardrobe improved dramatically. Doris was good with a needle and thread and it was not only clothing that she brought home from her regular trips to Alwoodley on the tram. She picked up a flat iron which she could heat on the range. She laundered, mended and altered the clothes she bought, the only item which cost more than threepence being the iron, and well worth the sixpence she spent on it. Doris was a bright girl. Her parents had encouraged correct speech and good manners and were thrilled when she had passed for the grammar school, even though they knew they would not be able to afford to let her stay on after the age of fifteen. Now, when the chips were down and competition for jobs so fierce, she knew she would have to use the full arsenal of her skills to impress Mr. Uttley. She knew she was overqualified for this position as a cleaner in an office. Mr. Uttley knew it too, and engaged her on the spot. She would be expected at six forty-five the following morning and not a minute later. She would present herself to Mr. Dobbs at the rear entrance to the property and receive instructions about her duties. Mr. Dobbs acted, explained Mr. Uttley, much as would a butler in any household. He was responsible for the efficient running of the premises, had charge of the domestic staff and, during opening hours he was guardian of the impressive front door through which he politely ushered clients. Doris would be answerable to Mr. Dobbs at all times and would receive her wages from him at the end of each week. Prompt and regular attendance at work was expected of her and failure in either would result in immediate dismissal. She would complete her morning duties well before the daily business of the office began and she would attend after the close of business, between five and six p.m., to help with the cleaning. Her wages would be nineteen shillings and sixpence, her working week Monday to Friday.

'Joe, Joe, they took me on! I start tomorrow!' she shrilled at the top of her voice as she burst into their rooms. 'Almost twenty shillings a week!' Doris danced about the dingy room until Joe caught her, a smile, for once, lighting up his dour expression.

'Well done, you!' he said. 'Maybe it was that hat that did the trick.' She pulled out the hatpin and took off the scarlet hat with the dainty veiling which came over her eyes. She placed it carefully in its original hatbox in the bedroom, calling out to Joe, 'Yes, it's certainly a lucky hat! Thre'pence, including the box, it was. It beats me how some of these women can throw out such good stuff. They must have more money than sense. Time Trudi and I took another trip over to Alwoodley. I'll be needing some decent clothes to wear to work.' She and Joe laughed for the first time for weeks.

And so it was that they began the long haul back to the respectability that they both, particularly Doris, yearned for. Not long afterwards Joe, too, found work. His affinity for horses had led him, on occasions when he had nothing better to do, to wander round the parkland of a nearby estate belonging to a wealthy landowner. Here the gentleman's horses were allowed to graze, albeit on the far side of a strong wire fence and Joe would go and talk to them. The public was welcomed into the outer park for recreation, even though the land was privately owned. It was towards the springtime by now and the horses were out more often enjoying the freedom from their stables. A lively little colt had tried to leap a low wall and had become wedged by one foot between loose stones. It was very alarmed, whinneying loudly and struggling to get free. Joe could not stand by and see it in pain. He climbed over the fence, went to the head of the horse and began to calm its panic. There was no doubt about it, he had a way with horses and shortly he managed to stop the animal's struggles long enough to move the stones with his foot. The horse scampered off as Joe straightened up, rubbing his leg where the horse had bruised it. A voice and the galloping hooves of a rider closed on Joe and he braced himself for a telling off for trespass.

'Young man, I am forever in your debt,' came the breathless words of the rider. 'That little fellow shows great promise as a riding pony, not broken yet ... but high hopes. I saw the way you dealt with him as I rode over. Good show, I say ... most impressed. Work with horseflesh, do you?'

'No, sir, not now, anyroad.'

'But you did? Whose stable?'

'Oh, no, sir. I were a blacksmith afore. I kept 'em shod, sir. Lovely creatures, 'osses, sir.'

'And now? Are you not employed?' Joe shook his head.

'Come with me,' said the man, dismounting and leading his tall chestnut mare. 'If you're as good with the animals as it seems, I feel sure we could make use of your talents here, that is if you'd be interested? I can't say how grateful I am that you had the presence of mind to intervene when you saw that pony in trouble. Not many would have known how to go about it, far less have bothered to try. We've need of an extra hand in the stables. My name's Edward Lazenby, by the way. We live just over the rise at Upton Hall.

Come and see whether you like the look of us.'

Joe was not sure how you were supposed to address the gentry, especially when they seemed to be offering you a job, but when he saw the stable-blocks ranged round three sides of a cobbled square, with housing for, he judged, at least twenty horses, his grin said it all. Then he remembered to doff his cap to his new boss.

Joe could not wait for Doris to come home from work that night to tell her of his good fortune.

'Fifteen bob a week and me dinner an' all,' he crowed, 'and me and two other lads tek it in turn ta work Sat'days an' Sundays.'

'Wonderful! That'll keep you out of mischief! Things really are looking up at last. We'll have that house before you know it, Joe.'

For several months it seemed as if life had, at last, settled into a regular pattern. Joe was more agreeable to live with. They found they could put a little money away instead of being always in debt at the end of every week and they even managed the occasional visit to the pictures. At the solicitors' offices Doris made it her business to ingratiate herself with Mr. Dobbs. She was always a few minutes early, never late, always neat and clean, polite, obliging, conscientious and, above all, respectful to Mr. Dobbs. She was determined to remain a char-woman not a minute longer than was necessary, for she had been there less than a week when she realised the opportunities that could lie within the walls of this elegant establishment. Play your cards right, she told herself, and you could rise to equal Miss Cheadle. She could see herself already, sitting behind the reception desk, answering the telephone, showing well-heeled clients to the partners' rooms. Oh, yes, dedication to the mop and bucket for a while is a small price to pay for such a goal thought Doris.

Mr. Dobbs was in his late fifties, a widower, very dapper in the morning suit he wore to work. He was a stickler for correctness and the offices of Uttley, Uttley and Ross were run on oiled wheels. Doris saw to it that she became more and more indispensable to Mr. Dobbs, turning in extra shifts when other staff were ill, staying a few minutes longer, polishing the brass that much brighter, but most of all finding time to talk to him. Like many lonely men he was susceptible to female charms and he was more than happy to make an ally, indeed a confidante of this delightful young lady. He was justly proud of the grand rooms, the gleaming woodwork, the comfortable furnishings and Doris appeared to share his pride. It was her idea to place fresh flowers on the table in the lobby and magazines for the waiting clients. It was Mr. Dobbs who took the credit.

'I really do not know how we managed before you came, my dear,' he would say. 'Quite a little ray of sunshine, you are, indeed.' And Doris would blush prettily and say nothing.

She should have been on the stage such was her acting prowess.

By the end of November 1933 Doris had her reward, access to the offices and contact, albeit still as a servant, with the partners and their secretaries. It was now her job to serve tea, coffee and sometimes sherry on elegantly laid trays whenever it was called for. Mr. Dobbs had the utmost confidence in his protégé and she was soon accepted by everyone as a trusted and reliable member of staff. Her working hours altered as did her uniform, a smart black dress, white apron and cap provided by her employer. She now attended during normal business hours and stayed on for another hour after closing to tidy up the consulting rooms and see everything ready for the next morning.

'You see,' she said to Joe, 'all that toadying up to the bumbling old fool's paid off. My wage has gone up and the work isn't as hard. I like seeing all the toffs. You should see what some of those women wear! Money no object.'

'Aye, well, it's all very well for them,' Joe's tone was bitter, 'most of 'em never 'ad to lift a finger, not like the rest of us, putting in all the hours God sends for a pittance, just to keep a roof over our 'eads and food in our mouths.'

'Listen, Joe! We've come a long way in the last twelve months. Think about it. A year ago we were almost destitute and look at us now. Most of the debts paid off, you're earning a bit at the stables and I'm well on track to finding my way to a fortune. Don't ask me how. I don't know yet. But that place is alive with people's secrets, Joe. If there's one thing the toffs'll pay to avoid it's their dirty linen being washed in public. These oh-so-respectful eyes and ears of mine are ever alert for a hint of scandal or skulduggery.' She laughed. 'There's not much that I miss, Joe. They're so used to seeing me now that they hardly stop their discussions when I take in the tea or whatever. I'm just part of the wallpaper and, believe me, I've put in some hard slog to make it that way.' It had been slowly dawning on Joe's mind just what his wife was talking about. He'd seen this sort of thing in a film once. Yes, they were gangsters, weren't they? James Cagney and somebody, he thought it might have been Cary Grant. There was a name for what they did. Even Joe, not known for letting scruples get in his way, was astounded.

'Blackmail! That's what you're talking about, isn't it? Doris?'

'Oh, I wouldn't use a word like that.' Doris smiled at herself in the mirror and smoothed down her newly bleached hair. She could afford to go to the hairdresser sometimes these days. Joe was hardly listening. A vague sort of panic seemed to have taken over his mind.

'Anyhow, you wouldn't have any idea how to go about it,' Joe protested, 'no idea at all. You'd never get away with it. You'd get caught, just like Jimmy Cagney did, and taken away to prison.' Doris was unperturbed.

'What's all this "you this" and "you that"?' she said airily. 'This will be a job for both of us. I shall need you, Joe. We'll be working together. There has to be someone who's not known at the firm. It'll be easy, you'll see. But we won't need to make proper plans until I come across the right information. Forget it, for the moment, Joe. And forget the word "blackmail" ... horrible word.' Joe grunted, unconvinced.

'What would you call it, then?'

'Hush money,' said Doris.

Chapter 16

Ever since the summer George Grange had pondered over the knowledge, just learned, and by accident too, that he had become a great-grandfather. It had come as a great shock to him and Edith but they were the last people likely to make judgements, apportion blame, chide or condemn especially when they were not in possession of all the facts. They had talked of it as they walked together on the wide expanse of Morecambe's seashore or sat in their garden late in the summer evenings. George was troubled.

'How Sarah must have suffered,' he had said to Edith, 'in keeping this from everyone. I'm just so glad that John and Alice stood by her, but it seems she was determined to shoulder the burden alone whether or not she had their support.'

'She is to be admired for that. Though I cannot help wondering at her foolishness in the first place.'

Born in 1871 Edith had been brought up in the strict Victorian code of morals when having babies out of wedlock was unheard of within her strata of society. She was worldly enough to know that it happened frequently in the lower classes; indeed she had, at one time served on a charitable committee whose sole aim was to help fallen women, as they were known. She felt an undercurrent of alarm over Sarah's fall from grace but she had to admit to herself that things were very different now in this modern world. Since the Great War women had tasted a freedom as never before. Even their figures seemed to have altered. Gone were the hourglass shapes, the corsets and stays of her own youth. Bosoms were a thing of the past during the twenties, when women had bound their breasts to accommodate the narrow, sack-shaped dresses, so fashionable and daring, whose hems had shot, alarmingly, up to the knee. Cloche hats hugged the head as the 'flappers' peeped cheekily from under the brims and the way they danced the Charleston and Black Bottom had shocked the older generation. Edith could not help but wonder whether all this feminine freedom from convention had played a part in diluting moral values but she had to admit that life for the young people in these modern times was far more fun.

'The worst aspect of our knowing of Sarah's child,' mused Edith over supper one evening, 'is that we must not admit to it, must not discuss it with anyone, may not accept the child as our own kin. He will be a three-year-old by now and part of someone else's family. I pray that he is happy and healthy, well cared for by his adoptive parents.'

'My dear, those have been my thoughts exactly. Today it occurred to me that if I cannot do something for the child at the present time, then I may be able to arrange that he benefit from my estate after my death. What do you think?'

'Would not your knowledge of his existence then be made known to all and sundry?' A note of alarm sharpened Edith's voice. 'A Will is public property, it seems to me. They publish them in the newspapers, for goodness sake, though I really wonder why they have the right. At the very least it is read aloud to the family and beneficiaries.'

'Yes. Yes, you are right. But I think I have found a way around it. I shall need to discuss the details with Tom Ross.' George's blue eyes held a sparkle as he explained his plan to his wife. 'So, you see, all the grandchildren will receive exactly the same as far as anyone can tell, a sum of money and a personal letter from me. The fact that Sarah's will lead her again to Tom's office will be known only to her.'

'And Sarah will be guardian of the child's legacy until she finds him? Well, it's certainly an ingenious idea. I'll be interested to hear what Tom has to say about it.'

George had never been one to gallop headlong into action as soon as an idea struck him. His success as a businessman bore witness to his circumspect and canny approach to any undertaking and he made sure that, as far as he could, his preparations for changing his Will left no stone unturned. He gradually, over several weeks gathered from a number of sources sufficient funds to furnish the special envelope that he intended to leave with Tom for Sarah to administer.

It was the second week in December when he and Edith finally made the journey to Leeds to their appointment with Uttley, Uttley and Ross. As their taxi drew up at the kerb Mr. Dobbs was already opening the doors, ready to usher them inside. He melted away as Miss Cheadle came forward with a smile. She was the epitome of smartness and oozed efficiency from the top of her carefully smoothed head to her high-heeled black patent shoes.

'Mr. Ross is expecting you, Mr. Grange, Mrs. Grange. Would you care to come this way?'

'It's good to see you again, sir,' said Tom Ross. 'You'll take some refreshment after your journey? A glass of sherry, perhaps, or tea?'

'I believe a cup of tea would be most welcome,' answered Edith. Tom glanced at Miss Cheadle who nodded her assent and withdrew, closing the door behind her.

'Shall we get down to business while we wait,' said Tom, 'I have your papers ready. I understand from your letter that it is just a matter of making a few amendments to your Will. As I recall we last looked at it when you retired from the mill in '25. Ah! Here we are. Perhaps you would both look over this copy,' he said, handing over the document and keeping the original for his own reference.

'We need to concern ourselves only with the section that deals with my grandchildren, Tom, beginning at the top of page three. There is nothing else that needs review.' George glanced at his wife. 'But, before I outline the plan I have in mind, I need to confide in you some information of a highly sensitive nature. My wife joins me in asking for your word of assurance that what passes between us this afternoon will remain close.' Tom Ross' expression showed no surprise. It was part of his job to be party to his clients' private matters, though he could not help wondering what George Grange could have to tell him, that he did not already know, that would have any bearing upon his Will.

'You can rely entirely upon my discretion,' said Tom. There was a gentle tap on the door. 'Come in ... this will be our tea, I expect.' The tray that was set before them on the wide desk was laid with a dainty, white lace cloth and china cups and saucers edged with gold, as elegant as would be found in any drawing room.

'Would you like me to pour, sir?' asked the smart girl who carried the tray.

'Thank you, Doris. I believe we shall manage very well.'

'Yes, sir.' It was not exactly a curtsey. Everyone knew that such formality was no longer expected, but Doris' slight inclination of the head as she stepped backwards before turning to leave the room was, nonetheless, deferential. Her grasp of the form required of the perfect servant had been gleaned in part from her observation of Mr. Dobbs and in some degree from a little book she had come across in the Public Library. (Lately she had discovered that membership of her local library was an inexpensive way of educating herself in a whole range of subjects.)

Now she closed the door quietly behind her and bent down to adjust the buckle of her shoe that had, mysteriously, become loose. Doris Smithson's luck held as no-one had occasion to pass by during the next fifteen minutes. Her eavesdropping was undisturbed though her heart beat fast against her ribs, every sense alert to the dangerous game she was playing. Several previous attempts had almost succeeded but she had been baulked, obliged to beat a hasty retreat before she had heard any useful information. It was a frustrating sort of gamble but she was not about to give up just yet. Thankful for the thick carpets and good floorboards that provided soundless movement about the building, she crouched, tensed for flight yet still and silent, listening.

'You will remember our granddaughter, Sarah? John's eldest child?'

'Yes, of course. She went to the Continent, did she not?'

'She is still there,' said Edith. 'She writes that she hopes to spend another year there at least. She finished her time at the school in Lausanne and was befriended by a family who were taking a holiday there and who were in need of a nanny. Sarah was persuaded to stay with them and travel north to their home in northern France, Lille in fact. It's a city built on the wool trade so she feels quite at home. She so enjoys the children and in her spare time she tells us that she is able to study the local textiles. I think John hopes she'll accept a job at the mill when she comes home.'

'Yes, yes, dear,' interrupted George, impatiently, 'but this is all beside the point, if I may say so. What Tom needs to know has little to do with all that.

'Briefly, Tom, we have come to discover that Sarah, before she went abroad, gave birth to a child. This makes me a great-grandfather and, although I am not supposed to know, I find I cannot ignore the fact. Therefore, in perfect secrecy, I need to provide for the child.' Tom Ross was listening intently, a thoughtful expression on his face and as George paused he said, quietly, 'You must be aware that, under these circumstances, you are in no way obliged to recognise this child.'

'I know that, Tom. I have spent many hours arguing the case with myself and discussing it with my wife and I have made my decision.'

'I take it that the rest of the family know nothing of this?' George nodded. 'And the source of your information cannot be divulged?' He shook his head.

'To reveal it would neither help nor hinder.'

'You are quite sure of your facts?'

'Of course, without a shadow of doubt. All I need is for you to confirm that what I propose to do about it is legal and water-tight.'

On the far side of the door Doris strained her ears as George Grange outlined his plan. A large sum of money in cash to benefit the child to be paid over to its legal guardians by Sarah herself. She hardly dared to breathe as she listened to the discussion between the solicitor and his client, the questions he asked them, the answers they gave. She committed all the details to memory, already beginning to formulate ideas about how to use this intelligence.

Tom Ross's eyebrows crept up over the tops of his spectacles as he considered George's proposal. It was novel, indeed, but when he had considered it he could see no reason why it could not be done.

'Have you any idea where the child may be living now?'

'No. None at all,' replied George. 'We believe that an adoption was to be arranged by St.

Faith's but that it took place well after Sarah left for Switzerland.'

'And you are quite decided that it is through your Will that you wish to make this gift?'

'Yes, I am certain that this is what I must do. This envelope contains £5,000 and my second note to Sarah. These are the other personal letters to my grandchildren ... all to be left with you as executors of the Will.'

At the mention of such a sum of money, in cash and only a few feet away from her, Doris' mind flew into flights of fancy as she crouched beyond the door. For a brief moment she imagined herself knocking at the door, walking in to collect the tray and accidentally scooping up that envelope under it. She had to smile as she realised how ridiculous an idea it was. No, there would be far more subtle ways of using this invaluable material. They had paused in their conversation and Doris' acute hearing had detected a note of finality in Mr. Grange's last remark. She was on her feet and moving swiftly out of sight as her ears took in the sound of papers being collected up and the voice of Mr. Ross, obviously on his feet too, moving towards the door.

'If you will excuse me for just a moment I will take these straight to the safe in the inner office. Do take another cup of tea while I'm gone. We can complete the revisions to the Will as soon as these are secure.' Tom Ross was pensive as he deposited the eight envelopes, carefully catalogued, labelled and tied together with the red tape so beloved of legal practice. This was an odd affair but who was he to question the old man's wishes. He hurried back to his clients. He and George Grange together drafted the new arrangements for bequests to the seven grandchildren while Edith looked on with interest. She had been privy to the letters composed with such care by her husband. They were full of his love and words of encouragement as each set out on life's journey but they were sealed as he gave them to Tom. The contents of only one of them was revealed to the solicitor, and that only in part, so that he should know that Sarah would return to collect her second instruction from her grandfather. The winter afternoon light was fading as the draft was completed to their satisfaction.

'You'll not be thinking of returning home this evening?'

'No. We shall stay with Annie and Jim tonight. Edith is keen to see this new film *"The Private Life of Henry the Eighth"* while we are here. It may be months before the Morecambe Picture House shows it.'

'Ah, yes, Charles Laughton is much praised for the part, I understand. Well, then, rather than waiting for this to be typed today, perhaps you would like to drop in tomorrow to have it formally signed and witnessed?' They were happy to agree to this arrangement since it was already nearly four o'clock and almost dark. George was relieved to have the legalities completed. It had been on his mind far too long.

Doris watched from a window as the taxi, hailed for them by Dobbs, collected them from the door and sped away. She needed a better look at them. She would have some homework to do on this family and to have a clear picture of these two was essential.

'What are you doing, Doris, loitering about by the window?' She was so intent on her own business that she jumped violently and only just stopped herself from retaliating sharply. Only just in time she saw that it was Mr. Dobbs beside her and quickly replaced her mask of docility.

'I am sorry, sir.'

'Yes, indeed! Make haste, Doris and fetch the tray from Mr. Ross's office. He has no further appointments today so you may begin work in there before you clean the secretary's office.'

An hour and a half later she was on the tram and making for home. In her purse lay the rough draft of part of George Grange's Will, the section that he had altered earlier in the day. It had fallen unnoticed behind the desk and had avoided being put into the waste paper basket when Miss Burton was rushing to finish the typing of it. It was Friday and she was anxious to be off home as quickly as possible to meet her young man at the bus stop. It was Doris' job to take all the paper from the baskets to Dobbs who would see that it was all burnt at the end of each day. No risks were taken with the paper-work at Uttley, Uttley and Ross. And because it was Friday Doris had to pull out the desks and clean behind them with the new-fangled electric vacuum cleaner. She remembered having seen one in the window of a large department store but never dreamed she would be required to use one herself. They were tremendously expensive she recalled, having gasped at the price label that declared £4.19.6d. That was almost six week's wages. She would soon be quite accustomed to owning such luxuries as this, she assured herself as she made the office shine.

She clutched her bag as if it contained the Crown Jewels and the journey home felt like floating on air. People looked at her. She knew they were looking and wondering why she had such a dreamy smile on her face on a cold, wet December evening. By the time she reached home her mind was in a ferment. Ideas, like bubbles rising in the washtub, jostled for prominence, floated or burst while others reformed and rose again. It was impossible to walk from the tram. She had to run, then slow down to catch her breath and run again until she burst in through the door of the basement flat. She could not wait to share this with Joe. The living room was lit only by the fire in the range and Joe was dozing in a chair, his work finished for the day. Being home early in the winter made up for all the nights when he had to work until the daylight faded during the summer months. He was, as a rule, reluctant to share in the domestic tasks but he knew that he would have to sit and shiver if he did not light the fire. Doris was rarely home before six-thirty. The sudden commotion at the door had him on his feet almost before his eyes were open.

'What the...?' His wife, who generally toiled in at the end of the day with dragging feet and weary look, was actually skipping across from the door to fling her arms around his neck and whirl him around the room in a frenzy. The woman must have lost her senses. She was jabbering away incoherently, her eyes sparkling, finally throwing herself onto the shabby sofa, completely out of breath. He took hold of her shoulders and held her still. Doris looked up into his face, her own shining with excitement.

'It's happened ... at last, Joe. It's what we've been waiting for.'

'What on earth are you talking about, woman? For God's sake slow down.'

'Yes, alright, Joe. But first find me some paper and a pencil. And light the gas! I'll tell you about it but I must write it all down, just as I heard it, whilst it's fresh in my mind. I did it, Joe! I listened at the door and you'll be amazed at what I heard. It could make us rich beyond our dreams. Go on, find me something to write with.' Joe's stomach willed him to ask when his meal would be ready but the look on his wife's face and the mood she was in persuaded him that this was the last thing on her mind and that mention of it would be futile, foolish, even. He found what she needed while she took off her coat and hat, changed her shoes for slippers and threw more coal on the fire.

'Now, Joe, sit down and listen to this. Today a Mr. Grange and his wife came to see Mr. Ross. He wanted to change his Will...' Doris began to write, beginning with today's date. She knew from snippets gleaned from working for the solicitors that every small detail of an event or situation required noting. She knew that the partners at Uttley, Uttley and Ross would be astounded if they knew how their maid listened and absorbed information on a daily basis. And now she played back to Joe the scene in Tom Ross's office that afternoon, starting with the moment when she carried in the tea tray. Having just caught the words 'information of a highly sensitive nature' and having paused for a few seconds, her ear to the door she had knocked.

'Mr. Grange was a kind-looking man, not very tall, with a lot of silvery hair and a full set of whiskers to match. He wore a dark grey suit, waistcoat and wing collar. Mrs. Grange had on the loveliest fur coat, dark brown, soft and shiny, with a little hat to match.'

'What does it matter what they had on?' Joe was already becoming impatient as Doris stopped again to write.

'I have to know what they look like, don't I? And this'll help me to remember.' Bit by bit Doris recounted and recorded all that had been said that afternoon. Gradually Joe's preoccupation with the state of his stomach waned as his interest grew in what his wife was saying. His chief fascination to begin with was the insight he was getting of the life of the wealthy. That was enough in itself to make him forget his hunger.

'This chap, Grange, how come he's so rich? He's not a Lord or anything?'

'Not that I know of. Mr. Ross called him Mr. Grange. We'll need to find out who he is, where he lives and all about the family.'

'How d'ya think we can do that?'

'Oh, Joe, just hang on with all the questions, will you. You're putting me off. I don't want to forget anything. Now, he told Mr. Ross that he'd found out a secret. His grand-daughter had had a baby. It was born three years ago, only he just found out a few weeks ago. Well, she wasn't wed! And she was only just sixteen at the time, an'all.'

'Pretty much a disgrace for such as them, I reckon.'

'Yes, well, they only found out by accident, he said. Only the girl and her parents knew, they thought. Now, let me see. What came next? You've interrupted again, Joe. Just shut up, will you, until I've finished.' Doris continued to tell and to write all that had passed between client and solicitor and Joe held his peace, though his mind was busy lining up questions to put to Doris as soon as she had done.

'They said the baby was born in January, 1930 at somewhere called St. Faith's wherever that is.' Doris was still writing her careful notes and now slowed down to chew the end of her pencil. 'I think I've got most of it down. There's such a lot to remember, Joe.'

'And what happened to it then? Is it a boy or a girl? And where is the mother ... the one that's going to get all this money?' Doris threw down her pencil, stretched her aching limbs and gave Joe a long look.

'If we don't get to it first, you mean? They referred to the baby as "him" ... I'm sure,' she said thoughtfully. 'Mr. Grange said he was going to be adopted. Sarah, the mother, went to Switzerland after he was born and now she lives in a place called Leel, or something. In France, I think.'

'Right! First tell me how we're to make our fortune out of all this. Are we going to blackmail the old couple, the grandparents? Is that your idea? Or the girl herself? Or her parents? I can't see how we can get our hands on that money in the safe. Are you sure you heard it like you think you did? And who's going to believe such a far-fetched story, anyway?' Doris took from her handbag a folded paper. Slowly she spread it out to show to Joe. He did not look impressed. It was a foolscap sheet covered in someone's rather untidy handwriting.

'Perhaps this'll help to convince you, then. I found this when I was cleaning the office. Just had time for a quick look before I hid it down my blouse. I've not read it properly but I know it's what Miss Burton was typing for Mr. Ross.' They pored over the spidery writing that revealed George Grange's revision to his Will. It had been set to paper by Tom Ross in accordance with his client's instruction. Joe read it slowly and carefully. He was puzzled. These words said nothing about a baby nor about money to be left to a child.

'No,' said Doris, 'that won't be mentioned here. The secret is in his letter to Sarah. But, don't you see? this proves that I haven't dreamed it all up! And, look, here on the back, a note to Miss Burton, telling her which page to replace ... and there ... just there, at the bottom George Grange's address. Good Lord! He lives in Morecambe.'

'Where the deuce is that?'

'I'm not right sure. I think it's by the sea, but I guess he used to live round here.' Suddenly she felt dog-tired. It had been a long day. The tension and thrill of the last few hours had left her drained.

'Do you think we could afford fish and chips for supper?' she asked Joe, knowing full well that they could, since it was she who held the purse strings. Doris was wise enough to let Joe believe he still had status as the head of the family.

Doris was tired yet she could not get to sleep. Joe, already snoring beside her, had no such problem. Hush-money! How much would this family pay to prevent the broadcast of their bastard child? How were they to go about it? Where do you start on a thing like this? She sighed. It was all very well in theory. Putting into some kind of action plan was another matter. And it had been a stressful day. Her brain seemed to have ground to a halt. She fell into a light doze at last her mind still dwelling on all the conversation she had overheard that afternoon. She had even considered trying to find a way to steal the money from the safe. But, no, there seemed to Doris a subtle difference between the clear dishonesty of theft and the trading of money for secrets.

She woke suddenly. Her luminous alarm clock stood at three-thirty. The room was bitterly cold as she pushed her feet into her slippers and dragged the eiderdown round her body. She went to the window and looked out. A bright, full moon shone in as she pulled back the curtain and an indignant howl came from the bed where Joe was woken by the cold air.

'What the hell's going on? I'm frozen. Where's the covers gone?'

'Come through to the room,' she said. 'There'll still be a bit of fire left. Come on Joe!' With loud and vociferous objections Joe allowed himself to be dragged into wakefulness as they huddled within the eiderdown in front of the remains of the fire.

'If this works,' said Doris, 'it'll be the answer to all our prayers.'

'If what works?'

'Well, Joe, I've been thinking. Nobody seems to know what happened to Sarah Grange's baby for sure. What if he wasn't adopted? What if he's still waiting, in an orphanage or something, for some childless couple to give him a home? Don't you see, Joe? You and me, we've been hoping for a baby ever since we got married and one hasn't come along. If we find him and adopt him we'll be in for the money as well! Two birds with one stone! No need for any blackmail. No risk of prison. All above board! It's perfect!' It was taking Joe a while to absorb and comprehend what his wife was suggesting. Slow and steady, was Joe.

'Well?' She shook him, trying to elicit some response. 'Well, Joe, come on, what do you think?' Joe was clearly having trouble focussing his attention on her words. He made a great effort. He knew that if he did not there would be little chance of returning to his warm bed.

'What if he's already adopted? He'll be somebody else's son.'

'We'll face that if we have to. Change the plan if he is. But, Joe, just imagine a son of our own and £5,000 to go with him. And all we have to do now is find him.'

'You make it all sound so simple. Can we go to bed now? I'm cold.'

Chapter 17

1936

John Grange allowed himself a late arrival at the mill so that he could drive Sarah and his mother to the station. He thought Edith had been wonderful throughout the past few difficult days, and he told her so.

'Well, thank you for that, dear. We all feel the loss in our separate ways. George was a remarkable person and I'm so thankful to have been able to share his life. It will be very different without him.'

'I'm glad he didn't suffer a long illness,' said Sarah. 'He would have hated to have become an invalid.'

'Very true,' said Edith, 'he would have been impossible. He could have his cantankerous moments, even when all he had was a cold. Ah, here we are and in good time for the eight-fifty.' They hurried to the platform and Sarah bought a couple of newspapers at the news-stand. 'I shall welcome the clean air of the coast after a week amongst the "dark, satanic mills."' Edith kissed her son goodbye, knowing that she would always have a soft spot for the smoky old city wherever she lived. John stood on the platform, waving until the train was out of sight, then walked slowly back to his car. Only he knew how much he would miss the wise counsel he had always relied upon from his father and his heart was heavy again as he drove to the mill.

The early train dashed across the county border into Lancashire, at its heels the snowstorms that, by the end of the day, had closed most of the roads in Yorkshire.

Sarah felt a shudder run through her as she turned the page of her paper and saw pictures of the wreckage of the Penzance to London GWR night express. The driver and twenty-six other people killed and many more injured; another disaster, just a week after her own narrow escape. Her mind flew back to that night and she wondered for the umpteenth time what had happened to Daisy.

'Is something the matter, dear?' asked Edith.

'No, Gran, nothing at all.' She closed the paper. 'Did you hear about the little girl I met? You know, the night I broke my ankle?'

'No, dear, who was she?' The strange tale of Daisy passed the time as they clattered down the track and Sarah found herself puzzling afresh over the effect the child and her disappearance had on her.

'When my ankle is mended and the winter weather is over I think I shall look her up. It shouldn't be too difficult, should it, Gran?' But there was no reply. Edith had succumbed to the gentle rhythm of the train and had nodded off. Sarah returned to the newspaper. Why was there only bad news in the headlines? There was an Epidemic of Influenza Striding across the Country. Mr. Rudyard Kipling, Poet and Storyteller has Sunk into a Coma after a Serious Operation at the

Middlesex Hospital. His Majesty King George has a Cold and will remain at Sandringham. (Subheading, No Cause for Concern). The Prince of Wales and the Duke of York have arrived at Sandringham. Lord Dawson of Penn and Sir Stanley Hewitt, the King's doctors are also there. The Queen is at his bedside. Sarah put down the paper. It did not sound like 'no cause for concern'.

She had had enough of doom, gloom and bad weather. She was going to enjoy the next few days. She would walk by the sea, yes, even if it rained, and she would blow the cobwebs out of her mind. Too much had happened to her, and too quickly, during the last seven days. She needed space and time to herself, time to think. Morecambe in the winter was just the place for a bit of solitude. The summer visitors were long gone and the residents stayed indoors as much as they could, gathered round their firesides. Her musings were rudely broken off by the squealing of brakes as Morecambe station platform slid alongside.

'Come along, Gran. Shake a leg. We're here.' Wrapped in her mink coat with the little matching hat Edith, without appearing to do a thing, had a porter rushing to see to the bags while another offered to hail a taxi. Of course she was not unknown at Morecambe station and some of them would know the reason for her journey and why she was not in company with her husband. There were flowers, several lots of them, waiting for her at the house. Edith had given up her live-in staff when they had moved away from the big house in Yorkshire and now she just had Ellie.

Ellie was a treasure, said Edith. A young married woman, about thirty, strong and cheerful, she came on a daily basis from her own home and saw to the general upkeep of the house, did a little shopping and cooking and helped when Edith and George had entertained. She was there when they arrived from the station, ready with a welcoming smile and a cup of tea for the travellers.

'We've been thinking of you, Mrs. Grange,' said Ellie, simply. 'Welcome back. It's good to see you, Miss Sarah. I've put you in the green room at the front.'

She could see the sea from her window in all its changing moods. Today it looked silver-grey and smooth, like a huge pewter plate. The sky was mirrored in its surface, full of heavy clouds. Sarah gazed, unseeing, through the window as tears trickled down her cheeks. She thought she had done crying for Grandpa Grange but being in this house without him set her off again. She turned to find Edith standing in the doorway and she ran to put her arms round her grandmother.

'I'm glad you're here,' said Edith as they pulled themselves together with an effort and went downstairs to drink Ellie's tea. The house, which Sarah had first visited two years ago on her return from France, was very modern and comfortable. When they had sold up the family house to retire to the coast they had made the new start, as they had called it, in style. Sold was the heavy Victorian furniture that they had had since their marriage, some of it handed down from the previous generation. Sold, too, the oil paintings in their ornate gold frames and all the clutter and fussiness of their former home. Edith and George had embraced with enthusiasm the clean, sharp lines of the Art Deco with its lightness of style, its functional design and its splashes of vibrant colour. They tempered this a little with the gentler ideas of the earlier Art Nouveau and Arts and Crafts Movements. Everything was of the highest quality, from the elegant dining room table and chairs, made of finest English oak, to the simple lines of the bedroom suites, all supplied by Gillows of Lancaster. Sarah loved this house and never ceased to admire the exquisite taste with which Edith had arranged it. Yet it was not a showroom. Every room had signs of human activity. Books, music, needlework, a chess-board, tennis racquets, walking boots, umbrellas, buckets and spades in the hall, waiting for the next invasion of youngsters. Untidiness of a practical and useful kind, thought Sarah, all speaking of a place where people lived and breathed.

'Do you mind if I take myself off for a walk this afternoon?' Sarah asked.

'Of course I don't mind. You must do whatever you wish while you're here. I need to telephone a few friends to assure them I am back in circulation and there is plenty more needing to be done.' Sarah felt a little guilty and immediately offered to stay and help. 'There is nothing you could do just at present, thank you, dear. But you might help me in a little while, to sort out some of your grandpa's things. I can't face it yet, though. Off you go and get some of that fresh air you came for.'

''Bye then, Gran. I'll go and see what the Morecambe breezes can do for my befuddled brain. I have quite a few knotty problems to think over.' Yes, thought Edith and I know what one of them is at least.

Striding along the promenade Sarah had to lean against the wind that whipped the tops of the incoming waves and threatened to sweep her off her feet and throw her onto the rocky foreshore. It was exhilarating, the very effort of walking taking up all her attention, filling up her lungs with oxygen and bringing colour to her cheeks. All thought of puzzling out her problems disappeared as she gave herself up to the sheer enjoyment of battling with the elements. It was the first physical exercise she had had for well over a week and she knew that it was doing her good. As she swung her heavily plastered leg expertly between the crutches she realised just how quickly a person can adapt to a situation that, formerly, would have seemed utterly daunting. Perhaps this was the lesson to be learned from this afternoon's jaunt, to accept what you cannot alter, just as she could not alter the force of the wind. She must accept with equanimity both the task set by her grandfather and the decision of her first love to turn his back on her. These, she realised, were the two events that she had shrunk from acknowledging. Whatever the outcome might be she knew she had to face them head on, just as she was facing this gale, and go forward with purpose; to stop looking back and wishing things were different. Her spirits rose as she neared the house. She was suddenly ravenous. The Bisto Kids would have been proud of her as she poked her head round the kitchen door, relishing the aroma coming from the cooking pots.

'Mmm... Smells delicious!'

'It's sure to be. Ellie made it before she went home. Ready in ten minutes,' said Edith.

They sat together when the meal was over, sipping a glass of George's excellent port. Sarah wondered whether it was too soon to talk about the Will. Edith was glancing idly at the paper that Sarah had bought at the station and her attention was caught by the report that the King was unwell. An ardent Royalist, Edith read on. It was unusual for comment on the health of any of the royal family to be published unless it was something of a serious nature. She read that the King had a cold, had taken a chill while out riding, that it was nothing serious. She read also that two eminent doctors had arrived at Sandringham, as well as the Duke of York. There was a picture of the little princesses playing in the snow. She did hope that His Majesty would soon be well again and said as much to Sarah who agreed that these winter coughs and colds could be very troublesome.

'You're very quiet this evening, my dear. Has your bracing walk tired you out?'

'No, no. But I need to talk to you, Gran, and I don't know how to begin.'

'Then let me help you. It's about your letter from grandpa, yes? It's alright, I know all about it.' Edith moved over to sit beside Sarah on the sofa. She had known it would be hard for Sarah to bring things out into the open.

'George shared with me all the letters he wrote and the reason behind them, you know.' Still

Sarah was not sure how to begin. Finally she said, very quietly, 'How long have you known ... about ... my baby? I thought nobody knew, except mummy and daddy. And Maddie. Oh, Gran, I am so sorry.' Silent tears flowed down Sarah's face. She was not really aware of them as the memory of that time came back as clearly as yesterday and she was suddenly lost in a sea of emotion. Edith placed gentle arms round her granddaughter and allowed the quiet and deep waves of anguish to surface and disperse into salt tears and sobbing. Sarah knew that, for the first time, she was truly grieving over the loss of her child. Edith sensed this, too. This was a different kind of weeping. It spoke of helpless despair, of self-reproach and irreparable loss. When she finally managed to pull herself together there was a haunted expression in her eyes and Edith's kind heart went out to her.

'Oh, Gran, for the very first time in six years I feel full of doubts and regrets.' She was so consumed with countless confusing feelings that she could not put them, properly into words. That sounded so tame. It came nowhere near the truth. Edith took hold of her shoulders and made her sit up straight.

'Look at me!' she said. 'Listen, Sarah. Whatever happened six years ago I am sure that you dealt with it in the best way you knew how at the time. Today is no time for doubts and misgivings. It is done. Right or wrong, you cannot have that time over again, do things differently. The only way in this life is forward. Come, I'll make some coffee. The port is making you maudlin, my love.' While

Edith clattered about in the kitchen Sarah took a deep breath, recalling the thoughts she had had, only this afternoon, as she returned from her windswept ramble. What had caused her to forget so soon all that positive thinking? As if in answer to her own question she spoke to Edith as she came in with cups of steaming coffee.

'It's just that I'd never really thought of the baby as a person. Not until after I'd read grandpa's letters. A child, needing to be raised, guided into adulthood ... all that.' She sipped at her coffee and looked at Edith, then adding quietly, 'I never knew that it was a boy.'

'Oh, my dear girl.' Edith was lost for words and placed a hand over Sarah's.

'I don't know how long you've known nor who can have told you, but my whole world has been turned over since I sat down and read Grandpa's letter. How many other people know, I wonder? We did everything possible to avoid a family disgrace. I was so sure that only my parents and Maddie knew.'

'And you were right, my dear. And you mustn't be angry when I tell you that it was through Maddie that we found out. No, no! She did not tell us. You know she would never have done that.'

'Then, how...?'

'It was while you were abroad. Maddie was working with the Concert Party on the pier and she and a friend stayed with us for the summer season. Perhaps she told you? Well, late one night, the pair of them came home after the show. George and I had retired early and were reading in bed. As they came upstairs I realised that someone was crying. She sounded so distressed that I put on my robe and went out onto the landing to ask whether there was anything I could do to help. Maddie was supporting her friend who was blinded by her tears, poor girl. She thanked me for my concern, but that she would go down shortly and make Josie a cup of chocolate, if I didn't mind. Maddie insisted that I go back to bed. All would be well, she said. Josie was overtired and upset, that was all. It was one of those summer nights when there's hardly a breath of air, hot and humid still, even in the early hours. We needed every window open. If it had not been for that fact we would not have heard the girls talking quietly in the next room.' Edith paused before continuing as Sarah's expression began to take on that of disbelief. Surely Maddie would not have betrayed her trust. 'In the still air their conversation carried to our room, Sarah. We could not help overhearing. Josie had been crying because she knew she was pregnant and her fiance had, just that day, broken off their engagement, saying that Josie must have been with another man. The girl was distraught. Maddie spent a long time trying to calm and comfort her, suggesting this or that course of action. I remember, at one point, Josie saying angrily, 'What do you know about it, anyway? Nothing, Maddie. You've never been in this position, have you?' And Maddie answered that she had not, but that her best friend had, three years ago. Her best friend had got herself into trouble when she was only fifteen. No, it was nobody you know, Josie. Anyway, if she could cope and see it through, Josie could, too. She had the advantage of being much older. What had this friend done about it? Had she got rid of it? Maddie explained to Josie how the girl had stayed at a convent in Scarborough for five months, had the baby there and left it to the nuns to arrange a home for it. The nuns were very kind at St. Faith's. Then, Maddie had said, she had gone to Switzerland to finishing school. She had stayed there afterwards and got a job as a nanny. There was no doubt that Maddie was talking about you, Sarah. But she did it with the best of intentions and she could not have realised that her words would carry as far as our room. George and I stored away the information that should never have reached our ears, but, by the end of the year, the knowledge of his great-grandchild bothered George so much that he went to Tom Ross to alter his Will. The rest you know.'

Sarah listened intently and with growing understanding to her grandmother's explanation. It all made sense now. One, at least, of her puzzles was solved.

'Thanks, Gran. I really don't deserve such wonderful grandparents, you know. Some would have disowned me, I know.'

'Nonsense. Now you can concentrate on tracing the baby. Do you feel better now?'

'Much, thank you. Did I tell you that Maddie offered to drive me over to St. Faith's next week? That's going to be my first port of call. I hope they'll be able to help.'

'I'm sure they'll do their best. Now, how about a little music, dear? There's usually something worth listening to on the Light Programme on a

Friday evening.' Edith felt that a change of subject was called for.

They sat, each with their own thoughts, as they listened to the wireless. Sarah tried to imagine how she would feel going back to see the nuns. Tomorrow she would write a letter asking for an appointment to see Sister Ruth. It would be good to see her again. Sarah would never forget her gentle concern and kindly common sense.

The programme on the wireless finished earlier than expected, the last piece of music being faded out to allow time for a special announcement. Sarah and Edith listened as the announcer, in grave tones, informed the nation that their King's illness was giving cause for concern. 'His Majesty remains at Sandringham with his personal physicians in attendance. The bronchial catarrh from which the King is suffering is not severe but there have appeared signs of cardiac weakness which must be regarded with some disquiet. A heart specialist has been consulted. Queen Mary watches by his bedside as other members of the Royal family travel to Sandringham today. The King was able to see his Private Secretary this afternoon. A further bulletin will be issued in the morning.'

'My goodness,' said Edith, 'he must be far worse than we thought for them to issue daily bulletins. The newspaper reports that he was seen riding his pony only three days ago. He must have taken a serious chill.' They were both startled by the telephone shrilling in the hall. Edith went to answer it, surprised by the lateness of it. She came to tell Sarah that the call was for her.

'Who is it?'

'Someone called Sam,' she said. As Sarah hobbled out of the room a look of grim determination crossed her face.

'Hello, Sam.'

'Sarah! Your mother gave me the number. I was surprised when I found you had gone away.'

'My grandmother needed company. We came over early to escape the snow.' Her tone was cool.

'There's plenty of that here now, and it's still coming down. Quite a number of roads are blocked. Are you alright? I wanted to talk to you. I came to your house this evening. Your mother told me you had gone away for a few days. Is there something wrong?'

'No, Sam, nothing at all. But I really did not think that there was anything more to be said between us. You made your feelings perfectly clear, I think, when you left on Wednesday.'

'I've done a lot of thinking, Sarah. Perhaps I was wrong to run out on you like that. I think we need to talk it through, straighten things out. I don't want to lose you again, Sarah.'

The note of pleading in his voice was not lost on her and she had to steel herself once again for her reply.

'I'm sorry, Sam, but the damage is done. I should never have told you. I realise that now. On the other hand I could never have taken up with you again without telling you. I think that's all there is to say.'

'Wait a minute, Sarah, please. Don't go.'

'It is very late. I really don't want to talk any more. I'm sorry, I have to go now. Goodbye.' She hung up the receiver. She felt relieved as she let go, with a long breath, the tension that had built up during that short conversation. It was time to go forward again. It was the only way. She knew that she must not weaken or ever look back with longing at the hope that had filled her soul during those few short hours before he had walked out of her life a second time. There would not be a third. He must understand that.

'Is everything all right, dear? You look thoughtful.'

'Everything is fine, Gran. I was just thinking about the Queen and how worried she must be,' she lied smoothly. 'This is so sudden, isn't it, this illness. Let's hope for better news tomorrow.'

Chapter 18

Sarah slept late the following morning. The bed in the green room was deep and comfortable, the curtains heavy and thick and it was somehow easier to relax here, away from all that had gone on at home these past few days. Edith roused her with a cup of tea.

'Good morning, sleepy-head.' Edith was glad of Sarah's visit. It had given her something to think about, dulling the stark emptiness of the house without George, someone to talk to, someone to care for. She sensed that Sarah, too, had need of support. There was something on her mind quite apart from the problem of the broken bones in her ankle and the sadness of losing her grandpa. Different even from the task set for her by George. She smiled at the tousled head in the bed as Sarah opened her eyes and stretched,

'Thank you, Gran. But tea in bed should have been my job. How could I have slept so late?'

'Oh, I'm always up before seven, my dear. Breakfast when you're ready. No need to hurry.' Sarah drank her tea and soon joined Edith at the breakfast table.

The morning had brought no better news of the King. Edith read out some of the headlines.

'The anxiety expressed in the last bulletin persists... Grave words from the medical advisers... Queen's watch by his bedside. Oh, dear, these are solemn words. I do hope he will rally. Maybe I shouldn't say this, but I really don't think our crown prince is ready, yet, for kingship. Shooting parties, holidays and pretty girls are more to his taste, though he is extremely popular wherever he goes on his public engagements. They say he's an absolute charmer.'

'Yes, I know. Mummy was utterly enslaved by him when he came to the dedication of the old queen's statue and paid a visit to the mill. You'll remember that, too. What had you planned to do today, Gran?'

'I shall go through the huge pile of correspondence that waits my attention. George was known and liked by so many people. There must be almost a hundred letters or cards of condolence.' She sighed. 'I expect it will take me most of the morning to deal with them, but it's a comfort to know how well regarded he was. Only a handful will need replies, of course.'

'Then I shall leave you in peace, Gran. I have a couple of letters to write, too. I must ask Sister Ruth if I can visit St. Faith's next week. I'll drop a note to Maddie as well.'

'Oh. Will you tell her about the hot summer night when I overheard her conversation?' Edith looked anxious. Sarah smiled.

'I shall tell her, but not today and certainly not in a letter. Don't look so worried, Gran.'

The heavy clouds threatened more rain and Sarah was content to stay indoors. She had difficulty in clearing from her mind the conversation with Sam last evening. Her common sense told her to let go yet her heart was telling her otherwise. Had she been too terse, too hurtful? For the life in her she could not quite remember what she had said to him. Perhaps she would write to him, explain more kindly that it was over between them; that it would never work; that it was too late to pick up the pieces. After all, she thought, she had hit him with quite a thunderbolt when she had told him he was a father. Little wonder his reaction had been as it had. She could make things quite clear in a letter whilst she could neither see him nor hear his voice.

Morecambe,
Saturday, January 18th, '36
Dear Sam,

This note is by way of an apology for the way I spoke to you on the telephone last night. I realise I must have sounded curt and I regret that, my only excuse being that recent events have been emotional and tiring. It is clear to me that any attempt to return to the relationship that we once had would be impracticable. Too much has happened during the intervening years and we are both very different people now. It is too late to pick up the pieces, Sam. Please do not try. Perhaps, in time, we may be able to become friends again, but that is all.

Yours,
Sarah.

She was not satisfied with it. Still doubtful she re-read her words. Should she have referred to the secret she had shared with him? If so, what should she have said?

Should she have told him that she was seriously considering Andrew's offer of marriage? Would that be true, or would it simply have been a ruse to deter him? She decided to leave it as it was, put it in the envelope and addressed it to the hospital.

Morecambe
Saturday 18th Jan., '36
Dear Maddie,

The weather over here is pretty awful but we have no snow. I came to keep Gran company and I expect to be home again on Wednesday. I wonder if the snowfalls have been bad enough to close the theatre? Probably not, the show must go on, eh?

You remember offering to drive to Scarborough with me? I hope to go next Sunday and would be glad if you can come too. If the snow's still on the ground we can go by train. I do hope you can make it. I'll tele-

phone when I get home. We can decide then whether or not to go by car.
Love, Sarah

Just one more to go. What should she say to Sister Ruth?

Morecambe,
Saturday, January 18th, '36
Dear Sister Ruth,
It is six years since I left St. Faith's. I wonder whether you remember me. I came to stay at the Convent in the summer of 1929 to wait until the birth of my baby. I was a terrified schoolgirl at the time, full of guilt and fear. The Sisters were so kind to me and I was so very grateful for the care I received.
Now I write to ask yet another kindness. For legal reasons, which I will explain to you, I need to ascertain some details surrounding the birth of the baby and, to this end, I request permission to call on you. I hope to travel to Scarborough on Sunday next, accompanied by a friend. You need not trouble to reply to this letter because I will telephone you on Thursday to find out whether our visit will be acceptable. I do hope that it will be. I look forward to seeing you and the Sisters again.
Yours affectionately, Sarah.

She omitted her surname. Although Sister Ruth was aware of it, nobody else at the Convent was told the family name of any of the girls who stayed there and you never knew who might see her letter. Sarah got up stiffly. She found that her potted leg prevented her from sitting comfortably for any length of time. A walk to the post box would help. She found Edith taking a break from reading the kind notes. Her eyes were moist. She stood looking out of the window. The rain had stopped and a watery sun was trying to shine.

'Come to the post with me, Gran? You could do with a breath of fresh air.'

'A splendid idea. You're right. I need a change. Can't read any more of those at present. It's not that I don't appreciate them, they're just rather sad.' At sixty-five Edith was very fit and would regularly walk five and more miles along the coastline before the sudden death of her husband. The post-box was just around the corner but Edith declared that it was far enough for today. As they walked back Edith took Sarah's arm.

'I think I shall have a rest, dear, when we get home. The other letters can wait.'

'And I'll practise my kitchen skills and rustle up some tea for us. How's that?' Sarah was seeing at first-hand how deep grief could affect a person's physical as well as mental state. She would encourage her to rest today and tomorrow she would help Edith with the 'sorting out' that she had mentioned, whatever that entailed.

While she prepared the meal Sarah listened to the bulletin on the King. He was no worse, they said, though he was no better. More members of the Royal family had arrived at Sandringham. The Prime Minister, Mr. Baldwin, was to remain in London over the weekend. Special prayers would be said tomorrow at every church for the recovery of the King.

Edith and Sarah went to church together the

next morning and took part in the nationwide prayers along with a church rather fuller than usual with anxious people. There seemed to be a fervent hope that mere force of numbers would persuade the Almighty to spare the life of George V. Little change was reported from his majesty's sickbed during the day. Sarah, determined to lighten the atmosphere in the house, got out the gramophone after lunch and played an eclectic mixture of music, anything she could find amongst the collection of records she found in the cupboard. The lively songs and dances of the mid-twenties were just the thing to have Sarah and Edith smiling, not to mention the popular airs of Gilbert and Sullivan operettas, of which George had built a full collection of recordings.

Grandmother and granddaughter were getting along famously with the sorting out of George's possessions during the afternoon, joining in at times with the songs and choruses. Sarah, determined not to let Edith become morose, had suggested a system of piles ... one for clothes to donate to charity, probably the Salvation Army, one for keepsakes for members of the family, one for things Edith wished to keep and one for disposal. They were dealing only with clothes and smaller items. All the rest Edith would want to go through later at her leisure.

'Now I realise how sensible it was to clear out all the dross before we moved over here. It has made today's job so much easier.'

'Do you want to open this box?' asked Sarah. It was a fairly small box, much like the jewel boxes so beloved of the older generation, inlaid with different coloured woods and mother-of-pearl.

'Yes, do open it, dear. I really cannot recall what's in there. Some very old things of your grandfather's I suspect.' Sarah lifted the lid. The box was lined with red satin and was fitted with a tray in the top to allow both small and larger items to be kept inside. It was altogether a very pretty thing.

'I remember now. That belonged to George's mother. It's years since I saw it. George must have put it away himself when we moved here.'

'It's full of all sorts of items,' said Sarah. Bits of costume jewellery shone dully, their metal tarnished with neglect. A collection of Whitby jet sparkled against the red lining, telling of former days of mourning when Queen Victoria had favoured this as her only adornment. The court and the people had followed suit, making the black jewellery vastly popular. An old golf ball, some military medals and a set of ivory buttons sat next to some tiny leather boxes, neatly stacked in one corner. Two of these contained rings. One was a plain gold band, the other a child's ring, judging by its size, set with tiny pearls in the shape of a flower with a yellow stone in the centre. Sarah was fascinated as these things saw the light of day for the first time, Edith said, for at least forty years.

'That was my mother-in-law's wedding ring. It was left to me along with the pearl one. I never wore it because it was too small for me. She was a very petite woman, George's mother. The tiny ring was hers, too. She had it when she was a child so it's even older. I doubt it's very valuable since the pearls are split ones. Do you see? Just halves, and the yellow stone is semi-precious. I used to know the name of it, but I forget now.'

'It's very dainty, though. A charming piece,' said Sarah, replacing it in its box.

'And that other box, Sarah, the oval one. Pass it to me, would you, dear. I think it is what I have been hoping to find, though I feared it to be lost. Thank you.' She opened it. 'Yes. My goodness, I haven't seen this since before the children were born. Look, Sarah, it's a miniature. It belonged to George's mother, too. It is painted so beautifully in oils on ivory. He told me it was his mother's portrait, done by a well-known miniaturist when she was about eight years old. Isn't it pretty?' Edith handed it to Sarah and she held the little work of art in her hand. The head and shoulders of a young girl, framed in gold filigree, looked out at her, the colours as fresh and new as the day they were painted. The child's face was exquisitely done, the fine detail so clear from the dark curls on her head, the brilliant blue of the eyes to the delicate lace collar round the neck. The clear, gentle tones of the complexion were masterly.

'This is really beautiful, Gran.' She turned it over to admire the neat gold setting and clever arrangement that allowed it to be worn as a brooch or as a pendant. As Sarah looked again at the picture she was puzzling over where she could have seen it before. Suddenly it came to her.

'How strange! I have seen a little girl like this before, Gran. She is so like Daisy. It's quite uncanny.'

'Daisy?' said Edith.

'The child who sat with me before the train crash. The one who disappeared, you remember, I told you about her.'

'Well, well, that is a coincidence.'

'I expect there are millions of little girls with dark curly hair and blue eyes but it did give me a start. At first glance it looked just like her.'

'You seem to have been quite taken with her, this little girl on the train I mean,' said Edith, laying the portrait onto its dark blue velvet pad.

'She was so frightened but once she'd decided she could trust me she was quite self-assured. I heard from one of the police that she had been collected from the hospital by the people she was travelling with. And, yes, she made quite an impression on me.' Sarah sounded wistful.

'You're just too soft-hearted for your own good, you know. She was probably playing up, running away like that, causing no end of worry to her people. She obviously had you wrapped round her little finger.' Edith's voice held undertones of disapproval. She was of the opinion that children should obey their elders without question, no matter what the circumstance.

'I expect you're right, Gran,' said Sarah, closing the subject but privately thinking that Daisy, far from wrapping herself round her finger, had wrapped herself around her heart. She would stop thinking about her this instant. They were busy for the rest of the afternoon and Edith was pleased to have achieved so much of a task that she had dreaded tackling. Sarah's presence had made such a difference. Instead of feeling disconsolate she admitted to Sarah that she had enjoyed sharing with her the parts of George's life that were represented by this collection of his belongings. Each of her grandchildren was loved but there seemed to exist a special bond with Sarah, a closeness that neither could explain. Perhaps it was that they shared the same independent spirit. Edith's, having been constrained by the conventions of her day, enjoying watching Sarah's success as a working woman, fulfilling dreams that she might have had. As a mother Edith knew the sacrifice that Sarah had made in giving up her baby. Though she would have wished it never to have happened, she, nevertheless, admired the way that Sarah had handled the situation and the determination with which she had got on with her life.

'Have we finished now, Gran? Hello?' Edith was miles away and pulled herself up with a start.

'Sorry. In a dream. Yes, that's all I want to do today. Come along, let's have a cup of tea.'

Andrew Marsden telephoned during the evening. West Yorkshire, he told Sarah, was being blanketed by snow once more. He would be walking to the mill tomorrow since that was the safest and easiest way of getting about at present. If there were a break in the weather he would drive over to Morecambe on Wednesday to collect her. Sarah was grateful. It would be so much pleasanter to travel by car, but that she would catch the train if the roads remained snowbound. She was pensive as she returned to the sitting room after they had agreed to speak again on Wednesday morning.

'Andrew is very attentive these days,' said Edith. 'Do I detect romance in the air? I couldn't help noticing how he looked after you at the funeral. He's an extremely attractive young man, don't you think so, Sarah?'

'He's both good looking and very kind. In fact he's everything a girl could want in a boyfriend, Gran, but ... well ... it's hard to explain ... I seem to take fright every time he suggests putting things on a more formal footing. I am very fond of him ... yet...'

'He doesn't ring the right bells, is that it?'

'Something like that. He offers me love and security. I feel I should be grateful for that. But I don't think that's enough, do you?'

'You certainly can't marry him out of gratitude. That could be a recipe for disaster, and no mistake. Unfair to both of you.'

'I keep hoping my feelings will change, that I will learn to love him.'

'Oh, Sarah, take care my dear. Remember you have known what it is to be in love. Don't be tempted to settle for second best. You're still very young. If Andrew is not the right man for you, tell him so. Don't keep him hanging on in fruitless hope. That's a sure way of hurting him, and you said yourself, you don't want to do that. I firmly believe there is a soul-mate somewhere for each of us. You will find yours.'

She knew that Edith was right. With Andrew that certain spark, that excitement, that enjoyment at simply being together was missing ... on her part at least. She must find a way to tell him without ruining their friendship and, perhaps just as importantly, their working relationship. She also knew, without a doubt, that withdrawing from any romantic association with Andrew would mean that she would be spared the need to reveal her past to him. She could not have married him without doing so, yet she knew the risk she would take in telling him.

A letter was delivered for Sarah on Monday morning. Although she had not seen his handwriting for many years she knew straight away that it was from Sam. His was, like hers, in response to the telephone conversation on Friday evening. It appeared they had both sat down to write at the same time. Their letters had crossed.

Doncaster
18th January, '36
Dear Sarah,

I cannot, even now, believe what I did, what I said to you last Wednesday. My reaction to what you told me was unforgivable and to run away as I did was nothing short of cowardly. I have regretted my actions from the moment I left your house.

Neither here nor anywhere, at any time, will I repeat what passed between us. You may rest assured of that.

I am truly sorry to have caused you distress and I understand your decision not to discuss things with me any further. I regret it because there are a number of questions I would like to have asked, as you can probably imagine, but I respect your decision. I came back to the hospital this morning realising I had spoilt my chances of renewing our friendship. That makes me more wretched than ever. My only hope is that, in time, you may be able to forgive me. Perhaps, all is not entirely lost between us.

Yours ever, Sam

Sarah was touched by his apology but did not weaken in her resolve. Life was complicated enough and she was convinced of the wisdom of letting sleeping dogs lie. She put the note into her handbag and went to join Edith at breakfast. The morning paper had one topic of news only, the anxiety over the King's illness. The radio was to broadcast the latest bulletin every few hours throughout the day. Edith's *'Times'* reported that a Council of State had been set up by the King in Privy Council in a room adjoining the King's bedroom, the connecting door left open. Sarah wondered what this meant.

'It explains here that the Council of State will deputise for the King in matters of State during his illness which may be prolonged,' Edith read. 'Some of his engagements will be cancelled while others will be carried out by other members of the Royal Family. Oh dear. It sounds more serious every day.'

Indeed it was. The King had become gravely ill and the comings and goings at Sandringham, reported by the B.B.C. at regular intervals, revealed the alarm with which the situation was now viewed.

The following morning sombre music replaced the usual programmes. Edith and Sarah listened as the voice of the announcer repeated the words that everyone had feared to hear. His Majesty the King had passed away at eleven-fifty-five p.m. on Monday, January 20th, 1936.

As the news had spread through London during the early hours of the morning parties ceased, music faded out, night spots, theatres and cinemas closed their doors and large crowds gathered, standing in silent sympathy outside the gates of Buckingham Palace. By the time the western world rose to greet that Tuesday morning flags flew at half-mast in every city, town and village to mourn the passing of a loved and respected monarch. By lunch time they had heard that the Prince of Wales, now King Edward VIII, had flown with the Duke of York, from Sandringham to London for the Proclamation of the Accession at St. James's Palace at 4.00p.m. It was the first time that a reigning monarch had used this form of transport. Sarah tried to imagine how he must have felt when, stepping onto the tarmac at Hendon Aerodrome, he was greeted with a deep bow and addressed as Your Majesty. Later she spoke to Alice on the telephone and found her mother close to tears as they talked of the King's death.

'When can we expect you home?' Alice asked her.

'Tomorrow. I shall be home tomorrow, mummy. Would you tell Andrew not to risk driving? I know the snow is still thick in places. I'll catch the morning train.' She thanked her guardian angel that the weather had not cleared. It meant that she had a perfect excuse to go home by train, thus postponing the next encounter with Andrew. She had not decided what to say to him yet.

'Thank you so much, dear, for your help and support,' Edith said as Sarah took her leave. 'This visit has meant more to me than I can say.'

'I was glad to come, Gran. I needed a break. I've really enjoyed being here. Now you take care of yourself and I'll come over again before I go back to work.'

'Mind the doors!' called the guard. Edith took out of her handbag a small package and pressed it into Sarah's hand.

'I want you to have this. It will remind you of our few days together and it's a keepsake of your grandpa. Goodbye, dear. Safe journey.'

'Goodbye, Gran. Take care of yourself.' Sarah waved from the carriage and then settled back into her seat and opened the packet that Edith had given her. It was a small, leather-bound case and inside, on its bed of blue velvet, lay the miniature of Marguerite Grange. The large, blue eyes that looked straight out from the portrait immediately put her in mind of the child she had befriended on the night of the railway accident. Daisy Francis, who danced and whose dark curls framed her face in just the same way. It was an uncanny likeness, even though it must have been painted nearly a hundred years ago. Sarah smiled as she looked at the painting. A strange coincidence, she felt, probably caused by her own thoughts which returned so often to wondering where the child had gone that night. It was typical of Grandma Grange to think of such a kind gesture. She would treasure it always. Sarah placed it carefully away in her bag.

Chapter 19

Having hoped to avoid seeing Andrew by travelling home by train, Sarah was alarmed when he rushed down the platform to meet her. She had pushed out of her mind all thoughts of him, so busy was she with plans for the following weekend, plans that were to do with finding her son, plans that she could not, would not share with him. She composed her face into a pleasant smile as he came and put his arms around her, glad that her own were both occupied in carrying, for the moment, her luggage. She returned his greeting with a kiss on the cheek as he took her case.

'I persuaded your father to let me come to the station in his place.' Sarah made suitably grateful noises.

At least they would not be short of a topic of conversation during the drive home, Sarah thought with some relief. The death of the king seemed to be on everyone's lips. As they passed civic buildings council workers could be seen already draping lamp-standards and railings with mourning black. This proud and prosperous city would not be found lacking when it came to expressing its loyalty and its support of the monarchy. During his twenty-six year reign this grandson of Queen Victoria had endeared himself to his people, none more so than those who lived and worked in the northern counties. His decision, in

1917, to change the family name from Saxe-Coburg-Gotha to Windsor in recognition of the strong anti-German feeling among the British was a symbolic gesture much appreciated by his people. He had been a king who took his role seriously and, with the elegantly beautiful Queen Mary at his side, had done much to regain for the royal family the popularity that had waned somewhat since Victoria's decline.

Sarah looked out at the remains of the snow, now dirtied by the traffic on the road, as they passed through the city and out to the leafy suburban lanes. She was glad to see that the weather seemed to be setting for a thaw. If this continued they would be able to drive to Scarborough without difficulty on Sunday. She dragged her thoughts back to the present as she heard Andrew's comments about the Proclamation of the Accession.

'Life will have to change pretty drastically for the Prince of Wales now that he's the King,' he was saying. 'He's quite the "Playboy", you know, popular with the ladies and fond of spending his time at the races or on holiday in the south of France.'

'I expect he'll be quite prepared to take up his duties. After all, he must always have known that he would become king at some point.' Sarah was trying hard to seem interested in Andrew's conversation. It was not easy. Her thoughts were elsewhere. She wondered what Sam had made of the letter she had sent him. She was anxious for Thursday to come so that she could telephone Sister Ruth. She wanted Sunday to come quickly, to be off to the convent with Maddie. None of this could be discussed with Andrew. Now he was regaling her with some gossip he had heard about the Prince of Wales, how he had been keeping company with an American woman, and a married woman at that. Apparently the foreign Press was full of such stories. It was rather worrying, some said, how this woman seemed to have captured the attention of the Prince.

'I've read nothing about her,' said Sarah, making a supreme effort to respond to Andrew's remarks with something approaching interest. 'Who is she, anyway?'

'Her name is Wallis Simpson. She and her husband are well in with the Prince's London set. According to my cousin Peter the American papers are making a great fuss about her, telling stories about her being forever in his company and his being besotted with her.'

'Oh, well, you can trust Americans to exaggerate! Considering their battles to cut free from the old country, they seem mightily interested in the royal family they once spurned. This can't be anything but salacious gossip or we would have heard about it here. The poor Prince, I expect he only needs to smile at a woman and he's accused of having an affair with her. Anyhow, if she's married, what's there to be concerned about? It's not as if the Prince was courting her, is it?'

'No, I suppose not. But cousin Peter says there's no end of talk about them.'

'How does your cousin know so much about it?' Sarah asked only to prolong the conversation, not because she really wanted to know. As far as she was concerned this topic was a far safer one than any that Andrew might introduce concerning their own relationship.

'Peter's been over there for a couple of years, didn't I tell you? He works on the *New York Times*. They seem to find out a lot more than our newspapers.'

'Well, as I said, I've never heard of this person. Wallis, did you say? Whatever kind of a name is that, I ask you?'

Andrew laughed.

'I'd agree with you there. I'm quite surprised he's still unmarried you know. Peter's latest cuttings from his paper point out that he's forty-two this year. You'd think he'd have found a princess by now. There can't be any shortage of eligible young ladies of noble blood floating around the fashionable resorts of Europe.'

'Well,' said Sarah, 'finding himself a suitable lady will be the last thing on his mind just now. He is our proclaimed king. He has to take over the reins of the monarchy, not to mention coping with all the ceremonial of a State funeral and learn to deal with the politicians in matters of running the country. I should think that's quite enough for the moment. There'll be time enough to find us a queen. Have you heard when the funeral's to be?'

'I think next Tuesday, but I'm not altogether sure. Well, here we are!' Sarah was relieved to see the familiar stones of the high garden wall of her home and to hear the crunch of the gravel as the car drew up the drive. No, Andrew would not stay for a cup of tea, he must return to the mill. Things were very busy there he said. Sarah felt a tinge of guilt at her pleasure on hearing this. Alice's voice, welcoming her home, could be heard approaching from the back of the house.

'I'll be off, then,' said Andrew as Alice thanked him for meeting the train. 'See you later, Sarah. Perhaps we can arrange dinner at the weekend?' Sarah managed to avoid answering his suggestion by reiterating her mother's thanks for his kindness in meeting her from the train. 'My pleasure, of course,' he smiled. 'Toodle-pip!'

Sister Ruth had been delighted to hear from Sarah and assured her of a warm welcome on Sunday and would she and her friend care to take lunch at St. Faith's? Maddie's little car chugged cheerfully along the old turnpike road from York to the coast and the girls caught up on each other's news. There was never any awkwardness between them no matter how many weeks, months or years passed between their meetings. A friendship forged in childhood is one of the most lasting, one that can survive separation, differences of opinion, taste and social standing. Theirs was one of these, the pair of them having met at the age of four in the Infants Class of the local Primary School. From that day they had shared the trials and tribulations, the joys and wonders of growing up until they were obliged to follow different paths at fifteen. Maddie valued Sarah's friendship more than any other and the trust that existed between them was total.

'Did you bring a notebook with you?' asked Maddie as they drove into the seaside town of Scarborough.

'A notebook?' Sarah looked blank.

'Well, something to write on at any rate. There may be all sorts of information that Sister Ruth can give you. Who knows? I know if I relied on my memory I'd be sure to forget something! Like a sieve, it is, sometimes, especially when I'm feeling a bit anxious.' She stressed the last few words and Sarah realised she was, indeed, very apprehensive about the coming interview, and that the closer they got to the Convent the more jittery she became. Writing things down would be vital. Why hadn't she thought of this herself?

'Worry not! I have the very thing in the glove box. It's a bit tatty now, but I use it to jot down steps and moves when I'm starting on a new show.'

'Thanks, Maddie. What would I do without you!'

The rose bushes that filled the beds alongside the driveway had been pruned well before the frosts. The gardens were tidy and bare in their winter hibernation and Sarah was glad of it. There would be no heavy scent of the roses to waken her memory, as nothing else did, of those weeks of exile. As the car drew up to the door the small, bustling figure of Sister Ruth could be seen coming down the steps to meet them. Sarah had warned her about her plastered leg, so that she should not be alarmed as she emerged from the car.

'My dear, how lovely to see you again. You look so well and so grown up and elegant. And this is Maddie. I'm so pleased to meet you. Sarah used to talk about you all the time. Come in, do, out of the cold.' Over a hearty, though plain lunch, served to them by the nuns, the talk was mostly of the goings-on in London, of the preparations for the funeral of the King.

'I read that he's to be laid to rest at Windsor,' said Sarah. 'I went, once, to St. George's Chapel. It's very old and quite beautiful. I expect we shall see all the pomp and ceremony on the newsreels.'

'And now, tell me what this visit is all about,' said Sister Ruth when they were sitting beside a cosy fire in her room after lunch. Maddie had insisted on going off to take some photographs of the castle and what she called 'the winter face of the seaside'. She loved photography and had taken it up as a serious hobby. Maddie's pictures were far removed from the average family snapshots and her room at home was lined with her work. Secretly she had even wondered whether she might make her living from it. Sarah's uncle Arthur was a professional photographer. Maddie might ask Sarah to introduce her. But that could wait. Sarah had far more pressing matters on her mind, Maddie thought as she trudged along the Marine Parade that wintry afternoon.

Sister Ruth did not interrupt, listening intently to Sarah's account of the death of her grandfather and of his instruction to Sarah to see that his legacy was duly delivered for the benefit of her child.

'When I left here all those years ago I didn't dream that I would ever come back, nor that I would ever need to trace my son. I'm gradually getting used to the idea, beginning to feel less afraid, starting to think out where I should go to ask about him. But, naturally, you were my first contact. Oh, Sister Ruth, I hope you'll be able to help.' The nun sat with her hands folded in her lap and said nothing for several seconds, a puzzled look on her face. Sarah was alarmed, and it showed in the sudden high pitch of her voice as she said, 'I really don't know what I shall do if you are prevented, by some promise you made, perhaps, from giving me some details of the adoption.'

'Oh, no! Under the circumstances I'm sure I can help. I'll need to look up some of our records, of course and I shall do that presently. I hesitated because I suddenly begin to doubt my memory. Certainly one of us is mistaken. Something is not quite as it should be, I feel. Would you excuse me for a moment, my dear?' She went to her desk and picked up the telephone, while Sarah's heart felt to be turning somersaults, her palms became cold and clammy and her eyes never left Sister Ruth who then went to a filing cabinet and took out a folder. Every nerve in her body suddenly tensed. What was all this about? The only answer her confused brain could come up with was that the baby had died. That must be it. He had died after she had left the Convent. Oh, God above, what would she do now? She watched as the nun dialled a single number to connect with the office.

'Marjorie? Would you be so kind as to find Sister Josephine and ask her if she could spare me a moment? I am in my room with our visitor. Thank you.' Sister Ruth seemed a little absent-minded as they waited for the younger woman to arrive, glancing first at her guest and then at the door. She hurried to let her in as she heard her approach, too pre-occupied to notice that Sarah's face had turned ashen and that she was perched on the edge of her chair, the knuckles showing white on her clasped hands.

'Please sit down, Sister Josephine. You may be able to help us.'

'I'll try, and that's for sure.' Twenty years in Yorkshire had not diluted the Irish brogue or the twinkling smile. Vaguely, Sarah wondered why she was smiling.

'You must remember when Sarah's child was born. You were the one who took away the baby as soon as it was born. Yes?'

'Yes, Sister. Sarah, you remember, you insisted I should do that because you feared to hold the child yourself.' Suddenly she looked quite terrified. 'I didn't do wrong, did I?' Her face had lost its colour and her eyes stood wide open. Sarah waited, unable to move.

'No! No! You were gentle and kind. You did nothing wrong,' said Sister Ruth. 'But I am rather puzzled. Sarah has been led to believe, by whom I am not aware, that her child was a boy. I called you, as the one who had charge of the baby, to confirm the fact, if you can, for I wonder if my old memory is playing me tricks.'

'Oh! You had me in a fright, to be sure.' Sister Josephine glanced at Sarah and then flew to her side when she noticed how pale she was, how glazed her eyes. Indeed she wondered if Sarah was about to faint.

'Why, whatever is the matter, Sarah? Are you ill?'

Both the nuns were now beside her, looking concerned. She made a supreme effort, speaking very softly, 'No, not ill, but I think I have guessed what you have to tell me.' She looked from one kind face to the other. 'It's alright. It was all a long time ago. You're going to tell me my baby died, aren't you?'

'Oh, my dear girl, of course not! Whatever gave you that idea? No, indeed! I only sent for Sister Josephine because I was uncertain of my memory. You see, Sarah, I was pretty sure that it wasn't a boy.' Sarah looked from one to the other, relief gradually flowing through her body.

'Sister Ruth's quite right,' the younger nun smiled, 'you had a little girl, Sarah. I remember that week so clearly because we had two babies within the week. T'was a boy for that poor slip of a girl from York.' Sarah was hardly listening now. A girl! So, where had she got the idea that it had been a boy? A baby girl! And now she would be six. Her mind had taken flight, but now she must return to the present and the reason for her visit...

'You see,' she told Sister Josephine, 'I have to find my child, not to interfere in her life, you understand, but I do need to know where she is. Sister Ruth knows the full story. What else can you tell me about her?' It seemed strange speaking of her, a daughter and not a son.

'I was in charge of her until her adoption. I remember Doctor Bennett coming to check her over. I made up her bottles, fed her, changed her nappies and took her out for walks in the garden in that big, old pram. She was such a good baby, only cried when she was hungry. I...' she faltered and fished hurriedly into her sleeve for a handkerchief. 'I became very fond of her. It was a wrench to let her go after those two weeks. I shall never forget those blue eyes, so trusting. She had very little hair to start with, but you could see that it was going to be dark. Her eyebrows and lashes were almost black. She had a pretty little face.' She stood up to go. 'I must get back to my duties if I may, Sister.'

'Of course. I'll call if I need you again.' Sarah thanked her as she left, this kind woman who had loved and mothered her baby when she had rejected her.

'I can guess what you're feeling, Sarah,' said Sister Ruth, 'but remember, you did what was right for yourself and the child.' Sarah pushed aside the doubts, her practical nature coming to the rescue as usual. She took out the notebook, made a note of Sister Josephine's comments and waited.

'Your baby was adopted by a childless couple, Sarah. They were put forward by Dr. Constance Bennett. She was their family doctor and she had a keen interest in trying to match up unwanted children with couples who could not bear their own. She had worked closely with the Convent for several years since she had heard about our work with unmarried mothers. Their names were Frederick and Margaret Miller.' She was referring to a sheaf of papers held in a folder. Sarah's heart leaped as she heard the first really concrete information, the first proper clue to lead her in the search. 'The two of them owned a boarding house in the town, taking in visitors during the season and I seem to remember that he had another job, too. They were good, hard-working folk. They took the baby with great joy, I remember, and asked me to tell her mother that they would give her the best life they could. But, by that time you had gone and it was not our policy to contact our girls after they'd left.'

'What about her Birth Certificate? Do you remember what happened to that?'

'Oh, yes. We passed it to the Millers along with the Adoption Agreement. This was a document signed by the doctor, the Millers and me. It confirmed their promise to bring up the child as their own and give her their family name. I felt it best to have something in writing, though some agencies didn't bother.'

'Did I have to sign anything? I've no recollection of doing so.'

'Look, Sarah. Here it is, your side of the contract, as it were.' She showed her a short written statement made on the day she arrived at the Convent. 'I, Sarah Grange, agree to put myself under the protection of the Convent of St. Faith's, Scarborough, until the birth of my expected child, remaining here until it is delivered and working at such tasks as are deemed suitable by the Sisters. I agree to give up the child at birth to the care of the Convent for its subsequent adoption by persons approved by the Convent Council. I am here of my own free will and with the approval of my parents. I agree to abide by the rules of the Convent House.' The paper was dated June 20th, 1929. Sarah read it through, seeing at the foot of the page her own signature and those of her parents and Sister Ruth.

'I truly don't recall anything of this,' she said. 'I must have been so frightened.'

'You were, my dear. But you soon learned to trust us, didn't you,' smiled Sister Ruth. Sarah was scribbling furiously in Maddie's notebook.

'Can you remember what her Birth Certificate said?'

'It gave the mother's name, Sarah Grange, father's name unknown, place and time of birth and the name and sex of the child. We gave her the name "Frances" after Saint Francis who presides over our side-chapel where we give all our babies a Christening before they leave us. Of course, Mr. and Mrs. Miller were free to name her as they wished.'

'Well, it should all be plain sailing from here. All we need to do is find the Millers at their boarding house. I hope they're still there. Do you recall where it was, Sister?'

'No, dear. We made it a rule that all contact with our tiny visitors should cease when we handed them over to their new parents. I'm sorry, but you must understand that this was best for all concerned.' Sarah nodded her understanding.

'There will surely be a list of boarding houses and private hotels available?'

'I'm sure there is. Now, have I given all the information you need, dear?'

'You've been more than kind. Thank you for sparing me your time. Maddie will be here any minute now to collect me.'

It was after three when they finally said goodbye to the nuns. Sarah's mind was in a whirl, anxious to set off immediately to find the Millers' guest house. Maddie, ever practical, suggested starting with the telephone book. They found a public call-box. The directory gave them several Millers, only one had the right initial and when they rang it turned out to be a retired gentleman who had never heard of Margaret and Frederick Miller. Time was running out. It was already pretty dark and they would have to drive back in total darkness now. Maddie was anxious. She hated driving in the dark, yet she wanted to help Sarah as much as she could. She had heard from Sarah all that she had learned at the Convent.

'They wouldn't have a guest-house without a telephone,' reasoned Maddie. 'Perhaps they've moved away from Scarborough.' With all the shops and offices closed they were at a loss what to try next. 'What about the doctor? What was her name?' They consulted Sarah's notes. 'Dr. Constance Bennett.'

'Look here,' said Maddie, 'by the time we've tracked her down it'll be too late to ask for an interview today. She may take a lot of persuading to talk to you anyway. You know how seriously these doctors take their oath of confidentiality. How about checking in to an hotel for the night and trying her in the morning. Once she's heard the full story, it might be different.' Sarah's face looked drawn and tired in the half-light of the gas lamp as they stood outside the telephone kiosk. 'You look all in, honey, and it's no problem to me to stay until tomorrow, as long as I get home in time for the show. What do you say?'

'I say "Yes"! A brilliant idea! Drive me to the Cliffs Hotel. We'll call home from there to tell them we're staying.' Dinner at the Cliffs was a welcome island of peace and orderliness in what had been an exacting day. They would telephone Dr. Bennett in the morning and hope that she would find time to see them.

As they lay in the comfortable twin beds with the sound of the waves and the occasional hoot of a distant fog-horn to remind them they were not at home the girls took stock of the day.

'It's quite a lot to take in, 'commented Sarah. 'The biggest surprise was to learn I had a girl. I wonder what she's like now. I wonder where she goes to school. I wonder what they called her.'

Maddie voiced a word of warning. 'Be careful, Sarah. Don't go imagining she's yours. Don't forget for a moment that you gave up all interest in her. However hard that was, or is, remember she's somebody else's daughter.'

'You're right, of course, Maddie. It's just very new to me, this realisation that she's a person, but I assure you I won't get involved. Little Miss Miller! My, have I got a surprise for your family!'

Chapter 20

1933–1934

Christmas 1933 saw Doris and Joe in better circumstances than for some years past. With all their debts paid off Doris allowed a few small extravagances during the festive period but aside from these, she kept a strict hold on the purse-strings. Even with money in the bank she would not hear of moving house or buying new clothes. No, she knew they would need money for pursuing the idea of adopting the Grange child, money for travel, mostly, but also for paying for information, (this she was quite prepared to do without qualm), money, perhaps, even for the adoption itself, who could tell? A little prudence now would see them well rewarded in the end. Since the idea had first taken root in Doris' head it had not once occurred to her that carrying it out might be difficult, that any obstacle might get in her way.

The excursions to Alwoodley with Trudi continued every so often where she would buy good clothes and other items cast off by the wealthy and give them a fresh look At the solicitor's offices Doris was careful to maintain an exemplary record as a trustworthy and competent employee, making herself quite indispensable to Mr. Dobbs. It would not do, now, to risk losing this valuable position and she made sure that Joe understood that he must guard his own job with the same care. She had one aim in life at present for her and Joe. They would become adoptive parents of the Grange child and be ready and waiting to claim the prize when the old man died. Failure in this was not an option. It was going to take some time, this was certain, for she had only Saturdays and Sundays free and Joe had only Sundays on alternate weekends.

'I just hope that the old man's as fit as he looks,' she said to Joe one day. 'As long as we find the boy before he turns up his toes, we'll be fine. Nothing will be done about the legacy until then.'

As soon as Christmas was past and 1934 welcomed in traditional style Doris got down to work in earnest. She had found the public library a rich source of information on all kinds of subjects and so she went there first to find out, if she could, where was this Convent called St. Faith's. She sincerely hoped it would not be on the south coast or in the north of Scotland. Visiting somewhere as distant as that would be out of the question. It might even be across the Channel, heaven forbid!

Joe was working that weekend and Doris took the tram into town alone. She had become quite friendly with the librarian over the past few months, a pale young man named Anthony who immediately showed her to the section she needed. It was easy from then on to find a book which listed Religious Houses of the Roman Catholic Church and described their type and function. There it was. North Bay, Scarborough. A community of nuns devoted to teaching and working among the local people. No 'closed order' this, she was glad to read, but probably quite approachable. Doris wrote down all the details, including the telephone number, and moved on to look at the section labelled 'Local Studies'.

She felt she needed to find out as much as she could about the Grange family, though at present she was not sure how useful such knowledge might be. She went to ask Anthony to show her where the past editions of the newspapers were kept. Here she would surely find references to such a high-profile family. Today the library was holding an exhibition celebrating the manufacturing of wool in the area, and the people who had helped to make it flourish. Doris went to take a look at the displays as photographs of some of the larger mills caught her eye.

Each mill had its own section with artefacts, ledgers, bills, receipts, order books and pattern books that told of the progress of the wool from the backs of the sheep to the bale of washed wool; from the bale to the spinner; from the yarn to the loom and to the fine worsted cloth made in this part of Yorkshire. Grange's mill was there, of course, being one of the oldest and now one of the largest. One photo showed George, with Edith at his side, accepting a cut-glass rose-bowl on the occasion of his retirement in 1925. His four children and their spouses, along with the grandchildren were all there and Doris found Sarah Grange, aged eleven, among them. What a huge family, she thought, as she peered at the captions to decipher their names. The two whom she had seen and heard talking to Mr. Ross had changed very little in eight years. She moved on to another picture, this time a greatly enlarged one showing the Golden Jubilee celebrations four years ago. In spite of his having retired by then, George and his wife took centre stage in this one, too. She compared the two photographs. They showed the same group of people on these two very special occasions, the grandchildren, still very young most of them, obviously on their best behaviour and standing to attention. There was no sign of Sarah on the second picture and Doris, after a moment's thought, realised she would have been in Switzerland by then. No need to bother with the newspapers, she told Anthony, she had learned a great deal from the exhibition, thank you, and time was racing on. She treated him to one of her beaming smiles before running down the steps of the grand building.

Winter gradually gave way to early spring. Doris had spent many hours during the past weeks making plans that she might carry out as soon as the weather was better and the evenings longer and lighter. She made further visits to the library, looking up more details about unmarried mothers, their fate, the fate of their children and the religious and other agencies that made it their business to try to help these unfortunates. She found there was little help from the State, although some Local Government Authorities were making efforts to provide more and better orphanages and seeing that the children had access to the schooling to which they were entitled. This gathering of information set Doris thinking.

She was a great planner. At first she would try to discuss her ideas with Joe but he became impatient and tended to lose interest as first one scheme and then another were suggested and rejected.

'Look, leave me out of it until you've decided how to tackle it. I'm fed up of your hair-brained ideas that never seem to amount to anything. Let me know when you've settled on something and I'll go along with it.' Privately he doubted whether any of her notions for tracking down and adopting this child would stand a cat in hell's chance of succeeding. Thinking them out, testing them for flaws, researching the whole idea was keeping her occupied and he was happy to let her get on with it. It certainly kept her happy and out of his way. He was somewhat less agreeable about the whole thing however when, at last, she came up with her master plan.

'If you think you're getting me into an outfit like that, you've got another think coming. I never heard of such a wild idea in my life. Bloody stupid, if you ask me!'

'You might remember, Joe, that you told me not to ask you. You said...'

'I know what I said. And now I'm saying this ... you're crazy! How you expect to get away with it I can't imagine. What sort of a fool do you think I am?'

'Joe, if you would just listen ... there are things you need to know before you can do this ... obviously ... Joe...' He was striding up and down in front of the range, not really listening, muttering under his breath, something to the effect that she could take up play-acting if she liked, she'd probably be very good at it, but she could count him out and that the best place for him just now was the Bell and Bottle. Acting upon his own suggestion Joe grabbed his raincoat and hat from the hook behind the door.

'And that's just where I'm off to, for I'll not stay to hear such ridiculous nonsense.'

'But, Joe, don't you see? This is the only way we'll be able to get them to tell us anything at all.' She caught at his arm as he made for the door. 'Please, Joe, don't be so pig-headed. Give me a chance to explain it properly ... Joe...' The walls seemed to shudder as the outer door slammed. Doris flew to open it again and chased her irate husband down the drive, planting herself firmly between him and the gate.

'Alright! Alright, have it you own way. If you don't want to co-operate I can't force you. But Joe, promise me you won't blather what I told you all over the pub.' She grabbed his shoulders and held on. 'If you go talking about it, my plan'll be ruined altogether. Look at me! Keep it under your hat, so nobody knows, and I might be able to pull it off by myself. It's not impossible, but it would have been so much better with two of us.' She was frozen, out there in her indoor clothes and a pair of slippers but she would not let go of him until he had promised. Joe marched off as Doris made her way back into the flat, a rather curious expression on her face, quizzical and yet a smile was definitely there. She was pretty sure that, by the time he came home, she would have won the round. He was so predictable, was Joe.

The roses in the terraced gardens of St. Faith's

were in full bloom, their heavy scent filling the air, by the time Sister Ruth stood on the steps to welcome Pastor John Bateman and his wife from the Gospel Mission, West Leeds. It was late July and Scarborough was full of summer visitors enjoying the golden sands and making a kaleidoscope of bright colour on the promenade. Children with their buckets and spades skipped along in front of their parents, mum carrying huge bags of towels and swimsuits, sandwiches and pop, dad toting folding chairs and rugs to spread on the beach, all hoping fervently that this warm sunshine would last all afternoon. Families. This was exactly the subject on the minds of the two soberly dressed callers who now climbed the steps and shook hands with Sister Ruth. A young couple, in their early thirties, Pastor John carried his black, belted mackintosh over his arm, for it had turned much warmer since he began his journey this morning. He carried a briefcase and, in response to the glorious weather, he sported a straw boater which was quickly removed from his head as he entered the Convent door. His wife, Jane, wore a plain navy suit. It was well cut with a calf-length straight skirt and her blouse was startlingly white against the dark jacket. On her head she had a small, bonnet-type hat trimmed with navy satin ribbons, rather reminiscent of those worn by the Salvation Army ladies, though it did not tie under the chin as theirs do. Most of her fair hair was tucked away neatly in a bun at the nape of her neck and her sensible shoes and black stockings made her appearance quite severe. That was, of course, before she spoke and smiled. Her voice, when she responded to Sister Ruth's enquiry as to whether she would take a cup of tea, was gentle and smooth and surprisingly cultured.

'What could be better on a hot day. You are most kind,' she said, her face lighting up in a broad smile. 'Thank you, Sister Ruth.'

'I should introduce my wife properly,' said Pastor John Bateman, suddenly. 'This is Jane. She has recently been appointed a Deaconess at the Mission. It's wonderful as we work together as a team. She is now "Sister Jane", though not in quite the same way as you Sisters here.' Looking uncomfortable, he stopped.

'We are all brothers and sisters in the eyes of the Lord,' said Sister Ruth. 'And we are all here to do a very important job, don't you agree? The job of caring for the children of this world. Titles are of little importance as long as the work is done. Sadly there is still great need for such work.' The Deaconess nodded her agreement, taking up the briefcase that pastor Bateman had been carrying and beaming at the nun.

'I must tell you how pleased we are that you agreed to help us today. May I show you some of the work that we have achieved already and the type of information that we are gathering?'

'By all means,' said Sister Ruth. The Deaconess took out a folder containing papers and a ledger which she opened on the desk between them.

'You see, Sister, the Mission, as I told you in the letter, is anxious to discover how many young women may be in need of our help. We have set up a hostel in Leeds where we can care for them, but the very fact of motherhood out of wedlock is seen as such a disgrace that concealment of their sometimes dire circumstances seems their only option. We have all the means by which we can offer them help and support, but these women are too ashamed to come forward and ask for it. If we can help the mothers then these poor infants can be helped. The Mission is most concerned about their welfare, the babies who through no fault of their own have to carry the stigma of being illegitimate.'

'And you are saying that your Mission needs to know where these children might be?'

'Exactly. But we have to be very discreet. For instance,' Jane showed the first section of her book, 'the places we visit are shown here only as numbers. If these papers fell into the wrong hands they would mean nothing to anyone else. See, the findings from number one, here on the first page, will give you an idea.' Sister Ruth put on her reading glasses. She saw lists under headings detailing women who had borne children under the protection of a particular establishment, the birth date, the sex of the baby and so on.

'Many of these babies are adopted, but not all. A surprising number are brought up by the mothers of the girls and treated as the younger sisters of their own mothers. This can be difficult for them to adjust to when they find out in later life. We try to follow their progress, especially if they are sent to the orphanages, and step in to provide practical help, clothes and suchlike if needed. We check discreetly on those who were adopted, too, in case there are problems. Sometimes we can help these families to adopt a further child if the first has proved a success.'

Sister Ruth studied with interest the pages in front of her. She was impressed by the sincerity of the woman whose work she was seeing. Her initial doubts about talking to these people were put aside.

'I admire the work you are doing with the Mission, Sister Jane. I see no reason why we should not allow our girls to be added to your records, especially for the sake of the ones who take their babies home and try to raise them alone. They might be glad of assistance from the Mission.'

'We are so pleased to hear you say that, isn't that so, John?' She addressed her husband who had been silent throughout. He nodded and cleared his throat, ready to put in a comment. His wife cut in with one of her own, 'You will notice we have logged all the births during the last five years. Of course, these are only from agencies who have agreed to co-operate with us, but it is a start. Eventually we hope our work will become better known.'

Over the next hour or so three new pages were created in Pastor Bateman's ledger covering the last five years of the Sisters' work in caring for girls in trouble. Sister Josephine was set the task of copying the relevant information into Pastor Bateman's ledger while the visitors enjoyed a second cup of tea and a scone. Mothers were listed under their Christian name only, the date of birth and sex of the child followed. A third entry told whether the children went home with their mother, went into an orphanage or were adopted.

'I can only tell you where they went immediately after leaving us,' said Sister Ruth. 'We cease contact with them when they go.'

'Well, it is a great comfort to know that so much is being done to help these mothers and babies when society shuts them out. You have been so very kind, Sister Ruth. We shall write and inform you of any work we are able to do for those you have cared for.'

'Would you be kind enough to check this, Sister?'

'Of course,' answered Sister Ruth and she sat down beside her colleague and they were all silent until the entries were carefully compared with the original lists.

'Thank you, Sister. This is a correct copy.' Turning to her guests she said, 'I hope you find this useful, Sister Jane, and may God bless you in your work.'

Pastor John and Sister Jane Bateman took their leave of the Convent of St. Faith's at two-fifteen with Sister Ruth's kindly smiling face watching them as they walked down the long drive and out through the iron gates. She wished them well. Into the town they walked with a spring in their step, smiling at the holiday-makers until they came to a department store busy with Saturday customers. The cubicles where purchases could be tried for size proved the perfect place for the transformation and Doris and Joe emerged triumphant from their afternoon's escapade. Making for a busy quayside café they mingled with the crowd, their dark clothing safely packed in the briefcase and a shopping bag. Doris was elated. With her blond hair freed from its bun and tied with a flowered ribbon to match her cotton dress she was the complete opposite of Sister Jane Bateman. Her toes wriggled in her fawn sandals and she hung onto the arm of the man in the open-necked shirt with a straw boater perched at a jaunty angle on his head. He looked ten years younger without the moustache and the pair of them could have been taken for a honeymoon couple, so excited were they.

'Let's buy an ice-cream and go and sit on the beach,' said Doris. She could not wait any longer to talk to Joe about things and the cafés were all too crowded.

With the ledger resting on a rock they checked their findings, well away from prying eyes. Doris found it hard to believe that it had all been so easy, that the nun had been so trusting. Flicking past the unnecessary facts they found the details of Sarah's confinement.

'Look, Joe, look! Sarah ... January 3rd 1930 ... 7lbs 8oz ... a healthy female child!'

'What? I thought the Grange child was a boy, that's what you said.'

'I know I did, because the old man thought it was. But it's quite clear here ... "a healthy female child", named Frances by the nuns, and who should know better than those who attended the birth? In the last section it says that Sarah left soon after the birth, that's right, we know that, and the baby was put up for adoption.'

'That doesn't mean that she was adopted. Just that they hoped she would be. What else does it say?' His voice began to reveal his disappointment. They could hardly adopt her if she already had a family.

'Yes, Joe, she was adopted. But, hey, we are on the point of finding the Grange child! That's what's important! I said we'd change our plan if we have to. Don't look so glum, Joe.' She was still searching the document, eagerly.

'Here we are. Adopted by Frederick and Margaret Miller of Scarborough. Left the Convent January 23rd 1930 after being given a clean bill of health by Dr. Constance Bennett who was instrumental in arranging the adoption.' She scanned the other entries relating to St. Faith's, the only ones amongst the dozens of bogus names and details that Doris, herself, had made. She was still glowing with pride at the success of this afternoon's work and Joe, who said he was thoroughly glad they were out of there without being rumbled, had to admit that it had gone very well.

'By the looks of it this Dr. Bennett seems to have been involved with a number of the adoptions,' Doris remarked, checking down the list. Another idea was beginning to take shape in her head but she would say nothing about that just now. Joe would be hungry. It would be no use trying to interest him in a new venture, especially one that would be even more risky than the last, before he had a square meal inside him. There was a fish restaurant on the pier. From its windows you could watch the pleasure boats and fishing craft moving about in the harbour as you enjoyed delicious food. What was more, they served meals all day, regardless of the hour. With everything packed carefully away they made for the 'Flying Fish' and were soon enjoying their favourite haddock in batter with chips and a portion of mushy peas.

It did not take her too long to persuade him. Her strongest argument was that they had in their possession perfectly genuine documents from the Convent to prove to Dr. Bennett that they were bona fide persons and, if she was in any doubt she could telephone Sister Ruth.

With their religious garb once more in place and walking sedately these two were soon furnished with the address of the doctor whom they sought to consult, 'not for any medical reason, you understand, no, indeed, but in order to help the under-privileged.' It was amazing how easily people were fooled, thought Doris. And Dr. Constance Bennett was no exception.

When they presented themselves at the door of her large, imposing, Victorian house their ring on the doorbell was answered by a maid.

'Please come into the waiting room,' she said. 'Dr. Bennett is out visiting a patient, but she will be back fairly soon, I think. Is she expecting you?'

'No, but we have travelled quite a distance. I believe she will spare us a few minutes,' said Doris with more confidence than she really felt. Part of the house was given over to the doctor's consulting room and a waiting room for the patients and Doris and Joe spent the next fifteen minutes anxiously looking out of the window for sign of a car or examining the scenes of Scarborough that adorned the walls. They were startled when the door burst open and a portly woman dressed in tweeds marched into the room, her hand outstretched, her voice booming, 'So sorry to keep you waiting. Urgent call, I'm afraid. Can't be helped. How can I help you, Reverend?' Joe looked round to see whom she addressed. Doris was alert and ready to cover his confusion.

'This is Pastor John Bateman, Doctor. I am Sister Jane, his wife. We wondered whether you would be willing to help us in a matter concerning our unmarried mothers and their children.' It seemed as if she had managed to hit exactly the right note with this bustling, tweedy woman, for they were immediately ushered into the doctor's living room, pressed to take refreshment and commanded to explain their mission. There was no beating about the bush with this woman. Her time was precious. She did not waste it in formalities. She was forthright, decisive, plain spoken, and by her own admission had made some enemies in her fight to get a better deal for illegitimate babies. She managed to convey all of this to Doris and Joe in a few short, sharp sentences. Joe was terrified of her. Doris swallowed hard, straightened her bonnet and took a deep breath as she replaced the cup on its saucer with a hand that trembled slightly. The doctor's voice was still booming on,

'It's ignorance, that's all it is. These girls don't get themselves into trouble on purpose. The disgrace is never laid at the father's door, is it? Is it, I say? No, off they go when they've had their fun. If you weren't a man of the cloth I'd tell you what I'd like to do with them.' The greying hair was coming loose from its pins with the vehemence with which its owner was shaking it. She stopped to take a breath and to smile at Doris. She had quickly picked up who was the leader of this deputation and addressed her remarks to Sister Jane who was now speaking again.

'May I show you some of our work in finding women and babies who need our help?' Taking her cue from the doctor the Deaconess spoke quickly, taking out her ledger, flicking through the pages of bogus entries and showing those of St.Faith's.

'Splendid! Splendid! The Sisters do sterling work against all the odds. Splendid!'

'And you find people to adopt the babies?' enquired the Deaconess.

'Adoption is the best answer for most of the cases. You would be surprised how many couples come to my surgery saying they seem unable to have a family. I have made it my business to match 'em up with unwanted babies. Usually turns out for the best.' She let her eye trace the list from St. Faith's, noting with some evident pleasure her own name occurring there.

'And do you keep in touch with them, doctor?'

'Many of them, yes'

'So you would be in a position to let us know if hardship had befallen any of the children?'

'Very likely, unless they had moved from the area.' Doris was trying hard to lead the conversation to the Millers in an effort to discover where they lived. Failing to find a subtler introduction she pointed to their names, 'This family, for instance,' she said, trying make it sound like a random choice, 'are they still living in Scarborough?' Joe looked over her shoulder, making an effort to be included.

'Ah, the Millers, yes. They had a boarding house, Margaret and Fred.' A distant look came into the doctor's eyes and her voice lost its boom. 'Such lovely people. Such a shame. They had been so happy together, the three of them. So sudden and so sad.' The bombastic medical woman was melting into a large blue handkerchief. Doris, not forgetting her character part, put her arm around her and offered the comfort of the Lord while her mind raced ahead of the doctor. This must be serious. Did their search end right here? Right now?

'Do forgive me,' sniffed Dr. Bennett, blowing her nose with a trumpeting sound and pulling herself together hurriedly. 'It had been a most successful adoption. They were so happy, the three of them. They named the baby Margaret after her mother but Fred said they'd get confused so they gave her Daisy for short. Then they won some sort of competition run by the Hotels and Boarding Houses Association. The prize was a weekend trip to Paris by aeroplane. They were so excited. They left Daisy with Margaret's mother. Sadly, they never came back.'

'What?'

'Their aeroplane ditched over the Channel,' said Dr. Bennett. 'Eight people were lost. It was all in the newspapers the next day. Such a tragedy.'

'And what happened to the little girl?' Relief was slowly creeping into Doris' veins. 'Did she stay with her grandmother?'

'Not for long. She, poor soul, went out of her mind with grief and couldn't continue to care for "little Margaret". She was taken into a mental hospital and the child into an orphanage. So, you see, they are not all happy endings.'

'Oh, what a terribly sad story,' said the Deaconess. 'Poor little girl. Is she still living in Scarborough?'

'I really couldn't tell you, I'm afraid. I only know that I haven't been called to attend to her since the parents were lost.'

'You have been tremendously helpful, Doctor Bennett. We will not take up any more of your time today. Thank you so much.' They shook hands and left with what the doctor felt was unusual haste. Strange people, she thought, but with their heart in the right place. If there had been more time she would have recommended they visit at least two of the others with their offers of baby clothes and food. Odd that they left so suddenly, but, there again, they probably had a train to catch this evening.

Chapter 21

Walking sedately, Pastor John and Sister Jane Bateman left the doctor's house. Doris' head was awhirl with the new parcels of information that she had just received. With her arm linked through Joe's they waited at the bus stop for a ride into town, speaking in low voices even though they were the only people there. Most of the passengers at this time of day were travelling out of the centre, not towards it. The stores would be closed so they would have to find somewhere else to change their costume before going to the guesthouse where Doris had reserved a room and breakfast.

'Let's go down onto the front, Joe. If all else fails we can squeeze in between the beach huts. It'll only take a couple of seconds.' Holiday-makers were everywhere, still making the best of the sunshine of the late afternoon, reluctant to go home while it was still so warm, but gathering up chairs, children, left-over sandwiches. A young man with a camera was prowling up and down among the crowd, offering to snap the 'happy couple' or the 'lovely family'.

'Pictures ready for collection ten o'clock in the morning. No obligation, sir! If you don't like it you needn't buy. What about it, madam? A keepsake of a happy holiday?' Snap! Went his camera, over and over, while he managed to persuade a respectable number of folk to part with a down payment and give him their names.

'Your money back if not completely satisfied!' called the cheery chappie, his striped blazer and straw boater making him easily seen along the promenade. 'Come along, miss! Let's have you and your handsome young man! What about you, madam, and your little girl? Your granddaughter, you say? No, I can't believe that! Just a moment, stay still. There, that's perfect. Thank you, sir!' The two darkly clad figures wove their way between the mass of people, listening to the constant patter of the photographer.

'He works hard for his money,' said Joe. 'I wonder if he makes much.'

'He can only do it for about three months, and then only on fine days. Hurry up, Joe. I want to get out of these things.' Only a short distance away there began a line of beach huts and within a couple of minutes the Batemans were once again folded up as part of the luggage. Joe and Doris Smithson, a couple on a day out to the seaside sauntered back past the photographer with broad smiles on their faces.

'Here's a happy couple. Hold it! Now, sir, would you care to call back in the morning for your souvenir of Scarborough? Only sixpence altogether, can I have your name, sir?'

'Oh, go on, Joe,' said Doris. She was feeling pleased as punch at everything that had happened today. Joe paid thre'pence deposit to please her, thinking that he'd get it back tomorrow, say he didn't like the photo.

Doris's mind was busy the whole time assimilating and evaluating the situation regarding the Grange child which seemed to alter by the day. They were walking along a street of less fashionable boarding houses and came to number thirty. This was where they were to spend the night. They so rarely ventured from the flat that this was a real treat. Even Joe was enjoying himself now that he was back into his ordinary clothes. Supper could be had at the boarding house if required and they took advantage of this. It would be far cheaper than a restaurant and they could retire to their room to plan the next day's agenda. They must be back in Leeds by Sunday evening and ready for work on Monday morning. The watery soup, skinny lamb chops and lumpy mashed potatoes reflected the cheap price of the establishment but, with a half-decent rice pudding to follow, it served to fill their stomachs.

Up in their dingy room Doris took out the

paperwork that they had collected during the day.

'Well, we know far more than we did this morning. What's our next move?' She was addressing her remarks more to herself than to Joe.

'Whatever it is I don't intend to prance about as a clergyman again.'

'Why ever not? You were very fetching in your black moustache. I could quite understand why Sister Jane fell for you. I must admit I quite enjoyed playing the religious, it certainly opened doors for us. Don't worry, I think those costumes have served their purpose, for the moment, at any rate,' she added, under her breath. 'Now, let's take stock, Joe. When we were told that the child was adopted I had to start re-planning ways of getting our hands on that £5,000. I've got to admit I was still casting about for ideas. But now we know the Millers are dead, well, what's to stop us returning to the first plan. There's still a chance we might be able to go for the adoption, Joe. But, at the back of my mind, there seems to be another idea taking shape. All a bit vague as yet. I'm tired. I'll sleep on it. Think about it again in the morning.'

'Just as long as you don't start prowling about in the small hours, waking me with your scatter-brained schemes. We've had a busy day and I'm buggered.'

'Such language, Pastor Bateman. Tut, tut! Goodnight, Joe. Thanks for playing up so well today. I swear I'll make an actor of you yet.'

'Oh, sure. Move over James Mason. Humph!'

Doris was awake far longer than Joe, whose present outdoor life with the horses that he loved ensured a tired body and a calm mind when he came home from work. His tall figure seemed to have grown straighter, his skin browned with sun and wind and his outlook on life was altogether different. Doris could not remember the last time he had been out on a drinking binge or had truly lost his temper. She blessed the day when Sir Edward Lazenby had taken him on. She knew for certain that a couple of years ago wild horses would not have persuaded him to dress up and go along with her fancy schemes. Lying awake next to him she had visions of how they would live after Daisy Miller and her 'dowry' became theirs.

Sunday was not the best of days to go searching for orphanages. For one thing her favourite source of information, the local library, would be closed. That was a pity. Perhaps it would be an idea to chat to the people who live here in the town. Perhaps she ought to go to church in the morning. Dressed as the Deaconess she might do well talking to the local congregation of worthies. Yes, that was what she would do. The dark suit would not look amiss for church attendance, she could add the bonnet just before she went in. Joe could go off by himself. First he could collect the photographs from the man in the kiosk and then he could wander along to the Spa and listen to the orchestra. She would join him there after church. She fell asleep well content with the plans for Sunday morning.

The boarding house breakfast was vastly different from the previous evening's fare. The man of the house both cooked and served it, saying that it was his wife's one morning off. There was porridge and fruit juice, followed by the most delicious plateful of bacon, eggs, sausage, fried bread, mushrooms with toast and marmalade to follow. It was all freshly prepared and Joe and Doris made the best of it. They would not have funds to buy much more food before catching their return train.

With their bags packed they left at nine thirty. Joe had no objection at all to Doris's plans and went off to walk by the sea until the photo kiosk opened. Doris made for St. Mary's Church and was soon mingling with the worshippers there. She could not remember when she had last been in a church, never mind to a service. With great care and by watching others she got through the service without faux-pas and emerged to stand in the graveyard outside where there was an outstanding view of the bay and of the ancient castle walls that straddle the opposite cliff top. She was so impressed that she almost forgot the reason for her being here. The vicar had shaken her hand as she came out of church. Now she was approached by a lady who smiled and said, 'Good morning, Sister. Welcome to St. Mary's. A lovely morning, is it not? Are you here on holiday by any chance?' It was just the friendly greeting she had been hoping for.

'Just trying to mix a little business with the pleasure of being in this delightful resort, as a matter of fact,' answered Doris. 'My name is Sister Jane Bateman ... from Leeds. I have been collecting information about the provision of orphanages in this part of the country. I don't suppose you would be able to help me?'

Doris covered the distance to reach the Spa in record time. Joe was waiting for her and she used the ladies' facilities to change into her cotton dress and put away Sister Jane. The orchestra was playing and quite a crowd was enjoying the music.

'There's no time to lose, Joe. Have you got our photographs? Why ever not? Come on. We can call again on the way.'

'On the way to where?' Doris was gathering up the luggage and urging Joe to hurry while people around them began to shush them for disturbing the peace. They called for the photographs which Doris said were very good and well worth sixpence, and made for a bus-stop.

'Now, where are we going?' Joe was bemused as they climbed aboard the bus that followed the cliff top.

'We're going to find Daisy Miller, I hope. There's an orphanage on the Filey Road. Here's the address. Look out for Bay View.'

Doris was far from calm as she rang the doorbell at Bay View House. A smart maid invited them to step inside and she would fetch Matron and would the lady and gentleman take a seat for a moment. They were met by a woman of enormous proportions all dressed in grey with white collar and cuffs, a serious expression on her face.

'Is there something I can help you with?' asked the grey lady. Doris explained that they had come over from York. A dear friend had asked them to call and enquire as to the whereabouts of a little girl called Daisy Miller who used to live, she thought, in Scarborough, possibly now in an orphanage.

'You see, she knew her parents. They'd been friends years ago and she has only just heard the sad news that they lost their lives in an air crash. She wondered if there was anything she can do to help Daisy.' Joe looked on with admiration as Doris painted yet another scenario.

'And who might you be?' the grey lady demanded. Joe froze. What would he say? Doris quickly answered, 'We work with the Gospel Mission. We are on holiday this week My husband is Pastor John Bateman, from the Mission.' Here we go again! thought Joe. Is there no end to her fairy tales?

'And how old is this child ... Daisy, did you say?'

'She'll be about four, I think,' said Doris.

'Well I'm sorry to say I can't help you at all. We have no one here of that name, nor, in fact, of that age. Our children are all over five.'

'Oh.' The disappointment was clear. 'Is there perhaps another orphanage where they have the younger children?'

'I believe there was one, over on the north side. I have only been here six months; I'm not too sure. I would like to help. Just a moment, though. I believe that one of my staff used to work over there. I could ask her, if you would care to wait a little longer.'

'Oh, please...' said Doris. Matron left them. In a couple of minutes she returned to introduce Mrs. Dean.

'Yes,' Mrs. Dean answered, 'there was two orphanages until about a year ago. I worked at

Northside myself. I do recall a child called Daisy. She was only very little when she first came to us. Just a baby, really.'

'Tell us what you remember about her. Was it Daisy Miller?'

'Oh, yes, definitely Miller. Couldn't forget the day she came, poor little mite. Her gran were lookin' after 'er, ya see. 'Er gran come bangin' on t'door one night. Gone right off 'er 'ead, she 'ad. She 'ad all the baby's belongins with 'er and she shouts at our Matron that 'er daughter's dead and so's 'er 'usband and that she'd 'ave to leave the littl'un with us. She were quite barmy. I remember our Matron lookin' at the baby an' sayin', "Well, Daisy Miller, it looks like you're comin' to live with us, darlin'." Then they come an' took the gran'mother away to 'ospital, or asylum or somewhere. It were awful.'

'Well, then, all we have to do is go to Northside. That's where we'll find Daisy.'

'No, 'scuse me, you don't understand,' said Mrs. Dean, 'that wor then. That wor before the fire. There ain't no Northside now. It were all burnt down. There were nowt left burra few black walls.' There was a shocked silence broken eventually by Matron who voiced everyone's first question, 'Was anyone killed?'

'No, mam, we all got out alright, burrit were a miracle we did. It 'ad iron stairs on the outside, fire escapes. One on each landing. The big children carried the babies. They was all very brave. There was such a lorra smoke and noise.'

'Where did all those children go to, after the fire?'

'Some come over 'ere. Some went to York, I think. Nowhere else were as big as Northside, so they was spread all over.'

Doris was at the same time relieved and bitterly disappointed. Relieved because she could be reasonably certain that Daisy was still alive. Disappointed that her search was by no means at an end. She glanced at the clock on the mantel shelf and rose sharply to her feet.

'You have all been very helpful and we are most grateful. We have to leave now, have we not, dear? Or we shall miss our train.'

Indeed, it was only by extreme good luck that they caught the Leeds train at six-thirty-five, collapsing into the carriage, quite out of breath.

'She insists on playing hide and seek with us, this Daisy Miller. Phew! What a weekend!' said Joe.

'Yes, but we have learned a great deal more about her. As soon as I can I shall go to the library and find the reports of that fire. Something as big as that is sure to be well reported.

And, duly as planned, Doris was at the library desk, asking Anthony to help her to find the old papers as soon as she had another free day. There was no rush, of course. She was keeping herself acquainted as the months went by with the comings and goings of the Grange family. It was only last week she had seen a report of a wedding. The bride was the daughter of a leading mill-owner, the Granges were listed as guests and it was noted that 'Sarah Grange, recently returned from Europe', was among them. Anthony was at pains to be helpful, gazing at the pretty Mrs. Smithson with dewy eyes whenever she graced his counter.

'Here we are. The report that you wanted,' he said, spreading the newspaper out on the large desk before Doris.

SCANDAL OF FIRE
AT SEASIDE ORPHANAGE

'Today the Brigade has continued damping down at the site where fire gutted the Northside Orphanage in Scarborough. Thankfully there have been no reports of serious injury, a miracle when you stand and regard the devastation wreaked by this terrible fire.' (Doris gasped when she looked at the pictures. A bomb could not have made a worse mess, she thought.) *'An inquiry has been set up to try to ascertain the cause of this fire and the police have been brought in to examine the possibility of arson.*

'It has been suggested that it was through neglect of the regulations that the fire occurred. It is claimed that the orphanage was not being well run, the children were poorly fed and clothed, funding badly allocated and that there was suspicion of fraudulent use of public money. Subsequent to these allegations it had been arranged that Northside should undergo a thorough inspection. This was planned to begin at the end of the month. The fire has not only removed most of the physical evidence but has destroyed the entire set of records kept on the children and staff.

All the youngsters have now been re-housed with other orphanages or foster-homes. This has been overseen by Scarborough's Chief Children's Officer, Mr. Mark Backhouse.'

Doris made a note of the man's name. She supposed that he could be contacted at the Town Hall. He must be her next quarry. She looked again at the date of the newspaper report she was reading. It was longer ago than she had been led to believe by Mrs. Dean, the woman who had worked there. It just goes to show how time passes and how our memories fail to keep pace with accuracy. Mrs. Dean had described how Daisy had been brought to the orphanage by her distraught grandmother when she was hardly more than a baby. The date of the fire was the first week of February 1933, almost eighteen months ago, certainly more than the year mentioned by Mrs. Dean. Doris sat in a daydream with the newspaper spread out before her, its yellowing edges already showing signs of its age. She reckoned that Daisy had had more than her fair share of troubles for one so young, having been, in a manner of speaking, robbed of not one but two sets of parents by the time she was three years old. I wonder where she is, right at this moment, mused Doris.

'We have to close in five minutes, Mrs. Smithson.' Anthony's quiet voice made her jump violently and she gathered her wits into the present tense.

'Oh, yes. Thank you very much.'

'Did you find what you were looking for?' She nodded, smiled and left the library. Joe would be home soon, and wanting his meal. She hurried to the bus stop, noticing as she went that it was almost dusk. A slight chill in the air forecast autumn nights. By the time she opened the door of the basement flat half an hour later the street lamps were lit, small haloes of mist giving them an ethereal look, and she was glad to close herself inside and put a match to her own gas lights. Busying herself lighting the fire in the kitchen range she let her thoughts dwell on the wording of the letter she planned to write to Mr. Backhouse, the Scarborough Children's Officer. The water was boiling ready for the potatoes she had peeled and the sausages would fry gently on the hob while they cooked. Joe loved his sausage and mash and she had bought a custard tart on her way home yesterday. An easy meal to put onto the table, she thought. Taking out paper and pencil she began her letter, pushing out of the way some of the things she had set on the table. It was warm here, near the range and she was soon engrossed in her writing. She knew she must sound as if she had a right to be asking about the whereabouts of Daisy Miller and she found that it was far harder to act out a part on paper than in the flesh. Several sheets of paper fluttered to the floor, rejected. Doris gathered them up and placed them on the fire, at the same time checking on the potatoes. They were done and 'falling away' as her mother used to say.

She looked at the big clock that stood on the iron mantelshelf. It was almost seven thirty. Joe was never as late as this except if he was going with Sir Edward to a show or a special event. Where could he be? Feeling rather irritated she took off the potatoes, mashed them and put them to warm in the oven along with the sausages and turned back to her letter. But she could not concentrate on it. Every so often she would get up and go to the door, peer down the driveway, come back to the fire, walk round the room. Irritation gave way to agitation and agitation to fear. She began to invent reasons for his non-appearance and hoped that he had not fallen prey to the evils of drink again after all this time ... or to any worse temptation. Nine o'clock came and went. Doris put on her coat and hat and a pair of stout shoes and prepared to walk to Upton Hall. Surely his employers would know something. At least they might tell her whether her husband had left for home.

Clouds had gathered obscuring the moon and stars and she found the lane pitch black after leaving behind the last of the street-lights. It was a darkness that you could feel as if it was touching you. Sometimes things did touch her, branches, grasses perhaps? Thorny bushes caught at her clothes and tore her stockings, as she mistook the path and blundered into the hedge. Small animals scurried out of her way while larger ones threatened her, even though, judging by their noises, they were only cows.

She was at last able to fix her eyes on the lights from the windows of the hall and follow their lead. There were a great many lights, some moving about, lanterns being carried, she supposed. As she came closer, she could see a great many people too, all milling about in front of the Hall. Closer still and she could see a fire-engine and what looked like two ambulances and a horse-drawn vehicle, a large cart of some sort, moving slowly towards the stable block. What it was carrying she could not make out. She began to run. There had obviously been some kind of accident. Where was Joe? Oh, where was he? Breathlessly gaining the pool of light in front of the Hall she grabbed at the coat of the man who was rushing past her.

'What has happened?'

'Not now, miss. There's two still down there. Have to get back.' He disappeared into the gloom. Doris ran towards the portico, up the few steps to the door that stood ajar and into the elegant entrance hall. Regardless of etiquette she marched straight through and into a room full of light and voices. The sight of two or three injured people lying on the carpet being attended to by ambulance men stopped her in her tracks. A tall man in torn but expensive clothes and looking distraught was moving from one to the other. He seemed to be in charge. Doris planted herself in his path.

'Excuse me, please. Would you tell me what has happened? My husband works here. Joe. He hasn't come home.' The tall man looked at her, confused for a moment, then realising that this must be Joe Smithson's wife, took her aside and gently made her sit on a chair at the side of the room.

'My dear, I am so sorry. I should have sent a message but everyone was needed here and in the confusion it slipped my mind. You must be so worried. The fact is that there has been a landslip of some kind up near the ridge. A large hole appeared in the ground just as the horses were returning after their afternoon canter. My best hunter took the brunt of it ... fell down about twelve feet ... broke his legs. Your Joe was riding him. The following two threw their riders but avoided the chasm.'

'But, Joe! Is he ... is he? Where is he?' A man, covered in dirt, ran in.

'Excuse me, sir. Thought I'd better let you know it's confirmed that it's an old mine-shaft. Must be left over from the lead-mining they reckon. They're just getting Joe out now, sir. He's the last one.'

'Is he badly hurt? This is Joe's wife.'

'He's conscious, just about. He's been a cryin' over the loss of the 'orse. He had to watch them shoot it, both of them being in the shaft, like. We're not sure how bad he is yet, sir.' Doris had listened to all this and felt her blood turn to ice. Little pieces of what the man said had lodged in her brain, but the whole sense of it evaded her. A mental replay of the scene as she had run towards the Hall paraded itself before her mind. The large, horse-drawn flatbed cart that she had flown past she now recognised as carrying the inert body of a horse, the horse that Joe had been riding.

'Can I go to him?'

'Come with me, it'll do him good to see you.' She hesitated, even though she wanted to go with the man, fearful of what she might find.

'Try to give him a smile, Mrs. Smithson. And tell him he's not to blame.' And to the man Sir Edward said, 'Bring him in here. Then we can decide what needs to be done. Then bring everyone in here. I'll organise a warm drink and so on. It has been quite a long job for the rescuers.' He looked exhausted. He had been early to the scene of the accident and had helped until the Brigade turned up.

Doris followed the man through the darkness with a lantern to guide them. They met the last of the rescue party not far away from the house. Joe lay on a stretcher under a blanket, his face filthy and covered with blood. His eyes were closed.

'I'm here, Joe. Can you talk to me?' Doris lifted the edge of the blanket, terrified of what she might encounter there, yet needing to find his hand to hold it. Blood was everywhere, his clothing soaked and sticky. She could feel her heart thumping in her ears. He opened his eyes, painfully trying to turn his head to look at her.

'What are you doing here?' he said weakly and his eyes closed again. Through the dirt, grime and blood that covered his face Doris could see that his skin was a dull grey. His breathing was shallow. Sir Edward Lazenby came over and put a hand on her shoulder, his face full of concern.

'Make sure he remains still. Talk to him to keep him awake ... and try not to worry, Mrs. Smithson. Everything possible will be done for him, I assure you, as soon as we get him to hospital.'

Chapter 22

1936

There was a kind of hush pervading all during that week between the king's death and his funeral. It seemed that the whole country was in mourning and the newspapers carried very little other news.

Sarah and Maddie were sad, too, but they were young and alive and had things to do. This morning they were glad of a clear, bright and sparkling day as they ate breakfast in their hotel overlooking the south bay. It was clear enough this morning to see far beyond Filey Brigg to the south and the headland crowned by the castle to the north.

'What a view!' said Maddie.

'Yes. It's lovely ... makes you glad to be alive. Come on let's get started.'

Yesterday's conversation with the nuns at St. Faith's had encouraged her to feel that the search for the recipient of Grandpa's cash legacy might not be too difficult. She felt tremendously relieved that her baby girl had been adopted by a couple who would love and cherish her and she blessed the people who had brought it about. She had been able to thank the nuns. Today she hoped she would be able to thank the doctor, too. But it was not to be. Not today, at least.

They found the large Victorian house, from which Dr. Constance Bennett ran her Practice, situated just off the centre of the town and a mile or so from the sea front. It stood at the end of a row of similar detached houses, good, solid, respectable family houses they had been seventy years ago and quite the most desirable to be had in the then burgeoning seaside resort. Now they were rather too large for today's smaller families and for the changes in the social order that had taken place since the Great War. They were excellent properties to convert into private hotels or guest houses and perfect, of course, for a doctor's premises. The brass plate on the gatepost proclaimed that Dr. Constance Bennett, M.B., Ch. B., could be found here. But the young lady who sat behind the reception window shook her head.

'I am very sorry, Dr. Constance is away. Her nephew, Dr. Nigel is running the practice until her return. Perhaps he could be of help?'

'Thank you, but no. I need to see Dr. Constance Bennett. Is she on holiday? Perhaps I could call again when she gets back?'

'It's not a holiday, but she will be coming back, let's see now, it will be towards the end of August. She is in South Africa. She went to spend a year over there, working with abandoned babies.'

'I see. Thank you. I'm sorry to have troubled you,' said Sarah, her disappointment clear to see.

As Maddie drove them back to the hotel Sarah had observed that the visit to St. Faith's had more than made up for drawing a blank at the doctor's. She felt they could go home with a feeling of achievement, encouraged in the search for the child she had given up.

The woman at the hotel reception smiled as Sarah went to check out.

'I hope you have had a pleasant stay, ladies.' She busied herself preparing their bill while Maddie idly flicked through the leaflets left out to inform guests of some of the delights of Scarborough. 'Places to Stay, Smaller Hotels and Guest Houses' caught her attention.

'Ready, Maddie?' Sarah had picked up her case and was making for the door.

'Just a minute. Come and look at this, Sarah.' Their journey home forgotten for the moment the two of them searched the booklet for any sign of the name 'Miller' amongst the list of boarding houses and small hotels.

'Can't understand it,' said Maddie, shaking her head. 'All the proprietors seem to be listed as well as the names of the places but no sign of a Miller. You sure that's what Sister Ruth said?' Sarah let go a heartfelt sigh.

'Yes, of course. How could I forget it?'

'Hmm!' replied Maddie as she began to check through the names once more.

'Do you ladies need any help?' It was the receptionist who had noticed their puzzled expressions. Sarah thought quickly.

'We were hoping to find some, er ... old friends ... of my parents ... haven't heard of them for years ... but...' her words tailed off. She was not adept at story-telling.

'Perhaps I can help. What was the name?'

'It was Miller as a matter of fact. We thought they had a guest house.'

'Fred and Margaret Miller, you mean?' Sarah brightened immediately.

'Yes, that's right. Do you know them?' There was no answering smile from the girl.

'Not personally, no, but it was all over the papers when it happened. All of Scarborough knew. The pair of them won a trip to Paris on an aeroplane. It was a prize offered by the Small Hotels Association for the best run hotel of its size.' She paused. 'I'm sorry to have to tell you that on the way back the aeroplane crashed into the sea. That's why there's no longer a Miller listed in there.' Maddie and Sarah looked at the girl, stunned.

'How terrible,' said Sarah, hoping that the girl would know a little more detail.

'Yes, it was,' she went on. 'They were lost at sea along with the pilot and crew. I don't think anything was ever found of them. Their guest house had to be sold, of course.' She paused again, wondering whether she had said too much. She was not one to gossip but these two young ladies seemed really interested. 'They left a little girl. She was only a tot, as I recall. They had to put her into an orphanage because her grandmother was too ill to care for her. Or did the grandma die soon after? I forget. Sad story, isn't it?'

'It is, indeed,' said Maddie, 'very sad. Thank you for your help though.'

Sarah and Maddie began to walk away. Sarah turned back.

'Just a moment ... do you by any chance remember the name of the little girl?'

'I think they called her Daisy. Yes, that was it. Daisy Miller.'

They walked in silence towards the car and Sarah was still in no mood for chatter as they drove westwards towards home. Her mind was busy.

After a while Maddie asked, 'Are you alright, Sarah? You're very quiet.'

'Just trying to think things through calmly. You know, Maddie, since the day my baby was born I've been determined to leave that fact firmly and safely in the past. I've never doubted for an instant that what I did was the best for the baby and for me. I never imagined there being any future contact with the child and I left St. Faith's ready to get on with my life.'

Maddie answered, quietly, 'And now...?'

'I'm quite unprepared for the bewildering emotions that are threatening to turn my well-ordered life upside down.'

'I know,' Maddie's voice was full of sympathy and she briefly laid her hand on Sarah's where she sat anxiously twisting her handkerchief.

'It's been just one thing after another, what with the unexpected results of the will and that awful railway accident, a broken bone and my encounter with a frightened little girl. I'm finding it hard to remain detached ... to deal calmly with this barrage of new feelings. Sarah became silent and thoughtful as Maddie agreed that there had been a lot to deal with during the past few days.

Sarah could not share, even with Maddie, the tumult of emotions that had accompanied the sudden re-appearance of Sam in her life. Her mind was racing, connecting together events and knowledge gleaned since the night when the London express had left the track and a child named Daisy had hidden under her coat.

And now, the discovery that her own child had been given the same name. Was it all coincidence? The pieces began to fit together as in a jig-saw, but she was reluctant to allow the picture to emerge.

'Penny for them!' said Maddie, glancing across at the pensive face. Sarah answered slowly, as if hardly daring to voice the thought.

'My daughter, Daisy Miller ... Daisy, a child from an orphanage ... Maddie, you know what this could mean, don't you?' Maddie smiled and waited for Sarah to finish. 'The little girl on the London train, the child who clung to me ... could she be my own child? Somehow I feel so sure of it ... and yet I can't believe it!'

'You'd better believe it, Sarah. It's far too much of a coincidence. What did she tell you her name was?'

'Daisy Francis, she said, I think. Of course, Fran*ces,* not Fran*cis*. She was telling me her Christian names, not her surname at all. Remember? The nuns gave her Frances? The Millers must have kept it and added their own. Oh, how strange ... perhaps this accounts for how oddly I felt about that little girl, almost as if I knew her...' She began fishing in her handbag. 'Wait, Maddie, can you find a place to pull up. There's something...' She found the miniature that she had carried with her ever since Edith had given it to her as her friend stopped the car.

'Look, Maddie. I never showed you this, did I? Gran gave it to me when I went home with her after the funeral. She gave me it because I said it looked so like the little girl on the train.' Maddie took the pretty thing in her hand and admired the perfection of the painting.

'How beautiful,' whispered Maddie.

'If this coincidence turns out to be the truth, you are looking at the great-great-grandmother of Daisy Miller, my own great grandmother. Her name was Margaret.'

'I wonder if she had Daisy for short?' said Maddie. 'She's certainly very pretty. I'll take your word that she looks like your waif and stray from the train,' said Maddie as she started the engine and resumed the drive.

'Do you know, Maddie, Daisy told me quite a bit about the place where she lives. I had already planned to visit her when I have the pot taken off my leg. I think it's a foster home, but I could be wrong. It's run by a Mrs. Johnson with help from her husband. She sounds a very pleasant person and Daisy obviously thinks the world of her. I really can't think of anyone better to hand over Grandpa's legacy to. From the sound of her I suspect she would use it well.'

'Don't go jumping the gun, honey,' warned Maddie, ever cautious. 'There's going to have to be some discreet inquiries made and, most important, Sarah, even when you are sure of who's who, remember that you don't want the world to know your connection with Daisy ... do you? It could prove to be a very tricky situation for you to handle. Tread carefully and mind whom you talk to.'

'Oh, Maddie, trust you to keep my feet on the ground. Yes, of course, I must think things through carefully.' And the one person Sarah knew she could talk things over with was Alice. Sarah valued the close relationship she had with her mother. It was something that many of her friends lacked and envied.

Maddie dropped Sarah at home in the pouring rain. She called to her mother that she was home. Alice's voice called from the back of the house that she would be with her directly. 'I'm just brewing a cup of tea for the weary traveller!' She busied herself now setting a tray with tea and scones.

The teacups stood untouched and cold as Alice listened to Sarah's account of her visit to the Convent, her discovery that she had a daughter and not a son, and that the child had been adopted and then bereaved of her parents so soon. Sarah's belief that this child was the same as the one in the train crash, the scared little Daisy who had taken refuge with Sarah, came as a shock to Alice.

'But, darling, can you be sure of this? There must be more than one child called Daisy living in orphanages. And why would a child from the Scarborough area be found travelling on the main line from London?'

'I don't know, mummy. It's a great puzzle, I admit and there's much more I still need to find out about Daisy Miller. For instance, where did she go when her parents were lost? The woman at the hotel said that she was put into an orphanage but I have no proof of that.'

'I can see that you'd really like to believe that the child on the train was the same Daisy ... Daisy Miller. If it does turn out to be so, you'll be half way to completing your task for Grandpa, won't you? What I mean is you know the name of the woman who runs the Children's Home. Johnson, wasn't it?'

'Yes, but so far I've little idea where to start looking.' Sarah was quiet for several minutes, lost in thought. 'Like all the best sleuths I should work from established facts and there's one that's truly troubling me now. I've only just remembered it. The child on the train said she was called Daisy Francis and she was six and three quarters. If that's right, and she didn't seem like a child who wouldn't know her own age, then she is not Daisy Miller.' Sarah and her mother were both only too well aware of the date of Daisy Miller's birth. 'Oh dear, one step forward, and another back. This afternoon I shall write a list of all the known facts and see whether there are any more avenues to explore. One fact is certain I have to carry out Grandpa Grange's wishes. It's just proving a mite more complicated that I thought.'

One of the more tangible leads on Sarah's list was the red hat that lay almost forgotten at the top of her wardrobe. She took it down and placed it on her bed, remembering so clearly the first time she had seen it, worn by the blond woman who called herself Daisy's mother, remembering also, with a frisson of guilt the day she had stolen it from the hospital. There would be no use in having brought it home if she did not follow it up, in some way try to make use of it. She felt encouraged. This was something she could do today and without having to travel miles. She would go into Leeds and try to identify the wearer of this hat. If she could find the blond woman so many doors might open to her. She put on a pair of thick trousers to protect her plaster from the rain and packed the hat safely into a box. The label inside the lining read 'MarieAnne, Exclusive Millinery. The Headrow, Leeds'.

The mixture of trams, motor vehicles and horse-drawn traffic made the place noisy and dirty but

Sarah always enjoyed the busy city centre. The shops and bill-boards were so colourful and even in the rain it bustled with people, umbrellas adding to the crush. There were sales on at all the large stores as they tried to sell off the stock left over from Christmas and it was almost as hectic as it had been in December.

MarieAnne's elegant little shop was tucked in between a tea-shop and a department store. Its windows were of bowed glass and dressed with just a few carefully chosen model hats, very eye-catching and obviously expensive. Sarah wondered how her strange errand would be received.

'Good afternoon, madam. May I be of assistance?' The woman was all of six feet tall, dressed in dark brown crepe de chine and so thin that Sarah was tempted to laugh as she thought straight away of a telegraph pole. To add to this impression her black hair was piled high on her head and held by extremely long pins with shiny knobs at the ends. She was, Sarah discovered, also very obliging and had a thorough knowledge of her work. She had made only two hats of this particular red fabric, she recalled. Both were to special order of course. She made very few hats for sale 'off the peg', to quote a modern term.

'Yes, I would guess it must be at least five years ago. May I ask where you acquired this model? And why you are bringing it here today?' She was very precise, her voice a rich contralto when she spoke.

'I became acquainted with a lady travelling by train,' said Sarah, trying to stick as close to the truth as she could. 'It was very warm and we took off our hats. The lady left hers and I am at pains to return it to her. It is a very beautiful hat.' Sarah felt a little flattery would not go amiss. 'It was almost three weeks ago, but as you can see, I have my leg in plaster and have only just begun to get about again. If you could give me the address of your customer I would be glad to return her property.' The telegraph pole had to go and find an old order book.

'I never make two the same,' she said, proudly, examining the hat. 'Let me see ... this one was for Mrs. Aaron of Alwoodley Park. I must say, I am surprised she is still wearing it. She tends to buy new every year.' She wrote down the address for Sarah and wished her 'Good-day'. Sarah left swiftly, thankful that she had not been asked for any details about herself.

A taxi took her to the fashionable outskirts of the city to the address that she sought. Sarah doubted very much whether this could be the address of the woman on the train. Mrs. Aaron was just saying goodbye to some friends and Sarah was glad that she had not arrived any earlier. This was most definitely not the woman on the London train. Oh dear! How was she going to explain her errand to this smart Jewess who politely invited her to step inside? Nothing for it but to tell her the same story as she had told the milliner. Mrs. Aaron, short, pump, jolly with dark, greying hair, laughed out loud at Sarah's discomfiture.

'Oh, my dear, how very kind of you to try to return my chapeau! It is clear I am not the person who travelled with you. No, indeed. It must be three or four years since I got rid of this outfit. I give my things to the Jumble Sale, you know, down at the Village Hall. Someone has bought it there, but I wouldn't have any idea whom. And you have gone to all this trouble! You must let me give you a cup of tea, my dear.'

Mrs. Aaron would never know just how disappointed the young lady was at not finding the right owner of the hat, but Sarah was not about to give up.

'Where is your Village Hall,' she asked, 'and who runs the Jumble Sales there? My mother might have things to donate,' she added by way of explanation.

Sarah arrived home from her expedition still clutching the box with the scarlet hat. She could not wait to share with Alice her findings of the afternoon and to arrange to take some clothes to the ladies at the Alwoodley Jumble sale. She was bubbling over with ideas. Mrs Aaron had said that they held the sales once a month and that they were very popular events. People came from all parts of Leeds, she said, many indeed, she understood, were regular customers. So eager was she to tell Alice that she went straight through to the back of the house to find her. But Alice was not there. She could hear her voice calling from the sitting room.

'Sarah! We're in here, dear!' Wondering vaguely who could be with her mother, since no mention had been made of any expected callers, Sarah retraced her steps. She came to an abrupt halt in the doorway of the sitting room. For waiting there to greet her was Sam Pearce. He rose from the chair as she came in but made no move towards her. Sarah stood, rooted to the spot in the doorway, the box falling from her hands, the hat rolling across the carpet unheeded by Sarah whose gaze was fixed upon Sam's face. It seemed like minutes before Alice, whose presence Sarah had barely noticed, broke the spell-like silence with, 'I knew you would be home soon, dear, so I asked Sam to wait. We have been having a pleasant chat. If you two will excuse me I need to make sure that David's football kit is ready for his match tomorrow.' Alice disappeared. It would be hard to believe that it had not occurred to this astute woman that this young man was her daughter's first love, indeed, the father of her child. But if she did suspect it she was far too shrewd and wise to let it show. She had observed the reactions of them both just now, felt the electricity fill the atmosphere and the tension rise as Sarah had stopped, dead, at the door. Alice liked Sam. He had probably been very foolish but who was not so during their adolescent years. If she was honest with herself she would admit that he had twice the personality of Andrew Marsden. And, sitting in the kitchen, she crossed her fingers, hoping that whatever had come between Sarah and Sam would be settled.

The red hat stopped at Sam's feet and he stooped to pick it up.

'Sam!' 'Sarah!' They both spoke at once and the awkward silence descended once again. Sam retrieved the hat-box and put away the hat.

'Has it helped at all? The hat, I mean,' he asked. Sarah pulled herself together at last and found her tongue.

'Er, yes, a little I think. I'm still following a lead it gave me. What brings you here, Sam? I really didn't expect to see you again after ... last time.' The memory of that day, his last visit here, when he had upped and left so abruptly was still raw.

'Thanks for your letter from Morecambe, Sarah. It seems that we wrote to each other on the same day.'

'Yes, thank you for yours, too,' she said a little stiffly, coming into the room and sitting down on the sofa. He came and sat beside her.

'I hope you don't mind my barging in again like this. There's something I have to tell you and I was coming up to see father in any case. I decided to risk calling in to tell you in person. All I ask is that you hear me out. Then you can tell me to go ... and I will. Will you listen? Just for a few minutes? Please?' He looked about five years old, she thought, asking for the thing he wanted most for his birthday. He had the most amazingly long eyelashes. For a split second she saw Daisy ... those same eyelashes. She caught her breath and looked away. She found she could not bear to look into his eyes.

'Well? What is it that's so important that you could not telephone?' she said brusquely, doing her best to sound calmly in control.

'I could have telephoned, but ... I wanted to see you ... and this gave me an excuse. It's about the little girl on the train, Sarah. I've seen her again. In fact I've found out where she lives. Gerry helped.' All the time he was speaking he was watching her face. Suddenly she was really listening, turning towards him, eager to hear more. 'It seems the police departments have lists of places where homeless children are cared for. Gerry made enquiries as to whether any of them had a little girl called Daisy. It's amazing what you can do through official channels! He found one foster home near Retford, run by Mr. and Mrs. Johnson. When he 'phoned they told him that Daisy had indeed said something about a train crash and a hospital, but that they weren't sure just how true it was.' Sarah was hanging upon his every word by now. The problem she had with this man who had 'run out on her' when she had told him he was a father had receded into the background. This was important. This was so utterly relevant to here and now and to the job she had to do for George Grange that nothing else mattered. Even today's business with the search for Daisy's supposed kidnapper took a back seat. If Mrs. Johnson's Children's Home was found and Daisy was there it was a huge step in the right direction. All this passed through her mind in a split second while Sam was still speaking. 'So, Gerry rang them again at my request and asked if Mrs. Johnson would have any objection to a visit from the doctor who had seen Daisy after the accident. They said there would be no objection at all because they would like very much to speak to someone who was there that night. Daisy's story did not tally, they said, with that of the people who had charge of her that weekend who had made light of the accident.' He stopped, waiting for some reaction from Sarah.

'That would be the woman in the red hat,' she said, quietly. 'I still don't know who she is. I've just got back from talking to the hat's original owner but so far I'm no nearer to finding the woman who wore it three weeks ago on the northbound train.' It was the most she had said since she had come in and encountered Sam. He was sensitive enough to realise that the situation between them was still extremely fragile and that Sarah's response was a kind of truce. He would have to tread carefully if he were to regain her trust and rekindle her feelings for him. He had been desolate when he had returned to Doncaster and would have given anything to have had a chance to re-play the scene with Sarah that he had ruined in one selfish, unthinking moment.

'Gerry and I went to see Mrs. Johnson last week. Gerry's just passed his Sergeant exams so he's allowed to drive a squad car. His Inspector is still trying to find out why the number of people found after the crash did not tally with the number known to be travelling.

He was worried that someone had been hurled out from the impact, was lying dead or injured or was still wandering about in a daze, needing help. Anyhow, he thought it was legit police business to go and talk to Daisy.'

'And did you? Sam? Did you talk to Daisy?'

'Yes we did. She was very scared and shy at first when she saw the police uniform, but she remembered me.'

'What did she say?'

'She remembered running away from two people who had been taking her for an outing. They had been shouting, she said, and she didn't like it. She had run away to hide. She told me again about you, Sarah, how you were hurt in the train and how you looked after her when she was hiding.' Sarah's face became dreamy as she recalled some of the moments before the jarring and screeching of the crash, the eating of the biscuits, the child dancing and singing, the dark curls bobbing and those bright, trusting, blue eyes. 'I wish you could have seen her face when I told her I was a friend of yours ... um ... that I know you,' he added, weakly.

'She was a spunky little thing, and so pretty,' said Sarah.

'I was wondering if you would allow me to take you to see Daisy,' said Sam. He held up both his hands, the palms towards her. 'No obligation, no strings attached,' he added.

'When can we go?' said Sarah.

Chapter 23

It was a case of placing things in separate compartments in her mind and not allowing any overlapping, mixing or merging. It reminded Sarah of her early days in the office when she had to learn where different items were kept in the filing cabinets and that woe betide anyone who placed papers in the wrong folder.

On the one hand there was the fact that she had given birth to a child, now known to be a girl, and her goal was to find her. This fact was known to a select few people, now including Sam, (though he knew simply that there was a child; she remembered that she had not had time even to tell him that he had a daughter before he had left that day).

And then there was her suppressed feeling for Sam Pearce which she had begun to realise would not go away and which she was now terrified of admitting. Bearing the hurt that he had caused when he had walked out had been dreadful. At first she never wanted to set eyes on him again, hated him venomously for his doubting he was the father of her baby. What other reason could he have had for leaving so suddenly? What did he think she was, anyway? Some floosie who would go with any man who flattered her. Was that all it meant to him, that magical relationship that had filled the golden days of spring 1929? It made no sense at all to the logical side of her brain that she could still bear to be in his company, indeed that she felt incomplete without him.

Then there was the child called Daisy, in foster-care with Mrs. Johnson who might or might not be her own flesh and blood, and if she was, then she was of Sam's blood, too. Sam and Gerry had tracked her down for reasons which appeared to be entirely unconnected with Sarah, yet he had known of her concern when the child had gone missing at Doncaster Hospital. She had no way of knowing whether Sam had connected Daisy with Sarah's secret past. On the face of it there was no reason whatsoever why he should.

Then there was a couple seen on the train who seemed to have some claim of their own upon

Daisy. The file on them was extremely thin. She cast her mind back to that night when they had burst into her compartment looking, they said, for their daughter. A bossy woman, brittle and hard, sharp-spoken, she guessed, when she was not trying to impress, and wearing that red hat. The man, tall, dark, rather non-descript, seeming anxious to find the child. She remembered that she did not like his eyes. Shifty they were, she thought, not at all kindly.

And again, there was the conflicting information regarding the birthday of the little girl. This was to mention but a few of the things jostling for position in Sarah's mind.

It was all very confusing and Sarah could not help wondering how it would all end. Her grandfather had certainly stirred up a hornet's nest and Sarah could fairly feel the buzzing insects darting in all directions, threatening her with their stings and disturbing her with their unpredictable motion.

When Sam had asked if he might take her to visit Daisy she had had no hesitation. This was what she wanted above anything else, even though she knew she was in danger of stirring up emotions that may be hard to guess at and harder to deal with. She would have to be circumspect in how she spoke to Sam. There was much she knew now about Daisy Miller, not least of which was her growing conviction that Daisy was her daughter. What did Sam know about her? Had he discussed the child's circumstances or her origins with Mrs. Johnson? Indeed, would Mrs. Johnson feel at liberty to reveal how Daisy had come to be fostered with her? Did she, in fact, have the full story of Daisy's short life? And, although Sarah needed more than anything else to know for sure if Daisy was hers, the thought of spending a day in the car with Sam, censoring her every word before it left her lips, filled her with apprehension. What a pity it was that she could not invite Maddie to join them. Her clear thinking common sense might well protect Sarah from serious errors of judgement.

Oh, if only her heart did not jump and leap so when he was near, if only his smile would not make her weak at the knees. She was not a fool ... she knew what ailed her ... if only she did not love him so. But Maddie was working on the Pantomime and there were rehearsals even during the run from time to time for various reasons and they had at least two matinees a week. No, she would not even suggest it to Maddie. She would stand on her own feet. She must discover the truth about Daisy Miller, and the sooner the better. So, when Sam suggested going the following day, Sarah agreed immediately.

It was Tuesday, January 28th, a date to be noted by the whole country as the day when King was taken to his final resting place, King George's Chapel, Windsor. The country was in mourning and many businesses closed their doors as a mark of respect. Sam made sure that the train they needed for Retford was running and was told that the mainline services were as usual. He arrived to collect Sarah just after breakfast, driving his father's old car which he left at the station. They were on their way while at the other end of their journey Daisy Miller could not sit still for excitement because Sarah was coming to see her.

'Are you sure? Is it today? Will it be after dinner?' Daisy hopped about until she was told, quite severely, to settle down to the schoolwork she had been set by her teacher, since she would be missing school today. Daisy did not mind. It was reading and she loved reading. It was a nice change to have the place to herself with all the others at school. She curled up in the window seat to read and returned there after lunch to watch the drive for the arrival of Sam and Sarah. There had not been time to buy Daisy a toy but Sarah had stopped at the bookstall on the station and bought a few comic papers and some pencils and a colouring book. It was not much, thought Sarah, but she remembered enjoying colouring when she was little.

It had been a strange and rather silent journey on the train. It had not taken Sam very long to explain to Sarah how he and Gerry had first visited Idle House, having tracked down Daisy to Mrs. Johnson's. As soon as he had seen her Sam remembered those blue eyes and dark curls and Daisy had recognised Sam as the doctor at the roadside. Elsie Johnson had taken to these two young men, the policeman and the doctor and had welcomed them as people who had looked after one of 'her' children. She had plied them with cups of tea and homemade scones and said she was grateful for their help.

As to the couple who should have been looking after Daisy, she was not so sure. There was something odd about them. Sure, they could not be blamed for the railway accident, but she felt it very strange that they were not together with Daisy when the train crashed. She had not been able to get any proper account of that night from them or from Daisy. Daisy's story of her weekend seemed very confused. Elsie had not quizzed her too much for fear of upsetting the child. One thing was certain, Daisy would be thrilled to be re-united with Sarah. She had talked of no-one else, yet she did not know who she was. Elsie was delighted when Sam had promised to bring Sarah to visit, saying that she was an old friend from his schooldays and that their meeting at the hospital at Doncaster had been a happy coincidence. Once the background to this trip of theirs had been covered Sarah and Sam had sat in comparative silence until they arrived at Retford Station.

Idle House was a misnomer. A busier place would be hard to find. The house took its name from the river that tumbled down the slope at the back of the garden and ran through the town. Mrs. Johnson, six children, their ages ranging from five to eleven and her husband, a railway signalman, filled the house with noise and bustle most of the time. Lacking any children of their own, the Johnsons had decided to give a loving and secure home to less fortunate children. They had been very successful and all six of their charges had settled well and felt loved and cherished by this quite remarkable couple. Samuel and Kevin were a couple of tearaways who soon succumbed to the kindly discipline dealt out by Elsie and Ernest. Anna was

Daisy's special friend and very close in age. Jennifer, at eleven, was their big sister. Tom, aged five, was the baby and had only just started school.

'They're here!' Daisy's sensible shoes made a racket on the stairs as she flew down from the day-room and Mrs. Johnson appeared to answer the door. The child came to a halt at the foot of the stairs, suddenly overcome with shyness. Her cheeks were flushed and her eyes shining as she half hid behind the newel post, watching as Mrs. Johnson invited them in. Sarah had both heard and seen the child and her heart performed somersaults as she played the old game of pretending not to have seen her. The emotion that caused them came from somewhere deep in her subconscious only to be subdued immediately by her conscious mind. She knew she must not allow herself to become involved with Daisy on more than a superficial level. She knew that endless heartbreak could ensue if she was not careful to keep her distance.

She glanced at Sam. Was there ever a stranger group of people meeting here today? A mother, a father, a daughter, most of them unaware of the others' existence, only the mother in possession of all the facts and she obliged by circumstance to keep silent. She shook herself into the present as she heard Sam saying,

'May I introduce Miss Sarah Grange?'

Daisy's heart thumped as she saw Sarah shake hands warmly with her foster-mother.

'Oh, dear, what a shame. She is at school perhaps? I shall be so disappointed to miss seeing Daisy. Isn't that a shame, Dr. Pearce?'

And knowing it was a joke at her expense but enjoying it just the same, Daisy let out a cry, 'I'm here, I'm here!' and ran towards the lady from the train whose arms were held open wide to greet her. Sarah scooped up the child in her arms and hugged her, saying, 'How lovely to see you again, Daisy.'

And Sam said, 'There, I told you I would bring her to see you, and here we are.'

Daisy gave Sam a huge smile and said, 'Thank you, Doctor Pearce.' She held Sarah's hand, looking at her as if she could hardly believe she was real.

'Come and sit in here,' said Elsie, leading the way into the room she still called the parlour. 'I'll go and put the kettle on while you talk to Daisy.' The three of them sat together on the settee with Daisy in the middle. Sam said little but watched and listened as Daisy chattered away, asking Sarah about her damaged leg, what had happened after the crash, about her stay in the hospital and her finding an old friend called Dr. Pearce. In her turn Daisy had a lot to tell Sarah about her adventures that night and the following day. Somehow it was easy to remember and tell it to Sarah, though she had been reluctant to say very much to anyone else, even Mrs. Johnson.

With childlike simplicity she told the facts. From the safety of Mrs. Johnson's parlour she could almost forget the terrors of the crash, her fears of the Smithsons as they swung between kindness and harshness in their dealings with her. She told Sarah about staying at the flat overnight and of their visit to the beautiful house the next day, followed by the surprising revelations made by Auntie Doris in the café in the park.

Elsie Johnson had returned quietly while they were talking and her eyebrows raised as she listened. Sarah was saying, 'Tell me again what Auntie Doris said ... about the "big secret".' Daisy had picked up and remembered this phrase that Doris had used. It smacked of fairy tales and mystery and excitement, just the things that Daisy had begun to enjoy reading about.

'She said they might be my real mummy and daddy.' Daisy looked round at the three faces that watched her with concern as her smiles disappeared to be replaced with a look of doubt and distrust, her small arms crossed tightly, her body suddenly huddled close. 'But they weren't sure, yet,' she added. There was a pause while each of the three adults considered what had been said and wondered how to react. Sarah was stunned. How could this be true? How could the couple on the train be Daisy's parents? Daisy was here because her parents were dead, killed in an air disaster if her information was correct. And yet, she had no firm proof that it was. Sam did not know what to make of it, but if the child's parents had turned up from somewhere, that was good, wasn't it? Mrs. Johnson looked worried and anxious and was the first to speak.

'They said nothing to me when they brought her back about thinking that Daisy was their child.' She refrained from expressing her other doubts about these people, her instinctive distrust, for, if they did turn out to be genuine, she did not want to influence Daisy against them.

And Daisy did not miss a trick when listening to adult conversation. Daisy looked from one to another, seeing not hope but doubt and concern.

'But it's alright. I don't think they are and anyway I don't want to go with them. I want to stay here with you and Mr. Johnson and Anna and the others.' And, as if that simple statement settled everything, Daisy suddenly cheered up, jumped from the settee and ran to whisper to Mrs. Johnson.

'Yes, dear, of course you may, but you must remember that it's not polite to whisper in company. She'd like to show you her bedroom and her treasures, Miss Grange. Would you mind? Do take care on the stairs.'

Daisy shared a room with Anna. It was light and pleasant, frugally furnished but spotlessly clean. Their iron bedsteads were from an earlier age, serving well this generation of boisterous children and were covered with white cotton bedspreads. Brightly coloured blankets made from small squares of crochet-work lay folded at the foot of each child's bed to give extra warmth on winter nights. Favourite soft toys sat on the pillows. A shared bookcase held more toys and books. Daisy placed Sarah's presents here, saying that she would let Anna help with the colouring.

'Oh, Daisy, what a lovely room!' Daisy grew with pride.

'This is my special box. Would you like to see?' asked Daisy, shyly.

'May I, really?' Sarah knew she was being greatly honoured. It was a shoe-box, still bearing the name of a shop in Scarborough with an illustration on one end of the shoes it had once contained, high-heeled, elegant, ladies shoes made of black patent leather with a tee-strap, quite the height of fashion in the early years of the decade. Somebody had taken the trouble to line the box with wall-paper and had covered the lid with the same, adding Daisy Miller's name in large letters. Daisy carefully took out a little, brown teddy-bear, a miniature set of dominoes in its own tiny box, a set of rosary beads, a small Bible, a silver thimble, the comic that she had found in Leeds and several photographs. All these she laid out for Sarah to see on the cover of her bed. There was a small folded paper in the bottom of the box and Daisy carefully took it out.

'I can read this myself now,' she said. 'It says, "These things belong to Daisy Frances Miller. The Bible and beads were given to her by the Sisters at the Convent of St. Faith's. The thimble belonged to her dear mother, Margaret. The bear and the ivory dominoes are given by her loving grandmama. The photographs will remind her of her early life."' It was a poignant reminder of how alone in the world was this little girl. Once again Sarah's heart went out to her. What trauma she had had to bear. Was it all her fault? Not for the first time, she had to ward off the doubts that had recently begun to batter at the door of her complacency.

'Let's have a look at the photographs, shall we? Should we take them down and show Dr. Pearce? I'm sure he would like to see them.'

There were five photographs. Two were obviously taken in a studio, the first being a baby with dark curls, dressed in a smocked dress of pale, dainty fabric, and propped against cushions. She would be about three months old.

'This is me,' said Daisy, 'when I was little.'

'What a pretty baby you were,' said Sarah, turning the picture over to look at the back. 'Yes, here it says, 'Our darling daughter, Margaret (Daisy) Frances Miller, aged eleven weeks.' The photo was produced on stout card with the name of a Scarborough photographer embossed on the front and was about the size of a postcard. Another similar one showed the same baby sitting on the lap of a woman who appeared to be in her early fifties.

'That's my nan,' Daisy told them. On the back was written, in the same hand, 'Daisy with her grandmama, 1930.' In pencil was scribbled by another hand, 'Copy to Mrs. Partridge.' Sarah read out the words, glancing enquiringly at Elsie.

'I'm not entirely sure,' Elsie responded, 'but I had assumed that this was her grandmother's name.'

'Do you remember your nan, Daisy?'

'I think so. They said she looked after me for a little while. Then she was sick. I think she died 'cos she was very old.'

The other three photographs were more commonplace, taken with a home camera. The prints were quite small but very clear. One showed Daisy as a slightly older baby enjoying the beach with her parents. On the back was written, 'Margaret and Fred with Daisy'.

Another was a group standing on the steps of Miller's Guest House. This showed the same woman as on the studio portrait, clearly part of the family, holding Daisy in her arms and flanked by two younger women. On the back of this one was written, 'Grandma with Daisy, Margaret and Dot.' The third was taken several months later, when Daisy was walking with support between her parents along the Marine Drive as the sea broke over the wall, spraying across the road and wetting those brave enough to be out in the winter weather. The three on the photo were laughing and jumping over the puddles.

'They look so happy,' said Sarah rather wistfully.

'I think I 'member them,' said Daisy. But Sarah doubted very much whether she did. The child would naturally have some memories, particularly of feelings and emotions, and these she would attach to the photographs that she treasured as part of her past. Sam had said nothing as they pored over Daisy's pictures.

'It is good to see Daisy so happy here with you, Mrs. Johnson. She told me about you as we travelled on the train. She's obviously very fond of you. How long has she lived here?' Sarah asked.

'She came straight after the fire at Northside, February 1933 as I remember. Mr.Backhouse was desperate for placements for so many children. We all did our best to accommodate as many as we could.'

'I hope you won't mind my asking, but could you tell me whether Daisy had any papers; a birth certificate perhaps?'

'Oh, no, nothing like that. You see everything was burnt that was left in the building. Daisy was lucky to have rescued her treasure box.' Sarah could tell that she would have to get Mrs. Johnson on her own if she were to ask further questions about Daisy.

'May we speak in private for a moment, Mrs. Johnson? Sam and Daisy can amuse themselves I'm sure.' When the two women were out of earshot of the parlour Sarah said, 'Do you know anything more about Daisy's background? This is not idle curiosity, I assure you. I have good reason to be making enquiries, but at present I am not at liberty to tell you quite why.'

'All I know about her is that she was sent to Northside when she was about eighteen months old. Her parents were hurt in some sort of accident I was told and could not take care of the baby. For a short while she stayed with her grandma, the lady in the photograph, I suspect. But she fell seriously ill and Daisy was taken into Council care. I fancy there may still be a chance that her mother and father will find themselves able to take up parenthood again. I like to think so anyway.'

'Have you any idea what happened to the grandmother? Might she be still alive I wonder?'

'I'm afraid I don't know anything about her. All Daisy's roots appear to be in Scarborough and a long way from here. You certainly are asking a lot of searching questions, Miss Grange.'

'I hope I may be at liberty to explain before long. Please forgive my reticence. And thank you so very much for allowing us to visit. I trust we may come again?'

'With pleasure. It's good to see Daisy so happy.

I will give you my telephone number before you go. Whatever your enquiries are, Retford is a long way to come to make them. I shall be glad to help if I can. I have heard no more from Mr. and Mrs. Smithson as yet. Would you like me to let you know if they turn up again?'

'Indeed, I would. From what Daisy has said they sound like very unusual people. And yet one cannot disregard them altogether. They may well have a claim on the child.'

Sam and Daisy were playing a game of Ludo when Sarah entered the room. She stifled a gasp as both dark heads turned towards her, the deep blue eyes almost identical. Time had flown and they were all surprised when they discovered it was time to catch the train. Sarah promised that they would come again.

'I'm so very glad that we've found you, Daisy. One day soon we shall ask Mrs. Johnson if you may come to visit my home. Would you like that?'

'Oo! Yes, Sarah.'

'Then you be a good girl until we see you again.' There were hugs all round and just as they were leaving they met Mr. Johnson coming in from work. Daisy ran to him and began to regale him excitedly with the events of the afternoon as Sarah and Sam slipped away.

Both of them were thoughtful as they walked the short distance to catch the train. It was dark and quite cold. Sam offered his arm and Sarah took it without thinking. It just seemed the most natural thing to do.

Chapter 24

It was only a short walk from Idle House to the railway station and Sarah and Sam were soon on their journey northwards. Whilst saying very little to each other they were on the same wavelength, both considering what they had discovered during the visit to Retford and wondering what should come next. Neither had broached the subject that had caused their breakdown in communications, namely Sarah's claim that Sam had fathered her child. Sam was content for the time being to gently mend their relationship. Nothing else mattered to him than to regain her trust and friendship. He knew little of Grandfather Grange's legacy or of Sarah's need to locate her offspring and those who had her guardianship. Sarah realised as time went on that it was this fact, more than any other, which held her back from allowing any further closeness to develop with him. Her soul seemed to scream out to her that this was her man, that no matter how hurt she had been she loved him with all her being. The fact that he was obviously doing all he could to put the matter right lifted her heart more than she would have believed. But until the business of the Will was settled and Daisy and the Johnsons provided for via the legacy, she could not and would not fully confide in him.

The following day Sarah was spending the

afternoon with Maddie. Maddie came in from the kitchen carrying two steaming cups of tea.

'Here we are.' Maddie passed a cup to Sarah. 'Now! Come along – spill the beans. I'm dying to know how you two got along yesterday.'

'Well, it was a good day. Easier than I'd feared. Sam was doing his best to mend the rift and he couldn't have been more supportive during the visit. I suspect that he's been giving the whole matter plenty of thought since he walked out that day. He certainly seems keen to help in connecting with Daisy.'

'Have you told him everything?'

'About the will, you mean?'

Sarah shook her head. 'No. All he knows is that I was searching for the child I met on the train.'

'And how was it, spending time with him. How did you feel?'

'Look, Maddie, with Grandfather's money Elsie and Ernest and their six children could have a bigger house and so much more. Once it's proved that Daisy is mine the lawyers can get on with the business and I'll be able to take a back seat. Only then will I allow my thoughts to turn to Sam Pearce.'

'Yes ... and...?' Maddie questioned. Sarah gave a deep sigh and smiled.

'I guess you know the answer to that one already! If he still loves me I'll be willing to spend the rest of my life with him, simple as that ... but not yet.' A silence fell between them for a few seconds.

Sarah sipped her tea and went on, 'I've been wondering whether it might be possible to trace

Daisy's grandmother. Surely, if she's still alive, she could hold the key to all the secrets. She wouldn't be very old, hardly sixty. True, she had been ill after her daughter's sudden death, but she may well have recovered.'

'If she had, wouldn't she have tried to find Daisy?' asked Maddie

'Mmm, I guess so. On the other hand, with Daisy safely in someone else's care she may have seen no reason to interfere in the child's life. She would have known that to take up her care she'd have had to dedicate almost twenty of her later years to Daisy's upbringing.'

'Yes, rather a daunting prospect if her health wasn't good, I suppose.'

'Still I think it's quite possible that Mrs Partridge might be alive and well and able to shed light on the darkness.'

The trilling of the telephone in the hall interrupted their thoughts. Maddie went to answer it and was soon back to tell Sarah the call was for her.

'Who can be calling me here,' Sarah said, getting up.

'I'll give you three guesses,' chuckled Maddie as Sarah went to the phone.

'Sam! This is a surprise.'

'I rang your house and your mother told me Maddie's number. Hope she doesn't mind my calling. Sarah, I've been thinking ... how would you feel about another trip to Scarborough to see if we can find Daisy's grandmother ... Mrs Partridge wasn't it?'

'Are you a mind reader? I've just said the same

to Maddie!'

'We can go on my next days off, perhaps in a couple of weeks' time. With a bit of persuasion I guess the old man might lend me the car. What do you say?'

'I'd like that very much, Sam. Meantime I'll do some sleuthing of my own.'

Sarah was glad that her grandfather's will had not stated any kind of time limit by which Sarah must hand over the legacy to his great-grandchild. She could afford to go slowly and carefully about the task and had, indeed, already made more progress than she would have believed. There was no rush. The cash payment was sitting in her father's safe until the time should come when Sarah would hand it over.

Daisy's report of her weekend with Auntie Doris and Uncle Joe had puzzled and alarmed Sarah. Who were these people? What had they to do with Daisy? Where had they come from and why? In the dark recesses of Sarah's mind there lurked a deep fear and suspicion about this couple who had taken Daisy out to Leeds. She had seen them, briefly, on a moving train. She had felt an immediate distrust of them based solely on the sight of a frightened child. What if she had been mistaken? Perhaps she was doing them an injustice. Could it be that they had some bona-fide claim on Daisy? It was something that took control of her thoughts from the time she woke in the mornings to the time she closed her eyes to sleep. Until the planned visit to find Mrs. Partridge she would keep herself busy following other lines of inquiry, the first being another trip to Alwoodley and an effort to discover more about the buyer of the red hat. She knew this could come to nothing but it was worth a try and, more to the point, something to do. These weeks of idleness, waiting for her leg to mend, were tedious. She missed the stimulation of her work and the discipline of going there each day.

The following week Sarah collected together some clothing no longer needed by the family and arranged to visit the ladies who ran the Jumble Sales at Alwoodley Village Hall. She had been told that there would be somebody at the Hall on Wednesday afternoons to receive and sort the clothes prior to the Sale opening at six o'clock. Alice said that she would go along to keep Sarah company. It was Sarah's hope that the woman who had bought the red hat would be a regular caller at the Sales and that she might find out more about her. To this end she placed the hat in a separate bag, meaning to slip it onto the counter if anyone remotely like Auntie Doris should turn up. She would doubtless have been sorry to lose such a good hat and be very glad to find another like it.

A woman hurried over to them as they entered the hall and several others were arranging clothing and shoes, bags and bedding, lamps and records, in fact the whole gamut of human requirements for living.

Sarah's gaze swept the huge room where trestle tables were arranged in a large rectangle.

'Please come in. You must be the ladies who telephoned and offered help. Yes, we're most grateful for anything that will sell. As you can see we are all busy setting out for this evening.' She laughed at their amazed expressions. 'Oh, we shall sell all of this I can assure you. By the time we open the doors there will be a queue fifty yards long, the helpers will be safely on the inside of the oblong of tables and it will be non-stop bedlam for a couple of hours. Thank you for your donations ladies.'

'You're very welcome,' murmured Sarah, watching, mesmerised as the piles of goods grew and the women beavered about the room. 'Safely inside, you say?' She was puzzled.

'Yes, there is such a crush that we would all be trampled underfoot! We all stay behind the barricades and try to see that most things get paid for. You have obviously never been to a Jumble Sale before,' she laughed as Sarah and Alice shook their heads. 'Why don't you stay and see how it's done? We have great fun.'

'I'm not sure about that. I'd sooner have a job to do than stand and watch.'

'Well, we are short of help in the kitchen today. There's the hatch over there, you could serve the tea and see into the room at the same time. How about it?' This jolly woman assumed that they had nothing better to do than put themselves at her disposal as she took an elbow of each and steered them away to the kitchen. 'We all stop for our own refreshment in about ten minutes. You'll be most welcome to join us. Then there is an island of calm before the doors open and the hordes swarm in.'

'Halloo! Halloo! There, I said it was you,' came a

voice from across the room, and Sarah recognised the portly figure of Mrs. Aaron as that lady steered herself unerringly towards her. 'My dear, how nice to see you again!' Their fate was sealed. They stayed. Sarah confided in Mrs. Aaron the purpose of her presence here and the jolly Jewess promised to do her bit to help if she could.

They finally returned home at eight thirty after a memorable evening. Sarah had watched keenly but Doris Smithson had not appeared and the red hat was still in its bag. They knew they would have to go again. In fact, visits to the Jumble Sale and helping with the tea just might have to become part of their lives for the time being. They were both exhausted.

'How about a cup of tea?' said Alice, making for the kitchen.

It had taken Sarah the best part of two hours sitting beside the telephone to track down Mrs. Thelma Partridge to the Lilacs Nursing Home, Scarborough. The Matron of the home could not have been more helpful once Sarah had found her. She had lived in the town all her life and knew the background of the lady who now spent her days in room number five. Mrs. Partridge had not yet fully recovered from the shock of losing her daughter and son-in-law, though she was slowly picking up the threads of her life. What a tragedy it had been. Sarah wondered if she and a friend might visit her.

'By all means, Miss Grange. We welcome visitors to our ladies and gentlemen. It does them good to see different faces. I'll tell her to expect you on

Friday then.'

The Lilacs Nursing home was a pleasant enough place, situated on the cliff top with a view of the ever-changing sea. Matron came to greet these new visitors, leading the way to room number five.

'Of course, she will not know us you understand,' said Sarah. 'We will have quite a lot of explaining to do. You say she is well?'

'Physically she is very well,' said Matron, 'and she is generally cheerful and bright. Only occasionally these days does she fall into deep depression where we can hardly reach her. She is improving all the time. Here we are.' She knocked at the door and opened it.

'Hello, Mrs. Partridge! May we come in? Here are the visitors I told you about.' Sam and Sarah were ushered into the large room which served as both bedroom and sitting room. The slim lady with greying hair was sitting by the window watching the sea and she turned as they went in. Then, to the surprise of them all, she stood up and came across the room, her arms outstretched, an expression of tearful excitement on her face.

'Oh, here you are at last, my dears. I've waited so long but I knew they would find you. Matron, isn't this a marvellous day? Oh! I can hardly believe it, but here they are, Matron. This is my daughter, Margaret and her dear husband, Frederick!'

Thelma Partridge gathered Sarah up in her arms and smothered her with hugs and kisses, soon taking in Sam to her joyful embrace, crying and laughing at the same time. 'Oh, come and sit down do, both of you. Dear me! I've waited so long for this day to come. I knew it would. I knew if I waited long enough and prayed hard enough you would come back.' Over the shoulders of the ecstatic woman the three other occupants of the room exchanged alarmed glances.

'Humour her, please,' was Matron's whispered advice. And louder, to Mrs. Partridge, 'Yes, sit down with your visitors, dear, and I will order some refreshments for you all.' As she left them this kindly woman hoped fervently that this young couple would be able to handle the tricky situation in which they found themselves.

Thelma Partridge was bubbling over with talk. Sarah was glad of it, for she had no idea what to say, how to react. Sam busied himself arranging her cushions and seeing that she was sitting comfortably whilst his mind dug frantically for recall of the course in psychiatry that had been part of his training. Yes, Matron's right. We should not face her with flat denial of who she thinks we are. Too much of a shock coming close upon the heels of her joy.

The visit was a bizarre affair. Sarah was immensely sorry for this woman whose life had been shattered by the sudden deaths of her daughter and her son-in-law, yet she found it very difficult to go along with her belief that she was that lost daughter, even for the short time they were there. Matron was at pains to ease the situation as much as she could, coming in with cups of tea and staying for short periods throughout the visit to help the conversation along. Strangely, and to Sarah's great relief, Thelma Partridge appeared to have no desire to delve into the past, to enquire when and how her daughter had returned, nor did she seem fully aware of the circumstances of her absence. It was as if Margaret and Fred had been unaccountably delayed, were but a few hours late and, although she had made reference to their 'having been found', no further mention was made of their having been lost. Weird, thought Sarah as she fought to find the most suitable responses to Thelma's remarks.

Today the mother was picking up the threads of her life just where she had left off ... with one important difference ... there was no apparent awareness of Daisy and certainly no mention of the child. No, she was simply rejoicing in seeing Fred and Margaret again. And 'Fred and Margaret' were doing their best to fill the parts as kindly and thoughtfully as they could, being as they were, so deeply sorry for this woman whose mind was still so sick.

'Now, my dears, I must show you those photographs. I only picked them up the other day. Where did I put them?' Matron went to the chest of drawers and brought out a wooden box.

'This is what you want, isn't it, Mrs. Partridge?' and to Sam and Sarah she said, 'We have often spent time looking at these old photos and things. She'll enjoy showing you.' Matron was under the impression that these young callers had been acquainted with Mrs. Partridge's family some years ago, though Sarah had been careful to leave the details as vague as she dared. Thelma lifted the lid of the large deed box and began to lay the contents on the table in front of them. There were, indeed, many photographs but there were also many papers that Thelma quickly discarded in favour of snapshots and studio pictures of her family. Matron now excused herself.

'I have several things to attend to so I will leave you together for a while. I shall not be far away and you must feel free to ring this bell if you need me. Mrs. Partridge is quite happy at the moment.' She closed the door behind her. Her patient was, indeed, happily occupied, picking out photos to show them.

'Look, here we are, the three of us. This was the day you moved into the hotel. We were all so excited. Do you remember?' A similar snap to one of Daisy's was held up for them to see, taken on the steps to the front door of the Miller's Guest House in Columbus Ravine. As Thelma became more engrossed in the photographs she began to withdraw into a world of her own, becoming less aware of her visitors. Sarah watched as more items from the precious storehouse of memories were laid on the table, her sympathy overflowing for Daisy's grandmother. Sarah examined the pictures carefully, showing a genuine interest, especially in those that showed a small girl, little more than a baby. This was beyond doubt the same child they had visited in Retford, the same one who had turned up so dramatically on the night of the railway accident. The same bright eyes, the unmistakable dark curls, the shy smile. While the older woman's attention was elsewhere Sarah motioned to Sam, taking him on one side and saying in an undertone, 'We can be quite certain that this is Daisy, don't you think so? Just look at this one, the image of her.'

'Yes,' whispered Sam, 'no doubt at all. I wonder why she has not mentioned her though.' Sarah took the picture to Thelma.

'Do you know who this little girl is?' Thelma glanced at it briefly, but gave no reply. Sarah saw her hand begin to tremble and a pained expression took over from the smiling face.

'No, no, no, Margaret!' Her face became contorted and she began scrabbling madly with both hands amongst the contents of the box, finally upsetting the whole lot onto the floor, bursting into tears as she did so. 'No, no, no, Margaret!' she cried out again, a note of panic in her voice. Sarah took her hands, speaking to her quietly, while Sam knelt on the floor to gather up the flotsam of her life.

Gradually Thelma Partridge began to calm down. Sarah stroked her hands, telling her that all would be well, that no harm had come to her treasures, and watched with her as Sam returned the things to their box. As he did so something caught her eye. It was the unmistakable pink watermark that is typical of British Certificates of Birth. Sam saw it too. Sarah held her breath. The world seemed to stop revolving and the photographs became a grey blur. She found she could not move. Everything drifted into slow motion as Sam took out the paper and unfolded it.

Transfixed and frozen, knowing yet not knowing what was written there, Sarah watched, unblinking, as Sam's eyes scanned the brief but crystal clear message he held in his hands. Sam lifted his gaze from the paper with its elegant copperplate script and rested it on her own. For a long moment he looked into her eyes and the two of them seemed to be the only occupants of that room ... of the world. Quietly he passed the paper over to Sarah.

It was Daisy's Birth Certificate.

She was faintly aware of Mrs. Partridge's voice. It was as if it came from another room, talking about the figures she could see on the photographs, but completely unconnected with the here and now. She was back once more in that happy world of her own, safe from the realities of the present while Sarah's heart was performing somersaults and her mouth went dry.

Oblivious of Mrs. Partridge and her ramblings Sarah read the words that Sister Ruth had told her. When was that? It felt to be aeons ago. As time slowly regained its normal pace and the world began once more to turn on its axis Sarah let out a long sigh, glancing again at Sam. Though neither had spoken Sarah knew that the understanding between them was complete. He had read the words that told of the birth of Sarah's child. 'Mother's name, Sarah Grange. Father's name, unknown.' Sam had closed his eyes, wrapped his arms around his body and sank down into a crouch beside the treasure box. He remained there as Sarah gently folded the paper and replaced it in the box and when he straightened up again she could see the tears in his eyes spill over to be dashed away hastily as if he were ashamed of them. The uncertain magic of the moment was broken by a sharp, but laughing remark from Thelma.

'Good gracious, Fred, what on earth are you

doing there on the floor? Tell him to get up, Margaret, do. You make the place look untidy.'

'Well, it's been lovely to see you again,' he said, 'and we're both so glad to see you in good health.' He was trying desperately to keep his comments non-committal and dreading saying anything that might give rise to her distress or to her realising that they were not who she thought they were. Sarah took her hand.

'We will come again to see you very soon, if you would like that.'

'Oh, yes, indeed. Of course you must come, my dears.' She was fingering one of the photographs, absentmindedly looking at one of Margaret and Fred walking on the seashore holding the hands of a tiny girl. Pointing to her she said, 'I, I ... can't quite remember who this is, but ... I, I expect it'll come to me. I know my memory isn't all it should be.' She shook her head and a puzzled expression came over her face as she looked from one to the other of her visitors. There was a sudden blankness in her expression, a lack of recognition and fear, real fear, in her eyes. 'Oh, dear, oh dear ... Matron ... where am I? Who is it? Oh ... dear me ... I'm such a silly sometimes.' Her hands began to flutter and they could see tears start to fall on her flushed cheeks. Thelma Partridge was losing even the tentative touch she had on reality. Sam and Sarah were alarmed to see her becoming confused and distressed again. Sarah put an arm around the old lady's shoulders, kneeling on the carpet to look into her face.

'There, there, my dear, there's really nothing to worry about. Please don't be upset.' By this time

Sam had rung the bell and Matron was hurrying into the room.

'Now, what about a nice cup of tea, Mrs. Partridge?' The sight of the familiar face and uniform, the kindly voice, immediately calmed the agitated woman. Sam had collected up the photographs and returned the box to the sideboard. They made their exit from the room on tiptoe as Matron made comforting noises and plumped up the cushions for her patient. A couple of moments later she, too, emerged from the room, smiling rather ruefully.

'You can never predict when something will jog her memory and perhaps set her off. She obviously still has memories but most of the time something in her brain suppresses them ... perhaps as being too painful to bear. Poor lady! I think she will get better in time though. It may be a lengthy recovery, but she is quite young enough to make it, given the right help. I can't help wondering, in view of what has happened today, whether you might be just the people to bring her round. You will be calling again, won't you?' Neither answered straight away. Both were fully occupied with their own thoughts of what had turned up among the photographs and were hard put to fully concentrate on Matron's words.

'Yes, er, yes, we will come again, though I hope she doesn't continue to mistake us for her relations!' Sarah followed the Matron to her office, adding, 'There is something I must tell you before we go, if you can spare us a moment.'

'Certainly. Come into the office and sit down. I won't keep you a minute.' Sarah and Sam were both grateful for the short space of privacy this allowed them. There was much to be said but now was not the time. It was enough for Sam to take Sarah's face between his hands, look into her eyes and say, 'Sarah, I am so very sorry. I think I understand everything now.'

'Not quite everything,' she replied. It was, she thought, something of an understatement. Matron was coming back and Sarah just had time to smile and say, 'I think we can trust this woman, at least with part of our story. What do you say?'

'My instinct says she's alright. But don't tell her more than you need.' Matron was back in the room and declared herself ready to give them her full attention.

'Dr. Pearce and I would like to take you into our confidence. We do indeed hope that we shall be able to assist in Mrs. Partridge's recovery but that was not our prime reason for coming here. We are aware of some of her family history and we have looked her up hoping that she might help us in our search for ... well ... let us say ... help us prove...' Sarah was floundering for the right words, terrified to say too much, afraid to sound insincere. She looked at Sam for inspiration.

'What Sarah means is that she needs proof of identity of someone ... a person who you might say is connected both with Miss Grange and with Mrs. Partridge.' He held up his hand as if to check whatever it was that Matron was about to ask and went on, 'And, I believe that proof has been found, Mrs. Porter.' He used her real name for the first time as he prepared to ask of her the favour that Sarah needed. 'During our talk with

Mrs. Partridge we came across this.'

Sam took from his pocket the Birth Certificate, along with several of the photographs they had been shown. Sarah's swift intake of breath and shocked expression were not lost on Mrs. Porter. 'I had no intention of taking these without permission, please understand that. But when it became clear that the lady was so confused I felt sure it would trouble her further to ask for them. This is the Birth Certificate of Mrs. Partridge's adopted granddaughter, of whom she has no recollection at present. Miss Grange and I would be grateful if we could borrow it, along with these few photographs. It would only be for a short time and I assure you they will be returned in due course.'

Mrs. Porter looked from one to the other, unsure what to make of this, unsure how to respond. They seemed like trustworthy folk, but how could she tell? She knew herself to be a shrewd judge of character. You became used to the need to weigh people up pretty nimbly in her job and generally her gut feeling was correct. She had to be especially careful, however, where other people's belongings were concerned.

'Well...' she began, doubtfully. Sarah found her tongue again.

'Look, Mrs. Porter, how would it be if I write a statement to the effect that we have borrowed these documents and that we promise to bring them back. We can both sign our names to it in the presence of witnesses. That way you will have protected Mrs. Partridge's property as best you can. What do you say?'

'That would seem to cover it, I suppose. Yes, I think that will do.' Nodding her head she bustled off to find two members of her staff to witness their signatures.

Sarah was relieved beyond words that she did not read carefully the details on the birth certificate. She merely glanced at the unfamiliar entries, ensuring that the certificate was what it purported to be, that of a female child born in 1930.

Clutching in her hands the precious proof that her daughter had been born at St. Faith's and had apparently become a member of Mrs. Partridge's family, Sarah walked from the Lilacs Nursing home. She felt she had climbed a mountain during the past few hours. Emotionally drained, she was not really aware of anything as Sam guided her steps along North Bay Promenade towards the town. There was always a breeze up there and today it was a cold one, cold enough to make them shiver and hurry their pace, cold enough to bring Sarah's thoughts back into focus.

'Where are we going, Sam? It can't be too long before we'll need to catch the train.'

'We need to talk and we need to eat. We'll do both in comfort before we go home.'

Sarah was in no mood to argue as she allowed herself to be led into the small restaurant. They had two hours to spare before they needed to catch the train and she knew they would spend it coming to terms with the strange truth that she and Sam were the natural parents of Daisy Miller, and that this child had somehow blundered into both their lives. Willy-nilly they were now involved with and concerned about Daisy even though circumstance decreed they should be so at a distance. Sarah knew, too, that she would now have to take Sam into her confidence over the matter of Grandpa Grange's Will.

At the corner table near to the fire the waiters saw the two heads, dark and blond, close together, deep in conversation, with eyes for no-one but each other.

'Bit early in the season for a honeymoon-couple,' murmured the waiter to Jeff the barman as he polished glasses behind his mirrored counter.

'No accounting for taste, young man. Winter's as good as any time for such as those two.' And Jeff, whose great pride lay in his mixing of cocktails, swiftly shook and poured two of his best.

'Give them a Sidecar each with my compliments, will you.'

Chapter 25

1934–1935

Doris would always remember that terrible night when she was told that Joe had ridden headlong into the old mine-shaft. It ranked as being the worst moment of her life. The immediate terror about his injuries, quickly followed by fears over what might be the consequences of his accident had filled the dark night with dread. When they carried him in all that mattered was that he was alive and not dead like Sir Edward's beautiful hunter. Whatever injuries he had would surely mend, wouldn't they? She was sure of that and told him so over and over as the ambulance took them to the hospital in the centre of Leeds. She became impatient as the driver kept to a snail's pace as she watched Joe grow even paler.

'Can't you hurry?'

'Sorry, miss. Can't afford to jolt him, not with what's happened to him. You're never sure where his broken bones are. You just pray that his back's in one piece, m'dear and leave the driving to me, understand?' He spoke kindly but what he said filled Doris with new fears. His back? What if that was broken?

Visions of week after week in hospital for Joe, perhaps unable to walk, to sit up, even, filled her mind. How would they cope? Pain and suffering for the man who had never ailed a thing in his life, who had no patience with any kind of illness, who was impossible to live with when he had the merest cold in the head would be a daunting prospect indeed. Doris had a vague notion that hospitals and doctors cost money. Never mind, she would think about that tomorrow.

Joe was whisked away from her and she was asked to sit in a dreary waiting room until her husband's injuries were assessed. Nurses in stiffly starched white hats and smooth aprons bustled to and fro and Doris' heart missed a beat each time she thought that one of them might approach her. It seemed hours before a nurse in dark blue and white came and said, 'You can come and see your husband now, Mrs. Smithson. Follow me, if you please. You may find him sleepy. We had to give him some strong sedative.' The nurse chatted steadily to Doris all the way to Joe's bedside but she had little idea of what she had been told. Joe had regained some of his colour, the blood had been washed away leaving not a mark on the face that Doris was expecting to see gashed and badly wounded. She breathed a sigh of relief as he opened his eyes.

'Hello, Joe. Can you talk to me?'

'Very tired,' he said. So Doris sat by his bed and let him sleep until one of the doctors came to speak to her.

'He's had a lucky escape, it seems,' said the doctor. 'It could have been far worse. He has fractures to his collar-bone and his right elbow and his right leg has been badly crushed. It will take time, but he's young and fit. I've seen a lot worse than that recover during the war.'

'But, all that blood?' said Doris.

'Yes, I'll admit it did look bad when he was brought in, but it appears they had to shoot the horse he'd been riding while they were both down the shaft. Terrible for the poor chap, I'd say, but the blood came from the horse and not from your husband. Now, why don't you go and call a taxi and get yourself home. You look tired out and it's after midnight. We need to spend quite a time on Joe to get his fractures set and him patched up. Come and see him tomorrow and you'll see a big improvement.'

Doris let herself into the basement flat. She would have to be at Uttley, Uttley and Ross at the usual time in a few hours. Exhausted she dropped into bed promising herself that tomorrow she would think about all the problems that now gathered on her doorstep.

Riding to work on the tram the next morning Doris reflected on her situation, realising that, if she was to continue the search for the Grange child, which she had begun with such high hopes so recently, she would have to do it alone. She would have to do pretty well everything alone if it came to that. It would take many months for Joe's injuries to heal, she reckoned. Walking through the doors of the Solicitor's office was enough to remind her of what they had achieved so far, from that memorable day when she had eavesdropped upon George and Edith Grange's conversation and of how much more there was to be done.

A certain attitude of pique gradually began to infuse her thoughts. Now that Joe's life was no longer in danger she could allow the feelings of resentment and annoyance at his carelessness to come to the fore. And come they did. Sure, hadn't it been like this from the start? Joe falling about, getting into scrapes, drinking too much or spending all their money, turning to her to sort things out when he got them into mess after mess. Well, he had gone too far this time. This time he would do things her way or not at all, once he was on his feet again. In the meantime she would have to keep on track with the other business, the one that was going to make their fortune.

Keeping an eye on the comings and goings of the Grange family was not too difficult since there were often reports of their business or social lives to be seen in the local newspaper. She must keep herself up to date as the search for the child went on and hope that old Mr. G. remained hale and hearty in the bracing Morecambe air.

That day Doris left the office as quickly as she could, grabbed herself a sandwich and a cup of tea in the station buffet and walked over to the hospital to see Joe.

The curtains were pulled around his bed. She could hear undertones of conversation and she was alarmed to see the sister and two doctors talking gravely to Joe as she peered round the corner of the drapes.

'Ah, Mrs. Smithson.' It was the young doctor whom she had seen yesterday. In a very few minutes he and the other man, who turned out to be an orthopaedic surgeon, had explained simply to Doris just how serious were Joe's injuries. She paled. As well as the fractures to his elbow, shoulder and leg they had found several broken ribs.

'How he avoided head injuries I'll never know. He will need several weeks in hospital, I'm afraid. He must remain as still as he can until those ribs have healed.' He had addressed his remarks to Doris but Joe was not asleep.

'I'm not an imbecile, doctor. I can understand what you're talking about.' His tone was nothing short of nasty, reminding Doris painfully of how he had been before, before they had come to Leeds and he had found work on the estate.

'Joe! There's no need for that.' Doris was sharp and glanced apologetically at the other people round the bed. Joe glared and snarled,

'Well ... you can stop that whispering behind

my back.' The doctors and the nurse looked sympathetic and left Doris alone with Joe. Looking at him lying there in pain after what she knew must have been a frightening few hours she regretted her sharp tone of voice. She took his hand and said, 'They have been very kind, Joe. You just try to be patient and you'll get well all the quicker. Look, I've brought you the paper. You're quite famous, eh? There's a full report about the shaft collapsing. Someone says the old mine workings should have been clearly marked. Someone else says that nobody remembered they were there. There's a photograph of Sir Edward Lazenby.' But no matter what Doris talked about she could elicit no response from Joe other than grunts of disinterest. It was going to be a long haul. She had seen him in low spirits before and over far less than this.

It was towards the end of the following week that Doris arrived at Joe's bedside at the same time as Sir Edward Lazenby. His country tweeds and county accent set him apart. She guessed who he was. He told her he had been to see Joe several times and that he was devastated about the accident to his employees and particularly to Joe. He found his present truculent mood quite understandable, he said, and was at pains to ease matters as far as he was able. Would Doris be kind enough to spare him a few minutes before she left? Doris would.

'I feel so responsible, you see, my dear. Such a terrible thing to happen. I trust you and Joe will allow me to cover any medical expenses incurred?' His politely phrased question had Doris in mind to throw her arms round his neck, until she remembered her manners and accepted the suggestion with quiet good grace. Her ability to appear as something she was not was, as usual, quite masterful as she smiled disarmingly at Edward Lazenby. 'I have another proposal to put to you, Mrs. Smithson; one that you may like to think about for a while, since Joe will be here for some time yet. I understand you are employed at a solicitor's in the city?' Doris nodded. 'I'm sure that is a very agreeable job and I hesitate to suggest your leaving it, but I have an estate cottage available at present which I would like to offer to Joe, and you, of course. Joe could continue his recuperation there and you could care for him. The only stipulation is that you would work for me at the Hall in return. There, give it some consideration and if you think it worthwhile I'll leave it up to you to discuss it with Joe.'

Discussing anything with Joe in his present frame of mind was not something that Doris could entertain with composure. It took very little to set him off on one of his tirades and she was unsure how he would view the idea of moving to the Hall. For one thing he took unkindly to change of any sort in his life and for another he might not wish to feel beholden to the man who, indirectly, had been the cause of his present trauma. Cutting all ties with their present life without consulting Joe could be disastrous and she, herself, had doubts about surrendering their independence and tying themselves to the Hall. Perhaps Mr. Dobbs could be persuaded to allow her leave to nurse her husband back to health. It would be worth trying. If their stay at the Hall was a temporary arrangement Joe could hardly object, could he?

Doris sat up well into the night, huddled over the range, trying to decide on her answer to Sir Edward Lazenby. Getting out the papers from the bank she pored over the accounts that had been growing healthily ever since the pair of them had been in work and had paid off their debts. She smiled to herself. 'I think this is called hedging your bets' was her thought as she came to her decision. The following day she told Sir Edward that they would accept his offer. There was enough in the bank to keep the basement flat for several months if necessary and it would still be there for them if Joe wanted to go back. For the time being, however, she divulged nothing of this to Joe or to her new employer.

Events seemed to fly by in a hazy blur of activity, punctuated at intervals by short periods of extreme clarity that stayed with her for years, until Doris found herself living an entirely different way of life. She could recall as if it were yesterday the unpleasant scene with Joe when she had told him of Sir Edward's generous offer. How he had shouted and growled that he was quite able to look after himself and didn't require charity from such as that ... that ... well, Doris preferred to forget the language he had used. Nevertheless she had taken the decision herself to accept the cottage and the job that depended on it. It would not matter what was suggested to Joe these days. The reaction was always the same, belligerence and fury. Well, he could bellow and roar as much as he liked, Doris held the reins at present and she meant it to stay that way.

She remembered how Mr. Dobbs had a tear in his eye when she left, silly old buffer, telling her that she must return as soon as Joe was well. She smiled to herself at the way she had fooled him.

The day she moved their few belongings from the damp basement into the estate cottage she was already planning how she would ingratiate herself into this new society. Joe would just have to accept the new arrangements when he came out of hospital whether he liked them or not.

The cottage was a palace compared with their former accommodation. A living room, a kitchen, two bedrooms, one of which had been sliced in half to provide space for a tiny bathroom and toilet, plus a sizeable plot of land outside where someone had grown flowers and vegetables. Yes, the consequences of Joe's accident had not been all bad thought Doris as she settled in. This would do very nicely, thank you, for the next few weeks.

The work that she was expected to do was not particularly arduous. Even if it had been Doris was not one to shirk hard work if she could see a good reason for it. Her chief obligation was to the housekeeper, Mrs. Owen, who soon found that her new assistant was bright and willing. Doris knew well that pleasing your immediate superior was a wise move.

Cleaning, polishing, preparing vegetables for the cook, changing the linen and even helping out in the dairy occasionally were all jobs that fell to Doris. Once again she proved to be an ideal employee. She was storing up her good offices until such time, (she knew it would come), when she would need to ask for time off.

With typical single-mindedness Doris returned to the project in hand, namely the search for Sarah Grange's child, as soon as she was settled at the cottage. In all it had been delayed by only a couple of weeks and while she was occupied in seeing to their move and learning her new role at the Hall she was constantly thinking ahead and planning.

First she must contact Mr. Backhouse, having been so rudely interrupted in that purpose on the night of Joe's accident. She had decided to retain the pose as Sister Jane in her dealings with said gentleman, hoping to add a little kudos to her appeal, but even she was surprised at the speed with which she received a reply. She quickly scanned the opening paragraphs of polite preamble and thanks for her interest in these unfortunate children until she turned the page to find a list of the Northside children who had been relocated after the fire in Scarborough. Mark Backhouse went on to explain that they had called upon the help of Council Services as far away as London in their sudden need to re-house so many children.

And there it was. Miller, Daisy Frances, three years, transferred to 'Idle House', Retford, to the care of Mr. and Mrs. Johnson, foster parents.'

Joe had been in hospital for almost two weeks and, although his physical wounds had begun to heal, his frame of mind had not improved. If anything he had become more ill-tempered, morose and churlish. He showed no interest in anything apart from his own unfortunate situation. Assurances from the medical staff that he would make a complete recovery, given time, did little to lift his mood and Doris found herself dreading visiting times. She had tried to cheer him, to instil some optimism, to interest him in what had been happening outside the confines of the hospital ward, but she felt she was fighting a losing battle. Patience was a virtue held by neither of them in abundance and so it was not long before the lines of communication between them began to founder.

Even so Doris had arrived at the bedside breathless with excitement to share with Joe the news that she had finally tracked down Daisy Miller, wanting to discuss with him the way forward.

'What do you think, Joe? Should I go and see the girl? Should we wait until you're fit and go together?' This, of all subjects, she thought might strike a spark in him. She had tried telling him about their new home at the hall, her new job, how kind everyone had been, how so many people had sent words of sympathy and goodwill for his recovery, but to no avail. He was not interested. And now he turned away.

'How the hell should I know?' he growled.

'But, Joe, can't you see, we're getting nearer to the...' she looked around furtively but did not complete the sentence. 'You know what I'm talking about, Joe. Come on!' Her voice dropped to a whisper. 'Just think what a difference that money will make to our lives when you get out of here.'

'Oh, do what you bloody well like, woman! Just

leave me alonc, can't you. Just go away and leave me alone!' And he turned painfully to face the wall. Moving about was still difficult and added to his irascibility. So Doris took him at his word and stalked from the ward with her head in the air, looking neither to right nor left, holding her breath lest someone might see the tears welling up in her eyes. They were tears of anger and frustration rather than of sorrow. She brushed them aside and squared her shoulders as she rode home on the rattling, clattering tramcar. Fine, she thought, if that's the way he wants it she would leave him out of her plans for the time being. She only used him as a sounding board, someone to bounce her ideas off, someone to boost her own confidence. She could manage fine on her own.

Elsie Johnson picked up the letter from the doormat and examined the unfamiliar handwriting. She placed it in her apron pocket to read when the children had gone to school or, in the case of the younger ones, to play in the dayroom upstairs. She had a healthy distrust of unfamiliar handwriting. Her husband, coming in from an early shift at nine-thirty, found her engrossed in reading it.

'What've you got there?'

'Something quite out of the blue. Listen to this, Ernest. 'Dear Mrs. Johnson ... I was given your name and address by Mr. Mark Backhouse of Scarborough, the man who was in charge of rehousing the orphans from Northside Orphanage after the fire in 1933. Mr. Backhouse told me that you accepted two children from there, Anna Thorne and Daisy Miller. I am making enquiries on behalf of a close friend as to the whereabouts of Daisy Miller. Is she still with you? If she is still in your care I would be glad to be allowed to call on you to explain more fully my interest in Daisy and, if possible, to meet the child. I assure you that I have the best interests of Daisy in mind and I wait eagerly to hear from you. Yours sincerely, Mrs. Doris Smithson.' What do you make of that?' asked Elsie, looking up at her husband.

'Well, I'm not so sure what to make of it, love. Where's the letter come from? This person seems to have her facts right, as far as it goes.'

'The address is 6, Hayfield Cottages, Upton Hall Estate, nr. Leeds.'

'Mr. Backhouse must have considered her to be straightforward and honest to have passed on our address,' commented Ernest, thoughtfully.

'I suppose so. Well, the least we can do is to send her a polite reply and tell her that she may call by prior arrangement. As far as Daisy's concerned, perhaps we should not involve her until we're sure what this woman's about? She hasn't said much, but what she does say is quite intriguing, don't you think?'

'Hmm! Let's talk with her first. Nothing like a face to face chat, I always think.' And Ernest went off to change with a doubtful look on his face. He was guardian of these unfortunate children and guard them he would, especially little Daisy who had suffered so much in her short life and who had won the hearts of everyone in the household.

They moved Joe to a convalescent home at the

beginning of November, saying that he would be able to go home by Christmas. It was while he was there that Doris paid her first visit to 'Idle House'.

She dressed carefully for this excursion, quite determined to make a good impression on the Johnsons. Living and working so closely to the landed gentry she had ample opportunity to study their dress and manners, especially those of Sir Edward's mother and his sister who was a frequent visitor to the hall. He was, they said, the most eligible bachelor in the whole of the Ridings and there were many social events at which Doris would attend the guests and learn to mimic their ways. The purchases at the Alwoodley sales continued to swell her wardrobe though she was careful to dress suitably plainly when working. The journey by train to Retford took little more than an hour and Mrs. Johnson's directions were easy to follow as she found her way to Idle House on foot.

Both Elsie and Ernest Johnson were at home and both were curious about Mrs. Smithson. As she approached the house they noted her smart, almost fashionable clothes, the fox fur stole about her shoulders, her pert little red hat with the veiling that contrasted sharply with her otherwise black outfit, the gloved hands, the neat clutch-bag she carried. They were not to know that these finishing touches had been added in the railway station's ladies' room, well away from the prying eyes at Upton Hall. The formalities were soon over and Daisy's foster parents sat sipping tea with their visitor, not quite knowing what to make of her.

'You say you are interested in Daisy Miller. May we know why?' asked Ernest.

'Yes, of course. You see, my husband and I have recently become very friendly with a couple who came to live near us. At first I just went over to be neighbourly, to ask if she needed anything ... you know the kind of thing. But in no time we were firm friends and I discovered that she had been very ill, so ill, in fact that they had had to move to Leeds in order to attend the hospital there. She is getting better all the time. I should think she might be completely well again within the next few months.' Ernest was starting to fidget. He felt uneasy. He was not sure why.

'Has all this something to do with our little Daisy, then?'

'Quite possibly,' answered Doris. 'My friend, you see, has had some tragedy in her life. It has been the cause of the illness that she's now recovering from. I don't know all the details myself, but she told me that she had had a little girl some years ago. For reasons she has not yet explained to me the child was taken away. I guessed she was unable to care for her. But now that she is getting better my friend is anxious to find out where her baby is and if she is happy and well looked after. The doctors think that she'll be able to have her home again eventually. To cut a long story short, I offered to help in the search for the little girl. There's just a chance that Daisy is the one.'

'What has led you to our door?' asked Elsie.

'It was through an orphanage in Scarborough, to whom I wrote for help, that I found this place.'

'Yes, well, Daisy was in Scarborough, wasn't

she, dear,' said Elsie to her husband.

'Yes, though I have very little knowledge of her background other than that. I know she had been at Northside about eighteen months before the fire forced them all to leave. I know nothing about her parents at all, though once Mr. Backhouse mentioned that he thought there was a grand-mother somewhere in Scarborough.'

'Oh, really?' said Doris, veiling her sudden interest.

'Then your friends have never mentioned that one of them has a mother living in Scarborough?' Ernest threw her a searching look and for once Doris was unsure of herself for a split second. It was enough to alarm Ernest even more.

'No, but I am sure they would have done so if there was.' Elsie was at pains to lighten the atmosphere which had become rather strained, so she asked, 'What are their names, these friends of yours, Mrs. Smithson? Can I assume their name is Miller?'

'I am sure you will understand, Mrs. Johnson, that they wish to remain anonymous, just for the time being. These enquiries are so sensitive, you know, and she is still in something of a delicate state herself.'

'Quite so,' said Elsie, 'and with your enquiries at such an early stage, I suggest that it would not be advisable to let Daisy meet you as yet. It's cruel to raise their hopes of finding a family when one is not sure of ... anything. Perhaps you could call again when you become surer of your facts?' She could see that the woman was disappointed but her reply was easy and polite.

'Of course. But we do agree that Daisy came from Northside in Scarborough to live with you and that she is four years old. That's a good start. Tell me, has the child blue eyes and dark curly hair?' The Johnsons glanced uneasily at each other.

'Well, yes, she has both.'

'Then I'm sure I have something hopeful to report to my friends. We just need to look a little further and I feel sure we shall come back to you with positive proof. I would so love to re-unite these parents with their daughter. Thank you so very much for your time and trouble.'

Doris went over the afternoon's scene in her mind as the train took her home. She could not help smiling as she recalled the remark she had made about the child's eyes and hair. It had been nothing but a random choice. Surely luck had been on her side today. Once in the cottage she took out paper and pen and made notes so as not to forget any detail. It would not do to trip oneself up on a later occasion. What next? Another letter to Mr. Backhouse?

She must find out about Daisy's grandmother.

Chapter 26

1936

It was the day appointed for Sarah to attend the local hospital to have the plaster cast removed from her leg. The weather could not have been much worse but Sarah would not hear of postponement, pointing out that no-one knew how much longer these Arctic conditions might last.

'Andrew has promised to go with me. The sooner it's done the better and life can get back to normal. I'm thoroughly weary of dragging this weight along. One thing's certain, we shan't forget the winter of '36 in a hurry!' Now Jennie was watching from the window as they trudged into view looking like a couple of animated snowmen.

'Here they come, Mrs. Grange! Lord! What a struggle they must have had getting home. I'll get the kettle on directly.' Jennie made for the kitchen while Alice ran to open the door for Sarah and Andrew who was supporting her as she tried out her mended leg for the first time, free of its plaster casing. They stamped the snow off their boots in the porch and shook their clothing.

'How far have you had to walk?' asked Alice, looking anxiously at her daughter.

'Only from the tram stop, but that was far enough. The trams seem to be the only vehicles still on the move, apart from the odd horse-drawn cart. Oh, Jennie, thank you. That's exactly what we need right now.'

'Is your leg alright, dear? How does it feel?'

'I had trouble keeping it to the floor at first,' laughed Sarah. 'It felt so light, but I got used to walking in no time. Had to!'

'Tea for you, Andrew?' asked Alice.

'Thank you, Mrs. Grange. I'm needed back at the office. Sorry! Have to get a move on, you know how it is. 'Bye, Sarah.'

'Well, thank you so much for bringing...' But before Alice could finish speaking he had disappeared into the snow.

'Strange, he's usually only too pleased to stay,' said Alice.

'I'm afraid it's my fault. I've upset him, mother. You know I'm very fond of him and I hated to hurt him but it had to be done. I couldn't let him go on thinking that I would eventually agree to marry him, so, while we were trudging through the snow I told him.'

'Told him?'

'I told him about Sam.' It was a simple statement but it told Alice everything.

Sam had returned to Doncaster with full knowledge of the facts concerning the baby he had fathered and of George Grange's will. As he and Sarah had occupied the corner table in the little restaurant in Scarborough, following their visit to Thelma Partridge, she had told him everything including the steps she had already taken to carry out her grandfather's request.

During the journey home, and with a railway compartment all to themselves, they had admitted to each other that the feelings that had swept them along in a joyful delight at the end of their schooldays had remained and strengthened. Sarah's anger and reproach towards Sam for his apparent denial of his fatherhood was matched by his own at her keeping from him the knowledge of her pregnancy. But once they had faced these facts together and willingly forgiven, there was nothing to stand between them, nothing to prevent their taking up the romance where it had left off but now as older and wiser people. As the train rocked them gently through the wintry evening Sarah's heart had soared with happiness.

'I find it hard to believe that I've really found you again,' said Sam. 'I'm just so lucky. It's as if I've come home to where I belong.' He kissed her gently and Sarah snuggled into his shoulder.

'We found each other,' she said. 'And we found our daughter, too, even if she does belong to someone else now. Poor Daisy. She had a rough start in life didn't she, but I'm so glad she's living with such kind and loving people now. I'll be so relieved when I finally hand over Grandpa's money to them. As soon as this snow clears I intend to go and talk to Mr. Ross about the best way to go about it.' And they had talked about the series of events that had brought them together after more than six years and led them to find the child of their loving. Sarah knew that she would have to make matters straight with Andrew Marsden as soon as she could.

'Did Andrew take it very badly?' asked Alice.

'He just went very quiet. There wasn't much he could say without losing face and I did tell him that I truly value his friendship.'

'He must have known how much your father and I hoped the pair of you would get together, too. Poor Andrew, he's such a gentle fellow under that Viking skin.'

'I've tried to be fair with him, mother, for the past year or more. I didn't give him reason to think I'd be ready to settle down with him. It was his own idea to hang around hoping for all these months. I really think he'd persuaded himself that it was just a matter of time before I'd agree to marry him.'

'I expect he'll get over it, dear. He'll meet someone else, a man with his looks and personality. Bound to! And you were right to tell him before things went any further.'

The snow went on for weeks, heavy fall, slight thaw, heavier fall, making everyone's lives difficult except the children's. Sarah returned to her job at the mill, glad to be back to normal after so long as a semi-invalid. Not that she had been idle or even much disabled by the accident. She even had reason to be grateful for her injury for it had enabled her to travel to Scarborough and to Retford with Sam. Now he was back in Doncaster and did not expect any more leave for some considerable time. 'By the time I see you again I hope I'll have been able to organise the hand-over of the money to the Johnsons. I do hope that Tom Ross will be able to work out a way of doing it so that there will seem to be no connection with me. I really don't want Mrs. Johnson to realise that Daisy is my daughter.'

'There's no reason why she should.'

'The way things are at the moment you and I can see Daisy and the rest of her family as friends. I doubt very much whether we could go on doing that if they knew the truth about her parentage. In fact I'm sure we'd be obliged to disappear from the scene.' This was the practical view. And Sarah was an eminently practical woman.

But now that she had found Daisy, felt that tug at her heartstrings, looked into those eyes, so like Sam's, she knew that it would be the hardest thing she would ever have to face if she was prevented from contact with her. She knew she would follow Daisy's fortunes for the rest of her life, even if it meant she had to watch from afar.

While Yorkshire lay under a heavy blanket of snow its inhabitants curtailed their journeys to the briefest possible and almost entirely on foot. They went to their places of work and scurried home again. They trudged to church on Sunday and hurried back to firesides and roast beef dinners. Sarah decided that the interview with Tom could wait until the weather improved. Sam telephoned as often as he could. Sometimes he would call every day for a week and then the calls would stop for a few days and Sarah would know that he was on night duty.

Sarah had telephoned Elsie Johnson to ask after Daisy, and Elsie had assured her that the children were 'having a whale of a time' in the snow and that she was having a job keeping up with a supply of dry clothes.

Although the two women were from very different walks of life they had liked each other from the first. Sarah had wondered if Elsie Johnson's closeness to Daisy had influenced the way she viewed her, but each time they spoke together Sarah became increasingly sure that Grandpa Grange's money could go to no one better. Those six children were cared for with love. It showed in their faces though they lived in cramped quarters and had a minimum of playthings. Sarah could see that they had learned to create their own entertainment from very little. The house was full of books, albeit second-hand, and the children's minds and souls were nurtured as much as their bodies. They were good people, Elsie and Ernest, and she was so grateful that Daisy had been sent to them. With the money that was coming to them they would be able to buy a bigger house with a garden where the children could play safely, have more bedroom space and room to do homework or follow their chosen hobbies.

The thaw began at last to everyone's relief. Late snowdrops, daffodils and primulas hurried into flower after their long winter wait. Sarah was happy. She knew that Sam's year as Junior House Officer would soon be over and they would become officially engaged. She was anxious now to get on with the task set by her grandfather.

Tom Ross was the youngest partner in the law firm but still Sarah did not relish having to confide her most private secret to him. Tom smiled as Sarah explained the lengths to which her grandfather had gone to conceal her past.

'That's just like the old man, Sarah. He had a heart of gold. Yes, I assure you that what you've told me will go no further. I can arrange for the foster parents to receive the legacy through the firm. You will need to come and see me again in a few days when I have drafted out some paperwork and let me have the envelope containing the cash. Between us we can sort things out to everyone's satisfaction I'm sure.' He consulted his diary. 'Let's see, could we meet again on Tuesday week? Ten-thirty, say?'

'Yes, I'm sure that will be fine and thank you, you have been most understanding.'

Later that day she told Alice and John what had been said and what she had arranged with Tom.

'Once I'd showed him Daisy's Birth Certificate he had no hesitation in agreeing to my request. It'll all be settled within the next two or three weeks.' Sarah sighed. 'I hadn't realised how much it's been pressing on my mind. I'll be glad to have it all done and dusted.'

A couple of days later Sarah, with David and her parents, were sitting round the table, when there was a telephone call for Sarah. She fully expected to hear Sam's voice and it took her a while to recognise the caller. It was Elsie Johnson.

'Oh! Mrs. Johnson. It's good to hear you.' Elsie was always conscious of the expense when she used her telephone and never spent time on trifles. She launched into her message without delay.

'Ernest said I should speak to you right away, you being so interested in our Daisy. We're not quite sure what to make of it so we haven't told Daisy yet. But it could be very exciting for her. You see, yesterday those people who took her on a day out before, you know, when the train crashed. Well, they came to the house again. It came as such a shock to us, Miss Grange, I can tell you. They say they are her real parents. They're going to claim her as their daughter.'

'What?' Sarah almost shrieked.

'Ernest isn't too sure about them even now. We didn't really take to them and Daisy was quite upset when she got home after that weekend with them, but then I reckoned that could be down to the train crash and all.'

'But ... Elsie, just a minute...' but there was no stopping her.

'Anyway, I thought I should let you know. It would be lovely for Daisy to go home with her real parents after all this time. She deserves a bit of luck, poor little thing.'

'Wait! Let me get this clear.' Sarah's brain was having difficulty making sense of Elsie's message. 'They claim Daisy is their own child, is that what you're saying? And these are the same people who were with her on the train?'

'Yes. Well, not their own child exactly. Their adopted daughter.' Sarah took a deep breath, trying to clear her mind of confusion. Elsie's voice carried on.

'There doesn't seem much doubt about who they are. They showed us the Adoption Certificate. Their names are Frederick and Margaret Miller. Miss Grange? Are you there?'

'Yes ... yes, I'm still here. Do forgive me. This has taken me by surprise to say the least.'

Sarah needed time to think. 'Would you do me a great favour, Mrs Johnson? Would you allow me to telephone you back and talk to you more fully? And, meantime, would you be so kind as to say nothing to Daisy about it?' Elsie must have picked up the note of anxiety in Sarah's voice.

'Yes, of course you may.' She hesitated. 'Is something wrong, Miss Grange?'

'Maybe, I can't be sure. I'll ring back within the next couple of hours. You did say it was the same couple who took Daisy on the Leeds train early in January?'

'Yes.'

'I'll call you back. Goodbye, Mrs. Johnson.'

Sarah excused herself from the rest of the meal and went up to her room. The events and circumstances that had brought her into contact with Daisy Miller had seemed to her like a series of coincidences, difficult to believe at first, but which had, so far, stood up to scrutiny in every respect. This little girl it would appear was none other than her own daughter whose short history had unfolded unbidden before Sarah's eyes. Now, without warning, comes this bizarre twist to set her emotions jangling and her thoughts to confusion. Sitting on the window seat where so often she had found peace of mind she watched the watery, late afternoon sun making shadows and patterns on the garden. She tried to recall everything she knew about the people whom she had first met briefly in a railway carriage so short a time before the train had come to grief. At first they had seemed merely strangers who had happened to cross her path but gradually they had begun to feature in the course of events that followed the night of January 9th, events that had led to her reunion with Sam and to the discovery of her daughter.

Sarah must have sat there, thinking, for well over half an hour until her head felt clearer and she was ready to talk to Elsie Johnson again. The more she thought, the more disturbed she became. There were questions she needed to ask. More than that, she needed to know how all this might affect the business that was even now being undertaken by Tom Ross. Slowly Sarah went downstairs.

'Hello, Mrs. Johnson, this is Sarah Grange speaking...'

'Oh, yes, Miss Grange?'

'I want to thank you for your call this afternoon. You know that I've become extremely fond of Daisy during the weeks since the railway accident. No-one would be more pleased than I to see the child settled with her legal parents, though I must say she seems very happy indeed living with you.'

'Thank you, we try to do our best for them all, you know.'

'I realise that I have no right to interfere, but there were a couple of things that worried me about your news. For instance, their name. I felt sure that you had mentioned a different name ... something beginning with "S" I had thought ... and Daisy called them Auntie Doris and Uncle Joe. Now you say their name is Miller?' Sarah had to be very careful about what she said to Elsie Johnson. She must not reveal the details that she had unearthed about Daisy's history. That would be both foolish and dangerous.

'They explained it all to us,' answered Elsie. 'It was a strange tale, but it seemed to make sense in the end. Ernest was very sceptical to start with. He said it was hard to believe such a story, but eventually he had to agree that it was just odd enough to be the truth and, in any case, he said, why would anyone want to make up something like that?'

'Like what?' enquired Sarah.

'Well, they told us they had been using the name of Smithson for the past few years, that their reasons were quite complicated but that their real names are Mr. and Mrs. Miller, Frederick and Margaret. They had adopted a little girl about six years ago, there had been some sort of accident and the baby had gone to an orphanage, and they had lost touch. Now they were sure they had found her and produced the Certificate of Adoption to show us. Up till then my Ernest was having none of it, I can tell you, but he had to take notice then.' As Elise paused for breath Sarah framed her next question with care.

'Did you think it seems genuine, the certificate I mean?'

'Ernest made a note of the details. I can read you what it says if you like but I don't think I could tell if it's genuine or not. It's written on paper from a Convent in Scarborough.'

Sarah felt as if someone had poured icy water over her. She listened, motionless as Elsie read out the details she herself knew so well.

'It's signed at the bottom by Sister Ruth and by a doctor ... yes ... Dr. Constance Bennett.'

Sarah shook herself out of her stupor. Either these people were genuine, (in which case what happened to the story that the Millers had perished in an aeroplane crash?) or there was something dreadfully wrong in all this.

Once again she felt she needed time, time to investigate, but it would be hard to explain to the

Johnsons why all this had anything at all to do with her. As far as they were concerned she was just an interested acquaintance of Daisy. What business had she offering advice or opinion? Nevertheless she must persuade Elsie to hold her horses before allowing these people to lay claim to Daisy Miller. Ideas flew through her mind like some crazy, speeded up silent movie until she grasped one as it passed.

'Mrs. Johnson, I can tell that you still have doubts about this couple. Do you mind if I make a suggestion?'

'Not at all, I'd welcome a second opinion.'

'Until you are both entirely sure that these are really Daisy's adoptive parents I feel that you should protect Daisy from contact with them and get proper legal advice about the Smithsons or Millers or whoever they are. Personally I'm suspicious of anyone who uses an assumed name.' She dare not say more.

'That's what Ernest said. But lawyers are expensive, Miss Grange, you'll forgive me.' This was exactly what Sarah had hoped she would say.

'It so happens that I have a friend, a solicitor quite used to dealing with family law, who might help us with this. Probably he would do it as a favour to me. If you like I could mention it to him?'

'Oh, Miss Grange, would you?'

'Of course. We may have to wait a little. You know how busy these people are. In the meantime perhaps you could tell the Millers that you are taking legal advice. If they're genuine they won't mind waiting, I'm sure. Where are they, by the way?'

'Gone back to where they live, somewhere in Leeds, I think.'

'As soon as it can be arranged I'll ask my solicitor friend to see you. Give Daisy a hug from me. Tell her nothing. I'll call again very soon.'

'Thank you so much, Miss Grange. You have taken a weight off my mind. I'll go and tell Ernest. Goodbye.'

A weight off your mind perhaps, thought Sarah, but a considerable one on mine ... and just when I felt things were coming to a successful conclusion. Are you watching all this, Grandpa Grange?

Chapter 27

Sarah's first step, after confiding Elsie's alarming news to Alice, was to tell Sam. It was about eight thirty in the evening when she eventually managed to get through to him and it took him a few moments to tune in to who was calling.

'Sarah! Darling I wasn't expecting to hear from you tonight. Is something the matter? You've that worried tone in your voice.' This she thought was quite astute of him since all she had said so far was 'hello' and that she had been trying to reach him for some time.

'I've had a call from Mrs. Johnson.'

'Mrs. Johnson ... who...? Oh, yes, I know, Daisy's foster mother, you mean? Sorry, darling, you'll have to excuse me. I've just come off an eighteen-hour shift and the brain cells are moving like slugs. Carry on! I'm with you now.' And she relayed the message that had come that day from Elsie Johnson. Sam listened with growing surprise and concern.

'So those people who had Daisy with them on the train are now claiming to be her adoptive parents?' he questioned.

'That's what Elsie said. Their real name is Miller but they've been using assumed names for some unknown reason, calling themselves Smithson for years. They said something about a serious accident and having had to place their child in an orphanage. It could fit with the history that we know about Daisy's past. Strange, isn't it, that they've turned up now, just when you and I have discovered Daisy ... and ... everything,' she added vaguely. Sam became thoughtful and Sarah wondered whether the line had gone dead.

'Yes ... sorry ... I'm still here. Did Mrs. Johnson say what these two looked like? Remember, we saw Daisy's photographs of her parents.' And, though he refrained from mentioning it to Sarah, Sam had seen other photographs of the family while looking through Thelma Partridge's box. Sarah's mind flew back to the day they had both visited Daisy, only a week or two ago and she was suddenly excited.

'Sam! You're a genius! Of course we have seen their picture. But I'm afraid I didn't take very much notice of the details and, anyway, the figures are so small on those tiny snaps.'

'Why don't you have another word with Mrs. Johnson. Remind her about Daisy's photographs.

Looking at them might help her to decide whether they're bona fide people.'

'Yes, a good idea. I'll speak to her tomorrow. You know, Sam, each time I learn something else about Daisy I feel closer to her, more involved, more concerned about her. All I want is for her to be safe and happy. I know she is that now with Elsie but how much better it could be for her if these people turn out to be the Millers. I find it hard to believe that they are the couple I saw on the train. You know, their strange behaviour after the crash when they left the train in such a hurry. As if they didn't want anyone to know they were passengers. Very odd.'

'But, if they were using assumed names, perhaps they were reluctant to be interviewed by the authorities,' suggested Sam. 'Who knows?'

'One thing is sure. The handing over of the legacy is going to have to be postponed until this is all sorted out. I have to be sure who is Daisy's legal guardian before we can proceed with that.'

'Will you contact Tom Ross in the morning?'

'Yes. I told Elsie that I have a friend who might help her to prove Daisy's parentage beyond doubt. I'll pick up the bill for any work Tom does, but really I was just trying to give us some time in which to make discreet enquiries. I'll put Tom in the picture as soon as I can.'

'I would like to help, darling. I wish we knew more about the Millers.'

'So do I. I was stunned when I heard they had shown up at "Idle House" when I thought they were dead. But I really had no proof of that. We were told of it by the receptionist at the hotel in

Scarborough. After all, she may have got it all wrong or been referring to some other couple named Miller.'

'Look, Sarah, I reckon you've enough to cope with in dealing with Tom and Mrs. Johnson. Leave that other matter to me, will you, darling? I'll see what I can find out.'

'But I thought you were up to your eyes in work just now.' There was a slight pause before Sam replied, very gently, 'Have you forgotten whose child she really is, my love? I am as concerned as you are that Daisy stays with the right people and that the legacy follows her. Let me do my bit for her if I can ... and for her mother.' There was such a depth of feeling in his voice that tears sprang to Sarah's eyes. Not for the first time did she feel sharp pangs of regret and guilt that she had kept from Sam the knowledge of his child all those years ago. It could all have been so different.

'Thank you, Sam,' she managed to stammer out through the emotion that threatened to overwhelm her. 'Thank you so much. We'll speak again soon.'

Tom Ross was surprised when Miss Grange requested another appointment to see him. He had been occupied in drawing up papers which would legally transfer certain monies from the trusteeship of Sarah to the foster parents of Daisy Miller, nee Frances Grange but he readily agreed to see her at eleven thirty that morning. Sarah explained to colleagues in her office at the mill that she would not be in to work until after lunch at the earliest and, before going to see Tom she made another call to Elsie Johnson.

There was a conflict raging inside Sarah. On the one hand the emergence of Daisy's legal parents was to be applauded, indeed she could think of nothing better for the child than the prospect of returning to a stable life with the Millers. On the other hand she could not help harbouring doubts, probably borne out of the instinctive dislike she had felt for these people on the one occasion she had met them, and from the knowledge that Daisy herself had been so afraid that she had run to hide away from them on the train. There was some intangible sense or notion that bothered her, a presentiment that something was wrong, and she could not put her finger on what it was. Perhaps, she thought, it was just her own maternal instinct fighting, even at this late stage, against the process of adoption. She sighed deeply as she walked to the telephone and dialled the number that would reach 'Idle House'.

Elsie answered straight away. Sarah needed a good excuse to call again so soon. She crossed her fingers to protect herself from the wrath of the Gods and the displeasure of Tom Ross as she took it upon herself to tell Elsie that he would be only too pleased to call and advise her and Ernest. She was sure that Tom would agree but, nevertheless, she knew she was taking a liberty.

'Oh, Miss Grange, that is so kind of him, and thank you for arranging it.'

'No trouble at all, Mrs. Johnson, I assure you. You told me something about Mr. and Mrs. Miller when last we spoke. I wonder, did they tell you their reasons for waiting so long before looking for their daughter?'

'Oh, yes, Miss Grange. They made no bones about telling us the full story. They both went through a terrible time, I can tell you, before they decided they could try to get Daisy back.'

'What made them decide?' Sarah wanted as much information as she could learn from the kindly foster mother.

'This was not their first visit, you know, but it was the first time that they told me their real names. We thought it was because they were now ready to be Daisy's parents again. You see they've only been back in England for a couple of years or so.'

'Back in England?' Sarah was baffled.

'Yes. You see, they had adopted Daisy in January 1930 and took her to live with them in the small hotel they ran in Scarborough. In September the following year they had won a competition, something to do with the hotel business. The prize was a trip by aeroplane to Paris. On the return journey the aeroplane had run into a storm over the Channel and crashed into the sea. They were close to the French coast when they came down and they clung to wreckage until they were picked up by a French fishing boat.' So, the story she had been told had been right thought Sarah as she asked, 'They came out alive from a crashed aeroplane?'

'Yes, apparently so. Mr Miller had serious injuries to his head, back and legs and he still walks with a limp. He thinks he might have been unconscious for a time. Mrs. Miller escaped more lightly from physical harm but the terror of the whole accident affected her mind. She didn't know who she was or that she had a baby waiting for her at home. In fact, she said that neither of them could remember very much to start with. They were given shelter and care by sympathetic local folk and stayed in the French fishing village while their injuries healed.'

'Were they the only survivors from the plane?' Sarah ventured to ask as Elsie paused to take a breath.

'I don't know. They never said. Mrs. Miller explained that her husband was afraid for her state of mind when he recovered somewhat himself. He felt she would not be strong enough to cope with the child or even accept it as her own until her memory returned, if it ever did, and so he decided they would stay in France for the time being, hoping that time would heal her. He told everyone that their names were Joe and Doris Smithson.'

'Why did he do that?'

'He didn't want to be found and taken back to England. He knew that neither of them could cope with life and certainly not with a small baby. That's why they stayed away for four years.'

'And then? They did come back?'

'Yes, when they were both quite well again. Mrs. Miller said they decided to remain as the Smithsons for a while, until they were ready to look for their little girl. She said they felt they must earn some money, set themselves up properly, before they could offer Daisy a home again.'

'Did she tell you where they had left her when

they went off to Paris in an aeroplane?'

'Yes. They weren't worried about her because they'd left her with her grandma, Mrs. Miller's mother.'

'I see,' said Sarah, her mind overcrowded with all that Elsie had told her. 'Well, there seems to be little doubt of who they are but I still think you would be wise to wait until Mr. Ross has looked into things before you say anything to Daisy. By the way, has Daisy ever showed you the photographs of her family?'

'Oh, yes, Miss Grange, several times. I must say the Millers have changed a bit but you'd expect that, wouldn't you, with all that they've been through?'

Alice popped her head round the dining room door as Sarah rang off.

'You've been a long time on the 'phone, darling. Is everything alright? Your father said you weren't going to work this morning.'

'I've an appointment with Tom. I was talking to Mrs. Johnson. It's a long story, mummy. I'll tell you all about it over lunch. Must dash now.' And Sarah hurried to her meeting with Tom Ross, her head full of the Miller's tale of disaster and recovery.

Tom Ross sat opposite his earnest and worried young client, his hands clasped and resting on the desk, his expression full of concern as he heard of the sudden resurrection of Daisy's adoptive parents. He listened without interruption as Sarah quoted Elsie's words to her that morning.

'You say they have the Certificate of Adoption?'

Sarah nodded.

'Mrs. Johnson read it to me. It appears to be signed by the right people ... and yet ... I know it's a lot to ask, Tom, but would you ... er ... could you arrange to go and see the Johnsons, take a look at the document, do whatever's necessary to make sure all's well before the money's signed over?' Sarah was so nervous that her words fell over each other as she spoke. Tom Ross smiled.

'Don't look so worried, Sarah. You can rest assured that your grandfather's money will only be handed over when I am absolutely certain of the legitimacy of persons involved. And yes, I believe I could make it my business to meet with Mr. and Mrs. Johnson ... since you are such a special client of mine.' There was a twinkle in his eyes, but Sarah still looked solemn. 'What is it, my dear?'

'It's ... well it's a trifle delicate, but you understand that the Johnsons need legal advice, but ... well they ... what I mean is that I will see to the...' Tom stood up and came round the desk, chuckling. Taking her hands he raised her from the chair.

'Our firm has been serving the Grange family for over eighty years. We trust each other and I may say that we are friends, too. There will be no talk of bills for the Johnsons, my dear. It will all be part of the execution of George's will. Now, go home and leave everything to me. You'll hear from me the moment I have anything to tell you.' Sarah thanked him. She thought it sounded inadequate, just 'thank you, Tom'.

After Sarah had left Tom sat for some time jotting down notes and musing over the situation.

Sometimes he felt that his job was more like that of a detective than a lawyer. He would need to check the veracity of the Miller's story. On the face of it, though unusual, it seemed quite credible. But there were parts of it that worried him, for example, what sort of person was it who survived an air crash and chose not to inform his nearest and dearest of the fact? Perhaps not the sort of person you might want to take over the bringing up of a little girl. Tom returned to his list of notes with renewed vigour. It would be easy to verify the aircraft accident. He would begin with that. He gathered his papers and picked up the telephone.

Ten days had passed since Sarah's visit to Tom's office and she was beginning to feel anxious again. Not only that, but she had not heard anything from Sam, either. Each time she had tried to contact him at the hospital in Doncaster there had been some reason why he could not come to the telephone. Going to work each day and immersing her thoughts in textile design helped to keep her from fretting but it was with great relief that she saw on the doormat an envelope addressed to her with Uttley, Uttley and Ross stamped on the back Sarah rushed to open the envelope and, with very mixed feelings, read Tom's words.

'Dear Miss Grange,

I have now completed the enquiries regarding the matter of Mr. and Mrs. Miller and I have pleasure in informing you that, in my opinion, these people seem to be the genuine adoptive parents of the child now named Daisy Miller. The Adoption Certificate is, without doubt, authentic and the loss of the aircraft has been confirmed by the Civil Aviation Authority as on the date specified in September 1931. Further details I will not commit to this letter, but these may be discussed with me at your convenience.

I feel that we are now in a position to proceed with the business required by your Grandfather's will. As I await your further instruction, I remain,

Yours sincerely,

Tom Ross

Sarah knew that she should be pleased. It was the right result for Daisy, wasn't it? And Tom Ross knew what he was about; she trusted him entirely. So what was holding her back? She needed to talk to Sam but he was still busy each time she rang.

Reluctantly she drafted a reply to the solicitor, suggesting that Tom should arrange to travel to Idle House to oversee the official transfer of Daisy into the care of the Millers. Sarah knew that his presence was not legally required but she knew also that Elsie and Ernest would be more content to let Daisy go if he were there. He could use this pretext to save himself a further interview with the Millers, killing two birds with one stone, in fact, and delivering George Grange's legacy at the same time. Much as she would have liked to be there herself she realised that leaving all to Tom was the wisest move. Or was it? Her pencil came to a halt over the paper, her gaze settling blankly on the flowers on the wallpaper as her mind mulled over what had to be done. Some of the details, she now realised, had not been made clear to her. For instance, had her grandfather stated whether or not his name should be put to the legacy or whether he was to remain an anonymous benefactor, only to be known to Daisy's guardians as her great-grandfather? She really must check this point with Tom. He would know, wouldn't he? Oh, dear, how confusing it all was.

She returned to the drafting of her letter which soon ran to a second page. She read it through, not altogether satisfied with it but too tired to think any more. She would finish it later. One thing was certain, if Grandpa Grange's name was to be revealed it would not take a genius to make the connection with Sarah herself. Bang would go her plans to keep in touch with the child. She would have to beat a hasty retreat, keep out of sight. It would never do to let Daisy or the Millers guess her identity. The upsetting of apple carts was not something that Sarah Grange had ever indulged in and she did not intend to start now. Nevertheless, the prospect of cutting ties for a second time filled her heart with sadness tinged with dread. Oh, where was Sam? She yearned to talk things over with him.

Sarah took herself off for a walk as far as the edge of the moor. The fresh air revived her and, as always, she thanked the powers that be for providing the beauty and space of the Yorkshire countryside, right on her doorstep, with its solid stone walls straddling the fields, the great outcrops of millstone grit, the houses spreading up the hillsides, clinging to them for security. She turned and looked down across the valley where smoke from a hundred mill chimneys blackened buildings and sat upon the city like a cowl on a still day. Straightening her shoulders she made for home and the letter that was still incomplete.

An hour later the draft was done. She had confided to Tom her disquiet at the outcome of his enquiries about the Millers but added that her acceptance of his decision was total. (She still privately felt she would have much preferred the money to have gone to Elsie and Ernest Johnson to help Daisy and the wonderful home they strove to provide for their charges). Her letter also asked Tom whether it would be possible to make Daisy's legacy anonymous, merely naming the benefactor as a great-grandparent. It was imperative, she wrote, that her own connection with the Will was not revealed. Sarah re-read what she had written a dozen times. The words sounded as ill at ease as she was feeling. Even now she was not sure that it was an acceptable request to make. The letter, still in rough, lay on the table full of crossings out and alterations as Sarah went down to join her parents for dinner.

'You've been up there a long time, darling. Been reading?' asked her mother.

'I've been trying to compose a letter to Tom Ross. Just a bit tricky!' Sarah smiled.

'I expect he'll see to everything, won't he, dear? Have you finished it?'

'Almost. It will need copying before I can post it but that's all. Better get it over with, done and dusted, all tickety-boo, you know, make Grandpa proud of me.' She tried to make light of things.

But Alice could still hear the sadness in her

daughter's voice and her heart went out to her. Part of her wished that Grandpa Grange had left well alone.

Chapter 28

The weeks of bitter winds and deep frosts of winter 1936 had exceeded those of earlier years in severity and had done their best to turn the ground to stone. The recent snowfalls had been memorable, transforming the land into a Christmas card scene and, although Joe had been declared fit to return to light duties, there had not been much for him to do apart from the daily care of the horses. They were exercised briefly each day in the paddock next to the home farm to give them a breath of fresh air but they were not ridden for sport or pleasure in this weather.

The Smithsons' recent excursions in pursuit of Daisy Miller had been doubly difficult since public transport had been so badly disrupted by the arctic conditions. One journey, indeed, Doris reflected, could have cost them and Daisy their lives, had they been travelling in another part of the train. But they had managed this last, this one really essential trip without any mishap. They had carefully presented themselves at Idle House, for the second time, as the Millers. They had met with the lawyer, Mr. Ross and had shown him the proof of their identity. They had come home well pleased with themselves.

The pair of them sat close to the fire in the cottage on the Upton Hall estate. Doris watched the flames dancing up the chimney. It was almost a week since their meeting with Mr. Ross. Now all they could do was wait, wait for the letter that would tell Doris whether or not her months of investigations, her devious collection of evidence, her frantic preparations during the past couple of weeks had borne fruit. It had been a sudden and complete reversal of the leisurely pace at which she had been working when, on that fateful weekend of the derailment, she had learned of the death of George Grange.

She and Joe had returned to Leeds to spend the night at the flat before returning to their cottage and it was as they were crossing the station to catch the tram that Doris had seen the newsboard that proclaimed the mill-owner's passing. She had gripped her husband's arm.

'Joe! Stop, Joe'. He had looked bewildered as she dragged him to the newspaper stand where he saw the headline that had caught Doris' attention. Swiftly paying for the paper she had moved to an empty bench where she sat down, her face quite pale and shocked. She had only read the first few lines and had turned to Joe.

'Yes, it is him! How could I have missed it? This is a tribute to his life and work. He died last week, Joe. The funeral's on Monday!' She had jumped up and begun slowly to pace the pavement as she read the details, hardly believing that this death could have overtaken her with such stealth. Why, it was only just before Christmas, hardly a month ago, when she had read the report and seen him photographed as guest of honour at one of the Masonic dinner-dances. He was frequently over with his wife to play golf or Bridge, whichever the weather permitted. There had been no hint of ill-health, though he was getting on a bit now, she reflected.

She was glad that she was now almost ready to reveal herself as Daisy Miller's legal mother. There was no harm in being ready well before the will came into effect. That would, of course, require her and Joe to be ready to take on full parenthood of Daisy, a situation she had been putting off because of Joe's attitude. She was working on that and felt she needed more time to bring him round. But there was no more time.

She stole a glance at Joe as he sat behind his newspaper. He was better tempered these days but still prone to fits of depression when he would withdraw into a world where she could not follow. She recalled with a quick surge of anxiety the conversation they had had only a few days ago. She had been laughing, boasting of how clever they had been, how easy it was going to be to claim the legacy that came with Daisy.

'Just imagine, Joe,' she had said to him, 'soon we'll be able to buy that house we both like so much. We'll be able to buy whatever we like. Think of it, Joe!' Both of them had their sights firmly on the Grange money. It was the be-all and end-all of their existence for the time being. Both had pushed into the far recesses of their minds the thought that they would also be parents if this plan came to fruition. If Joe thought about it at all his mind backed away and refused to contemplate such a state of affairs. Doris would find a way round it, he thought, vaguely. On the one and only occasion when the subject had been broached openly between them Doris had quickly closed it again for fear that Joe's views would scuttle the whole scheme. She had no idea that he had such strong feelings nor where they had come from but they frightened her thoroughly. Joe had made it crystal clear that he had no intention of becoming a father to Daisy Miller. Not in the long term. He was adamant.

'Oh no, lady,' he had said, menacingly to his astonished wife, 'you can forget it if you thought that I'd take on the child for good. Bloody hell, woman, what use would that be, tying ourselves to bringing up the girl? No fear! As soon as we get the money we're off! Those Millers can disappear as quickly as they came and the brat can fetch up in some other orphanage a few hundred miles from here.'

And Doris had to make do with the conviction the she could always, in the end, get her own way with Joe. Well, she always had, up to now. She never again referred to this conversation. She would pretend it had never taken place. This present, urgent need to finalise their plans had her wondering just how difficult Joe was going to be.

The waiting was not easy. As each day passed Doris imagined the deceitful fabric of her story, so meticulously woven, so cleverly executed, being gradually unravelled, her lies being exposed by an over-zealous solicitor or some other busybody at pains to see justice done. The waiting was making her irritable and she could feel tiny icicles of fear begin to prickle into her confidence. Why Mrs. Johnson had needed to make such a fuss over checking all their details Doris did not know, but it had produced an anxious delay for her and Joe. What if...? Her fertile mind began to turn somersaults trying to devise some kind of escape route should the worst occur and everything go wrong. She pondered over the last few hectic days, wondering whether they had been convincing enough in their identities as Fred and Margaret Miller. Had she covered each and every eventuality in her account of their adventure in France, their years there and their return to claim their daughter? Was her new hair-colour and style enough to pass for Margaret's own? She held onto the thought that she held a trump card in the Adoption Papers. Even if, by some miracle, the dotty Mrs. Partridge should miss the items she had taken there was nothing to link their theft with Doris. Yet, after so many months of slow, careful and even leisurely planning, this latest whirlwind of activity had come as a shock. It would have been so easy to make mistakes. Doris got up and looked at her reflection in the mirror. She saw a tidy, respectable young woman, dark-haired and altogether different, even in the way she walked, from Doris Smithson.

No! Away with the doubts, she must not let them weaken her now. She and Joe would have to possess their souls in peace until they heard the opinion of Mrs. Johnson's lawyer, however long that might take. Then they must both be ready to play their parts convincingly. They had come this far without creating suspicion. There was no reason why anything should stop them now.

Sitting cosily, watching the flames in the grate, her thoughts once again drifted back ... back to the summer of '35 when Joe had been finally released from the convalescent home. She had had so much to tell him then.

During his stay there and in the hospital she had refrained from talking about the search for Daisy for fear of being overheard. The months spent recovering from his appalling accident had been a trial to him, especially at first when he had been in such pain. Doris remembered how difficult it had been to cope with his moods, his outbursts, despondency and tempers. But gradually, as the injuries to his body began to heal, so did his mind. It had taken many months but by the end of July 1935 they had allowed him home to complete his recovery. Doris had been living and working at the Lazenby estate for over six months. Joe's initial anger when he was told of the move was soon forgotten but he declared himself glad that Doris had kept on the flat. He was not at all sure that he would be able to carry on working with the horses. He had yet to try his skill in the saddle. If he had lost his nerve or even his love of the beasts ... well, he would know as soon as the weather improved, wouldn't he? But he had to admit that the thought of returning to the dingy basement flat did not appeal.

Doris enjoyed recounting to Joe how she had made two visits to Scarborough and one to Retford during his recuperation. She told him how she had contacted Mr. Backhouse again by letter, and in the guise of Sister Jane Bateman, asked him for any further information he might be in a position to give her about Daisy Miller. She even had the audacity to tell him that, through his previous helpful advice, she was hoping to be instrumental in providing Daisy and her guardian with some welcome news on the financial front. She did wonder, however, whether he might be able to tell her the whereabouts of Daisy's grandmother, the one who had looked after her briefly before she had been taken into the orphanage? His reply came at length. He had needed to make some searching enquiries but he was led to believe that she was now at 'The Lilacs' nursing home in Scarborough. Her name was Mrs. Thelma Partridge.

Joe had listened in growing admiration to Doris' account of her visit to the 'Lilacs'. There seemed to be no end to this woman's daring. Armed with a pile of second-hand paper-backed novels, some magazines and a basket of fruit Sister Jane Bateman had been made most welcome. She had chatted briefly with all the inmates of the Old People's Home but she stayed the longest with Mrs. Partridge. When she left it was with gleeful satisfaction at the trophies she had won.

'Well Joe, I found her! I went to see the grandmother and look what I got,' she crowed as Joe had peered at the items that Doris spread before him on the table. It took him several minutes to realise what they were.

'How on earth did you manage to lay your hands on these?'

'It was easy, Joe. I just got her talking about her family. She's completely do-lally, Joe, nutty as a fruit cake most of the time. They told me that she only remembers occasional flashes of what truly happened. She would have given me the whole boxful of stuff if I'd asked for it. She thinks her daughter will come back some day, but she's forgotten about the child. I took a picture of Daisy from her box ... this one ... see? She must be about a year old there, sitting on someone's settee. The other photo's of the Millers. But Joe, this is the real prize, Daisy's Certificate of Adoption!'

'Now let me get this straight,' he tapped the photograph, 'these two adopted Daisy, yes?'

'Yes,' said Doris, patiently, 'and left her with dotty Mrs. P. when they went off and got themselves killed in an aeroplane crash.' She thought for a moment. 'But I don't suppose she was dotty then. It was the shock that sent her off her rocker.'

Joe had studied the picture of the handsome young couple. They stood, hand in hand on a summer day with the sea and the jutting headland of Flamborough clearly visible in the background, smiling at each other without, it seemed, a care in the world. He turned it over to see the inscription on the back, 'Fred and Margaret, Summer 1929'.

'To think that they'd only two or three years to live after this was taken. Makes you think, doesn't it?' said Joe whose own mortality had so recently been threatened.

'Yes, and it makes me think we should go for all we can get out of this life while we're here, Joe. It's quite clear, now, how we can get our hands on that money. Forget trying to adopt the child. We have to turn ourselves into...' she checked the Adoption Certificate, 'this Frederick and Margaret Miller. We have to claim Daisy as our own. And here's the proof.' Doris had danced around and around the tiny sitting room until she collapsed into a chair. She had become pensive then, picking up the photograph and examining it closely.

'Actually we're roughly the same height and build. That's a bit of luck. Just my hair colour and style will need changing. That's no problem to see to with some of that new dye that Wella have advertised on the billboards. But I won't change it until I'm ready to tell them who I really am ... Margaret Miller! Now, Joe, you had better get used to being called "Fred".'

The autumn of 1935 saw Joe Smithson taking up the reins, quite literally, of his work for Sir Edward Lazenby. He had lost none of his aptitude for the horses, though he would walk with a limp for the rest of his life. During harvest time the work horses had to be kept up to scratch as they worked non-stop through the daylight hours and the kitchen, where Doris did much of her work, was occupied in feeding the extra mouths of itinerant labourers. It was by far the busiest time of the year at Upton Hall and everyone was expected to give one hundred per cent effort from dawn until after dusk. Doris did not mind. She had completed her plans and now all they had to do was to invent the best account of the Miller's apparent return from the dead. It would have to be a credible story, this tale to support their claim to be Daisy Miller's long lost parents.

One after another ideas would be tossed about,

considered and rejected in the privacy of the cottage. Joe was soon infected with his wife's enthusiasm and applied himself eagerly to the plotting. He it was who came up with the notion that they might have escaped, injured but alive, from the aeroplane. This was the ideal explanation for 'Fred's' bad leg. They could easily have been washed up in France and stayed there for a while. Yes, with suitable embellishments it could become the perfect history of a couple lost at sea and now returned. Doris would spend the next few weeks polishing it. Surely, thought Doris, nothing could go wrong. They had the Certificate to prove who they were. They knew for a fact that it was genuine. They were almost ready.

But Doris wanted to be sure of Daisy, too. What did she remember of her early life? Hopefully not very much, since she had been so small when she went to the orphanage. She really needed to see the child, to question her, make quite sure that she recalled nothing of those first eighteen months. She thought it would smooth along the whole process of the claim if they had already set up some kind of rapport with Daisy. And so it had been a last minute decision to take Daisy out for the weekend, try to befriend her, get her on their side. They would have to wait until the winter season to do it. There would be no chance of taking days off work until then. After that they would be ready. They would be ready to make the claim, to transform themselves into the Millers.

As Joe nodded and dozed in the warmth of the fire he failed to see Doris smiling ruefully at the memory of that disastrous first trip out with Daisy. It had begun badly with Joe losing his temper and scaring the child into running away from them. And as if that had not been enough, the steady, reliable express from London had chosen that evening to leave the tracks. They had been forced to duck police questioning and as a consequence the girl had been whipped away from under their noses. To cap it all she knew they had mismanaged their questioning of Daisy, (they knew nothing at all about six-year-old children) and to avoid further calamity, had to take her home a day and a half early. No, it had not been an auspicious occasion.

Doris winced at the memory of the Johnsons' attitude of doubt and distrust. They had not set eyes on Daisy since the day they had been to tell Mrs. Johnson that their real names were Margaret and Fred Miller and to make the claim that they were the child's adoptive parents. Elsie's protection of her had become complete as she explained that it was for the little girl's benefit that all should be legally proven before she was told that her parents had come to find her after all this time. A solicitor would be called. Mrs. Johnson was sure that they would bear with them as they made quite sure that all was in order for them to take Daisy away.

And they had met with Mr. Ross with their hearts in their mouths that day. The only piece of evidence that they could rely upon thoroughly was the Certificate of Adoption. Would it be enough?

And so they waited to hear from 'Idle House'. They did not know how long it would be before they could go and 'collect', as Joe put it. A secret corner of Doris' heart occasionally dwelt upon a picture of herself as a mother, buying dolls and pretty clothes for her daughter, watching her grow into a woman, guiding her steps. But always there was the shadow of Joe's antagonism to this scenario. He was bitter that nature had seen fit not to furnish him, (or so it seemed) with the ability to father a family. Doris thought that she had overcome the grieving that she had done in her younger days at their failure to produce a child, but now she was not so sure. These things were hidden deep inside. They were not dead.

Chapter 29

The draft of the letter to Tom Ross had lain upon Sarah's writing table for two days awaiting a fair copy and a stamp. Something was bothering her about this whole business and she found herself putting off the task. If Tom had assured her that these people were truly the Millers who had taken her baby into their care in the winter of 1930, then she must accept his decision. Why did she still harbour this uncertainty? There was no obvious reason for it, only a feeling deep down inside her that she did not want Daisy to spend the rest of her childhood with the woman in the red hat.

'What in heaven's name are you talking about, girl?' Maddie had said when she had confided her fears to her friend. 'What could be better than a reunion with her parents? After all, from what you've told me it's clear they can't be blamed for what happened and they have come forward now that they're able. You should be pleased it's all turned out so well.'

'I know, Maddie, really I do. The sooner it's all settled the better. Then I can begin to look forward again. For the last few weeks I seem to have been living my life in retrospect and I can tell you it has opened old wounds and brought back memories I'd rather forget.' Maddie looked at her friend as they sat at the kitchen table sharing a pot of tea. Sarah looked drawn, she thought, as if she had the cares of the world on her shoulders.

'What does Sam think about it?'

'That's just it, I don't know. I haven't been able to contact him for ages. I wanted to tell him about this letter from Tom Ross. He knows about the Millers but not Tom's opinion of them ... that they're genuine, I mean.' There was silence between them.

'You know, Maddie, I think that is what's stopping me from posting that letter to Tom. You've asked the right question ... hit the nail on the head ... as usual. I should bring Sam up to date. I'll do it now!' And Sarah made for the hall and dialled the hospital number. Maddie could not hear what was said but Sarah came back in less than a minute, shaking her head.

'What's up?'

'They told me that Sam has taken some leave, unexpectedly. He's been away almost a week now and they're not sure when he'll be back. It's assumed that it's a family matter but I would know if Mr. Pearce were ill, wouldn't I? He lives not fifteen minutes from here, for goodness' sake.' She sat down heavily at the table and stared at Maddie. 'What's he playing at? Why can't he telephone?'

'Look, honey, whatever he's up to there must be a good reason for it. Judging from what I've gathered he's just as dotty about you as he was seven years ago and I know you feel the same. He's hardly likely to ride off into the sunset at this stage. Think. What did he say to you the last time you spoke?' Sarah was lost in thought for a moment or two, recalling the conversation she had had with Sam almost two weeks ago.

'I remember he said he wished we knew more about the Millers. In fact he said he would see what he could find out.'

'Well, there you are, then. He's probably doing just that. Lord! Look at the time! I'll have to fly. I'll call you tomorrow. 'Bye, darling!' Maddie's high heels sent the gravel in all directions as she ran down the drive. Sarah smiled. Maddie was a tonic. She had been with her through good times and bad and never failed to instil in her a sense of optimism when problems loomed. A complete philosopher and pragmatist was Maddie and Sarah knew she was right. She should cease worrying about Sam and get on with the job of settling Daisy's future as best she could. Squaring her shoulders she went upstairs and set about copying her letter to Tom Ross. Within the hour it was in the post. She knew that her instructions would be carried out faithfully and quickly and that she could safely leave the rest of the business to Tom.

Elsie Johnson felt nervous. She was glad that Ernest would be home by midday since the prospect of singly entertaining Mr. Ross as well as Mr. and Mrs. Miller had filled her heart with dread. That today they would be losing Daisy after four years of cherishing her young life was hardly bearable. Daisy had become very special to them both and Elsie knew that the child herself was beset by fears and anxieties since the evening, just twenty-four hours ago, when they had told her what was to happen.

Daisy's blue eyes had darkened, become wide and finally had filled with tears and she had clung to Elsie, wetting her flowered apron as she sobbed.

'I ... want to ... stay with you ... I want to stay here with Anna. What about Anna?' The child had been beside herself, yet had found it impossible to put into words all the emotion and fear that was churning up inside her. Elsie knew this. She knew also that there was nothing she could do about it, nothing she could do to stop them taking Daisy away. All she could do was to hold the child closely, stroke her hot forehead and promise that all would be well in the end. Her heart was breaking, too.

And here they were, waiting for the people to come who were to take her away. A new life, Elsie had said to her, a new home and real parents to love her and bring her up. Oh! It would be wonderful. Just you wait and see. Ernest came down from washing and changing after his morning shift in the signal box. There was a strange quietness about the house as if it was holding its breath. The younger children played softly in the day room, the older ones, apart from Anna and Daisy, were at school. To pass the time and to keep Daisy's mind occupied Elsie played a game of Ludo with the children and Ernest joined them. In the kitchen trays were laid with dainty sandwiches, Elsie's date and walnut loaf, sliced, buttered and arranged fan-like on the best china. Battenberg and chocolate slices added colour to the array of refreshments while the teapot waited to be scalded and the tea freshly made as soon as the formalities were over.

'I want you to play here in the day-room, Daisy, just for a little while. The grown ups will need to have a talk first and, perhaps, sign some papers. As soon as that's done I will come and fetch you.' Daisy nodded, her expression solemn, her eyes like dark pools. It had already been explained that she would be going away with the Millers and her clothes and few belongings were packed and ready. Daisy was not at all sure that she could leave here without crying but she had promised Mrs. Johnson that she would be brave in return for her assurance that she may visit whenever she liked. The fact that the distance between Retford and Leeds might be too great for this to be a frequent or even occasional event did not occur to Daisy. Elsie felt it better left unsaid at this juncture; better to let things take their course, wait and see.

'Can we go and play now?' asked the anxious child.

'Of course you can,' Elsie said. She knew full

well that Anna was the one person above all whose company and affection Daisy would miss. They had been as close as sisters and the break would be hard. It was for this reason that Anna had been allowed to miss school today.

A car was heard as Elsie and Ernest entered the hallway and they took hold of each other's hand momentarily for moral support. Through the stained glass panel of the front door they could discern the figure of a bowler-hatted man as he raised his hand to ring the bell.

'It's Mr. Ross,' whispered Elsie, smoothing down her dress with perspiring palms then patting her hair into place. 'You go into the sitting room, dear. I'll answer the door.' Ernest did as she asked and stood before the fireplace drawing upon his cigarette and trying to look nonchalant, as if he was accustomed to entertaining gentlemen of the law during the afternoon. The churning of his stomach and his need to keep moving from one foot to the other told its own story. He knew that this was best for Daisy, yet he could not imagine Idle House without her. For four years he had watched her grow from babyhood to schoolgirl and had come to love her dearly. His heart was heavy.

'Please take a seat, Mr. Ross. No doubt Mr. and Mrs. Miller will be here directly. Will you take a glass of sherry?' Tom said that he would and Ernest was glad of something to do as he poured a glass for the solicitor and one for himself and Elsie.

'And how is Daisy? Keeping well, I hope? I expect she is very excited today.' The polite conversation continued as the three of them waited for the arrival of Daisy's parents. Afterwards Elsie confessed to remembering nothing of what was said, so on edge was she. Another taxi, another ring of the doorbell and the waiting was over.

Margaret Miller smiled as she shook hands with each of the others. Frederick's tight expression, as he was welcomed by Elsie, revealed his unease with the situation. He had become quiet and withdrawn, quite unlike himself, ever since the letter from the solicitor had arrived just a few days ago.

'Here it is, Joe!' Doris had torn open the envelope with a mixture of excitement and dread. 'Oh, Joe, we have to go to Retford.' Relief flowed over her like a warm shower. 'We can go and collect Daisy.' She had sat down, the colour draining from her face, and held out the letter to Joe.

'And what does it say about the money?' Joe did not take the letter, merely giving it a cursory glance and walking to the window of the cottage and gazing out.

'Well, nothing, yet,' said Doris. For a second she had forgotten about it, her thoughts pinned on the prospect of having a daughter, her daughter back. She had worked so hard at the story she had invented, lived and breathed the part of Margaret Miller in her mind so often that she had begun to believe her own fabrications.

They were smart. Elsie had to admit that. Margaret was wearing a navy suit with a fur stole to shield her from the winter cold. A neat pillbox hat sat jauntily on her dark hair and matching gloves with silk stockings and navy shoes completed her outfit. She was the epitome of middle-class respectability. Her husband, walking with a decided limp was less assured, but was nonetheless equally well dressed. Doris had scoured the jumble sales for months so that they would be well turned out today. Joe had been tutored carefully for this event. He was prepared to allow his wife to do the talking. She had politely refused the offer of sherry, preferring to keep her wits as sharp as possible. Fred, on the other hand, had no such scruples, his only regret being the genteel size of the glasses.

Elsie tried to put herself into the shoes of this woman who now waited to claim her adopted daughter after surviving such a traumatic experience. Fairness had always been her watchword and, although her instincts were those of distrust if not active dislike towards the Millers, she could not account for them logically. Assured by the solicitor of their legitimacy she now felt she must make special effort to support Mrs. Miller if only for Daisy's sake.

'Before we settle down to business perhaps you would like to go up and see her?' asked Elsie addressing Mrs. Miller. There was an awkward pause, a blank look.

'See who?'

'Why, Daisy, of course. She's been so excited about your coming ... she's...'

'Oh, yes! Yes, please.' The woman's discomfiture was hurriedly covered up by animated chatter as the two women climbed the staircase. The problem of how they would approach the subject of the legacy should it not be mentioned by the solicitor had occupied the conversation between Joe and Doris throughout the journey to Idle House. Joe would not leave it alone and the reclaiming of Daisy had been eclipsed for the moment.

Daisy and Anna scurried back from their positions at the top of the stairs, feigning deep absorption in a game of cards in the day room.

'Come and say "Hello", Daisy.' Elsie had tried to prepare the child for this moment. They had had long conversations, just the two of them, when the story of Daisy's mother and father's disappearance was told and of how they had come to find her again. Elsie had made it appear like a fairy tale with a happy ending and Daisy had needed to hear it over and over. Now she looked fearfully at the woman whose appearance had altered so radically since the night of the train crash and whispered a greeting as Anna watched intently from behind the table.

'We'll have lots to talk about later, you'll see,' said Mrs. Miller, her voice a trifle highly pitched and falsely jolly. 'Everything will be alright.' She made a move closer to Daisy and the child backed away, then turned and ran to join Anna behind the table. From that safe position she remembered the words that Elsie had rehearsed with her.

'Thank you-for-coming-to-find-me-again-er ... er...' blurted out Daisy all in one breath but coming to an abrupt halt when she found she could not call this woman 'mother' or even Auntie Doris. (For it had been explained to her that the lady who had pretended to be Auntie Doris was really her mother. Daisy felt equally uncomfortable with both persons). The atmosphere in the room had become so tense that Elsie decided to end the interview quickly.

'The grown-ups have things to discuss now, Daisy. You carry on playing with Anna. I'll come for you when we're ready. After you, Mrs. Miller,' said Elsie as she held open the door for her visitor.

Whilst waiting for the two women to return Tom Ross had chosen a position beside the dining table which was covered, whilst not in use, with a green chenille cloth. In the centre stood a decorative glass epergne with seven flutes rising from its round glass bowl. In spite of its being well out of fashion in 1936 it was Elsie's pride and joy, a gift from her grandmother many years ago. Now, as Tom spread papers on the table Elsie moved her treasure out of harm's way. Tom cleared his throat and looked round at the expectant faces. Polite preliminaries were soon over and he addressed the Millers as they sat together on the settee.

'This afternoon's business will not be altogether pleasant for Mr. and Mrs. Johnson, I know, since they have become very fond of Daisy Miller over the past four years. However that may be, you will all have heard that my opinion of the Adoption Certificate is that it is genuine, proving beyond doubt that you are Daisy's legal parents. The child has had a difficult time, especially during her first three years. The prospect of a return to a proper family life for her is very good news though I am sure you will appreciate that she will take a little time to settle down. I understand you are to take her to live with you on the

Upton Hall estate?'

'Yes, that's right,' answered Mrs. Miller taking hold of her husband's hand. 'The cottage is quite large enough for the three of us and Sir Edward has no objection to Daisy's coming. She will be able to go to the local village school when she has settled in.'

'Quite so,' said Tom who was, through his own enquiries, fully aware of the Millers' domestic arrangements. 'Remind me, Mrs. Miller, of the child's date of birth if you would.' He did not look up from the notes he was making, his matter of fact tone belying the importance of his question.

'Daisy was born on January 3rd, 1930,' she said. 'We took her home towards the end of that month.'

'But ... excuse me, Mr. Ross, I think there must be some mistake...'

'It's quite alright, Mrs. Johnson,' Tom was smiling now. 'I know that you have her birthday as 26th March. That's due to a mistake that happened subsequent to the dreadful fire at Northside Orphanage when all the children's records were destroyed. The checks I was able to make at the Registry Office soon made it clear that Daisy's birthdate had been incorrectly recorded at her transfer to Idle House. I understand that most of those details had to rely on the memory of orphanage staff as they struggled to re-locate the children after the fire. I am relieved indeed that you, Mrs. Miller, know her proper date of birth.'

'Was it not on the Adoption Certificate?' asked Ernest with obvious concern.

'Strangely enough, no,' said Tom, 'though it may

have been an oversight at the time. These private arrangements for adoption are left, largely, to the agencies concerned. It seems that the nuns at St. Faith's went to some pains to guard the identity of the mothers. They designed the documents themselves. They did not always pass on the Birth Certificate to the adoptive parents, but in this case, so Sister Ruth recalls, they did. Do you, perhaps, have it with you today, Mrs. Miller?'

Doris was caught off her guard. This was a question she had not anticipated. She must produce a confident reply ... or play for time. Joe was no help, sitting there as if turned to stone. She chose the latter.

'I believe I did put it into my bag before we left but...' she said, starting to look through the pockets of her handbag.

'No matter, Mrs. Miller, for the moment. There is another circumstance that I must acquaint you of today.' The solicitor's tone of voice held a different timbre. 'I feel sure that this will come as a great surprise and, indeed, a pleasant one for you both.' He began to shuffle his papers and pulled out one in particular and laid it on top.

'Today you are to regain your little daughter, and take her home. But that is not all.' Joe and Doris glanced at each other, feigning puzzled astonishment but they remained quiet. Tom Ross beamed at them, enjoying the effect his words were having.

'It is with great pleasure that I can tell you now that there is a sum of money put aside for the use of Daisy Miller's adoptive parents to help in her upbringing.' Daisy Miller's adoptive parents sat up straight and paid close attention. Tom went on, 'This is a legacy from Daisy's great-grandfather whose identity will remain anonymous but whose generous gift of £5,000 will be yours to use for Daisy's benefit.' There was a silence in the room broken after a moment by Elsie Johnson.

'Oh! How wonderful for you, Mrs. Miller, Mr. Miller,' Elsie enthused as her husband nodded in hearty agreement. 'Wonderful for Daisy, too.'

Now that the moment had arrived for which she had been working for the best part of three years Doris was lost for words. She was saved from her confusion by the sound of the telephone ringing in the hallway. Elsie excused herself and went to answer it returning almost immediately to ask Mr. Ross to come to the 'phone.

'Might I be allowed to use your bathroom, please?' asked Doris, taking advantage of the break in the proceedings. A need to powder her nose and collect her scattered wits drove Doris plus a sixth sense that this 'phone call might have something to do with their business. What should she say? She felt it would be imperative to respond carefully to the news of the legacy. There must be no hint of any pre-knowledge of it. There must be no crowing over their good fortune yet they must appear delighted, grateful and, above all, thankful on Daisy's behalf. She must remember to place Daisy at the forefront of any discussion about how the money might be used. All these thoughts lined themselves up in her head as Elsie showed her the way to the W.C. situated at the far end of the hallway and adjacent to the telephone. Her ears, always finely attuned to the movements and talk of others, noted Elsie returning to the lounge via the kitchen where she put the kettle on the hob and carried the first of several plates of refreshments into the parlour.

'Time for us to celebrate your good fortune with a cup of tea,' she said to Joe as she pulled out a small occasional table for his use. 'Come along, Ernest, help me to bring in the rest of the things.' Doris, meanwhile, was preparing with meticulous care her words of acceptance, and hoping that Joe was continuing to keep his mouth closed while she was out of the room.

Tom had looked a little surprised as he went out of the room. Who but the office would call him? And what could be so important as to disturb him here? His ensuing conversation with Dr. Sam Pearce had been brief and to the point. Tom did most of the listening, much to Doris' annoyance as she tried to glean the gist of the call through the door of the toilet. Finally she heard, 'Yes... Yes, they are... Oh, that is quite genuine, sir... I can indeed... If there is any doubt at all... Only about half an hour?... Yes, that would be no problem since we are just about to break for a cup of tea, I think.' Tom smiled at Elsie as she passed him with a plate of scones. 'We'll expect you shortly, then? Goodbye.'

Tom returned to the parlour, soon followed by Doris, lipstick repaired.

'This all looks delicious, Mrs. Johnson,' said Tom, making no reference to his telephone call. 'You really need not have gone to so much trouble. Now, where were we? Ah, yes, the legacy, Mr. and Mrs. Miller,' he smiled disarmingly at them both.

'Yes, by the way, did you find Daisy's Birth Certificate in your bag?'

'No. I remember now. I left it with my mother when we went on the aeroplane trip. She had all Daisy's things.'

'And you discovered Daisy was in care when you were finally able to look for her. Why was that, Mrs. Miller?' Doris' face took on a suitably doleful expression as she announced, 'Well, you see, Mr. Ross, we found that, sadly, my mother had passed away whilst we were in France.'

'I see,' said Tom, a closed expression coming over his face. 'I'm so sorry to hear that.' Doris knew that this could be her fatal mistake. One lie too far. Would he know? Would he notice? 'Were you not informed of this fact?' Tom was probing now.

'No-one knew we were still alive,' she said. 'Everyone thought we had been lost at sea after the air-crash.'

'Ah! Quite so.' Tom, unable to shake her story had to admit that it still sounded thoroughly plausible.

Doris accepted her tea and sandwiches with her mind busy elsewhere. Why had Mr. Ross not given them the money yet? When did he intend to hand it over? She had to find out. The words she had prepared so few minutes ago somehow deserted her entirely in favour of, 'Er, might I ask, Mr. Ross ... er ... when we take Daisy home, will we take the money at the same time? I mean, it's such a big responsibility, isn't it. How will it be paid to us? We can get to the bank first thing in the morning, can't we, dear?' Doris addressed her silent husband. Tom, who had Sarah's envelope full of bank-notes safely in his breast pocket said, 'I will have to ask you to come to the office in Leeds once Daisy is settled with you at the Lazenby estate. It can all be seen to then, I assure you.'

'Yes, of course, I understand,' said Doris. Alarm bells began to ring in her head. This was not what she had expected at all. She looked at Joe. He seemed far more uneasy than before.

Tea and refreshments were passed to and fro yet to Doris the scene and conversation had dissolved into a blur. She fought to clarify her mind as she stood up to pass the ham sandwiches to Joe. Through the window she was sure she caught sight of a police car, just for a second. Where did it go? The neat front garden was small and bounded by a close-cut privet hedge a good five feet tall. Could that car have stopped outside this house? She could not track its progress farther up the road. It must have stopped. It would be easily visible from an upstairs window, wouldn't it? Doris hid the alarm she was feeling. She put down the plate, beamed at Elsie Johnson and said, 'Mrs. Johnson, may we go up and have another little word with Daisy? I want to tell her it won't be long now.'

'Yes, of course,' said Elsie. Doris took Joe by the hand and almost dragged him behind her.

'Come along, dear, she'll be getting tired of waiting.' The two of them made for the stairs as the others finished the last of the cakes and tea.

'Well, that was a most successful afternoon for Daisy, wasn't it?' remarked Ernest Johnson. 'I do hope they will all settle down happily together. The money will help so much. How very kind the great-grandfather was, don't you think, Elsie. I mean to say, many an old man would have cut the girl completely out of his will for disgracing the family. Good Lord, what was that?'

An urgent and loud knocking at the door brought those inside to the window and Elsie to answer the door. On the doorstep stood Sam Pearce, Sarah Grange and police sergeant Gerry Roberts.

Chapter 30

'Come in,' cried Elsie. 'This is a surprise.'

'Not to me, I assure you, Mrs. Johnson. I was expecting them,' said Tom Ross. He smiled rather grimly as he shook hands with them all. 'They telephoned earlier, Mrs. Johnson. I'm afraid that what Dr. Pearce had to tell me has rather turned today's business on its head. I wonder, would you ask Mr. and Mrs. Miller to join us please.' Elsie went upstairs while Ernest ushered his new visitors into the parlour. At the top of the staircase she came upon Daisy and Anna, their eyes popping, peering down into the hallway.

'Is it Sarah? I thought I heard Sarah,' whispered the little girl, her eyes shining.

'Yes, my dear. I didn't know she was coming. I expect she'll come up to see you soon. Just be patient a little longer. But I'm looking for your people, Daisy, Mr. and Mrs. Miller. They came up to talk to you a little while ago. Did they go into the dayroom?' The two children looked at each other and then at Elsie as if she were speaking another language. Their eyes followed her, wide open and solemn, as she hurried along the landing, peering in at each door she passed. The upper floor was empty but for the three of them.

'Haven't you seen them?' Elsie swung round to face the children before running down the stairs without waiting for an answer. They heard her burst into the parlour.

'They've gone! There's no-one upstairs,' Elsie was breathless.

'Sit down, Mrs. Johnson, please,' said Tom. 'I think, perhaps, we have all just had a very narrow escape.' Tom's own suspicions, never far from the surface throughout this strange case, had been raised once again when Mrs. Miller had begun to ask questions about payment of the legacy. Expressions of gratitude, surprise, disbelief at their good fortune, any of these he did expect. Somehow the mercenary tone of her question had disturbed him. 'Yes,' he repeated, 'a very narrow escape.'

Elsie fussed about the room, removing the used crockery, making room enough for them all to sit down.

Sarah was joined on the sofa by Sam. There was something different about them thought Elsie but she was too preoccupied to try to decide what it was. Ernest, quick to sense the change in the tone of the visit asked the question that was on everyone's mind.

'A narrow escape? Whatever do you mean, Mr. Ross?'

'It appears that we have been far too trusting and I am as much to blame as anyone. Dr. Pearce's telephone call revealed that the people we have been entertaining as the Millers are impostors, fraudsters only out to claim the cash that would come to Daisy's guardians.'

'Oh, my good Lord!' exclaimed Elsie. 'So that's why they disappeared so suddenly.'

'How they managed to fool us I'll never know but they are clever. And clever enough, it would seem, to detect that their cover was suddenly blown and to make themselves scarce before they could be faced with awkward questions.' There was silence as Elsie tried to take in Tom's words. He continued, 'The call from Dr. Pearce came just in the nick of time and I won't ask how many miles an hour that police car did in order to get you here so quickly.' He twinkled at Sarah and his little joke made them all relax. 'The child's legacy is still safe.' He patted his pocket. 'A few more minutes and I would have handed it over. Come along then, Sam, fill us in with a few more details before we all die of curiosity.'

'But, what about those two ... the Millers or whatever their names are. Shouldn't someone try to stop them?' said Sarah.

'They'll be well away by now,' said Gerry. 'But I'm quite sure we'll be able to catch up with them before long. Go on with what you were saying, Sam.'

'I'll admit that I am far from knowing the complete story. My interest in Daisy began when I met Sarah again the night of the rail crash. I'd better explain that Sarah and I had been friends years ago.' Here Sam took hold of Sarah's hand and the smile that passed between them told its own story to those watching. 'We hadn't kept in touch but neither of us had forgotten how we felt about each other.' He cleared his throat and continued, 'Sarah told me all about Daisy and of how concerned she was about her when she went missing from the hospital that night. I promised to help to find her. That's how it all began and that's how Gerry got involved.'

'It's a long story and there are still many gaps in our knowledge about the movements of the Smithsons. Yes, that is their real name,' said Gerry. Sarah, who had so far said very little, took up the tale.

'From the start, when you, Mrs. Johnson, told me that Daisy's parents had turned up out of the blue I've been uneasy, though I couldn't explain why. Just an innate feeling I suppose. Sam knew I wanted to find Daisy at first, just to be sure she was alright. It's amazing how close you become to someone when you're thrown together as we were, escaping death by nothing but good luck. And we did find her chiefly with the unwitting help of Daisy's grandma whom we tracked down to a nursing home in Scarborough.'

'Just a minute, Mrs. Miller has just told us that her mother died ... while they were recuperating in France ... unless you mean her other grand mother of course.' Ernest was following the conversation closely.

'No, we are talking about Mrs. Miller's mother,'

Sarah assured him. 'Her name is Mrs. Partridge. The air accident and the loss of her daughter and son-in-law gave her such a severe shock that she has a mental block about the whole event. But there's no doubt about who she is. She allowed us to look at her family photographs and letters. For a time she mistook Sam and me for Margaret and Fred, safely returned. It was very sad. Then when I heard that they really had come back I just didn't know what to make of it all, the recovery from the sea, the long stay in France...'

'That story becomes more far-fetched each time it's repeated' Sam said, flatly.

'Indeed it does,' added Gerry. 'However, the enquiries undertaken by Dr. Pearce have been far reaching. Between the police and his efforts we now have firm proof that these people told a pack of lies. Perhaps you'll excuse me. I need to go out to the car. No, please stay there, Mrs. Johnson. I'll only be a moment.'

Sarah was pensive hardly noticing that Gerry had left the room.

'If they are not the Millers then who are they? What are they up to? How have they obtained the Adoption Certificate, I wonder?' Sarah was also puzzling over how in the world anyone could possibly know about Grandfather's bequest.

In the police car parked outside Idle House sat a figure in a mink coat. Ten minutes ago she had watched carefully and with curious interest the well-dressed couple who emerged from the side entrance to the house and walked briskly past. As they approached the corner of the street she saw them break into a run, decorum thrown to the winds. The lady smiled to herself and took out of her bag a gold case and lighter and carefully lit a cigarette. She settled down into her corner and pulled the fur round her shoulders. She might not have too long to wait after all. She hoped not, for it would soon feel very cold.

Gerry Roberts came and opened the door of the car. 'Would you be kind enough to join us, Mrs. Benson? I trust we have not kept you waiting too long.' The elegant legs which stepped onto the pavement were obviously used to getting out of motor cars. Mrs. Benson was tall and slim, a stunning woman of about forty. As she approached the house Elsie hurried to the door.

'Why, Gerry, you haven't left someone out in the car? Please, come in, come to the fire and get warm.' It was Elsie's first concern, the comfort of her guest.

'Oh, I'm not cold. I'm quite used to winter weather, but thank you just the same.' Her voice had a slightly American inflection, her clothes obviously expensive. Sam stood up and, smiling, shook the lady's hand.

'Mr. and Mrs, Johnson, may I introduce Mrs. Dorothy Benson. Mrs. Benson lives in Canada. She is sister to Daisy's adoptive mother and she has spent the last week or so travelling from Toronto,' announced Sam.

'Yes, I'm Margaret's sister. I can assure you that the couple who left here a few minutes ago are not Fred and Margaret Miller.'

'And a signed statement confirming that fact is all I need before I return to the station,' said

Gerry. Dorothy Benson smiled and nodded her agreement.

Tom Ross had been observing the scene that unfolded before him in growing relief and admiration. The thoughts of the consequences of his giving George Grange's money to the wrong party made his blood run cold. The end of his legal career, he wouldn't doubt. 'Well, Mrs. Benson, I'm sure we are all delighted to meet you,' he said.

'It was the least I could do, to come over and meet the people who had worked so hard to prevent such an injustice. As soon as I received the first letter from Dr. Pearce I resolved to take a holiday in England not least of all to pay a long overdue visit to my mother. I wired him immediately. It seems my ship was only just in time,' she laughed.

'Letter from Dr. Pearce?' questioned Tom.

'Sarah and I had visited Mrs. Partridge together. She took us for her nearest and dearest, as you heard, and was glad to share with us her box of personal treasures, photographs and so on. We were then only conducting the search for Daisy, you understand, but I had noticed many letters from someone in Canada. Later, when the details emerged about the Millers' return from the dead and their claim on Daisy, I went back to Scarborough. I asked Mrs. Partridge who was writing from Canada but she could not remember, at least, not on that day. She had no objection to my borrowing some of the letters. We already had some photographs which tallied with those in Daisy's possession. Between letters and photographs I soon discovered Mrs. Benson and wrote to her.'

'Yes. It was a real surprise to me, I can tell you. I had often wondered what had happened to the baby after mother was taken into the home. But Canada's a long way off and we were heavily occupied with the business. Mother never wrote to me. She had forgotten who I was, or so I was told by the Matron at the Lilacs, who was kind enough to keep me informed. So I just went on writing, hoping that some day she might remember me.'

'I'm so glad you did,' said Sarah. 'We knew that Daisy had an aunt; we found you on two of the photos taken outside the Miller's Hotel. One had written on the back, "Margaret, Fred, Auntie Dot with Daisy."'

'That would have been just before I went out to join Peter, my husband. He was setting up the Canadian branch of the business,' said Mrs. Benson. 'I've been over there since 1931.' Tom Ross looked intrigued.

'Not Peter Benson of Benson's Brolly Company?' he questioned, eyebrows raised.

'Yes, the same,' she smiled. 'You've heard of us?' Tom laughed.

'Well, I should just think I have. He's about the most successful umbrella manufacturer in the country. All the best people have a Benson's Brolly.'

'Yes, well, I will admit the company has been a success, but only due to a great deal of hard work and struggle at the start.' Those gathered in Elsie's modest parlour could well imagine the extent of that success as the diamonds on Mrs. Benson's fingers sparkled in the firelight.

'My story is not important today,' said the lady. 'There is one more thing I can do to lay the ghosts of the bogus Millers. It's especially good that your solicitor is here. When my sister and her husband were lost in the air accident only the bodies of the pilot and co-pilot who had been trapped in the cockpit were found. It was assumed that the other four people had died as a result of drowning. No death certificates could be issued, because no bodies had been found. It was almost three months later when two bodies were washed up on the shore near Penzance. They were identified as Margaret and Fred Miller from the jewellery they wore, and their deaths were then registered in the county of Cornwall. These are the certificates. They were sent to me as next of kin when mother had become so ill.' She handed them to Tom Ross. The room was still and quiet. Tom passed the papers for the rest to see.

'Those wishing to impersonate my relatives for their own gain would assume there were no death certificates issued as is usual in case of loss at sea,' added Mrs. Benson.

'Even if the Smithsons did enquire about the deaths they would never have looked as far afield as Cornwall,' said Sarah as she handled the pathetic reminder of a young life lost.

Gerry Roberts had been quietly writing a simple statement on Mrs. Benson's behalf and now he asked her to read and sign it.

'Thank you, Mrs Benson. I'll be getting back to the station now, if you'll excuse me. It's time to start tracking down certain parties who left here in something of a hurry.' He addressed his last remark to Sam, 'Bye, old chap, I'll be in touch as soon as I know anything.' With a slight wink at Sarah, Gerry left. His work was by no means over.

Elsie, who had quietly removed the remains of their earlier refreshments, looked at the clock. The children would be home from school directly. There was no tea ready for them and she still had not asked Sarah to go up and see Daisy. There was little left of the afternoon and she wondered whether she should offer to provide her visitors with an evening meal. She looked at Ernest for help.

'Perhaps you would excuse Elsie and me? We have the children to attend to but please feel free to stay and talk. Later on we would be pleased to provide you with dinner.' Ernest prayed they would not accept. He found it a proper strain entertaining these people who, nice as they were, were not, well, quite his sort.

'That is very kind but you have enough to do and we must be making our way home very soon,' said Tom Ross. At the same time he did feel that there were one or two matters that still needed clarification and quite a few things that still needed to be said. They would do well to wrap up as much of this business as possible today while they were all together.

'May I make a suggestion, ladies and gentlemen? Rather than outstay our welcome here at Idle House, I would be happy to invite you all to join me for dinner at the Crown Hotel. It is a very comfortable hostelry which provides excellent food. What do you say?' It was agreed.

Elsie came back into the room and reminded them all of the central reason for their being here. Daisy. Had they almost forgotten about the child who was at the hub of all this discussion today?

'Excuse me, Mr. Ross. Am I to assume that Daisy will stay here with us after all? The child was expecting to go home with her parents this evening you know. All that has changed. What shall I tell her?'

'Oh, Mrs. Johnson, I am so sorry. We have entirely overlooked matters of the moment, I fear. Yes, of course Daisy must stay here tonight. The poor child, she won't know whether she's coming or going, will she?'

Sarah, who had moved to the window seat, was lost in thought, even Sam forgotten. She was considering the legacy. Now, she thought, now it can really go to the Johnsons where I always wanted it to go. She must find a way to speak to Tom Ross in private before the end of this momentous day. And yet, even as she rejoiced at this, the still small voice deep within her soul cried out to be heard. An instinct that truly yearned for a different outcome altogether, but one that would put at risk too many reputations, one that she could not entertain and must continue to deny. A deep sigh escaped her body and she turned resolutely to join Sam who was chatting quietly with Mrs. Benson. Tom was packing up his papers, a slight frown creasing his forehead. He must find a way to speak to Sarah in private before the day was out.

Now Sarah made for the door. It was time to see Daisy. She was surprised how fast her heart was beating as she opened the door and glanced out into the long hallway.

There was a squeal of delight from the landing above. Shoes that hardly touched the treads hurtled down the stairs. Dark curls with ribbons flying and skirts billowing behind ended up in one untidy bundle, scooped up from the foot of the staircase by Sarah's arms. Anna watched. Would this be the last she would see of her friend? Why had Sarah come? Where were Daisy's parents? When would they have to say goodbye?

'Sarah, Sarah, you've been such a long time!' Sarah sank to the floor, her arms enfolding the child. She could not speak. All of a sudden the strain of the afternoon, the swings of emotion she had felt but suppressed took her over entirely and all she could do was hang on to Daisy and hold her tight. To her own surprise she found herself sobbing, great, shuddering sobs that shook her being, whilst at the same time she was laughing, tears rolling down her face. There was a mixture of so many feelings that she would have been unable to name them all had anyone asked what ailed her. Anger that anyone should behave so wickedly in manipulating a child's life to their own evil ends; guilt that it was through her own actions that this little girl was now in this position and further guilt that she was still hiding her secret; immense fear of losing contact with Daisy; frustration at the escape of those two this afternoon; the elation that so frequently swept over her when she thought of her renewed relationship with Sam and the discovery of her daughter.

'Oh, Daisy, Daisy, how lovely to see you again.'

She finally pushed the child to arms' length and looked at her. 'How are you sweetheart? I have missed you. My! Don't you look pretty today? Is that a new dress?'

'They said I was to go home with my real mummy and daddy today. Anna and me stayed home from school. Have they come yet, Sarah?' Daisy hugged Sarah close again and whispered, 'I don't think I want to go. Sarah, I don't want to go with them. I like it here with Anna,' she began to cry. 'I want to stay here. Please, Sarah, tell them to let me stay here.' Sarah, with great difficulty, pulled herself together and stood the child on her feet. Kneeling beside her she said, 'Look at me. I promise you, Daisy, you need not go with those people. Not today, not ever... Now, dry those eyes and come and say hello to Sam. He hates to see a lady in tears.'

'Honest? Cross your heart and hope to die, Sarah?'

'Honest,' she said solemnly, suiting the action to the words. 'Come along, now.' Sarah took Daisy by the hand and led her into the parlour. She shrank back behind Sarah's skirts so that Sarah had to push her gently forward.

'Now, you mustn't be shy. You know Sam. This lady is Mrs. Benson and the gentleman is a friend of mine called Mr. Ross.' Daisy managed a small smile as she recognised Sam. She looked in awe at the beautiful woman whose presence seemed to overpower the room. Sam came and took Daisy's other hand and the three of them sat together on the sofa.

'I don't suppose there's been time yet to tell

Daisy what has happened?' asked Tom. Sarah shook her head.

'No, Tom, not fully. I did tell her that she won't be going away today, after all.'

'Well, young lady, it has been a day of surprises for everyone. And there is yet another surprise for you, Daisy.' Daisy was not at all sure she liked the sound of this, coming from that man with the black suit, even if he was Sarah's friend. 'Mrs. Benson has come a long way over the ocean to see us, and especially to see you. She is your aunt, Daisy, the sister of your mother who died when you were just a baby. She is your Aunt Dorothy.'

'That's right, dear. You are my niece, though I haven't seen you since you were terribly small, so I'm sure you won't remember me.' The lovely lady came over and took both her hands and planted a kiss on Daisy's cheek. Daisy was mesmerised. 'I live a very long way away now, with my husband, but we once lived quite close to you and your parents. It will be delightful to have our very own niece.' Aunt Dorothy gently eased herself onto the settee beside Daisy and put an arm around her slight shoulders. Daisy could feel the softness of the cashmere suit and smell the subtle, expensive perfume. 'You must call me Auntie Dot because that's what your dear mother used to call me. I do miss her so. It will be like having a little bit of Margaret still here.' She looked wistful. 'Your Uncle Peter and I were not lucky enough to have a family of our own.' She gave Daisy a little squeeze before returning to her chair.

Daisy had said not a word but her large blue eyes had never left Auntie Dot. From her immaculate make-up to her sparkling earrings, that pretty little hat and those diamonds on her fingers, Daisy had never seen anyone so wonderful. She was captivated. Dorothy Benson might as well have been the Queen of England.

Sam exchanged a look with Sarah.

'We really should be making tracks,' he said.

Chapter 31

The Crown Hotel offered an excellent dinner. Dorothy Benson had suggested that they should reserve rooms for the night because the journey home would otherwise be a very late and arduous affair.

'I should very much like to see Daisy again before I leave for Scarborough, and it will be far pleasanter to travel tomorrow when I can see England in her springtime greenery again. It's one thing I do miss, you know.'

Sarah and Sam managed to catch Tom alone for a moment or two before dinner as they all enjoyed a drink at the bar.

'Tom, I need a word if you can spare a moment,' said Sarah.

'Now here's a coincidence, I was hoping to catch you, my dear for a moment in private. What's on your mind?'

'Well, it's quite simple, really. I merely wanted to make sure that Grandfather's money will now go where I always wanted ... that is to the Johnsons. They're Daisy's guardians and they have made a wonderfully loving home for her. That can be arranged straight away, I'm sure, Tom.' Sarah smiled happily at the thought as she sat close to Sam.

But the smile began to fade as Tom spoke.

'My dear, I can understand your feelings on this but I think you may have overlooked the fact that Daisy now has someone with a stronger claim to her. As yet I've not had time to fully discuss the situation with Mrs. Benson but from some things she has said I would not be surprised if she and her husband were to take over Daisy's adoption.' Tom watched the emotions chase each other across Sarah's face. He took her hand. 'Sarah, my dear, she has told me of their sadness at remaining childless. I have little doubt that she will look into the possibility of taking her sister's child back to Toronto with her.' Sarah looked from Tom to Sam and back again, stunned disbelief filling her being. Ashen pale she stood up. They were no longer alone in the bar and other diners glanced in curiosity at the pretty blond girl whose words hissed at her older companion, her face now contorted with fury.

'No! I will not allow it. I will not agree to it. Weeks it has taken us to find her. Fate threw us together on that train. It was meant to be.' Sarah was finding it hard to breathe, her words punctuated by harsh, dry sobs, yet she was very much aware that she was in a public place. 'She's mine, Tom, mine, do you hear?' she rasped. 'I rejected her, yes, I was wrong. I will not let her go a second time.' She rose and walked unsteadily towards the stairs leaving Tom no opportunity to respond. With a tremendous effort she turned and said, 'I must powder my nose. I am going to my room. I will join you for dinner shortly.' With that she marshalled all her reserves of dignity and poise and made for the stairs, only to be confronted by Mrs. Benson, elegantly dressed for dinner, her cigarette in an ivory holder.

'Why, good evening, Miss Grange.' She received no reply except for what sounded like a strangled scream as Sarah lost all composure and fled up the stairs.

'I'll go after her, Tom, see she's O.K.' Sam knocked briefly on Sarah's hotel room door and went in. He found her prostrate on the bed, her sobs muffled by a pillow.

'Sarah, my darling, come here,' he said as he gathered her into his arms.

'Oh, Sam, what am I going to do? How can I ever bear it if they take Daisy away to Canada. How can I face that woman at dinner?' He sat and held her while she was oblivious to anything but this overwhelming grief. Tangled memories of the same grief undergone and overcome all those years ago swept her along in their wake. Her baby, given up and rediscovered by accident. The joy of knowing that she might be allowed to remain in contact with Daisy, if only as a friend, was fading as a photograph left in the sunlight. Why? Her heart cried out at the injustice of it.

Almost ten minutes must have passed before she began to quieten, her breath coming more calmly, her thoughts more clearly. A new notion was beginning to take hold, one that caused a surge of anger that erupted with a sudden violence as she jumped up from the bed.

'This is all your fault, Sam, your fault, do you hear!' She flattened herself against the wardrobe, getting as far from him as she could, her eyes blazing. 'If you hadn't written to her, fetched her here from Canada ... oh ... oh ... see what you've done?' She flew across the room, her arms outstretched to punch and batter whatever part of him she could reach. A resounding slap across his face found its mark before Sam caught her flailing fists and held them firm.

'Stop it, Sarah!' he was almost shouting now. 'Stop this! Don't you realise that without her your grandfather's money might have gone astray.' But she was not taking in his words.

Bitter, angry disappointment engulfed her soul and she needed someone to blame. She was quiet now, controlled, hardly raising her voice above a whisper.

'Get out, Sam!' He did not move. 'Get out, leave me alone!' She began to shout hysterically, 'Get out, get out, do you hear? Get out of my room! Get out of my life, Sam Pearce. For the second time you've destroyed everything.'

It was no use. Sarah would not listen to anything he tried to say. She seemed beyond all reason and obviously in no fit state to appear at dinner. He was at a loss what to do as he went down to the dining room. Tom and Mrs. Benson were already seated and consulting the menu.

'Do forgive me for keeping you waiting. I'm afraid that Sarah is not well. She will not be dining this evening.' It sounded contrived. He could not help it.

'I'm sorry to hear it. Is there anything I can do?' asked Mrs. Benson.

'Thank you, but I think she would prefer to be left alone. I'm sure it's only a bad headache. We have had a rather momentous day, after all.'

'Yes, you may well be right, Sam. Your arrival, Mrs. Benson, has really made a difference. Shall we order?'

Sam wondered how he managed to get through the meal. It was torture to carry on polite conversation knowing that his world was crashing to the ground. Not only his but Sarah's too. Tom's assumption, it turned out, had been right and Sam listened with heavy heart as Dorothy Benson, with growing animation, questioned Tom as to the possibility of her taking over her sister's role. Tom was not at all sure how to advise her and he was obliged to play for time by promising to consult a colleague who was more familiar than he with certain aspects of family law and adoption. Truth to tell his close association with this case, his knowledge of Sarah and Sam's secret could not fail to colour his approach to Mrs. Benson's enquiries. He felt his judgement would be clouded and knew he must bring in a clearer mind to the matter. His thoughts had wandered as Sam and Mrs. Benson talked and he, rather mechanically, spooned apple pie and cream into his mouth.

'That dessert was excellent!' declared Mrs. Benson.

'Indeed it was,' Tom agreed, bringing his attention back to the table and laying down his napkin.

'How long do you expect to stay in England,

Mrs. Benson?'

'I'm not certain. So much depends upon my final decision about Daisy and that will depend to some degree on what your colleague has to tell me. My first call must be to my mother and I shall go there tomorrow. I may stay a day or two, even a week. Then I can travel over to Leeds and speak to you at your offices there. By then I will have had time to contact my husband and discuss matters with him. And now, gentlemen, I must bid you goodnight.' They stood as she left the table. Sam's sigh of relief as he resumed his seat was not lost on Tom Ross. He had known this young man a comparatively short time but he had quickly developed both a liking and respect for him. Sarah and he seemed admirably suited and very much in love.

'Cigarette, Sam?' Tom offered his case. 'And what would you say to a night-cap?'

'Thanks,' said Sam as Tom ordered brandy. 'It's not often that I get to dine in such style.' He grinned ruefully as he recalled the rushed and basic meals he was used to in the Residency at the hospital. His thoughts, however, soon returned to the day's events.

'What are the chances of Mrs. Benson's taking Daisy home with her?'

'Well, I suppose there's every chance, given that her husband is equally in favour.'

'Hm-m.' Tom regarded the younger man, trying to read his thoughts. He remained silent, hoping that Sam would open up. The brandy was helping them both to relax after the rather formal atmosphere of dinner with Dorothy Benson.

'It would break Sarah's heart, you know ... and mine ... if she were taken away,' Sam spoke so quietly that Tom wondered if the comment was meant for him to hear. And although nothing had been said Tom's growing suspicion quite suddenly became a conviction. Of course, this is the father of Sarah's child. And then ... does the lad know it himself? And what if I'm wrong? Tom Ross had hoped the brandy would help him sleep but he was still pondering matters well into the early hours.

Sarah woke very early. She had been completely exhausted following her tirade against Sam and had fallen into a deep sleep that healed her shattered emotions. She woke full of remorse. How could she have ranted at him so? While the sun barely lit the rooftops she took a shower, dressed and packed her bag ready for the journey home. Somehow, during those few hours of sleep, she had come to a decision. This morning she was calm, determined and utterly sure of her plan of action. This was something she had to do entirely on her own yet, at the back of her mind the fear of failure sent icy tendrils through her throat causing her breathing to quicken and her heart to beat faster. She took several deep breaths, swallowed hard and went quietly downstairs to the lobby. At the hotel desk she surprised a sleepy clerk. 'Good morning,' she said, with her sunniest smile.

'Oh! Good morning, miss. You are bright and early. What may I do for you?'

'Could you tell me the number of Mrs. Benson's room?' He consulted the ledger.

'That would be room sixteen, miss.' He looked askance, hesitated, then added, 'First floor, front, just to the left as you leave the lift.' It was not his place to question the guests' movements.

Sarah made her way upstairs leaving the clerk looking at his watch, then shrugging his shoulders. After all, it had nothing to do with him. The passageway leading to the best rooms was wide and furnished with sofas and easy chairs. Here she settled down to wait. It was not yet seven. Far too early to disturb the lady, yet Sarah's ears were alert to any signs of movement from room sixteen. She heard none until about three-quarters of an hour later when a maid brought a tea tray and morning paper. She heard a sleepy 'come in' as the maid knocked.

'Your tea, madam.'

'Thank you, so much,' she heard Mrs. Benson's voice. Sarah waited another ten minutes before she approached the door and knocked.

'Who is it?'

'It's Sarah Grange, Mrs. Benson. May I please speak to you for a moment?' The door was thrown open.

'My dear, by all means. A tryst before breakfast. How exciting! But how are you feeling? Sam said you weren't well.'

'Oh, thank you, but it was just a bad headache. I feel fine this morning.'

'Good! Well, then, do come in. I've just been reading the newspaper. They were good enough to order the *Toronto Gazette* for me specially. There's quite a to-do, you know, about the King and this American woman he's so friendly with.

A married woman, too. Says here that he sent her to Ascot in one of the royal carriages and that he's forever at her side. He seems quite besotted with her.'

'Who? What?' Sarah's mind was so full with the things she had planned to say that the friendly chit-chat over the newspaper report sounded to her like some foreign language. 'I'm sorry?'

'Ah, yes, well I guess the English papers aren't writing about it. But there have been reports like this for months over in Canada, even more so in America. Seems they quite fancy the idea of an American woman as Queen of England.' Sarah was nonplussed. She hesitated, wondering how to bring this bizarre conversation back to reality.

'Mrs. Benson, I need to talk to you. I need to talk to you now, before the day properly begins. It's terribly important.' Sarah's earnest expression caught Dorothy's attention and the small talk was abandoned.

'Sit down, my dear. What is it?' she said, throwing the newspaper aside.

Meanwhile, Sergeant Gerry Roberts was back at his desk in the Doncaster Station sifting through all the information connected with the little girl who, it had been thought, had been separated from her parents during the night of the train crash. What had seemed at first to be a simple case of a lost child had sent out tentacles in many directions finally revealing a potential fraud. It had been a remarkable stroke of luck that they had turned up at Idle House with Mrs. Benson just in time to prevent that fraud, yet he was in no mood to congratulate himself and Sam. The business would not be tied up until the Smithsons were apprehended. And they were still on the loose.

Gerry discussed the case with his Inspector telling him that he needed to travel to Leeds in order to find the pair. He knew from Sam and Tom Ross that they lived on an estate called Upton Hall so he was sure that it would not be difficult to bring them in for questioning. With clearance from their boss Sergeant Roberts and a young officer called Peter Jones were now making good progress up the A1 towards Leeds. Once there they would confer with their colleagues in the West Yorkshire Force. It would all be settled in no time thought Gerry, as long as they stayed in the long grass and did not alert their quarry.

'Should be on our way back by this evening,' said Gerry. 'I can't wait to see those two safely behind a desk in the interview room.'

'O.K. So you'd better fill me in as we go,' said Peter.

Sam woke to find a note pushed under his bedroom door. When he saw Sarah's handwriting he was alarmed. Last night after her outburst and her refusal to come down to dinner he had decided to leave her to calm down. He had not called to wish her good night. He ripped open the envelope.

'My darling Sam,' he breathed a sigh of relief.

'Can you please forgive me for last night? I am truly sorry. I didn't mean all those things I said. I was just so scared. I went into panic mode and wasn't thinking clearly. Today I mean to do something about it and I'm asking you to go home with Tom just as planned. Please

don't question me on this. I promise I'll explain everything and I'll follow later in the day, but just for now I have to be on my own. Please ask Tom to hang on to the legacy a little longer and I'll tell him when it's time to hand it over to Elsie and Ernest. I won't see you at breakfast. There are things I must do, things that can't wait. Trust me, please, darling. Remember that I love you and always will whatever happens. Sarah.'
His feeling of alarm returned. What did she mean by that last remark? It seemed to cast a shadow of doubt on their future together. They had planned to spend the weekend together before his leave was up and he had to return to the hospital.

He flew down the corridor to Sarah's room. The door was open and a maid was already servicing the room. Down to the lobby, to the desk.

'No, sir. Miss Grange has left, quite some time ago. No, sir. No. She did not say where she was going. Oh, about an hour I should say, sir. I called her a taxi. Thank you, sir.' Sam re-read the note. What on earth did it mean? He joined Tom Ross at breakfast but had no appetite for it. Tom tried to chivvy him out of his gloom.

'Sarah's a very decisive young woman. I'm sure that whatever she's doing it is for the best. Forgive me for prying, tell me to mind my own business if you will, but I suspect that you and Sarah have, well, an understanding. Am I right?'

'She has promised to marry me, but she insisted it must be unofficial for the time being. Something's holding her back. I really don't know how I stand at all today.'

'Perhaps she just wants to make sure that Daisy's settled. You know how tidy-minded Sarah is. It would be so like her to want to tie up loose ends before embarking on the next part of her life. Don't worry, Sam. Do as she says and 'trust her'. My guess is that she has just gone to say her own goodbye to Daisy. That she really does need to do on her own.' Sam nodded his agreement and sighed deeply.

'Sorry, Tom! I suddenly feel so insecure somehow. I really don't know how I'd cope if I were to lose Sarah now. All I do know is that she's shutting me out.'

'Have you seen Mrs. Benson this morning? We should see if she intends to travel as far as Leeds on our train on her way to Scarborough.' They asked after the lady at reception.

'Mrs Benson had to change her plans and left to catch an early train. She asked me to give you this, Sir.' The short note said, *'Dear Mr. Ross. I have spoken to my husband on the telephone. I will be contacting you in a couple of days after I have visited my mother in Scarborough. Yours etc.'*

'Come on, lad. Let's collect our bags and get off to the station.'

'I wonder how Gerry's getting on,' mused Sam as the countryside flew past the carriage window. 'He's probably planning to pounce on the Smithsons at Upton Hall within the next few hours.'

It was early evening. John and Alice were sitting with Sam, all of them wondering when Sarah would return. Sam had dined with his father earlier and had come to Sarah's parents to tell them what had been happening during the visit to Retford. So much had changed since the day they had left to hand over to the Johnsons the legacy of Grandfather Grange.

'Sarah should be home soon, then?' said Alice. She could sense Sam's unease. He had no clear idea what Sarah was up to today. Understanding why she had excluded him was beyond him. John poured a Martini for Alice and asked if Sam would like a tot of whisky. Gradually the conversation faltered. The clock's ticking and the Light Programme's offering of pleasant evening music were all that could be heard when the wheels of a car crunched over the gravel driveway.

'I think she's here.' John was peering through the window into the darkness beyond. They got to the door just as Sarah was coming through it. Sam hung back to allow her parents to greet Sarah. She looked different. There was a light in her eyes yet she seemed apprehensive.

'Hello, everyone. Sorry I've been so long but here's the reason.' From behind her she pulled the small figure of Daisy Miller. 'Mrs. Johnson says that Daisy may stay for a few days.' The child glanced shyly at Alice and John but beamed when she saw Sam.

Sam took in more of this situation than Sarah's parents could. He was across the room in a flash to pick up Daisy with one arm and to gather Sarah in the other. As they hugged each other Sarah whispered,

'I've brought her home, Sam. I've brought her home!'

Epilogue

The boy swooped round the corner on his bicycle and rode through the wrought iron gates whose elaborate lettering proudly declared that this was the 'Toronto Home of Benson's Brollies'.

'Telegram for Mr. Peter Benson! Telegram!' he yelled.

Peter Benson opened the short message and read, *Taking next available passage home, stop. Mother with me, stop. Daisy with natural parents, stop. Best for all, stop.*

Love always, Dot

An air of excitement pervaded the Convent of St. Faith's that morning when the invitation was received from Mr. and Mrs. John Grange requesting the pleasure of the company of Sister Ruth and Sister Josephine at the marriage of their daughter, Sarah, to Dr. Samuel Pearce on May 1st, 1936.

Wrapped around the gold-edged, formal invitation was a letter from the bride-to-be.

'Dear Sister Ruth,

Much has happened, many problems have beset us, since the day I came to ask for your help in finding my daughter. But now the sun has come out on my life again. I am to be married to Daisy's father, which is wonderful. Best of all we have our daughter back with us where she belongs and she is to be Maid of Honour at our wedding.

I shall never forget the care, love and understanding I received from the nuns all those years ago and someday I hope to share with you and Sister Josephine the story of how we ended up as a real family.

Sam joins me in sending affectionate greetings and looks forward to meeting you both on our special day.

Sarah

The girl at the reception desk at Doncaster Hospital called to Dr. Pearce as he hurried by, 'Someone dropped in this note for you, Doctor.'

It was very brief but brought a grin to Sam's handsome face as he read

'Hi, Sam! We got 'em!

Gerry.'

Daisy and Anna were trying to keep still for the dressmaker. They were wildly excited as final touches were made to their bridesmaid frocks.

'And look what Sarah gave me,' Daisy said to her friend.

'Your mummy ... you mean,' giggled Anna.

'Yes, well ... I'm allowed to wear them on the wedding day.'

'It's a picture of you!' Anna breathed her admiration as he saw the miniature of Marguerite Grange and watched as her friend slid the tiny pearl ring onto her finger. 'It looks just like a daisy, doesn't it?'

Tom Ross was relieved when he could tell Sarah and Sam that he had completed the overseeing of the Trust Fund set up for Daisy with George

Grange's legacy. In addition there had been, at Sarah's request, the transfer of a certain sum to the Johnsons at Idle House in recognition of their care of Daisy for four years.

With a satisfied smile he closed the file containing the Last Will and Testament of George W. Grange.

The publishers hope that this book has given you enjoyable reading. Large Print Books are especially designed to be as easy to see and hold as possible. If you wish a complete list of our books please ask at your local library or write directly to:

Magna Large Print Books
Magna House, Long Preston,
Skipton, North Yorkshire.
BD23 4ND